C000098206

MURDER
AT THE MANOR

The Libby Sarjeant Series
by Lesley Cookman

MURDER IN
STEEPLE MARTIN

9781905170159

MURDER AT
THE LAURELS

9781905170845

MURDER IN
MIDWINTER

9781906125028

MURDER BY
THE SEA

9781906373306

MURDER IN
BLOOM

9781906373771

MURDER IN
THE GREEN

9781907016080

MURDER
IMPERFECT

9781907016462

MURDER TO
MUSIC

9781907726545

MURDER
AT THE MANOR

LESLEY COOKMAN

Published by Accent Press Ltd – 2011

ISBN 9781908192028

Printed and bound in the UK

Cover Design by Zipline Creative

Acknowledgements

Thanks to Graham and Kelly Waller for lending me Imogen, who should have been thanked in the last book, *Murder to Music*, and thanks to my friend Brendan, for allowing me to use his name. I must add that the character is in no way based on him!
I have used a Writers' Weekend in this book, but I have never been to any writers' event like this, nor have I ever met any writers who behaved as badly. The Romantic Novelists' Association, of which I am a proud member, gets a good press here, and I would urge any would-be writers who might be reading this to have a look at their website:
www.romanticnovelists

There is more police activity in this book, too, and I will apologise to members of the force everywhere for my cavalier treatment of their methods and procedures. This is not the way to run an investigation!

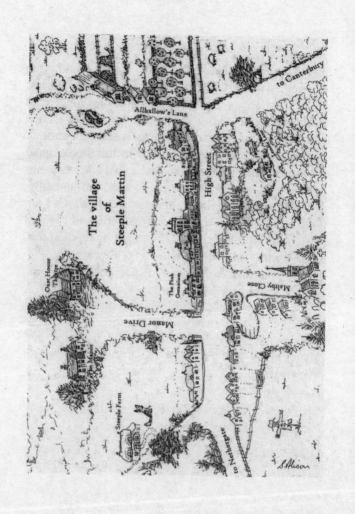

The village
of
Steeple Martin

to Canterbury

Allhallow's Lane

High Street

Maltby Close

Oast House
Theatre

The Pink
Geranium

Manor Drive

Steeple Farm

to Nethergate

S. Alison

DRAMATIS PERSONAE

Libby Sarjeant
Former actor, sometime artist, resident of 17, Allhallow's Lane, Steeple Martin. Owner of Sidney the cat.

Fran Wolfe
Formerly Fran Castle. Also former actor, occasional psychic, resident of Coastguard Cottage, Nethergate. Owner of Balzac the cat.

Ben Wilde
Libby's significant other. Owner of The Manor Farm and the Oast House Theatre.

Guy Wolfe
Fran's husband, artist and owner of a shop and gallery in Harbour Street, Nethergate.

Peter Parker
Ben's cousin. Free-lance journalist, part owner of The Pink Geranium restaurant and life partner of Harry Price.

Harry Price
Chef and co-owner of The Pink Geranium and Peter Parker's life partner.

Hetty Wilde
Ben's mother. Lives at The Manor.

Greg Wilde
Hetty's husband and Ben's father.

DCI Ian Connell
Local policeman and friend. Former suitor of Fran's.

Adam Sarjeant
Libby's youngest son. Lives above The Pink Geranium, works with garden designer Mog, mainly at Creekmarsh.

Lewis Osborne-Walker
TV gardener and handy-man who owns Creekmarsh.

Sophie Wolfe
Guy's daughter. Lives above the gallery.

Flo Carpenter
Hetty's oldest friend.

Lenny Fisher
Hetty's brother. Lives with Flo Carpenter.

Ali and Ahmed
Owners of the Eight-til-late in the village.

Jane Baker
Chief Reporter for the *Nethergate Mercury*. Mother to Imogen.

Terry Baker
Jane's husband and father of Imogen.

Joe, Nella and Owen
Of Cattlegreen Nurseries.

DCI Don Murray
Of Canterbury Police.

Amanda George
Novelist, known as Rosie.

Chapter One

'WHEN ARE THEY ARRIVING, then?' Ben Wilde stared up at the newly refurbished exterior of his family home. The sun had briefly pierced the grey sky and reflected in the brightly polished windows.

'Fran's bringing Rosie at about two, and the rest are supposed to start coming in dribs and drabs between four and six,' said Libby Sarjeant, referring to a large clipboard. 'I hope it works all right.'

Ben turned and gave her a hug. 'Course it'll work. It was your idea, remember?'

'I know,' said Libby, 'but I can't help feeling a bit uncomfortable. We seem to have done it so quickly. It's not so long since your father died.'

'If Mum had any objection, she'd have told you. She's as happy as Larry in her little flat, and she just loves having people to boss about.'

'I hope so.' Libby sighed. Ben's mother Hetty had accepted the death of her husband Greg with the stoicism she was famous for, but when Ben suggested gently that she should sell the Manor and retire to sheltered accommodation near her brother Lenny, she had refuted the idea with some vigour. No, she was going to stay at the Manor in what had once been the housekeeper's quarters, and Ben and his sister Susan could do what they liked with the rest.

Which was where Libby, Ben's significant other, had come in. Her idea, mooted some time ago, of turning The Manor into a venue for creative writing

1

and painting holidays was put into action. Their friend Guy Wolfe was an artist, married to Fran, who was taking creative writing classes with a best-selling novelist, Amanda George, known to them all as Rosie. They already had the contacts to make the venture work, and the first outing, a painting weekend run by Guy and Libby between them, had been a success.

Hetty had insisted on overseeing the cleaning and cooking and had recruited part-time help herself.

'She's thoroughly enjoying it,' said Ben, giving Libby a hug. 'Now tell me exactly what this weekend is all about. A reunion?'

'Apparently,' said Libby, letting him lead her indoors, 'this group met on a writing holiday in Devon and this is a reunion weekend. They've all kept in touch with each other by email, so there shouldn't be any awkward moments.'

'But Rosie's going to be teaching them? It isn't just a knees-up?'

'No. The organiser, –' Libby referred to her clipboard again '– Lily Cooper, wanted a proper tutor. Only for a couple of sessions. So Fran asked Rosie.'

'So they all eat together this evening, then what?'

'You haven't been listening to me for the last couple of weeks, have you?' They were in the huge kitchen now, and Libby put the clipboard down on the table and went to put the kettle on the Aga.

'Yes, I have.' Ben looked vaguely guilty. 'But I've been busy, too.'

'I know.' Libby turned with a smile. 'And a brilliant job you've done, too. The Hoppers' Huts are terrific.'

'Well, between them and Steeple Farm we've got plenty of letting properties now, and there's plenty of space for people on courses if they spill out of the main house.'

'Which they have done this weekend.' Libby checked her clipboard again. 'We've only got a couple in the Huts, both men. Oh, no – one woman. She was a late booker.'

'So, go on, then, what happens after dinner this evening?'

'This Lily Cooper introduces Rosie and then they all go off and do what they want. They can all go down to the pub if they want to, or sit in the sitting room and talk books.'

'Haven't they got drinks here?' Ben frowned.

'We're not licensed, are we? They get wine with their dinner and before it, that's included in their weekend price, but we couldn't afford to include any more, not for what they're paying us.'

'Then we need to do something about that,' said Ben.

'They can always bring their own. That's cheaper for them.' Libby poured tea into two mugs from the large brown teapot.

'Hmm.' Ben didn't look convinced. 'Shall I take a cup to Mum?'

'No.' Libby shook her head. 'She hates it. Thinks we're waiting on her. Anyway, she's not here, she popped down to see Flo and Lenny. Said she'd be back in time to start the dinner.'

3

'But we've got people coming in to do that,' said Ben.

'You know your mother.' Libby grinned at him. 'And tomorrow night you do remember Harry's bringing his food?'

'They're all going to be eating veggie Mexican, are they?'

'No, he's breaking all his own rules and cooking meat and chicken as well. Pollo Verde, my favourite.'

'I hope they all like spicy food, then,' said Ben. 'I can hear a car.'

Outside, Fran was helping Rosie George out of her little Smart car.

'Hello, both.' Libby went forward to take Rosie's overnight case from Fran. 'Good to see you.'

'This is lovely,' said Rosie looking round, her grey-blonde hair flying, as usual, in uncontrollable wisps around her head. 'You're so lucky, Libby.'

'Oh, we don't live here,' said Ben, coming out to give Fran a kiss and shake Rosie's hand. 'My mother still does.'

'I was sorry to hear about your father,' said Rosie.

'Thank you,' said Ben. 'He'd been ill for years, but somehow we didn't expect it.'

'No.' Rosie shook her head. 'One never does.'

Libby led the way inside and across the hall to the wide staircase. 'You're sure you want to stay overnight, Rosie?' she said. 'You can go home if you like.'

'No, I've arranged for Talbot to be fed, and I

want to immerse myself in the weekend.' Rosie beamed. 'It's quite exciting. Different from my adult ed classes. And Fran's staying, too.'

'I know.' Libby sighed again. 'I said she and Guy could come and stay with us, but she refused.'

'Getting my money's worth,' said Fran with a grin. 'The only writers I know are the ones in Rosie's class. I need to network a bit more.'

'Don't forget that most of these people know each other already,' said Libby. 'They may be cliquey.'

'If they see I'm best friends with their tutor I'll be welcome, I'm sure,' said Fran, with a smile at Rosie. 'After all, Rosie's quite a famous name.'

'We've got another quite famous name, too,' said Libby, consulting her clipboard again. 'Patrick Joseph.'

'Oh, I've heard of him,' said Ben, looking interested. 'Is he really coming?'

'Doesn't he write crime?' asked Fran.

'Yes, rather gritty urban stuff,' said Rosie. 'I've met him several times. Seems a nice enough man.'

'Well, there you are. He won't try and take over, will he?' said Libby.

'No, I shouldn't think so. I might ask him to field a few questions, just to be friendly,' said Rosie.

'Speaking of which,' said Libby, going into the kitchen to shift the kettle back on to the hob, 'I'm not being very friendly. You must be parched.'

'Could I go to my room first?' asked Rosie. 'Then I'll come and join you.'

'Come on, then,' said Ben, picking up her case. 'I'll show you.'

5

'How's it going?' asked Fran, following her friend into the kitchen and sitting at the huge, scrubbed pine table. 'Did you get the leaky shower pod fixed?'

Libby pulled a face. 'Just in time. After all that money they cost.'

The all-in-one bathroom pods, similar to those found in student accommodation, had been installed in all the bedrooms, Libby having stated unequivocally that en-suite facilities would be a necessity for the kind of operation they were trying to run.

'I know.' Fran was sympathetic. 'Especially after Ben had to buy Susan out.'

'That was awful.' Libby brought the tea to the table. 'She always said she couldn't care less what happened to the Manor, and she didn't want anything to do with it, until we told her what we were going to do.'

'You told me. Although I still don't know why he had to buy Susan out. Technically, it isn't even his yet.'

'I think it's his active conscience. It also makes sense, in that when Het dies, she can leave it to him alone.'

'As long as they've got that in writing,' said Fran.

'Well, of course. It was all done legal-like, but as you say, it was an expense he could have done without.'

'Pity you're not rich.' Fran grinned across the table.

'No, but I'm a fully paid-up director of the

company, so I'm a real person. And a grown-up.'

'Nearly,' said Fran, and ducked the tea cosy aimed at her head.

'Nice room,' said Rosie coming into the kitchen. 'Ben said to tell you he'd gone to the office.'

'Glad you like it,' said Libby. 'Tea?'

By half-past five, the rest of the group had assembled. Most were in their rooms, although some, including Patrick Joseph and Rosie, were in the sitting room renewing old friendships. With Patrick, sullen and rather bored, was the organiser of the weekend, Lily Cooper. A tall woman with highlighted dark hair and a striking figure, she was obviously unused to being ignored. On her way to the kitchen to see how the dinner was getting on, Libby paused in the doorway. Pasting on a professional smile, she went over to the little group.

'Everything all right?' she asked, addressing Lily.

'Fine, thanks,' she said, her tone implying that it obviously wasn't.

Patrick Joseph and Rosie both looked up.

'Yes, thanks, marvellous,' said Patrick, in a smooth, chocolatey voice.

'Have you met properly?' asked Rosie. 'Patrick, this is my friend Libby, who runs the Manor. Libby this is Patrick and – um –'

'Lily Cooper,' said the woman in an icy voice.

'Yes, actually, Rosie, I introduced myself when they booked in,' said Libby hastily. 'Well, if there's nothing I can get you, I'll see you for drinks before dinner.'

'If looks could have killed,' she said to Ben a

7

few minutes later, when they went to change in the privacy of the estate office. 'She couldn't bear it that this Patrick was enjoying talking to Rosie.'

'Rosie wasn't up to her old tricks, was she?' Ben's head popped through the neck of his collarless shirt.

'She wasn't flirting as far as I could see. Anyway he'd be too young for her. He can't be more than fifty.'

'Would that be a barrier?'

'Maybe for him, if not for her.' Libby grinned as she wrapped a long lilac scarf round her neck. 'Anyway, she doesn't flirt any more. Not now she's more-or-less settled into a semi-detached relationship with Andrew.'

'Like we used to be.' Ben opened the door. 'Come on, attached one. Let's go and make the party swing.'

Rosie, Patrick and Lily were nowhere to be seen when Libby re-entered the sitting room, but several of the other guests were drifting aimlessly around. She smiled round brightly.

'Please help yourself to a drink,' she said waving a hand in the direction of a chiffonier laden with drinks, glass and an ice bucket. Slices of lime and lemon were in a lidded glass dish. Immediately the guests converged and there was some fairly well-mannered jostling for position.

'Everybody, here, gal?' Hetty appeared in the doorway.

'I think one person was missing.' Libby went over to her. 'I left the clipboard in the kitchen.'

They went back to the kitchen together.

'Oh, no – look. All the names are ticked.' Libby frowned. 'Did you check anyone in, Het?'

'No, gal. Wouldn't have asked you if I had, would I?'

'Suppose not.' Libby put down the clipboard. 'Oh, well. I'll wait until the last three put in an appearance in the sitting room, then we can serve dinner.'

When she got back, Patrick had reappeared and was being lionised by several of the other guests. Rosie and Lily arrived a few moments later, and Libby clapped her hands.

'Dinner's served, everyone. If you'd like to follow Ben over there into the dining room, I'll join you in a moment.'

Fran paused by her friend as she watched the guests shuffle obligingly out of the room.

'So far so good,' she murmured.

'Keep your fingers crossed,' said Libby. 'Although I honestly don't see what could go wrong unless one of them gets food poisoning.'

'Don't tempt fate,' said Fran. 'With our record, that could be fatal.'

Libby gave her A Look.

Chapter Two

LILY COOPER DEVIATED SLIGHTLY from the programme she'd sent to Libby by welcoming the guests and introducing Rosie before dinner rather than after.

'Not that it matters,' said Libby to Ben as they went back to the kitchen to eat their own dinner with Hetty and the casual cooking and waiting staff. 'And, by the way, did you tick off the last guest? I was sure there was one to come, but when I looked they'd all been ticked off.'

'Not me.' Ben shook his head. 'After I'd seen Rosie to her room I went straight to the office.'

'I wonder who it was, then?' Libby frowned. 'Unless someone arrived, found the clipboard and no one with it and checked himself, or herself, in.'

'How would he have got his key or known where to go?'

Libby sighed. 'Oh, I don't know. Anyway, they all seem fine in there at the moment, and I'm sure if there's someone missing or something wrong, that Lily will be only too keen to tell us. She's the least happy of the lot.'

'She's jealous.' Ben smiled his thanks at his mother as she put a plate of food in front of him.

'Of what? Who?'

'Anyone, I would think.' Ben laughed at her puzzled face. 'Oh, come on, Lib. I would think they're having an affair – or at least she thinks they are, probably after a one-night stand at their last gathering. She'd be jealous of anyone he took an interest in, knowing her own precarious position.'

'Mmm.' Libby remembered the sulky-faced woman, and the way she had clung to Patrick Joseph's arm before dinner. 'You could be right.' She looked consideringly at her partner. 'He is quite attractive.'

He slapped her arm with a spoon. 'That's quite enough of that, woman.'

'Did you see that, Het?' Libby turned an astonished face to her mother-in-law-elect. 'He hit me! That's abuse, that is.'

'He don't deserve no pudding then,' said Hetty, laconic as ever.

After dinner, the guests gravitated to the sitting room, and Libby asked if they were all there, as far as Lily Cooper knew. Looking slightly surprised, she agreed they all were, why? Libby explained, but Lily, Patrick and the other guests all looked vaguely uncomprehending.

'Well, that's that.' Libby left the sitting room. 'Where are Fran and Rosie?'

'In the kitchen with Hetty,' said Ben. 'I don't think they fancied sitting in there with that lot.'

'I said they'd be cliquey,' said Libby, going back to the kitchen.

Hetty was waving a bottle of red wine around. Libby fetched glasses and she and Ben sat at the table.

'So, what do you think?' she asked Rosie.

'They're all right, as far as it goes,' said Rosie. 'Not really up for being taught anything though. It strikes me as more of a reunion than a writing weekend.'

'Well, that's exactly what it is,' said Libby. 'You sure you want to stay, Fran?'

'I'll stay to keep Rosie company.' Fran raised her glass. 'Cheers. Anyway, I've already paid.'

Libby felt herself colouring. 'We'd give your money back.'

'I know. But I am genuinely looking forward to talking to some of the others. The only writers I know are the ones in Rosie's class, and none of them are published.'

'I thought for a moment you were going to say none of them were real writers,' said Rosie. 'Anyone who writes is a writer.'

'It doesn't matter how many times you tell me that,' said Fran, smiling at her tutor, 'I shan't feel like a writer until I see my name in print.'

'I know what you mean,' said Libby. 'I knew a playwright in London who'd been writing for a living since he left university, but he said until he had a book published he couldn't call himself a writer.'

Ben snorted. 'Bloody artistic temperament.'

'No, I don't think it's that,' said Rosie. 'For instance, if someone asks you what you do for a living and you say you're a writer, their next question is either "What do you write?" or "Would I have read anything of yours?" or a combination of the two. If, as a friend of mine does, you reply "I'm a columnist for The Times" they say, "Oh, a *journalist*," as though it's a lower life-form.'

'Really?' Libby was interested. 'I wonder where I come in the life-forms.'

'You write?' Rosie looked astonished.

'Panto.' Hetty leaned forward with the bottle to top up glasses. 'Written dozens.'

'Not dozens, Het. Just a few.' Libby stood up. 'I'll fetch another bottle, shall I?'

'One o' the good ones gal, not the ones you bought.' Hetty nodded to wards the pantry door.

'Not good enough, Mum?' said Ben with a grin.

'Good enough for this lot,' said Hetty, sitting back in her chair. 'Good job our Flo ain't here.'

Flo Carpenter, oldest friend of Hetty and live-in partner of her brother Lenny, had been left as something of a wine connoisseur by her late husband, who, as the village would have it, "kept a good cellar".

'Some of them have started drifting off to the pub,' said Libby, coming back into the room with a bottle in each hand. 'There seems to be a bit of an atmosphere.'

'It's that Patrick Joseph,' said Rosie.

'I thought you said he was a nice enough man?' said Fran.

'He is,' agreed Rosie, 'but he is also the most dreadful womaniser.'

'Has he tried it on with you?' asked Libby.

Rosie shook her head and smiled. 'I'm ten years older than he is, and he tends to go for the younger ones, anyway.'

'Lily Cooper's not that young,' said Ben.

'No, but I expect she was the best of the bunch at whatever event they met at,' said Rosie, 'or even the only one who responded. Some young women aren't as dazzled by his celebrity status as they should be, you see.'

They all laughed.

Later, as Ben and Libby walked down the Manor drive on their way home, they met Patrick Joseph, Lily Cooper and two other writers coming back up.

'Sleep well,' said Libby. 'We'll see you in the morning.'

'Aren't you on site?' asked Lily in surprise.

'No, we live round the corner,' said Ben, 'but my mother is in the Housekeeper's flat should you need anyone in the night.'

'But – what about staff?' persisted Lily, looking more and more disgruntled.

'We aren't a hotel,' said Ben, rather stiffly. 'We're a rather small conference centre. That's why you got this weekend at such a bargain price.'

'And that told you, Lily,' said Patrick genially. 'Thanks – er – Ben, was it? See you tomorrow.'

'She's an unpleasant piece of work, isn't she?' said Libby, as they resumed their way down the drive.

'Yes.' Ben frowned. 'I hope I haven't made things worse. Good job we charged each delegate individually, we might not have got paid.'

'And should we have had someone staying on site?' asked Libby. 'It's not fair to leave your mum in charge.'

'We modelled it on that place in Wales, didn't we?' said Ben. 'They don't have anyone staying on site. And the guests cater for themselves.'

'True. I'd hate that, though, wouldn't you? At least ours get good food.'

'Nothing better than my mum's cooking.' Ben

squeezed her arm against his side. 'Apart from yours, of course.'

'Don't flannel. I'm not fit to lick Het's apron.' Libby gave him a reciprocal squeeze as they turned left into the high street and past The Pink Geranium, the vegetarian restaurant run by their friend Harry, and owned by him and Ben's cousin Peter. Libby peered in through the windows, but no one was in evidence.

'In the pub,' said a voice behind them, and Libby turned to face her son Adam, who worked occasionally for Harry, and rented the flat above the restaurant.

'Fancy joining them?' said Ben.

'Have we got time?' asked Libby.

'It's early yet,' said Adam. 'Come on.'

'Where's Sophie?' asked Libby, as they went into the pub, subject of many a calendar photograph. Sophie, Fran's stepdaughter, had been going out with Adam for two years and had recently finished her Art History degree at university.

'Away with some uni mates at a hen weekend,' said Adam. 'I don't want to know, quite honestly.'

'I can imagine,' said Libby, amused.

'Hello, petal,' Harry, tall, slim and blond, leant forward and kissed her cheek. 'Some of your punters were just in here.'

'Patrick Joseph.' Peter, equally tall and blond, although rather more patrician, kissed her other cheek. 'I've met him before.'

'You don't sound too enamoured.' Ben squeezed between them and waved at the barman.

'He's not a bad writer, but thinks a lot of

15

himself.' Peter leant back against the bar. 'Quite the renaissance man, he is. Finger in a lot of pies. Does a lot of broadcasting.'

'A true polymath, in fact.' Libby pulled a face. 'Yes, Rosie implied the same.'

'Oh, Rosie's up there already, is she?' said Harry. 'I thought she was the star turn tomorrow.'

'She is, but she thought it would be more friendly if she stayed with them. Fran's staying too, although I said she could come home with us.'

'Well, they didn't impress me,' said Harry, 'and there was some bird hanging off that Patrick who reminded me of an angry heron.'

Ben and Libby laughed. 'Lily Cooper.'

'Whoever.' Harry shrugged. 'Couldn't keep her hands off him. Very pissed off that he didn't pay her much attention.'

'As that's everyone's impression, I guess it's right,' said Libby. 'Is Patrick married, do you know, Pete?'

'Very.' Peter pulled a face. 'Although he keeps her very much in the background. She's something quite important in her own right, but I don't know what. I don't even know her name, but the word is he uses her as an effective brake on any little interlude that threatens to get out of hand. Your Rosie would know.'

'She does know him, but hasn't said much about him other than he's quite a nice bloke, but a terrible womaniser.'

'There you are then.' Harry wagged a finger in her face. 'So don't you get into any little corners with him.'

Adam snorted.

'Don't embarrass my son,' said Libby, hoisting herself onto a bar stool.

'So,' said Peter, picking up a new glass of red wine and nodding thanks to Ben, 'are any of the other writers famous?'

'No, they're all aspiring,' said Libby. 'Like Fran. They met on a writing holiday last year.'

'Isn't that what you want to do? Host writing holidays?'

'Yes, but small weekend ones. This was a big one.'

'Have you had any more feedback for tomorrow's dinner?' asked Harry. 'I don't want to poison someone accidentally with a prawn or a mushroom.'

'I sent you the food forms ages ago,' said Libby.

'But there will still be someone who says, "Oh, I can't eat dairy/seafood/red meat." Or "I don't like that foreign muck." You know there will.'

'No one's said anything yet,' said Ben, 'and Mum's food went down a treat.'

'Traditional British, dear,' said Harry. 'Bound to.'

It was nearly half-past eleven when Libby and Ben returned to Number seventeen, Allhallow's Lane. Sidney the silver tabby shot out between their legs and Libby tripped down the step. All was much as usual.

But in the morning, when the phone began ringing at half past seven, when Libby was only just out of bed, she knew the roof had fallen in.

There was a body in the grounds of The Manor.

Chapter Three

'I'M THE OWNER,' BEN said to the yellow-jacketed policeman, 'and we are co-organisers of the event going on here. Of course you've got to let us in.'

The policeman looked doubtful. 'Wait here a moment, sir,' he said and went over to a dark saloon where two men stood zipping themselves into blue boiler suits. All three turned and looked at Ben and Libby.

'All right, sir.' The constable lifted blue-and-white tape and beckoned them under. 'Would you go inside and wait with the other people?'

Libby looked at the ambulance standing with its doors wide open, the police vehicles and what seemed like dozens of people moving slowly around the forecourt in front of the theatre. Some in uniform, some plain clothes and some boiler-suited. And two with dogs, who wagged tails and grinned, their tongues hanging out. She shivered. This was a scene from television, not Steeple Martin.

'Come on,' muttered Ben, taking her arm. They were ushered into the Manor, where they turned left towards the kitchen.

'Sorry, sir,' said the constable, 'in here, please.'

Libby stopped. 'No, constable,' she said. 'I am going into our kitchen to make tea. Has anyone been given tea? Or coffee? Or have they all been turfed out of bed and barricaded in here without anything?'

The poor constable looked even more confused, as an older, more confident constable appeared at his side.

'Sorry, ma'am,' the older man said. 'You'll have to obey the rules. In here with the others.'

'Go and get your superior,' said Libby, calmly turning towards the kitchen. 'The body, about which I know nothing except that it wasn't found in this house, will not be compromised by my making tea. Nor will any of the so-called suspects.'

Ben was already ahead of her filling the huge brown kettle. Luckily, the oil-fired Aga was still on, but, to back it up, Libby filled the electric kettle while the two hapless officers stood in the doorway. By the time trays with mugs had been prepared and the two brown betty teapots filled, the older constable had disappeared, while the younger one stood unhappily in the corridor outside the kitchen.

'Now we'll go into the sitting room,' said Libby, smiling sweetly as she passed him.

There was a loud reaction to the sight of the teapots and Ben's cafetière from the inmates of the sitting room. Another constable, obviously to set to watch these dangerous insurgents, started forward frowning, but caught sight of constable one, who shook his head hopelessly.

While serving mugs of succour, Libby and Ben tried to find out what had happened.

'First I knew was the police at the door,' said Hetty, taking charge of the second teapot. 'One of them people in the huts come out and practically fell over her.'

'Her? It's a woman? Who?'

'None of us know, yet. The police woke us all up and herded us in here.' Rosie was looking resentful.

19

'One of the guests?' Libby looked at Fran.

'We're all here except the people from the Hoppers' Huts, and it was one of them who found the body, so I wouldn't think so.'

The door opened again and they all looked round. One of the men whom Libby and Ben had seen outside walked into the middle of the room.

'Ladies and gentlemen, I'm sorry to have kept you in here for so long. As a preliminary, we just need to take your names, then you can go back to your rooms, and I'm sure your breakfast will appear as soon as possible.' He turned to Hetty. 'Mrs – er – Wilde –'

'You don't want to speak to me,' said Hetty, loading up one of the trays. 'Them's the two you want.' She nodded at Ben and Libby. 'And her.' She jerked her head at Lily Cooper who was on her way to the door.

'Mrs Cooper,' called Libby. The woman stopped.

The detective looked at Libby. 'And you are?'

'Libby Sarjeant. My partner Ben Wilde and I run the Manor. Lily Cooper is the organiser of this weekend break on behalf of the delegates – guests.'

Lily Cooper approached reluctantly, pulling a somewhat frivolous dressing gown more tightly around her.

'DS Wallingford,' the detective introduced himself. 'If you don't mind, I'd like to get the names of all the guests present here over the weekend, and,' he looked at Libby, 'the staff.'

'All my paperwork's in the estate office,' said Libby. 'Perhaps Ben could show you while I go and help Hetty with the breakfasts?'

DS Wallingford was frowning. 'Yes, that'll be fine,' he said. 'And Mrs Cooper? Have you any paperwork?'

'Well –' Lily hesitated. 'Not as such. It was a very informal group. We did it all by email and phone calls and I just did the block booking. Everyone paid for themselves.'

'But you'd have a list of all the guests?'

'I could write one, I suppose,' said Lily, ungraciously.

'That would be ideal,' said the detective. 'Perhaps after you're dressed?' He turned to Ben. 'Would it disturb you too much if I borrowed your office for a while this morning? Or is there somewhere else I could use?'

Ben shook his head. 'Much the best place,' he said. 'There's an individual phone line in there if you need it, and the wifi works better in there than in the rest of the house.'

Wallingford was frowning again. He looked at Libby. 'Sarjeant,' he said slowly. 'Why does that ring a bell?'

Libby's heart actually lurched. 'I don't know, I'm afraid,' she said. 'I don't think we've met.'

'No reason why we should,' said Wallingford, still looking pensive.

'No,' said Libby. 'May I go now?'

'Yes, I'll come and find you in the kitchen if I want to speak to you,' he said, and looked hopefully at the cafetière.

'Here,' said Ben, retrieving an unused mug. 'There's still some left, and I'm sure Libby will

21

make more.'

'Thank you.' The detective took the mug, added milk and cast another thoughtful look at Libby before following Ben out of the door. Libby sighed and picked up her tray. Lily Cooper had already vanished.

'That detective thinks he knows me.' Libby put the tray down on the table in the kitchen. 'Bugger.'

'Bound to rekkernise the name, gal,' said Hetty without turning from the Aga where she was loading bacon into a huge pan.

'Not from Ian Connell,' said Libby, carrying mugs to the sink.

'You bin mixed up in all them murders already, you and that Fran. And you bin in the papers. They probly warn young coppers about you in training.'

Libby ran hot water into the sink. 'I know, but this is a bit closer to home. I'm in a different position.'

'It was just as close to home with that first one,' said Hetty.

Libby looked quickly over to Hetty's bowed head. 'Shit,' she said under her breath.

'Closer, actually,' she amended. 'But the others – well, I've got involved by accident, really, haven't I?'

'Or you was arst in. That young Lewis, he arst you, and Harry's friend did too.'

'Hmm. And Ian's almost made a career out of warning me off.'

'He's bin grateful for your help, though hasn't he?' Hetty turned and fetched a large basket full of eggs from the dresser. 'Look at these. Old Pritchett

22

brought 'em up last night, fresh yesterday. Good job he didn't leave it till this morning. He wouldn't have got in.'

'No, and they won't let the staff in either, will they?' said Libby, looking worried.

'We can cope with the breakfasts, gal. And we don't know what's going to happen after that. They might want them to stay, or they might send them home.'

'Surely they'll want them to stay, at least for today, until they've interviewed everyone.'

'In that case you just carry on with your programme, and they'll let Harry in all right. Or they'll send someone for the food. Don't worry. Nothing we can do about it, anyway.' Hetty shrugged and started cracking eggs.

'I bet some of the guests won't see it that way,' said Libby.

'Then more fool them. You already got the better of them constables this morning, you can hold your own with this lot.'

Somehow, Hetty and Libby got the breakfast out. The bacon, eggs and tomatoes stood ready in chafing dishes, toast wrapped in napkins on a warming plate and large insulated pots of tea and coffee. Libby made sure all the tables were properly laid and went back to the sitting room to see if any of the guests had reappeared. Only Patrick Joseph and another younger man were there discussing something earnestly by the window.

'Gentlemen,' said Libby, 'breakfast is ready in the dining room. Can I ask you to let the other guests know if possible? We have no staff this morning for obvious reasons.'

'What?' said the man who had been talking to Patrick Joseph. 'Why?'

Patrick looked at him pityingly. 'The police won't let anyone in, of course, Nick.'

'Oh.' He looked confused, then held out his hand to Libby. 'We didn't meet yesterday, not properly. I'm Nick Forrest.'

Libby took the proffered hand, remembering seeing the slight, dark man hovering in the background yesterday. And wasn't he with Patrick and Lily on their way back from the pub? She smiled.

'I wish I could say I hope you're enjoying yourself.'

'Oh, I was.' Nick Forrest shot a quick look at Patrick. 'Lovely place. And I was looking forward to hearing Amanda George speak. She seems very nice.'

'Oh, she is. And we hope the police will allow us to carry on with the programme as far as we're able, as I expect they'll want you to stay around today.'

'I'm sure they will.' Patrick gave her a warm smile. 'And we appreciate all you're doing.' He turned to Forrest. 'Come on, Nick, let's get to the breakfast before the ravening hordes.'

Libby made her way to the estate office and found Ben and Wallingford peering at Ben's computer together.

'Breakfast's served,' she said. 'Did you want some, Ben?'

'I'll get something in the kitchen later.' He looked up at her. 'Look at this, Lib.'

Libby peered at the screen. 'That's my late booking. I told you. And it had been ticked off on the form, don't you remember?'

'But have you ever seen her?' DS Wallingford straightened up from the desk.

'I – er – I don't know.' Libby was bewildered. 'I assumed she was with the group in the dining room yesterday.'

'Was there anyone there you didn't remember having seen before?'

Libby looked at Ben. 'Honestly – I don't know. I didn't greet all the guests myself.'

'So someone could have slipped through the net?' Wallingford sounded stern.

'We did wonder yesterday,' said Ben. 'But Lily Cooper would have known if someone was missing or if it was someone she didn't know.'

'I'll go and chase up her list.' Wallingford started for the door.

'Do you want a print-out of our list?' asked Ben.

'Please.' Wallingford disappeared. Ben and Libby looked at each other.

'Rude, or busy?' said Libby.

'Busy,' said Ben. 'And slightly rattled. He's nervous for some reason.'

'Because it's a murder investigation and he's only a DS? Wouldn't it normally be a DI?'

'That's always been our experience,' said Ben, retrieving the list from the printer. 'But maybe not always.'

'It's early days,' said Libby. 'I expect a DI will turn up sooner or later. Let's hope it's Ian.'

'It can't always be him,' said Ben following her

out of the office. 'It could be old what'shisname from Canterbury.'

'Murray. Our Donnie, remember?' Libby grinned over her shoulder.

'Oh, yes, his dreadful wife. Did they ever come to the panto?'

DCI Don Murray had been the senior investigating officer on the first murder case Libby, Ben and Fran had been involved in, and had been given tickets to the opening production at the Oast House Theatre. The theatre had been transformed from a no longer working oast house by Ben, a former architect, and opened with a play about his family's history by his cousin Peter. It had caused some distress to the family in the end, which was why Libby had been worried about Hetty's reaction earlier in the kitchen. She needn't have worried.

'Bloody hell, Lib, you ought to know her by now,' said Ben, when she voiced these concerns. 'She's put all that behind her. Now, where's that Wallingford?'

They found him with Lily Cooper in the sitting room.

'Here's the list for comparison,' said Ben, nodding at Lily Cooper, who was now dressed in an unsuitable pale blue outfit that looked rather as though she'd just got in after a night on the tiles.

The young sergeant bent over the two lists, frowning, then looked up.

'There's an extra name here,' he said to Libby. 'Do you know who this is?' He turned to Lily.

Lily looked at the list and scowled. 'No, I don't.' She looked up at Libby as if it was her fault.

26

'That's the late booking I told you about,' Libby said. 'Mrs Ann Marsh.' She put her hand to her mouth. 'Oh, God, is it her?'

'If no one admits to having seen her, we won't know, will we?' said DS Wallingford, standing up and scowling in his turn.

'She was booked into the last Hoppers' Hut,' said Libby. 'Have you looked in there?'

DS Wallingford shot her an irritated glance. 'No reason to, have we? And which one is it?'

'I'll show you,' said Libby meekly.

'First, I need to show a picture of the victim to all your guests. When they've finished their breakfasts.'

'Oh, dear,' said Libby. 'Couldn't I show you the hut first? We could find out first if she's my missing guest.'

Wallingford sighed. 'All right. Come on. Mrs Cooper, if you would not talk about this to anyone, please. I'll see you here when I get back.'

Outside, Ben led the way to where the Hoppers' Huts stood, past the ominous white tent and blue-and-white-suited figures that surrounded it. Libby, after one look, averted her eyes. This was a lot closer than she normally got to murder.

The hut let to Mrs Ann Marsh was a small one in the middle of the row. Ben tried the door and found it open.

A handbag sat on the bedside table, toiletries on the dressing table and in the bin a take-away carton.

'That's why she wasn't at dinner last night.' Libby frowned. 'But why not? She was ticked off before dinner.'

'This,' said DS Wallingford, who was going through the handbag with gloved hands, 'is not Mrs Ann Marsh.'

'Oh.' Libby was puzzled. 'But I took her name and that was the name on the credit card she paid with.'

'In that case,' said the sergeant, 'this is a different woman.' He held up a driving licence. 'That is the woman we found, but her name, according to this, is not Ann Marsh.'

'What is it, then?' asked Ben.

'Melanie Joseph,' said Wallingford.

Chapter Four

LIBBY GASPED. 'IT CAN'T be!'

'Why?' Wallingford was looking at her closely.

'One of our guests is Patrick Joseph. He's quite a famous writer.'

'Wife? Sister?' Wallingford looked at the driving licence again.

'But why did she say she was Ann Marsh?' asked Libby.

'We don't know that she did,' said Ben. 'Ann Marsh might yet turn up.'

Libby shook her head. 'No. Ann Marsh was ticked off on the form last night against Hoppers' Hut five – this one. And somehow she'd got the key. We still don't know how she managed that, either.'

Wallingford heaved a sigh. 'Well, we'll take this and show it to Mr Joseph and get a search party organised for in here.' He pulled a face. 'I'll be glad to hand this one over.'

Libby and Ben preceded him out of the hut. 'Is someone else coming, then?' asked Libby. 'As SIO?'

He sent her a sharp look, then paused. 'Ah. Now I remember.'

Libby's heart sank.

'You're DCI Connell's friend. Are you the psychic one?'

'No,' said Libby weakly. 'But she's here, too.'

'Saints preserve us,' sighed Wallingford. 'Well, you'll be pleased to know that yes, he was to have been the SIO, but he withdrew when he heard where the case was.'

'Did you say DCI?' said Ben. 'Has he been promoted?'

'Yes.' Wallingford strode forward towards the Manor. Libby raised her eyebrows at Ben and they hurried along behind him.

In the sitting room, Patrick Joseph was sitting near Lily Cooper, who looked hunted. Libby nodded. 'That's him,' she whispered.

'Mr Joseph?' said Wallingford. 'Could I have a moment, sir?'

Patrick Joseph looked up with his warm smile.

'What can I do for you – er – Sergeant?'

Wallingford looked uncomfortable.

'Would you like to use my office?' said Ben. 'You know the way.'

Wallingford gave him a smile which seemed to Libby to hold an appeal of some sort, but she knew neither she nor Ben could go with the two men and offer moral support to either. This was to be Wallingford's unpleasant job.

'Well.' Libby turned towards the kitchen. 'What happened?'

'How do I know?' Ben was frowning. 'Come to check up on him incognito?'

'That's what it looks like,' said Libby, 'but would he kill her just for that?'

'Someone killed her, and I can't see who else it could have been.'

'Lily Cooper,' said Libby with satisfaction.

'Just because you don't like her,' said Ben, moving the big kettle on to the hotplate of the Aga.

'Don't like who?' Hetty appeared from the pantry with her arms full of vegetables.

'The Lily Cooper woman,' said Libby.

'Wandering around at night in something I'd be ashamed to call a nightie,' muttered Hetty.

'What?' said Ben and Libby together.

Hetty dumped the vegetables by the sink. 'I get up early. I reckoned she'd bin in a room she shouldn't have oughter.'

'Where was she?' said Libby.

'In the corridor outside my flat. Lorst, I shouldn't wonder.' Hetty smirked.

'You must tell that detective, Mum,' said Ben.

Hetty sniffed. 'I will if he asks.'

'We'll tell him,' said Libby. 'Then he'll come and ask you.' She turned to Ben. 'Pity Ian isn't coming himself.'

'Because of "where it is" indeed.' Ben laughed. 'Because you're here, more likely.'

'He knows too many of us,' said Libby, 'not just me. It would compromise the investigation. I wonder who they'll send?'

'Might be our first guess, Donnie Murray.'

'Or someone entirely new. There must be more than two DCIs at Nethergate and Canterbury.'

One of the uniformed constables tapped nervously at the open kitchen door.

'Scuse me, but DS Wallingford said could I make some tea and take it to the office? Sorry to bother you.' He glanced at Libby as if waiting for her to refuse.

'That'll be for Mr Joseph,' she said. 'It's all right, we're just making some. We'll put it on a tray

31

for you.'

Hetty, looking curious, immediately got out a small teapot and laid up a tray with mugs, milk and sugar. Libby filled the teapot and handed the tray to the constable, who gave her a servile nod.

'For Mr Joseph?' asked Hetty.

Libby explained.

'Poor bloke. Bit up himself, if you ask me, but that shouldn't happen to anyone.'

'It might change who they put in charge,' said Ben, hitching himself onto the corner of the table. 'He's quite a famous author. The police might feel it's a higher profile case.'

'They won't put in a superintendent as an SIO,' said Libby, 'and they don't call in Scotland Yard any more.'

'Well, I suppose we'll find out soon enough,' said Hetty. 'I'm getting on with the lunch.'

Libby, clutching a mug, wandered off to find out what the rest of the house party were doing. She wasn't surprised to find Rosie calmly giving a talk in the small sitting room which had been allocated for the purpose. All the guests appeared to be there, except Patrick Joseph. Even Lily Cooper was at the back, although she didn't look as though she wanted to be. Satisfied, Libby went outside to see if the police presence had abated. It hadn't. In fact, there was a new car there now, a dark, top-of-the-range current model. She wondered if this was the new SIO. The ambulance had gone, but been replaced by what looked like a hearse in disguise. So the body was still there, then. She suddenly realised she had no idea how the woman had been killed.

'And I suppose we can't ask,' she said to Ben on returning to the kitchen.

'You know more about all the other cases you've been involved in, and you're closer to this one,' said Ben. 'It's a different prospect, isn't it?'

The young constable appeared in the doorway again.

'Could you come back into the – er – other room, please. The sergeant would like a word.'

Hetty dried her hands on a tea towel, Ben and Libby put down their mugs and followed the constable to the sitting room, where all the other guest had reluctantly reassembled. Libby went over to Fran and Rosie.

'Did they interrupt your talk?'

Rosie shrugged. 'Hardly matters. I don't think people were attending really. I was just giving them something else to focus on.'

DS Wallingford appeared from the direction of the office followed by another young man with a dark suit and a cheerful expression.

'Ladies and gentlemen, I'm sorry to disturb you again, but the officer in charge has asked that all of you be interviewed individually, as soon as possible, so myself and DC Sharif will talk to you one by one in –' he looked over at Libby.

'The dining room?' she suggested.

'The dining room.' He turned to Lily Cooper. 'Would you come with me, please, and could another of you go with DC Sharif?'

One of the middle-aged ladies got up to follow the other officer, and Lily Cooper reluctantly followed DS Wallingford. Libby filled Fran and

33

Rosie in with everything that had happened so far that morning.

'But don't say anything. I don't know whether they'll tell people it's Patrick's wife or not. Assuming it is.'

'That's why he isn't here,' said Fran, looking round the room. 'The new boss is presumably still interrogating him.'

'Or sympathising.' Libby sighed. 'I suppose they'll want to search all the rooms. What a nuisance.'

'More of a nuisance for Patrick and his wife,' said Fran.

'I know. Sorry.' Libby drummed her fingers on the back of a chair. 'Do you think we've really just got to stay here until we've been questioned? I wanted to bring coffee in.'

'Ask when the next person comes out,' said Rosie. At that moment the woman who had been in with DC Sharif came out and Sharif poked his head round the door. Libby put up a hand and went quickly towards him.

'I'm the host of this conference and I wanted to bring in coffee for everybody, so could you see me now? Then I can get back to the kitchen.'

DC Sharif looked doubtfully over his shoulder to where Wallingford sat with Lily Cooper.

'Oh, I expect it'll be all right,' he said. 'Come in.'

Libby followed him to a corner where he had set up two chairs well away from Wallingford.

'Now,' he said. 'Could I have your name?'

'Libby Sarjeant with a J.'

'Thank you. And you said you're the host? What exactly does that mean?'

Libby explained.

'And when did you last see Mrs Joseph?'

'Oh, so it is really Mrs Joseph, then? Only she booked in as Ann Marsh.'

Sharif looked up. 'Oh? And when did you last see her?'

Libby explained about the mysterious signing in. 'After DS Wallingford found her driving licence I assumed she kept out of sight because she wanted to confront her husband and didn't want to give him any warning.'

Sharif remained impassive. 'So you knew nothing about any of the other guests? You'd never met them before?'

'Only Mrs Wolfe and Mrs George. Mrs George is giving some talks and Mrs Wolfe is a friend of mine and a student of Mrs George.'

'Student? What does Mrs George teach?'

Libby raised her eyebrows. 'Creative Writing, of course. She's a famous author.'

'Patrick Joseph's a famous author, too, isn't he?'

'Yes, fairly,' said Libby.

'Did they know one another?'

'I believe they'd met before. But all the other guests had met before at a previous writer's holiday or something. They'd know more than I would.'

'And you can't think of anything else you've noticed? Anything that would help us? Were you here last night?'

'No, we went home.' Libby suddenly remembered. 'But my mother-in-law was here. That was when she saw Mrs Cooper outside her room.'

Libby and Sharif both looked over at Wallingford, who, somehow sensing their gaze, looked up. Sharif made a gesture and he and Wallingford both rose and went to the window out of hearing. Libby watched Lily Cooper who looked quite beaten, then Wallingford came back and bent towards her, speaking very softly. She reared back and stood up, knocking over her chair. Libby looked uncomfortably at DC Sharif.

'I'd better go, hadn't I?' she said. 'I'll make coffee. Do you want anyone else yet?'

'No, thank you,' he said. 'I think this might take both of us.' And he went across to the two figures facing one another at the other end of the room.

Chapter Five

LIBBY, WARNED NOT TO say anything to anyone, went straight to the kitchen and began assembling tea and coffee trays again.

'A police investigation runs on tea,' she said out loud, before carrying the first tray back to the sitting room.

'They called Hetty in, but Lily Cooper hasn't come out,' Ben murmured as he came to help her, 'but then the young DC went off towards the office. I guess they've gone to get the SIO. What happened in there?'

Libby told him. 'But I wasn't supposed to tell anyone,' she said under her breath, 'so don't let on. And now I'll go and fetch the other tray. We really should invest in a trolley.'

When she got back, Ben was over in a corner with Sharif; Wallingford was in another with Nick Forrest.

'Has Lily Cooper still not come out?' she asked Fran when she came to fetch her coffee. 'And what about Hetty?'

'Hetty's still in there with another officer and Lily was taken off to the office.' Fran looked round the room. 'I don't know what to make of all this. We haven't actually been involved in a murder case like this, have we?'

'Ben and I were, and the family. When he first brought you down here.'

'I suppose so. And I was, a bit, when my aunt

died.'

'Hetty's not going to be happy.' Libby handed a cup of tea to a white-haired woman in a padded gilet and pearls.

'She'll be fine.' Ben appeared at her shoulder. 'I don't think it's the SIO who's in there talking to her. I didn't recognise him.'

'I wonder who's talking to Lily, then?' said Fran.

'Don't know. All I know is I've just been grilled thoroughly.' Ben accepted a cup of coffee.

'By young Sharif?' Libby laughed. 'He was very mild with me.'

'I think what you told him has made a difference. He asked me a lot about the house and the huts.'

The door to the dining room opened and Hetty came out followed by a middle-aged man in a rumpled suit. He went straight out of the room towards the office and Ben and Libby converged on Hetty.

'Who was that?' asked Ben.

'What did they want to know?' asked Libby.

'Come and sit down,' said Fran.

Hetty sat down and accepted a cup of tea.

'Where I'd seen that Lily Cooper, who I was, what I was doing. Cor, you'd think I was the bloody murderer.'

'But you put them straight?' said Ben.

'Bloody right. I don't know who he is, another sergeant, I think, not too pleased at having to talk to me.'

At that moment, the rumpled officer reappeared followed by a harrassed-looking, balding man with the vestiges of violently red hair lurking over his

38

ears.

'Murray,' whispered Libby.

'I remember,' said Hetty grimly.

'He's got even less hair now,' said Ben.

'Well, it was several years ago now,' said Libby.

DCI Murray was coming across the room towards them.

'We meet again, Mrs Sarjeant, Mrs Wilde, Mr Wilde.'

'Indeed, Mr Murray,' said Libby. 'I don't believe you met Mrs Wolfe last – oh, yes, you did, didn't you?'

'When my aunt died,' confirmed Fran, holding out a hand. 'But I was Mrs Castle then.'

'Ah, yes.' Murray peered at her, eyes narrowed. 'I must say you manage to get yourselves involved in far too many murder investigations.'

'We hardly mean to,' said Libby. 'And we're always ready to help if ever we're asked.'

'Well, the only help we need right now,' said Murray, 'is anything you've heard or seen that might help us.'

'Where's Lily Cooper?' asked Fran, realising that she hadn't come back into the room.

'In her room, why?'

'I just wondered,' said Fran, with a tiny shrug.

'I take it the dead woman is Patrick Joseph's wife?' said Libby.

DCI Murray sighed. 'You can take what you like, Mrs Sarjeant, but don't expect me to start giving away information like some others I know. Now, what is supposed to be happening for the rest of this weekend? I gather you're in charge?'

'We own the Manor,' said Ben, 'and we're starting to run it as a conference centre. The organiser of this group is actually Mrs Cooper. We're just providing the premises and the food. Oh, and the guest author.'

'Patrick Joseph?'

'No, he was simply one of the guests. It was a reunion, apparently, from a writers' holiday last year,' said Libby.

'So I've been told. So what had been set up for the rest of the day?'

'Well –' Libby looked at Hetty 'we were going to serve a cold buffet lunch, but we haven't got any of the casual staff who we'd booked to come in. And this evening Harry from the restaurant – remember him? – is bringing up a Mexican Feast. Or was.' She frowned anxiously at DCI Murray. 'Will he be able to?'

Murray looked thoughtful. 'If the rest of the guests want to carry on with your plans it would suit me very well,' he said. 'And I'll arrange a police escort for the Mexican Feast. Let me know what time.'

Libby was surprised. 'Well, thank you,' she said. 'Harry was going to bring the food up around seven. It's another buffet, which is lucky, with no staff, but I expect his partner Peter Parker will help.'

'I remember Mr Parker and Mr Price perfectly well,' said Murray, 'I'm sure I can trust them. And now, Mrs Sarjeant, if I could have a word?' He held out an arm indicating the dining room once more. Libby sighed.

'I'm told Mrs Joseph booked in under a false

name?' Murray wasted no time.

'Yes, and paid by credit card over the phone, so she must have had an account in that name.'

'And she doesn't appear on Mrs Cooper's list?'

'No, but all the guests booked individually, so the bookings all came in at different times. It never occurred to me that this one wasn't genuine.'

'Why do you think she did it?'

Libby was taken aback. 'I don't know! I assumed she didn't want her husband to know she was coming. There was a take-away carton in her room so she planned to keep out of sight.'

'And you never saw her?' Now Murray was frowning. 'How did she check in?'

'I've no idea. I just found her name ticked off on my clipboard and her key gone. How she would have known about the keys I don't know. Her room number was beside her name on the list, but how did she find the Hoppers' Huts?'

'And you'd never met her husband before?'

'No.' Libby was getting exasperated. 'Look, Mr Murray, I've told all this to DS Wallingford and DC Sharif already –'

'But you also told DC Sharif a very important fact,' interrupted Murray. 'I'm hoping you might remember another one.'

'When I first spoke to DS Wallingford I didn't know Hetty – Mrs Wilde – had seen Mrs Cooper this morning. Or last night, or whenever it was. She only told me when we came back after showing Wallingford the Hoppers' Huts.'

'And nobody's told you anything else since?'

'No! I've only spoken to Ben, Hetty and Fran.

None of us know any of the others.'

'You said you arranged the guest author?'

'You must have been told all this by now,' said Libby.

'I'd like you to tell me again. How do you know her?'

Libby narrowed her eyes at him. 'DCI Murray,' she said. 'I'm quite sure you know all about our little escapade at White Lodge that Inspector Connell investigated, so you know perfectly well how I know Amanda George.'

If this answer discomfited him, DCI Murray didn't show it, he just grinned.

'Look,' said Libby, 'you know I'll do everything I can to help, we all will. It's not as if we don't know the drill. I won't interfere –' Murray's grin grew broader '– and if we find anything out we'll tell you immediately.'

'Just don't get yourself into trouble.' He stood up. 'I'll tell the guests they're free to carry on with the weekend as planned. I've still got to question most of them again, so they couldn't go, anyway.'

'How's Mrs Murray?' asked Libby as they went to the door.

'Very well, thank you. She comes to all your productions now.'

'Does she?' Libby smiled smugly. 'Excellent. Tell her we're doing Cinderella this year.'

Murray made his announcement and then carted Rosie off for questioning. Libby stood and clapped her hands.

'Mrs George won't be long, then you can resume the session you were having earlier. We'll be having a cold buffet lunch as we have no staff, but the Chief Inspector has said there will be no problem with our Mexican meal tonight – in fact he's going to give it a police escort.'

This raised a ripple of laughter, then one of the women said:

'Do we know who it is? And how she died? It is a woman, isn't it?'

Libby, shocked, looked at Ben and Fran. She hadn't realised that the rest of the guests wouldn't necessarily have been told who the victim was.

'Yes, it's a woman, but I'm afraid I don't know anything else about her.' She looked round the room, 'And, by the way, did any of you meet her yesterday? A woman you haven't seen since? Only she was ticked off on my clipboard and she'd got hold of her key, so someone must have seen her, or helped her.'

'The police asked that,' said Nick Forrest. 'I don't think anyone did. And where's Patrick? He hasn't come back.'

'Gone to his room I expect,' said Libby, feeling a bit hot under the collar. 'And now, if you'll excuse me, I've got to help prepare lunch.'

'Phew!' she said as she went back into the kitchen. 'That was close. And I think they all deserve alcohol with their lunch. Have we got enough wine?'

'If we haven't I'll get Harry to bring more when he brings dinner,' said Ben. 'What did Murray say to you?'

After ascertaining that no police were occupying the dining room, Libby, Ben and Hetty laid out the

43

buffet, and set wine and beers on the chiffonier as the night before. Libby crept in at the back of the small sitting room, saw Rosie acknowledge her by the slightest move of her head, and slunk out again.

'There,' she said to Ben. 'I've done all I can. Now I'd like a drink.'

'What about them bedrooms,' said Hetty when they got back to the kitchen. 'We need to do the bedrooms.'

'I don't suppose they'll let us,' said Libby. 'Thank goodness.'

'Why?' Hetty raised her eyebrows.

'The police will want to search the rooms, I expect,' said Ben.

'She weren't killed here,' said Hetty. 'She was outside. Anybody coulda done it.'

'But she was part of this group – even if the rest of them didn't know, and she was Patrick Joseph's wife. They're all suspects, particularly Patrick himself and Lily Cooper.' Libby sighed. 'I shall have to get them talking.'

'Libby!' warned Ben. 'You are *not* to get involved.'

'I told Donnie Murray I'd help all I could and tell him everything,' said Libby, her eyes wide. 'And anyway, I expect Fran will have talked to several of them by now.'

Ben sighed and shook his head.

Libby decided to eat with the guests and when she'd loaded her plate managed to find a chair which she dragged over to where Fran and Rosie were sitting with three of the guests, the lady with the gilet and pearls, whose name was Jennifer

44

Alderton, a younger woman with very long fair hair and a huge smile, who was introduced as Nina Etherington and one of the only other men in the group, apart from Nick Forrest and Patrick Joseph, Daniel Hill, a round man with the grumpy face of a bulldog and a scattering of ash down his knitted waistcoat.

'So are you all writers?' asked Libby ingenuously. 'Sorry, that's silly, of course you are, or you wouldn't be here.'

'We're all here because we want to write novels,' said Fran, 'but some people are already writers in other genres.'

'Oh?' Libby smiled round brightly.

'I write features for the womags,' said Jennifer, smiling back.

'The what?'

'Sorry – the women's magazine market. We call them the womags.'

'I write for *Scriptus*.' Daniel Hill took a large swallow of his white wine.

'Ah.' Libby looked round for help. Jennifer smiled again.

'*Scriptus* is a quarterly literary magazine. Daniel's a contributor.'

'I see,' said Libby, thinking that he couldn't exactly live on an income from that.

'And you, Nina? What do you write?'

'I'm trying to write a romantic novel,' she said. 'I was really pleased that Amanda was coming to talk to us.'

Rosie smiled. 'And what I've seen of your writing you're doing very well,' she said. 'Pity you live too far away to come to my classes.'

'So you don't write for magazines or anything like that?' said Fran.

'Oh, no! I work for a vet.' Nina gave her lovely wide smile again.

'And you all met at the writers' holiday and kept in touch? That's great.'

Daniel Hill grunted and finished his wine, before standing up and waddling over to the chiffonier.

'What did I say?' said Libby.

'He only came because he was trying to get Patrick Joseph to get him in with his publisher,' said Nina. 'He's a horrible old man.'

Jennifer shook her head. 'I'm afraid that's right. Last time he just attached himself to Patrick as though he was on an equal footing with him, boasting about what he'd done. Patrick was too nice to slap him down, which he should have done, but he tried to avoid him as much as possible.'

'Not only him,' muttered Nina, looking down at her plate.

'Writers do get lionised a bit, Nina,' said Rosie, 'although usually only by other writers.'

'Oh, I didn't mean –' Nina looked, looking confused. 'But some writers are jealous, aren't they? They think they should have been published, or sold more or something and they resent the successful ones.'

Rosie looked quickly at Libby and Fran. 'Yes, that does happen sometimes. But no one here's like that are they?'

'I couldn't say,' said Nina, but they all knew that she probably could.

Chapter Six

'SO WHAT'S REALLY GOING on here?' said Libby as Fran helped her carry dirty plates into the kitchen. 'Somebody's jealous? Resentful? Nina thinks so, and that Daniel Hill, revolting though he is, obviously does too.'

'More likely he's the jealous resentful one,' said Fran.

'And when I saw Nick Forrest with Patrick this morning it didn't look much like a friendly chat, either,' said Libby. 'Although maybe I'm thinking that with hindsight.'

'Anyway,' said Fran, beginning to load plates into the dishwasher, Hetty having finally conceded that washing up for this many people was best left to others, 'whoever's resentful or jealous the target of that resentment and jealousy is surely Patrick. So why wasn't he murdered?'

Libby frowned. 'His wife was murdered to get at him?'

'I can't see that being the case,' said Fran. 'Do we know how she was killed?'

'No. And she was out in the open, too. Could you mistake her for someone else in the dark? Perhaps the killer thought it was Patrick?'

'He's quite a big man. I don't see how, unless she was a very big woman.'

'I wish we could *ask* someone,' said Libby, viciously scrubbing a serving dish too big for the dishwasher. 'We've always been able to before.

People have *known*.'

'We'll just have to talk to all the guests,' said Fran. 'Perhaps you ought to stay over tonight? There's room isn't there?'

'Ben's still got his old room.' Libby looked up from the sink. 'That's a good idea, actually, Fran.'

'The police will probably let everyone go tomorrow, and I can't see anyone wanting to stay on longer than necessary, so we've only got tonight.'

'To do what?' Libby grinned at her. 'Solve the crime?'

Fran went faintly pink. 'Well, yes, actually. I mean, we can't go charging off all over the country to talk to these people. The police can, but we can't.'

'That's true.' Libby looked thoughtfully out of the window over the fields. 'Perhaps we're just going to have to let it go. I can't see how we can get involved with this one after today.'

'That's not like you,' said Fran.

'I know. Perhaps I'm getting sensible in my old age.' Libby perched on the edge of the table. 'When do you think the police will let the others know it was Patrick's wife who was murdered?'

'No idea. He didn't come in for lunch, did he?'

'That young uniformed constable came and fetched plates of food for Patrick and Lily Cooper.' Libby stopped, struck. 'Goodness. Do you suppose that means they've arrested Lily Cooper?'

'Well, she was wandering about at night – or was it early morning? And we think she was having an affair with Patrick.'

'A fling, we thought,' said Libby. 'A one-night

48

stand last time they met which she wants to turn into a full-blown relationship.'

'We don't know that for certain.'

'We could ask young Nina. She knows more than she's letting on.'

'Or thinks she does,' said Fran. 'She's much younger than all the others. She may not have been taken into their confidence.'

'That's a thought,' said Libby. 'If he's such a womaniser, why didn't he go for Nina instead of settling for Lily?'

'What was it Rosie said last night? Lily was the only one who responded? Some of the younger ones didn't take his celebrity status seriously?'

'Of course! And what did Nina say just now?'

'Not just him, or something. Patrick tried to avoid someone else? Was that what she meant?'

Libby jumped off the table. 'Where is she now?'

'In Rosie's talk, I expect. Most of them decided to go to it just for something to do. Daniel Hill tried to go to the pub, but the police wouldn't let him leave.'

'Right.' Libby stared at her feet and chewed her thumb. 'Well, I suppose I'd better get the afternoon tea and coffee ready and we can lie in wait for Nina when Rosie lets them out.'

'But we've only just had lunch,' said Fran.

Libby sighed. 'It's just a constant round of food and drink, this lark. It breaks things up for them.'

Thus an hour later, when the small sitting room door opened and the guests filed out, Libby and Fran were on hand to offer milk, sugar and biscuits. Rosie and Nina came last. Rosie took a cup from

Fran with a grateful smile.

'Nina?' Libby offered a cup.

'Oh, thank you. Is that coffee?'

'There's tea if you prefer.'

'No, coffee, thank you.' The girl smiled. 'You know Amanda well, don't you?'

'Fairly.' Libby smiled back.

'She's a brilliant tutor. I wish she'd been on the holiday last year.'

'Who was?' asked Libby. 'Apart from the group here, of course.'

'There were a couple of other writers taking workshops, you know the sort of thing.'

'I don't actually,' said Libby, moving away from the tables and sitting on the arm of a chair. Nina sat down opposite and leant forward.

'Well, they give you things to do, subjects to write about, exercises. There was a short-story writer – she was really good – and a thriller writer, who wasn't. Patrick of course, he was doing thrillers, or crime, I suppose you'd say, and a romance writer. There were other delegates of course, but we were all in Patrick's group and we tended to stay together.'

'I'm surprised at Daniel Hill being in your group.'

Nina pulled a face. 'Because he attached himself to Patrick. We told you.'

'Oh, yes, and Patrick tried to avoid him.'

'Yes.' Nina's head was bent, but Libby was sure she was blushing.

'Did he have to avoid anyone else?' she asked gently.

The head came up. 'Oh, no! that wasn't –' she stopped, once more looking confused.

'That wasn't what you meant?' suggested Libby. 'What was it? That someone else was trying to avoid Patrick?'

Nina swallowed, her eyes sliding away from Libby. 'Where is he, anyway? They haven't arrested him, have they?'

'Why should they?'

'He hasn't been here since this morning. Was the murdered woman something to do with him?'

'Lily hasn't been here since before lunch, either,' said Libby, avoiding the question.

Nina stared at her. 'You know something we don't. Is that why you're asking me these things?'

Libby shook her head. 'I'm just trying to get the feeling of the group, as Fran, Rosie and I weren't there when you all met.'

'Rosie?'

'Sorry, Amanda George. Rosie's her real name.'

The door from the hall opened and DCI Murray appeared followed by DS Wallingford and DC Sharif.

'Ladies and gentlemen,' said Murray. 'You all agreed to a search of your rooms, which is now being undertaken. I shall ask to speak to you all after each search is completed, but in the meantime if you could stay in the public rooms I'd be grateful.' He took a deep breath. 'It's my sad duty to tell you that the murder victim found this morning was Melanie Joseph, Patrick Joseph's wife.'

There were gasps and exclamations and Libby's eyes darted from one to the other of the guests

51

trying to gauge reaction. She realised she wasn't the only one, Fran, Murray, Wallingford, Sharif and even Rosie were all doing the same thing. But the reactions were in no way surprising, except for Daniel Hill, who looked merely irritated.

'So,' continued Murray, 'obviously I shall want to know if any of you had any connection to Mrs Joseph and when was the last time you saw her, if so.'

'But we didn't.' That was Nick Forrest. 'None of us knew Patrick apart from the holiday last year. We weren't friends.'

There was a murmur of assent, but Jennifer held up a hand. 'I knew them, Chief Inspector. I live in the same village.'

All eyes turned to her. She stood up. 'Would you like to talk to me now?' she said. 'And perhaps, if Patrick would like to see me, I could see him. I've known him since he was twelve.'

There was another gasp, as Murray ushered her out of the room, then a buzz of talk.

'Well,' said Nina, looking shocked. 'She never said!'

'I expect she thought it wouldn't do to be seen to be on intimate terms with a course leader, especially a famous one.' Libby looked across at Fran and raised her eyebrows. Fran turned and spoke to Rosie and they both started towards Libby and Nina.

Nina shook her head. 'Poor Patrick.' She looked up at Libby. 'You said "intimate" terms. You didn't mean – surely not!'

'No, but Jennifer said she lived in the same village and had known Patrick since he was twelve.

That means she's known him, and probably his family, a very long time. That's intimate.'

'I just thought – well, he did – er –'

'Try it on with you?' suggested Fran, and Nina looked up at her with shocked, wide eyes.

'That's what you meant,' said Libby. 'That you tried to avoid Patrick.'

Nina looked as though she would get up and storm out, but suddenly subsided.

'I don't know why you're asking me all these questions,' she said plaintively. 'That's all that happened.'

'Last year? So why did you come on this weekend?' asked Rosie.

'To meet you,' said Nina. 'I've read all your books, and they're exactly the sort of books I'd like to write. And after Patrick took up with –' she stopped and looked at the three of them nervously.

'Lily Cooper,' Libby finished for her, 'you thought you'd be safe.'

'Yes.' Nina looked down at the coffee cup she still held in her hand. 'How do you know all this?'

'Sheer nosiness,' said Libby cheerfully. 'And observation. Rosie knew Patrick a little before, on the writers' circuit, and knew he was a bit of a lad.'

Fran snorted.

'And we worked out the rest ourselves, partly because we did know a bit more about it all than you or the other guests did,' supplied Rosie.

'And we've done it before,' said Fran, patting Nina's hand, 'so if there's anything you'd like to tell us that you don't fancy having to tell the police, we'd be happy to help.'

Nina frowned. 'You're not – er – whaddyacallem – private detectives?'

'No, but we have helped the police several times.' Libby slid off the arm into the chair. 'Even DCI Murray.'

'But I didn't think that really happened, you know, ordinary people helping the police,' said Nina, puzzled. 'Only in books.'

Fran and Libby looked at each other. 'Well, yes,' they said.

Rosie touched Nina's shoulder. 'Honestly, dear, if there's anything you know, you can tell them. They really can help, you know. They helped me.'

Nina looked up at her. 'Did they? Then perhaps ...'

'Think about it,' said Libby. 'I'd better go and start washing the cups and getting the kitchen ready for tonight. Are you doing any more talks, Rosie?'

'No, I'm not!' said Rosie. 'Half of them hadn't got their minds on what I was saying anyway. I'm going to sit here for a bit before I go up and change. If I'm allowed into my room, that is.'

Fran and Libby left Nina and Rosie and collected cups and urns.

'I'm definitely going to buy a trolley,' said Libby after the third trip to the kitchen.

'So I should think,' said Fran, easing her back. 'What have you got to do for Harry?'

'Not much. Plates warming in the oven, napkins and cutlery, a few serving dishes, I think. You shouldn't be helping.'

'I want to leave Nina with Rosie. I think she'll be telling her everything. Bit of hero-worship there.'

'She doesn't know Rosie like we do,' said Libby with a giggle. 'But you can help me with the dishwasher in that case. Hard work, this catering stuff.'

They had just finished reloading the dishwasher with cups and putting the plates into the warming oven of the Aga when Rosie came into the kitchen.

'Is it too early for a drink?' she said, sitting at the table. 'I've got quite a bit to tell you.

Chapter Seven

'I SAID SHE'D TALK to you,' said Fran, when Libby had provided glasses of a rather nice Sauvignon Blanc.

'It was a bit difficult. I think she's been taught it's rude to gossip or talk about her betters.'

'Her betters!' repeated Libby. 'Good God!'

'You know what I mean,' said Rosie, taking a large sip. 'But you were right, at this holiday last year Patrick made quite a determined play for her, and she said quite candidly that it was only because she was the youngest there. Then she thinks he went on to someone else who obviously rebuffed him, and ended up with Lily Cooper right at the end.'

'What we thought. And Lily thinks it's a proper affair?' said Fran.

'Nina doesn't know, but in the emails Lily sent round to the group she was always dropping little hints about "Patrick" as though she knew him really well. Nina felt uncomfortable about it, but she'd got quite friendly with Jennifer and when she heard I was booked for this weekend she decided to brave it.'

'So nothing we didn't know so far,' said Libby. 'You said there was a lot.'

'Apparently several people, including Daniel Hill and Nick Forrest tried to get Patrick to look at their manuscripts, and some were more persistent than others. He had read and given a critique on the first – oh, I don't know – ten pages from everybody before the holiday, so there was quite a lot of muttering and backbiting, I gather, because he refused.'

'Why would he refuse?' asked Libby. Rosie and Fran turned incredulous and scornful faces to her.

'How long do you think it takes to read a manuscript, Libby?' Rosie asked. 'And comment on it?'

'I don't know. A couple of days?'

'Much longer. And if the manuscript is awful, either you have to frame a very kind comment, or actually pull it to pieces. Neither of which is what people at conferences want. They want you to love it and offer to pass it to their agent or publisher with a strong recommendation to publish.'

Libby frowned. 'But don't you pull things to pieces every week for your classes?'

'Only short pieces – homework which I've set. A proper manuscript evaluation service costs a lot of money, at least five hundred pounds for a full manuscript.'

'Really?' Libby gasped. 'Blimey!'

'Unless you join the Romantic Novelists' Association,' said Fran.

'Eh?'

'They have a new writer section and you can get a full report for a very modest fee. And it's a report from a published member in your particular genre,' said Rosie. 'I'm a member, but I rarely do the evaluations as I have enough to do with the classes and getting a book a year to the publishers.'

'Right, so don't other writers understand all this?' asked Libby.

Rosie sighed. 'You'd be surprised. I've lost count of the conferences and talks I've given where someone asks exactly the same question time after time. People who are destined to be published learn quickly. Like Fran.' She gave Fran a quick smile. Fran made a face.

'OK – so neither Daniel Hill nor Nick Forrest understood this.'

'No, and they did the unforgivable, which was to try and make Patrick into a friend, instead of a conference speaker.'

'But he's here as part of a group of friends.' Libby frowned.

'There's a difference,' said Rosie. 'I don't suppose I can explain it, and the fact that he's here could be misconstrued by some of them. As far as Nina's concerned he's here to sleep with Lily and have a bit of fun.'

'And Daniel and Nick think because he's here, he really is a friend and they can renew their onslaughts.' Fran took a sip of wine. 'I can see how they might think that.'

'Well, none of that is a reason to kill Mrs Patrick,' said Libby.

'No, but it shows a certain underlying atmosphere in the group. And Nina said that there were a couple of other women who were after Patrick and could be –' Rosie paused.

'Women scorned?' suggested Fran.

'Exactly. She didn't say who.'

'Well, I can't honestly see any of this helps the murder enquiry,' said Libby. 'It's Mrs Patrick who was killed, not him.'

'Sounds a little as though Nina's not above dramatising a bit,' said Fran. 'There's nothing in what she's told Rosie that couldn't be found in any group of people, especially a group of potential rivals.'

'Of course!' Libby topped up the wine. 'They are rivals. Resentment against Patrick for being top dog must be there somewhere.'

'Oh, yes. Daniel Hill in particular apparently felt that he was a much better writer and there must be strings being pulled for Patrick to be such a best-selling author when he, Daniel, couldn't even get an agent,' said Rosie.

'Well, interesting though it all is, it doesn't get us any further,' said Fran. 'I've a feeling we ought to just leave it to the police after all, as Libby said.'

'I just wish Ian was in charge,' said Libby. 'We'd at least get some of the low-down.'

'And he knows that, which is why he stepped back,' said Fran. 'Unfortunate that DCI Murray also knows of the connection and will be on his guard.'

Libby sighed. 'Oh, well. Disappointing, though. I thought Nina was really going to come up with the goods.'

'Maybe she has and we haven't spotted it,' said Rosie. 'Although it doesn't seem as though there's much motive there apart from petty jealousies.'

'Sexual and authorial,' agreed Fran. 'And nothing for poor Mrs Patrick. Oh for heaven's sake what was her name, Lib? Can't keep calling her Mrs Patrick.'

'Melanie. And who was it said she was important in her own right?'

'Did someone say that?' Rosie looked surprised. 'I didn't hear it.'

'Maybe I dreamed it. Anyway, no one's likely to tell us, and we can hardly ask Patrick, if he ever reappears.' Libby stood up. 'I'd better start getting things ready for Harry.'

'I wonder if he *will* reappear?' Rosie also stood up and swallowed the rest of her wine.

'I wonder if he'll be charged?' said Fran.

'Maybe we can ask Jennifer when she comes back.' Libby was getting plates from a tall cupboard.

'Hardly,' said Fran. 'I think we'll just have to wait and see. Difficult for us, isn't it?'

Libby grinned over her shoulder. 'Dreadful.'

Harry and Peter arrived later laden with dishes and containers.

'Great fun having a police escort,' said Peter, pushing back the lock of hair that always fell over his forehead. 'Where's Hetty?'

'Laying up in the dining room,' said Libby, who had found time to change and tell Ben all they had learnt during the afternoon.

'So what's the goss so far?' said Harry.

'I assume you mean what's the state of play with our murder?'

'Of course. You always have the inside stuff.'

'Not this time,' said Libby. 'DCI Murray's in charge and they aren't telling us anything. All we know is the victim is the wife of one of the delegates, Patrick Joseph.'

'Oh, yes, he was in the pub last night,' said Harry. 'He's the famous one.'

'You might as well tell us what you do know, old trout,' said Peter, sitting down at the kitchen table, his legs stretched out elegantly in front of him.

Libby repeated the day's events while Harry pottered around decanting food and Peter opened wine bottles.

'So, no inside knowledge, then,' said Harry.

'No, except we took the sergeant to Mrs Joseph's room this morning, so we knew right from then that she'd arrived under an alias.'

'And you don't even know how she was killed?' said Peter.

'No. One or other of us has been keeping an eye or an ear on the news all day, but so far nothing's leaked out. I'm surprised, because Patrick is quite well known and a frequent broadcaster on the BBC.'

'What does he write?' asked Harry.

'Thrillers, I think. Gory stuff.'

'He's had a couple serialised on TV,' said Peter. 'Remember *Cold Death*? That was his.'

'Oh, I remember!' Libby was surprised. 'He wrote that, did he? Very nasty.'

'Perhaps this is based on incident in one of his books?' suggested Harry.

'Why would it be?' said Peter.

'Oh, I don't know. A mad, obsessed fan, you know – like that film.'

'That film was also a book first,' said Peter. 'I wish I could get you to read more.'

'Too busy,' said Harry cheerfully. 'And when I'm not, I devote myself to you, dear heart.'

Peter patted him on the bottom. 'So you do.'

'If I could interrupt this lovefest,' said Libby,

'what have I go to do with this food, Hal? And are either of you staying for the evening?'

'We both are.' Peter grinned wolfishly. 'You don't think we'd let an opportunity like this pass us by, do you?'

'Go on, petal,' said Harry, giving her a gentle shove. 'Go and get the guests tanked up before dinner. I'll come and announce it when it's served.'

Libby went to fetch Ben from the office and joined the guests who were milling around the chiffonier. Jennifer was there, looking the same calm person she'd been earlier in the day, although now attired in a lace jacket and velvet skirt. Nina stood close to her, looking nervous.

'How was Patrick?' asked Libby, going up to them.

Jennifer shook her head. 'How you'd expect. Asolutely shocked, devastated, uncomprehending. He can't understand what she was doing here, especially under a false name.'

'Really?' Libby looked sceptical and Jennifer sighed.

'Yes, I know. He was an incredibly naughty boy and she obviously decided to check up on him. At least I assume so. I gather the police do, too.'

'Have they said so?'

'He said that what they said to him sounds as if they do.' She sighed again. 'Such a silly boy.'

'Boy?' Nina said.

'To me he is,' smiled Jennifer. 'I was an adult when I first met him. I used to babysit.'

'But he was twelve! You said so earlier.'

'He had a younger sister and a twelve-year-old

boy wasn't considered a fit babysitter in those days.'

'I don't think he would be now, either,' said Libby. 'You'd have social services on your back.'

'So he's not coming back to join us?' Fran came up on Jennifer's other side.

'No, I'm taking a plate up to him. And he'll leave as soon as the police let him. He's already had to identify the body, poor soul.'

Fran, Libby and Nina all nodded in sad agreement.

'And what about Lily?' asked Nina. They all looked at her in surprise. 'Where's she?'

'I don't know. In her room, I suppose.' Jennifer looked round. 'I don't know why she was singled out for treatment.'

Libby managed not to catch Fran's eye. 'Oh, I expect because she was closer to Patrick than anyone else.'

'You think so? Apart from the fact that they were sleeping together?' said Jennifer.

'Er – well –' Libby slid her eyes sideways to Fran.

'She was no closer than any of his other conquests,' said Jennifer. 'He really was devoted to Melanie. And he hadn't seen Lily since last year.'

'Oh.' Libby frowned. 'Do you think in that case she *was* murdered to get at him?'

'Why not just stab *him*?' said Jennifer.

'Stab?' said the other three.

'Yes.' Jennifer looked confused. 'That's what he said.'

'Stabbed.' Libby was thoughtful. 'Out there in the field.'

'No, apparently,' said Jennifer. 'The police think she'd been moved.'

Libby, Fran and Nina stared at her.

'Dinner is served,' said Harry.

Chapter Eight

HARRY AND PETER WERE relishing being in the spotlight. The older ladies, including Jennifer, Libby was surprised to see, were twittering around them like elderly moths, agreeing to be tempted by some of the more exotic dishes Harry had brought.

'I though Mexican was just chilli con carne,' said one, adjusting her multiple necklaces and patting her wispy hair.

Libby watched as Jennifer bore away a tray with a covered dish and a bottle of Harry's best Cabernet Sauvignon.

'Up to the condemned man,' Harry whispered as she took her place at the serving table in front of him.

'Don't,' said Libby. 'Apparently he's devastated.' Harry looked scornful. 'No really. I'll tell you later.' She filled her plate with Pollo Verde, refried beans, salad and rice.

'Got enough there, dearie?' Harry handed her a full glass of wine.

'Cheek,' said Libby, and went to find Fran and Rosie, who were, unsurprisingly, at a table with Nina.

'Where's Ben?' asked Fran.

'He's opted to eat in the kitchen with Hetty. I think he's a bit overwhelmed with all these writers.' Libby turned to Nina. 'Is Jennifer all right? She must be very shocked as she knew them both.'

Nina nodded. 'She seems to be. I didn't know

she knew him. She didn't say last time.'

'I can understand that,' said Rosie. 'She didn't want him to feel pressured or to be seen to get preferential treatment.'

Nina's eyes slid to Fran.

'Yes, I know it's obvious we're friends,' said Fran, reading Nina's mind. 'But I'm not expecting any sort of treatment.'

'But that's exactly what a lot of the other people did think they would get if they befriended Patrick, wasn't it, Nina?' Libby forked up Pollo Verde and assumed an expression of bliss.

'I think so.' Nina was looking nervous again, and Fran shook her head slightly at Libby. Just in time, Jennifer reappeared and sat down with them.

'How is he?' asked Rosie.

'A bit more normal. He said he wanted to come down for a drink after dinner –' she turned to Libby '– if we're allowed to have a drink after dinner? We'll be drinking far more than was included in the price.'

'Well, of course you're welcome, but would he want to be surrounded by a lot of inquisitive well-wishers?'

'Oh, I think most people will be sensitive enough to leave him alone,' said Jennifer. Nina looked doubtful.

But before Patrick could make an appearance downstairs, it was Libby who was accosted by another of the guests, a small, slim, dark-haired woman with an intense expression and skin-tight black jeans.

'You're one of the organisers, aren't you?' The

woman had sidled up to Libby almost without her noticing.

'Not exactly. My partner owns the Manor and we host this sort of thing.' Libby found herself looking down on the woman, not something she normally had to do.

'But you know Amanda George?'

'Ye-es.'

'Could you introduce me? I'm sure my work would be of more interest to her than to Patrick Joseph.' The name came out like venom from a snake.

'You could introduce yourself,' said Libby. 'No introduction from me would make any difference, and I don't even know you.'

'Dee Starkey.' The woman held out a thin hand. 'I write erotic fiction.'

'Oh.' Libby swallowed and shook the hand gingerly. 'Well, Rosie – I mean – Amanda doesn't write that sort of thing, you know.'

'I know, but she writes women's fiction, doesn't she? Nearer my market than gory bloody thrillers.'

'You could,' said Libby, inspiration striking, 'join the Romantic Novelists' Association. I bet they've got people who write that – er – well – your sort of thing.'

'Them!' Dee Starkey was scornful. 'I'm not going to join a bunch of wannabes and old women.'

'Really?' Libby's brows drew together. 'You're published then?"

'I have a regular slot in *Spank Monthly*.'

Libby bit the inside of her lip hard to stop herself from laughing. 'I'm sorry,' she said in a shaky voice, 'I don't think I've heard of that.'

'It's an online erotic fiction magazine. So you see, I'm hardly a beginner.'

'No, I quite see that,' said Libby, 'but what makes you think Amanda could help you?'

'I need an agent. She could introduce me to hers.'

Libby was beginning to see what Rosie and Fran had meant. 'Oh, I don't think she could do that,' she said, improvising, 'her agent doesn't deal with your sort of fiction either.'

Dee Starkey let out something between a snort and a sigh. 'That's what the other bastard said.'

Libby located a wine bottle and held it up. 'Can I top you up?' she asked, realising that Dee's other hand held an empty wine glass.

'Is that red? I only drink white.'

Libby picked up another bottle, turning the label in case this strange little woman had the widespread and fashionable dislike of Chardonnay.

'So, Patrick refused to help you did he?' Libby topped up her own glass.

'Said more-or-less what you did. And that he couldn't be seen to be showing favouritism.'

Another tick for the theory, thought Libby. 'You were friends, were you?'

'Yes.' Unattractive colour seeped into Dee's thin cheeks. Oho. Another conquest? Or another refusal?

'Perhaps this sort of thing isn't quite the right place to try finding an agent,' suggested Libby. 'The holiday you went on where you all met, isn't that more the sort of thing?'

'Oh, writers' holidays, conferences, you name

them, I've been to all of them.' Dee fidgeted, her eyes turning to the door. 'I suppose I can't very well ask Patrick again.'

'Hardly,' said Libby. 'He's just lost his wife.'

'Much he cared about her.'

'Really? Jennifer said he was devastated.'

'Jennifer?' Dee laughed. 'What does she know?'

'Quite a lot, actually,' said Libby, beginning to get annoyed. 'She babysat him when he was a boy.'

'Well,' said Dee, obviously not wanting to give ground, but with little left to say.

'I'm sorry I can't help you,' said Libby, 'but I don't know enough about your business to suggest anything else.'

'You're not a writer?' Dee looked surprised.

'No, I'm an artist.' Libby didn't mention pantomime. She didn't think Dee would appreciate it.

'Oh, well, of course you wouldn't understand. I'd better talk to Amanda George myself.' Dee sighed, as though this was one inconvenience too far.

'I'll wa– tell her,' said Libby, hoping Rosie, Fran, Jennifer and Nina had done as they said and gone to sit in the small sitting room. 'Why did you ask Patrick in the first place?' she asked as a delaying tactic.

The colour seeped back into Dee's cheeks. 'He - er –' she cleared her throat, 'looked at something of mine.'

'A story? A – um – manuscript?'

'A short, actually.'

'Oh, so he didn't downright refuse, then?'

Dee looked hunted. 'Er – no.'

'So what, then?' Libby wasn't going to give up now.

Dee pulled herself up to her full five feet and threw back the last of her wine. 'If you must know,' she said, putting her glass down with a bang, 'he asked to see it because he said it turned him on. And it did. With me. And then had the fucking nerve to say it wasn't his sort of thing. I tell you – it was his sort of thing while he was doing it!' And with a furious glare at the unsuspecting Harry, who had arrived to collect plates, she stamped off towards the hall. Libby subsided against the table.

'Here,' said Harry, taking her glass and topping it up again. 'What was all that about?'

'Another of Patrick's little peccadilloes,' said Libby. 'Did you see where Fran and Rosie went?'

'Into the small sitting room with those other two, I think.'

'I shall get them to convene in the kitchen in a minute, I think. You and Pete can come too, if you want to hear a bit more gossip.'

'You know I don't like gossip.' Harry wagged a finger in her face. 'But I might stretch a point.'

But before Libby could convene anyone, Patrick Joseph appeared in the doorway.

The buzz of conversation gradually faded away as he walked between the tables towards Libby.

'I don't suppose you know where Jennifer is?' he said.

Libby knew now what was meant when it was said someone had aged overnight. Or in this case over one day. Patrick's rather long but normally jovial face was haggard, his cheeks sunken and the wrinkled shadows under his eyes a chalky grey.

'Er – yes. She's in the small sitting room. I'll show you.' She put down her glass. 'I'm very sorry about …' she stopped not knowing how to go on. He gave a tired smile.

'I know. No one knows what to say. But I've known Jennifer nearly all my life. I thought I'd like to have a drink with her.'

'What can I get you?' said Libby. 'Wine? Whisky? Gin?'

'Red wine would be lovely, thank you. I had a very nice Cabernet Sauvignon with my dinner. Which,' he turned to Harry, 'was excellent. Thank you. I gather you're the chef.'

Harry, who also didn't appear to know what to say, inclined his head and produced another bottle of Cabernet. Libby took it and led the way to the small sitting room.

'We'll leave you to it,' she said, when the others had expressed their sympathy and Jennifer had pulled a chair up for Patrick. 'I'll send Harry in with a couple of glasses.'

'Fran and Rosie, could I speak to you for a moment in the kitchen?' she said, once they were outside. 'Nina, sorry this is a family matter.'

'That's all right,' said Nina, with a resigned expression. 'I think I'll go up to my room.' She turned to go, then turned back. 'Do you know if any of those policemen are still here?'

'I don't think they are, except perhaps a couple guarding the – er – the hut and the front door. Why?'

71

Nina looked nervous. 'I – well, I wanted to talk to one of them.'

Libby raised an encouraging brow. Nina's pale skin began to change to a delicate pink. 'I just – just thought of something,' she said, and rushed out of the room.

Hetty and Ben were sitting either side of the Aga and Hetty had opened the door to show the glowing red fire inside. Peter was in a chair at the table, his legs stretched out before him as usual. Harry came in bearing plates almost as soon as Libby, Fran and Rosie had sat down.

'OK,' he said. 'What's happened now?'

Chapter Nine

'SO IT APPEARS,' LIBBY concluded, 'that Patrick asked to read one of Dee Starkey's stories purely as a seduction technique and then turned down her manuscript. Or the chance to read it.'

Rosie shook her head. 'So that makes three of them, Daniel Hill, Nick Forrest and Dee Starkey. All of them turned down by him.'

'But he hasn't been killed,' said Fran. 'His wife has been killed.'

'But not where she was found,' said Libby. 'And we know now she was stabbed. So she could have been killed here, in the house and moved.'

'And we know Lily Cooper was wandering around during the night,' said Rosie.

'Morning,' said Hetty.

'Eh?' All heads turned towards her.

'It was morning. About half five. Told you in the first place – I get up early.'

'Does that make a difference?' asked Ben.

'It would if we knew when she was killed,' said Libby.

'Your inspector will have asked everyone if they heard anything, won't he?' said Harry.

'The sergeant asked me,' said Ben, 'but I told him we weren't here.'

'If she was killed here one of those people could have mistaken her for him,' said Peter.

Rosie shook her head. 'No, he's quite a big man.'

'Now, if it had been poison,' said Libby, 'it

could have been mistaken identity.'

'It wasn't, though,' said Fran. 'I think we should be looking into Melanie's own life.'

'How exactly? We aren't looking into this at all, Fran.' Libby sighed and leant back in her chair. 'Oh, I wish Ian was here.'

'I shall start getting jealous if you keep saying that,' said Ben.

'We asked him when we started looking at White Lodge last year,' said Libby.

'That wasn't a murder case,' said Rosie.

'Then,' murmured Peter.

'Anyway, I bet Murray doesn't know about Dee Starkey's fling, or that she, Daniel Hill and Nick Forrest were all turned down by Patrick,' said Libby. 'People are far more likely to talk to us than to the police. Mind you, young Nina wouldn't tell me just now what she wanted to tell the police.'

'What?' said several voices at once. Libby explained.

'And he made a pass at Nina, so this could simply be getting her own back,' she concluded.

'Libby, once and for all, it wasn't Patrick who was murdered,' said Fran.

'Oh, all right,' grumbled Libby.

'Anyway, all the guests will be leaving in the morning. They've been told they can go,' said Rosie.

'Oh, well, that's that then.' Libby sighed.

'I hope the police go as quickly,' said Ben. 'We don't need this sort of publicity.'

'This was a private booking,' said Libby, 'it isn't as if it'll go on the website.'

'Have you got any more bookings?' asked Peter.

'Not until later in the year. No one knows us yet,' said Libby.

'But we have got a lot of lettings for the Hoppers' Huts and Steeple Farm,' said Ben. 'Something to do with people wanting to holiday in the UK rather than spend money on going abroad.'

'Where do all the guests live?' asked Fran suddenly.

'Why?' Libby looked taken aback. 'You're not thinking of tracking them all down all over the country?'

'No, but I wondered how well they *really* knew one another.'

'Except for Jennifer, no one knew Patrick,' said Rosie. 'Except me, I suppose, and I only met him on the circuit.'

'I still find it odd that if all these people are aspiring novelists, why they didn't know anything about the etiquette of a gathering like this, or the previous writers' holiday,' said Libby. 'And that Dee Starkey was scathing about your Romantic Novelists' Association, Rosie. I asked why she hadn't joined. I was sure there must be erotic writers there? Or wouldn't they be allowed?'

'Of course they are. It's a very broad church and much more inclusive than most of the other organisations. I mean, we allow unpublished writers. No one else does.'

'That's what I thought. She seemed to think you were all twinset and pearls or wannabes.'

Rosie laughed. 'If you knew how many times that's been said. Most journalists like to perpetuate the pink, fluffy image that's about fifty years out of date – if ever it was the right image in the first place, which I doubt.'

'I suppose we shall just have to wait for the police investigation to sort it out,' said Fran, standing up. 'I'm sure there's more to this than meets the eye.'

'There could hardly be less,' said Libby, following suit. 'I don't think I want to stay here tonight after all, Ben. They'll let us go home, won't they? Sidney needs to be fed.'

The constable detailed to stay on guard at the door confirmed that he had instructions to let Harry, Peter, Libby and Ben leave the Manor and they strolled down the drive together.

'I can't believe it was only twenty-four hours ago we walked down here and said goodnight to Patrick Joseph,' said Libby.

'You have had a busy day, haven't you?' said Harry. 'Do you want a nightcap with us?'

'I think I'd like to go home if you don't mind,' said Libby. 'You can go if you want, Ben.'

'No, I'll come home, too,' said Ben. 'Thanks all the same, Hal.'

Peter turned right to go to their cottage, while Harry popped into The Pink Geranium to see how the evening had gone under the stewardship of Donna, his right-hand woman, recently married to her doctor husband. Ben and Libby walked along the dark village street arm in arm.

'What made you change your mind about staying?' asked Ben.

'I'd had enough,' said Libby. 'It seemed to be

questions all day, either the police asking them or us asking each other, and getting nowhere. If we'd stayed it would have meant sitting up with Fran and Rosie and carrying on talking about it.'

'And the alternative is going home and talking about it with me?'

'No, I shall try and find something mindless on the telly.' She squeezed his arm. 'I want to feel normal.'

'I know what you mean. I'm wondering how normal I'll ever feel at the Manor after this.'

'Oh, Ben! Don't say that. Do you think we should shut down the operation and just stick with the lettings?'

Ben sighed. 'I don't know. Now we've done all the conversion it seems a waste.'

'Let's just see how it goes.' They turned the corner into Allhallow's Lane under the lilac tree. 'They'll all be gone tomorrow, so it'll look completely different.'

Ben frowned and took out his key. 'It's odd having your childhood home overrun like that, though.' He opened the door and Sidney shot out.

'I thought it would be Hetty who'd be unhappy, but she isn't, is she?'

'No. And it's been good for her since Dad died.' Ben switched on a table lamp. 'Takes her mind off it. Nightcap?'

'Do you know what I'd really like? A cup of hot chocolate.' Libby went kitchenwards. 'That proves I'm not an alcoholic.'

The following morning the casual staff had been

allowed back and by the time Libby arrived in the kitchen of the Manor Hetty had breakfast well under way.

'Half of 'em ready to go,' said Hetty pouring a mug of coffee and handing it to her. 'Can't wait.'

'I don't blame them,' said Libby. 'What a start to the business.'

Hetty gave her a look. 'Art weekend went well. Not half so much trouble. Stick to them.'

Libby sighed. 'We could. I don't think I'm quite in tune with writers.'

'More bloody artistic temperament than artists,' said Ben, coming in and giving his mother a kiss.

'I don't think so. More jealousy, perhaps, and a murder's enough to make anyone throw a temperament,' said Libby. 'But Rosie says they're not all like this.'

'And we mustn't forget, as Fran said, that it wasn't a writer who was killed, but a writer's wife.' Ben poured himself some coffee. 'Come on. We'd better go and check the guests and the police. See what the situation is.'

The situation was clear. All the guests except Patrick Joseph were assembled in the large sitting room, their bags neatly piled against the wall.

'Is breakfast ready?' asked Lily Cooper. 'I need to get away.'

'It's on its way,' soothed Libby. 'If you'd all like to go into the dining room, the staff will bring it in.'

There was a muttering and sighing and the guests gradually got to their feet. Dee Starkey gave Libby a hard look as she passed, and Jennifer and Nina came up to speak to her, followed by Fran and Rosie.

'We'd like to thank you,' said Jennifer. 'You coped admirably.' She turned to Rosie. 'And you were brilliant. I wish I lived nearer and could come to one of your courses.'

'Oh, yes,' said Nina, 'so do I. And will you sign my book before you go?'

Rosie smiled. 'Of course. Now? Or shall we do it after breakfast? I'm not rushing off.'

Nina looked at Jennifer, who said, 'After breakfast, I think. And I've got one too, if you wouldn't mind.'

Rosie beamed. 'Delighted,' she said. 'Let's go and eat.' She walked off towards the dining room between them.

'Andrew's coming to take her home,' said Fran, 'so I thought I'd hang around and see if you need a bit of help.'

Libby sighed. 'Stay by all means. I only hope all the food we had in for lunch today won't go to waste. I expect Hetty will insist on cooking for us, so will you stay for that?'

'Of course. Guy might drive up, too.'

'That means neither of you can have a drink,' said Ben. 'Oh, well, I'll go and see if our resident policemen are in my office.'

'I'll come too.' Libby waved a hand at Fran and followed him out of the room

DCI Murray and DS Wallingford appeared to be in the process of leaving, too.

'We're done here for the time being, Mr Wilde,' said Murray. 'We need to keep a presence and there are more forensics to be done, to make certain we know where Mrs Joseph was killed.'

'So you think it was in the house?' said Libby. 'We heard you thought she'd been moved.'

Murray's lips tightened. 'That we're not sure of, Mrs Sarjeant. But you'll understand the investigation will take some time.'

That he'd wanted add "You of all people" was quite clear.

'But you're letting the guests go home?'

'I can hardly keep them here when not one of them's a suspect,' said Murray.

'Not even Lily Cooper or Patrick Joseph?' said Libby.

'Mrs Sarjeant,' Murray sighed, 'please don't start trying to solve this case. Try and believe we do sometimes know what we're doing.'

'You know where we are if you need us,' said Ben, hastily stepping into the breach. 'If not here, at home on Allhallow's Lane.'

'You live there now, then, Mr Wilde?' Murray raised his eyebrows and looked from to the other.

Ben bristled.

'Thank you for your help,' said DS Wallingford. 'We'll be in touch if we need to. All right if we leave the SOC officers here? And don't let anyone touch any of the guests' bedrooms until we give the all-clear.'

'Or the public rooms,' added Murray.

'But there's already been a certain amount of clearing up,' said Libby. 'Washing up and that sort of thing.'

'That's fine,' said Wallingford. 'Just don't do any cleaning yet, if you don't mind.'

'Does that include the Hoppers' Huts?' asked

Ben.

'The–?' Murray frowned.

'Surely you remember the Hoppers' Huts, Mr Murray?' said Libby.

He scowled.

'Oh, and did young Nina whatsername manage to speak to either of you?' Libby looked from one to the other of the policemen, who looked at each other.

'Not to me,' said Murray.

'Nor me,' said Wallingford. 'What did she want?'

'She didn't say,' said Libby. 'Shall I ask her?'

'No!' said Murray and Wallingford together.

'That went well,' said Ben, as they watched Wallingford and Murray get into the large sleek car Libby had noticed yesterday. The other police vehicles and bodies in blue-and-white boiler suits were still scattered across the forecourt. One of them was reading the poster on the front of the theatre.

'Let's go and tell Hetty the good news she can't start spring cleaning,' said Libby. 'She'll be furious.'

Chapter Ten

HETTY WAS PHILOSOPHICAL. SHE made arrangements with the casual staff to come in as soon as the police allowed, and set about preparing lunch, refusing all offers of help.

Fran and Libby waited until Andrew Wylie, Rosie's occasionally significant other, came to pick her up, then wandered down the drive on their way to number seventeen Allhallow's Lane.

'Well, that's that,' said Libby. 'The murder case we've been closest to for ages and it's all over.'

'It's hardly all over,' said Fran. 'Just as far as we're concerned.'

'It's so frustrating. We know absolutely nothing about it and we can't find out.'

'Libby, you're positively ghoulish.'

'We could look everyone up on the internet,' said Libby, with an air of inspiration.

'What good would that do? And who would we look up?'

'We–ell,' said Libby slowly, 'how about Melanie Joseph? Peter said she was quite important in her own right. She might be quite well documented. And we might find a clue as to why she was stabbed.'

'I'm not sure about that,' said Fran, equally slowly.

'What, that we might find a clue?'

'No, that she was stabbed.'

Libby stopped and turned to her friend.

'A "moment"?' she asked.

Fran's occasional psychic "moments" had played a part in most of the investigations in which they had been involved, and were the source of the help given them by Detective – now Chief – Inspector Connell, who, despite the scepticism of his colleagues, had not infrequently asked for her help – and by extension, Libby's.

'I'm not sure.' Fran frowned. 'I keep getting one of those pictures.'

'Of what?' said Libby, excitedly.

'A woman drinking.'

'Oh.' Libby began walking again. 'No suffocating feeling?'

'No.'

'Poison?'

'No idea. But poison's a bit dramatic and passé these days, isn't it?'

'Shades of Miss Marple, you mean?'

'Well, yes. And I don't know if it has anything to do with murder, or contradicts the stabbing theory, really.'

'But you feel it has?'

'Yes.' Fran sighed. 'You know I can't be sure of things. But what I don't understand, if it does contradict the stabbing theory, is why Jennifer was so certain Melanie was stabbed.'

'Patrick told her. And that the police thought she'd been moved.'

'I wonder?' Fran was still frowning. 'Would the police have volunteered that sort of information to someone who must be the prime suspect?'

'So you think Patrick was lying?'

'Or Jennifer was.'

'Jennifer?' Libby was wide-eyed with surprise. 'Why would she lie?'

'By her own admission she's the only one with any previous knowledge of them both.'

'But she was really nice. She couldn't possibly have a motive for killing Melanie.'

'If she knew them as well as she said, how do we know she didn't have one?'

Libby shook her head. 'I don't believe it.'

'She's one we could look up when we get back. She writes for the women's magazines. She's bound to have an internet presence, or at least be mentioned.'

'I still think it's something to do with mistaken identity,' said Libby, getting out her key.

'You can look all the others up, too. Daniel Hill's a contributor to *Scriptus* and Dee Starkey to *Spank Monthly* –'

Libby snorted and opened the door.

'– so they could be there, too.' Fran narrowly avoided Sidney and followed Libby into the sitting room. Libby woke the laptop and went into the kitchen to put on the kettle. Fran sat at the table in the window and put Jennifer Alderton into the search engine.

'I don't know what we're going to do with this information even if we do get any,' she called to Libby.

'We'll think of something,' said Libby. 'Tea or coffee?'

'Loads of information about Jennifer.' Fran turned the screen to show Libby as she set a mug down on the table. 'But no website of her own, which surprises me. Most writers have one, even the struggling ones. Daniel Hill has one – or rather, he has a blog, look.'

Daniel Hill had ideas of aggrandisement. His blog reflected the fact that he was convinced of his superiority as a writer, and his attacks on others, popular or literary, were scathing. There was little about either his history or his personal life, except the suggestion that he lived in Dickensian surroundings with his cat – 'Poor cat,' said Libby.

Of Nick Forrest there was no sign. Many Nick – or Nicolas – Forrests appeared in the results, several of which could be their Nick, but none were writers.

'Of course,' said Fran, 'he could have a blog under another name.'

'Yes – lots of them have odd names, don't they?' said Libby. 'But we don't know, so he's a washout.'

Nina didn't come up in any searches, either, so Fran typed in Patrick's name. There was, of course, a plethora of information, including, coming first, a news report about the death of Melanie.

'Oh, bugger,' said Libby. 'I didn't think they'd released it yet. Now we'll be besieged by reporters.'

Fran was reading the reports. 'No, I don't think so. There's no mention of how she died, just "Melanie Joseph, wife of thriller writer Patrick Joseph, has been found dead. Mr Joseph was unavailable for comment. A friend said he was devastated. Mrs Joseph was chair of the environmental charity Green Country and served on various government committees.'

'Well, there!' said Libby. 'Pete was right, she

was important. And there could certainly be motives for her murder there, couldn't there?'

Fran nodded. 'Environmental subjects seem to rouse the beast in everybody, for and against.'

'All those demonstrations and marches,' agreed Libby. 'So perhaps it wasn't anything to do with the writers, after all.'

'I expect that's why they let all the writers go and there's no mention of the Manor in the report. Hang on, let me look at the other reports.' She scrolled through the reports from the BBC, Reuters and CNN. None of the papers appeared to have got the news in time to go to press. 'No, you're safe for the time being.'

'I bet someone gets wind of it, though,' said Libby morosely. 'You know what the press are like.'

'Never mind.' Fran was comforting. 'Come on, let's have a look at Jennifer Alderton. She seems to be a regular not only for the women's weeklies, but some of the glossies, too. Not such a nonentity.'

'I wonder how old she is?' mused Libby. 'Not as old as she looks. Rosie's age?'

'She said she babysat Patrick when he was twelve. I wonder how much older than him she was?'

'Need only have been a few years. She dresses like someone Rosie's age, though. Odd for someone who works in the magazine industry.'

'And I wonder why she came on the weekend?' Fran sat back in her chair. 'She's an experienced writer.'

'But she went on the original writers' holiday. I

expect she just wanted to write a novel. There's a huge difference, I should have thought.'

'But she didn't make anything of it, not like Daniel Hill or Dee Starkey, who thought their limited experience put them on the same level as Patrick.'

Libby pulled the laptop towards her. 'Ooh, yes. Let's look up *Spank Monthly*!'

There was a warning that the following pages contained adult content and should not be viewed by anyone under the age of eighteen. When they clicked through to the *Spank Monthly* site, they could see why.

'Bloody hell!' said Libby, wide-eyed at the images. 'Do people actually read this stuff?'

Fran nodded. 'Very popular. Erotic ebooks are huge sellers, especially, believe it or not, in America.'

'This is erotica? It's positively pornographic.' Libby sat back and shook her head. 'So Dee Starkey was going to write a pornographic novel.'

'Erotic,' corrected Fran.

'Whatever. So why was she anxious for Patrick to help? He doesn't write that sort of thing.'

'The basics of writing a novel are the same whatever genre it is,' said Fran. 'You know, characterisation, story arc, over- or under-writing, setting – all sorts of things.'

'Hmm,' said Libby, 'but if she wanted help with contacts, Patrick wouldn't have had the right ones for this sort of thing, would he?'

'He might have known where to go – you know which agents or publishers might be approached.

Once you're in the industry you can find out a lot. There are newsletters and websites with up-to-date publishing news that come out daily.'

'She could do that on her own, surely? Any of them could.'

'But if you're on the outside it's much more difficult. Introductions are worth their weight in gold.'

'Cliché? Fran – and you call yourself a writer!' Libby grinned at her friend and picked up her mug.

'Clichés are there because they are a good way of putting across an idea,' said Fran. 'It just doesn't do to overlard your writing with them or it looks careless and lazy.'

'I should imagine there are quite a lot of clichés in *Spank Monthly*,' said Libby, 'or it might simply be rather unpleasant biological description.'

'Let's see if there's a list of contributors,' said Fran going back to the laptop. 'Yes – see? Dee Starkey, and a picture of her looking like a vampire.' She scrolled down. 'But nothing much about her except a list of other erotica she's had published online. Not a lot, it seems.'

'And has she got a website of her own?' asked Libby.

She did. But as with Daniel Hill's, it gave little away about her personal life.

'Well, it wouldn't do to say "I live in a three-bedroomed terrace with two point four children and my hubby who's a double-glazing salesman" would it?' said Libby. 'Ruins the image.'

'Hang on,' said Fran, 'look. She's a member of a pressure group to save some ancient monument.'

'So?'

'I wonder if there's a connection to Green Country? That would be their sort of thing, wouldn't it?'

'I'm not sure what Green Country actually does,' said Libby. 'Are they like the Green party?'

'They have the same basic aims but disagree on things like nuclear fuel and some preservation issues. They stand for "best use", which doesn't always chime with the ecologists.'

'I'm confused.' Libby put down her mug. 'Perhaps we ought to find out more.'

'But not now,' said Fran. 'There's Guy pulling up outside and Ben's with him.'

Guy kissed his wife and explained that he'd gone to the Manor to pick her up, where instead he'd found Ben.

'Mum says lunch at one thirty,' said Ben, 'and we're to see if Peter and Harry are coming.'

'He's been opening Sunday lunchtimes for weeks,' said Libby. The Pink Geranium closed on Sundays for the first months of the year, but usually began opening at Easter.

'What have you two been up to?' Ben swung the laptop round to face him before Fran could do anything, and whistled. 'Guy, look at this! Our women seem to have developed rather exotic tastes.'

'Erotic, rather,' said Guy, laughing. 'Go on, then, what's this all about?'

Libby and Fran explained.

'I don't know what you think you can achieve now the suspects have all gone home. It's nothing to do with us at all. We're only on the periphery due to being the place where the body was found,' said Ben.

'We're a bit more involved than that,' said Libby. 'Don't forget she booked in with us using a false name.'

'I don't think the police are considering that an "involvement" exactly,' said Ben.

'But Libby and Fran are,' said Guy. 'And after all, what would you expect? It's like expecting a cat to ignore a whole salmon left on the floor by mistake.'

'So what have you found out about your suspects?' asked Ben.

'Not a lot, except that Melanie Joseph was, as Pete said, quite important and there are probably far more motives for her murder than for her as an adjunct to Patrick.'

'Yes.' Guy was frowning. 'Of course. Here, can I have a look?' He pulled the laptop towards him and typed Melanie Joseph into the search engine. Scrolling down the entries, he clicked on one. 'There,' he said. 'I knew I remembered. She received death threats.'

Chapter Eleven

'NO WONDER THE POLICE were not that interested in the writers,' said Libby.

'I expect they are,' said Fran. 'They'll be looking into all their backgrounds to see if they have any connections to organisations which might be in opposition to Melanie Joseph or Green Country.'

'See? We were on the right lines with Dee Starkey,' said Libby. 'Her and her ancient monument.'

Ben and Guy looked confused.

'It's all right, we'll tell you about it on the way,' said Libby.

'It's not time to go back to the Manor yet,' said Ben.

'No, but it is time to go the pub,' said Libby. 'Come on.'

'I remember one thing Green Country were against,' said Guy, as they strolled back towards the high street. 'And that was defiling ancient monuments. They took the position that they should all be preserved and the public should not be allowed anywhere near them, except at a safe distance.'

'Like Stonehenge? Where the only time they let people in is Midsummer and Midwinter? That's right, isn't it?' said Libby.

'Something like that. Their idea was that the general public damage these monuments, and they disapproved of the solstice gatherings.'

'But a lot of the monuments are protected,' said Fran. 'The public can only look from a safe distance.'

'But some, like Stonehenge, are focal points for pagan ritual,' said Libby. 'I mean, they even do the May Day and summer solstice thing around Grey Betty in Steeple Mount, don't they?'

'But· that's not real druid celebration, it's an excuse for a jolly,' said Guy.

'Some of those Cranston Morris people took it very seriously,' said Fran. Libby and she had got involved in a murder that had taken place during May Day celebrations some time ago.

'If Dee Starkey is involved in protecting ancient monuments, I bet she's a druid or something. A lot of them seem to be into the Goth look,' said Libby.

'That really is stereotyping,' said Ben.

'Let's shelve the subject,' said Guy, pushing open the door of the pub. 'What's everyone having?'

An hour later, they trooped back up the drive to the Manor.

'Fewer Socos,' commented Ben.

'Fewer we can see,' said Libby. 'I bet they're all over the house. And the huts.'

'There aren't so many vehicles,' said Fran, as DC Sharif in a boiler suit emerged from the house. He smiled brightly at them.

'Be out of your hair soon, Mrs Sarjeant.'

'Have you combed every inch, then?'

'Every millimetre.' He grinned. 'Just finishing off over in those bungalow things, then we'll get the go-ahead from the boss and be away.'

'Thanks,' said Libby. 'Not being nasty, but I shall be glad to see the back of you!'

'Might pay a couple of visits if there's anything else comes up,' Sharif said, 'but I think the investigation's moving away from here, despite being the murder site.'

'Ah. That would be Mrs Joseph's own life, rather than the connection to her husband?' said Libby.

Sharif's eyes narrowed. 'And what would you know about that, Mrs Sarjeant?'

Libby opened her eyes at him. 'Only what everyone knows. The death threats, that sort of thing.'

'Ah.' He relaxed. 'Anyway, I'll come and find you when we're ready to go.'

'We'll be in the kitchen,' said Ben. 'Thanks.'

'Honestly, Lib, why did you say that?' he muttered, as they went inside.

'Why shouldn't I?'

'Because they might start taking a closer look at you if they think you knew too much about Melanie Joseph,' said Fran.

'But I don't,' said Libby as they entered the kitchen. 'I don't even know about the death threats because Guy didn't tell us. Hello, Het.'

Hetty was laying the table. 'Them police are still about,' she said.

'But they'll be gone soon, Mum,' said Ben, his arm round her shoulders. 'You should have let us help with this.'

'You can clear up after,' said Het. 'Go and get the wine. 'There's a white Bordeaux in the fridge and a claret open on the dresser.'

During Hetty's perfectly roasted rib of beef and vegetables, the conversation turned once more, as it would, to the murder, and the death threats to the victim.

'I remember that,' said Hetty surprisingly.

'Do you?' Ben stared at his mother.

'Why wouldn't I? Made all the papers and the telly. Bomb under her car and everything.'

'Who did they think it was?' asked Libby. 'Or did someone claim it was them? You know, with one of those coded phone calls.'

'No one claimed responsibility, as far as I remember,' said Guy, 'but there were various theories. Anti-nuclear protestors were the favourites, I think.'

'But I thought the Greens were anti-nuclear?' Libby frowned.

'Some are, but Green Country are for it and against the coal-powered systems,' said Ben. 'I remember that bit.'

'So they're a bit divisive?' suggested Fran.

'A foot in both camps, it seems to me,' said Libby. 'Not all out Green at all.'

'No, they're not,' said Guy. 'They purport to be the green face of the government, but independent, of course.'

'So there could be lots of people with a motive to get her out of the way politically?' said Fran.

'There could,' conceded Guy, 'but doing it here doesn't seem to make sense, unless one of your guests was a member of an opposition organisation and took the opportunity on the spur of the moment.'

'That's what the police will be looking into now,' said Libby. 'The guests' backgrounds.'

'Treacle pud?' said Hetty, standing up.

Hetty, now having relinquished doing the "pots" herself for good, retired to her flat, leaving the rest of them to clear up and load the dishwasher. Young DC Sharif interrupted them.

'You can get on with cleaning the rooms, now,' he said. 'We've finished, but we've cordoned off the room Mrs Joseph occupied for the time being. DCI Murray will be in touch.'

'Thank you, Mr Sharif,' said Libby. 'Would you like a cup of coffee before you go?'

He looked longingly at the cafetière and shook his head. 'Thanks all the same, but they're waiting for me.' He looked round the table. 'Thanks for all your help. Sorry if we've been a nuisance.'

'Goodness,' said Fran, when he'd gone. 'Fancy the police apologising for being a nuisance.'

'Wouldn't get Ian doing that,' giggled Libby.

'Speaking of which,' said Guy, 'when are you going to phone him and ask for the low-down?'

'Don't think we haven't thought of it,' said Libby, 'but apparently he turned down this case because we were involved, so he's hardly going to be amenable to being pumped. Anyway, according to DS Wallingford he's now a Detective *Chief* Inspector.'

'I might be able to tell him something off the record, though,' said Fran thoughtfully.

'You mean your "moment"?' said Libby. 'About seeing a woman drinking?'

'Doesn't sound much though, does it?' said Fran

apologetically.

'What did you see?' asked Guy, who was still coming to terms with his wife's occasional psychic ability.

Fran told him.

'No, it doesn't sound much,' said Ben, 'but he always looks into anything you tell him, and you could hardly tell Murray. Ian might think it's worth pursuing, like he did with White Lodge.'

White Lodge was a building Libby and Fran had investigated on behalf of Rosie.

'We could try,' said Libby. '*You* could try.'

'I'm not ringing him today,' said Fran. 'It's Sunday. He might have the day off.'

'I know,' said Libby, 'we've got his email address, haven't we? Wasn't it on that card he gave us last year?'

'That's an idea,' said Ben. 'You needn't tell him what it is, just say you think you might have some information that DCI Murray wouldn't listen to.'

'That way we're not putting him on the spot. He can come back to you or not, as he chooses.' Libby nodded in satisfaction.

'Poor Ian,' said Guy with a smile. 'I bet he regrets ever having met you.'

'We've been very helpful,' said Libby indignantly.

'Do you want to do it now, Fran? You can use the computer in the office,' said Ben.

'Yes, come on, Fran. I'll come with you,' said Libby.

In the office, Fran logged on to her email account and Libby found the card with Ian's contact details in a drawer in Ben's desk.

'There. I've just said exactly what Ben suggested,' said Fran sitting back so Libby could see. 'And added congratulations on his promotion.'

'That should do it,' said Libby. 'You could send my regards.'

'Let's not make it too personal,' said Fran, and hit *send*. Libby switched off the computer.

'We can't do any more,' said Libby. 'We'll just have to sit back and wait.'

After they'd been to say goodbye to Hetty, Guy and Fran left and Ben and Libby walked back down the drive. Passing The Pink Geranium, Peter waved to them from the sofa in the left hand window. 'Coming in?' he mouthed.

Harry appeared in his whites and waved a bottle. They went in.

'We do nothing but drink alcohol these days,' said Libby, eyeing the bottle.

'You don't have to drink it,' said Harry, nevertheless producing four glasses. 'You can have coffee if you like.'

'No,' sighed Libby, 'I'll have wine.'

'Under duress, of course,' said Peter. 'Now tell us what's been going on up there today.'

Libby and Ben told them.

'So you're going to get poor old Ian into hot water again,' said Harry. 'I have to hand it to you, petal. You never know when to give in.'

'I don't know what you mean,' said Libby.

'It never occurred to you that Ian's still carrying a torch for your mate? That's why he jumps when she says jump?'

97

'No.' Libby felt colour rising up her neck. 'Anyway, I'm always more worried about Guy being jealous. After all, he pinched her from under Ian's nose.'

'I don't think Ian would get involved if he didn't think it was important,' said Ben. 'He's a nice bloke, and a very dedicated policeman.'

They finished the bottle, then Ben and Libby went home. Time enough to do any final administration for the weekend tomorrow. Tonight it was mindless television and an early night.

But at nine o'clock Fran rang.

'Ian just called,' she said.

'Was he cross?'

'No, just interested. I said what I'd seen, stressing it could be nothing. He checked and said the post mortem isn't being done until tomorrow morning, and he'll look into it. He knows nothing about the case, as we thought. He didn't want to get mixed up with us again.'

'Poor Ian,' said Libby. 'But he's quite happy to do this?'

'Yes. He's going to suggest they do a complete tox report even if they do find she's been stabbed. I don't suppose DCI Murray will like it.'

'And did he say anything about his promotion?'

'Just thank you when I congratulated him.'

'Oh.' Libby was disappointed. 'Well, did he say he'd let you know about the results?'

'Not exactly, but I expect he will, though it will be strictly on the QT. Otherwise I shall be given the third degree by Murray who will be convinced I know more about it.'

'Let me know as soon as you hear,' said Libby.

'As if I wouldn't,' said Fran and cut the connection.

Libby relayed this to Ben. Sighing, he stood up and went to pour himself a restorative whisky.

'Here we go again,' he said.

Monday morning was grey and drizzly. Ben and Libby went back to the Manor to finish the work of the weekend to find all the casual staff turning out the bedrooms and cleaning the public rooms with a certain amount of ghoulish zeal.

'Ben,' said Libby, looking up from her guest list, a copy of which they'd given to the police. 'Look at this. All the guests' car registration numbers are here, but nothing next to Ann Marsh's name.'

'Well, as she was being secretive about everything else and she seems to have checked herself in, it stands to reason she wouldn't leave a car registration about to be recognised,' said Ben.

'But if she came in a car,' said Libby, 'where did it go? There was no extra car in the forecourt, nor up by the huts. In which case, how did she get here?'

Chapter Twelve

BEN SAT BACK IN his chair. 'That's a point, but I can't think the police wouldn't have thought of it.'

'But they haven't asked me about it, and surely they would have done? Especially after we found that Melanie's name – or false name, I suppose – wasn't on Lily Cooper's list. And they had a copy of our check-in sheet, so they should have noticed the lack of registration number, too. Why didn't they ask?'

Ben frowned. 'True. But I'm sure they wouldn't have overlooked something as crucial as this. Could she have come in a taxi?'

'Wouldn't someone have noticed a taxi outside? And come to that, *when* did she arrive? We still don't know that. When exactly did I notice her name had been ticked off?'

'Before dinner on Friday. While the guests were having drinks.'

'And I asked Lily Cooper if everyone was there.'

'So while you were checking things were OK and then we were changing. How much time is that? And no one was in the hall?'

'No.' Libby shook her head. 'But the odd thing is, if she was checked in, why didn't the guests in the huts see her – or hear her? They would have seen if there was a car near the huts.'

Ben thought about it. 'Suppose,' he said slowly, 'one of the other guests gave her a lift?'

'How would that work, though?' said Libby. 'I

greeted everyone else. I would have noticed someone else in a car, and it would have meant slipping back to tick the check-in sheet and somehow give Melanie the key to the hut. And how would she know how to get to it?'

'Ah.' Ben tipped back on his chair and gazed at the ceiling. 'You don't think someone knew the back way into the estate?'

'What, up to the top of Allhallow's Lane and on to the track?' Libby was incredulous. 'Hardly anyone, even in the village, knows about that.'

Ben tipped his chair back on to two legs and grinned. 'Don't you be so sure! People have been using it for years. Especially when we kept game.'

'Poachers?' said Libby. 'How feudal.'

'Everyone who had an estate kept game. Large estates still do, you know that. As the Manor estate grew smaller we stopped. It didn't help that Dad didn't hunt or shoot and was rather against blood sports. Not the thing to do for a Squire.'

'So someone could have found out about the back way in, dropped her at the Huts – no, that won't work. They'd have to know which hut she was in.' Libby made a face. 'God, this is difficult.'

'Did someone take his, or her, car out again after he'd checked in?'

'I don't think so.' Libby shook her head. 'And if he or she did, that would mean Melanie would have had to stay hidden until the person came back to the car. No,' she said, 'I can't see any of this working at all. I reckon the murderer drove the car away after the murder.'

'But why?' asked Ben. 'What possible reason

would there be to do that? All the evidence of her real identity was in the hut.'

'I know what I'm going to do,' said Libby, sitting forward and picking up her guest list. 'I'm going to ask the guests who were in the other huts if they saw a car.'

'How can you do that?'

'I've got all their phone numbers, haven't I? And their addresses, come to that.'

'Should you be doing this?' said Ben dubiously. 'The police might not like it.'

'Bugger the police,' said Libby. 'I'm sure this is something they've overlooked.' She pulled the office phone towards her and punched in the number of the guest who'd stayed in one of the other huts. There was no reply until an answerphone kicked in and Libby was required to leave a message, which she did merely requesting the guest to call the Manor.

'That way it simply sounds as if we've found an item they left behind or something,' said Libby, punching in the number of the other guest, who turned out to be Nick Forrest. But the same thing happened and Libby was left frustrated.

'It's Monday morning,' said Ben, 'they'll be at work.'

'Both those guests are men,' said Libby thoughtfully. 'I put them there because I thought it would be better for men to be roaming about in the dark than women. The only reason Ann Marsh – Melanie – was put there was because she was a late booking.' She stopped and thought a bit more. 'Do you know, when I went to tell the guests that breakfast was being served, Nick Forrest was talking to Patrick in the sitting room. He didn't seem to know anything about what was going on, so it must have been the other guest who found the body. That was what Hetty said, wasn't it?'

Ben nodded. Libby checked the list. 'Paul Fisher.' She looked up. 'Haven't come across him before, have we?'

'Not as in spoken to,' said Ben, 'except you must have done when you checked him in.'

Libby was frowning. 'Hang on, let's see. Nina, Jennifer, Fran, Rosie – no discount Rosie –'

'And not Fran?'

'No – I'm counting guests. Start again. Nina, Jennifer, Fran, Lily Cooper, Dee Starkey, Patrick, Nick Forrest, Daniel Hill – those are the only ones I had any real contact with. Then there's this Paul Fisher and two women who shared a room, Audrey Glenister and Bernice Weldon. And then Ann Marsh. That's it, that's the twelve.'

'How did you manage not to talk to them?' asked Ben.

'They were often with Lily Cooper. Ladies of a certain age,' said Libby with a grin. 'Mine. Probably susceptible to Patrick. He had quite a fan club, didn't he?'

'The aura of glamour.' Ben turned to his computer. 'What's the other bloke's name? Paul Fisher, wasn't it. Let's look him up.'

But of the many results that came up for the name, none quite seemed to fit the Paul Fisher Libby remembered only as a vague presence.

'Not a published writer, then,' said Libby,

'although he could have a pseudonym.'

'But they were all aspiring writers,' said Ben. 'You told me.'

'Aspiring novelists,' corrected Libby. 'Some, like Jennifer, were published in other spheres.' She giggled. 'Like *Spank Monthly*.'

Ben waggled his eyebrows at her. 'Shall I take out a subscription for you?'

'Thanks, but I think I can manage without.' She giggled again, stood up and dropped a kiss on her beloved's forehead. 'I'm going to see if Hetty needs me to do anything, then I'm going back home for lunch. Going to join me? I feel the need to get back to normal.'

'Go on, you go. I've got more stuff to do here,' said Ben. 'I'll grab a bite with Mum if that's OK? And can we have something normal at home tonight? At the kitchen table for instance?'

Libby gave him another kiss. 'You bet. Back to pipe and slippers today.'

But later that afternoon, Ben called to say Paul Fisher had called back and what was he supposed to say?

'Give me his number and tell him I'll call him straight away,' said Libby, scrabbling for pen and paper.

Paul Fisher's voice was cautious when he answered the phone.

'I'm sorry to bother you, Mr Fisher,' said Libby, 'and I'm sorry I didn't manage to speak with you over the weekend, but there were rather difficult circumstances.'

'You can say that again.' Fisher's voice was

unaccented, cool and very slightly hostile.

'I gather you were the unfortunate person who found Melanie Joseph's body?'

'I was.'

'I just wondered whether you'd noticed anything the day before?'

'The police asked me that. No.'

Definitely hostile.

'And the car?' persisted Libby.

'The car?' The hostility slipped a bit.

'There must have been a car each for all three of you guests in the Hoppers' Huts.'

'Oh … I see.' There was a pause. 'No, I don't think so. Nick and I came by taxi.'

'So you did. No car Saturday either?'

'Not as far as I remember,' said Fisher, now sounding a little more friendly. 'Why? Is it important?'

'It might be,' said Libby cheerfully. 'Did the police ask you about the car?'

'No, they didn't.' Fisher sounded surprised now.

'Thank you, Mr Fisher, you've been a great help, and I'm sorry to have intruded on your day.'

'Not at all. Is there any way we can keep up with developments? Having been involved with a murder, I'd rather like to know what happens.'

'Of course,' said Libby. 'Tell you what, if you send an email to the Manor's website, I'll collect the other guests' e-addresses and I can send a group email to keep you all informed. Not,' she added, 'that I'm likely to be able to tell you much, but it'll be more than is in the papers, I expect.'

With further expressions of goodwill, they said

their goodbyes.

And Fran phoned.

'We were right.' She sounded weary. 'She didn't die of the stab wound. It was done post mortem.'

'Lordy, lordy!' said Libby.

'So Murray didn't need to ask for a full tox screening, it will be done automatically.'

'Was Ian surprised? Did he go to the post mortem?'

'Not his job, but he's been to see Murray, apparently, and he wants to speak to me.'

'Murray, or Ian?'

'Ian. He didn't tell Murray about my involvement.'

'Hooray! So we can get the low-down.'

'No, Libby, we can't. Ian's still not on the case.'

'When are you seeing him?'

'In the morning. I suppose you want to come?'

'Well, duh! Will he mind?'

'I don't suppose so. He might be a bit tetchy.'

'He often is,' said Libby. 'Thing is, I've got something to ask, too.'

'Oh? What?'

Libby explained about the missing car. 'And the police didn't ask about it,' she concluded.

'You're right,' said Fran slowly. 'That is odd.'

'So I can mention it to Ian?

'Definitely.' Fran sighed. 'I do hope he won't get annoyed with us, though.'

'He will,' said Libby. 'What time?'

Half an hour later Ben arrived with Nick Forrest's number.

'He left a message just now, so I thought you

may as well phone back.' Ben gave her the piece of paper. 'I hope it's worth it.'

Nick Forrest was initially more forthcoming than Paul Fisher, and confirmed that he hadn't seen a car.

'But I did hear one in the middle of the night.'

Libby felt the sensation usually described as her stomach turning over.

'On Saturday?'

'Early hours of Sunday, I would have said,' said Nick Forrest.

'Did you tell the police this?'

'No, they didn't ask anything about cars.'

'Mr Forrest –' began Libby.

'Nick, please.'

'Nick, this may be very important. I'm not sure, but I think the police may want to talk to you about this.'

'Fine.' He sounded puzzled. 'Will you keep me informed?'

Libby repeated her suggestion of a group email. 'And I'll let you know if the police need to speak to you. I'm seeing them tomorrow.'

'Right.' He sounded even more puzzled, but Libby wasn't about to enlighten him.

'Thank you so much, Nick. I'll be in touch.' Libby switched off the phone and went to report to Ben in the kitchen.

'Looks as though you're getting involved again,' he said, stirring the contents of a saucepan on the Aga. 'Is this bolognese?'

'Yes,' said Libby, affronted, 'and just for that you can cook the spaghetti.'

The following morning, Fran and Libby met

outside Canterbury Police Station and were shown to Ian's new office.

'Bit different from last time I was here,' said Libby, looking round. 'Being interviewed by our Donnie.'

Ian's lips twitched.

'Well, this time it's me, Libby. And I don't remember inviting you.'

'But you'll want to hear what I've got to tell you,' said Libby brightly. 'Betcha.'

Ian sighed. 'Right,' he said. 'Tell me the whole story, right from the beginning. I don't know anything, remember.'

'You should have taken the case in the first place,' said Libby.

'Libby!' said Fran.

'Maybe I should,' said Ian, 'but I really couldn't. I had to claim personal knowledge.'

'Of us?' asked Libby.

'And the Manor. And DCI Murray had investigated there before, hadn't he? So it made sense that he took it. However –'

'However?' prompted Libby.

'I've spoken to him this morning and told him I might have some information. It's extremely irregular, and we've not worked together that well before, but he's not interested in keeping it to himself. He's on the downward road to retirement, and Mrs Murray's getting impatient for her Spanish villa on the golf course.'

'She'll miss our pantomimes,' giggled Libby.

'So you haven't read the case files yet?' asked Fran.

'No. I'm relying on you two.' He looked from Fran to Libby. 'Although I didn't invite you, I knew somehow you'd be here.'

So they told him the whole story as they'd seen it from their point of view, including Fran's feeling that Melanie hadn't been stabbed and she'd seen her drinking.

'And you don't know where it was? It didn't look familiar?' said Ian.

'No. I was just certain she hadn't died from a stab wound.'

'And you were right. Now, Libby, what did you have to tell me?'

Libby told him.

'And no one asked them about a car?' Ian was frowning. 'Right. Stay here.'

He left the room and Fran and Libby looked at one another.

'Castle and Sarjeant to the rescue again,' said Libby.

'Wolfe,' corrected Fran with a sigh.

'But Castle and Sarjeant go together so much better, don't you think? Could be the name of a detective series on tv.'

Chapter Thirteen

IAN CAME BACK INTO the room, swivelled a computer towards him and tapped something in.

'Right,' he said. 'DS Wallingford appears not to have seen the significance of the missing car, and obviously no one else did. Tell me again, Libby, why there should have been a car, or why you should have seen or heard one.'

Libby repeated the conclusions she and Ben had reached the day before.

'So,' said Ian, frowning, 'she had to arrive by car or taxi. Any other way?'

'Helicopter?' suggested Libby.

'By bus,' said Ian, exasperated.

'Well, yes,' said Libby doubtfully, 'but there's only one an hour from Canterbury to Nethergate – and that's an improvement. Never used to be able to go direct.'

'And would there have been one at the relevant time?'

Libby looked at Fran. 'There must have been one sometime during the afternoon, but I left my post at the front quite late and she hadn't checked in then. And it was just before dinner I noticed she *had* checked in. So between half five and just gone six. You could check the bus timetable.'

'Don't worry, we will,' said Ian. He sat back in his chair and looked at them. 'If it wasn't for the body, I'd say she was a fantasy guest.'

'Who ate takeaways,' said Fran.

'Takeaways?' repeated Ian.

'In the bin in her room,' said Libby. 'When Ben and I showed him her room. We assumed she didn't want her husband to see her until she confronted him – or something like that.'

'Confronted him? What about?'

Libby sighed. 'You really don't know much about the case, do you? Patrick Joseph has a reputation with the ladies. Apparently, he and the organiser of the weekend had a thing going. We thought his wife had come to find out for herself. I'm sure that's covered in the case notes. This woman was seen wandering about the house in her nightclothes in the very early morning. They questioned her quite thoroughly, I know that, because I was the one who told them about it.'

'You saw her? But I thought you stayed at home overnight.'

'Hetty saw her and told me. So I told DC Sharif, and he told Wallingford.'

'Right.' Ian frowned down at his desk. 'Anything else you can tell me? Don't tell me you haven't been doing some investigations of your own.'

'We looked up everyone we'd met on the internet,' said Fran. 'We couldn't find anything much. There were plenty of motives for trying to hurt Patrick, although I wouldn't have thought any of them would resort to murder.'

'What sort of motives?'

'Mainly concerning books he wouldn't help them with,' Fran explained. 'But, unless Libby's theory that it was mistaken identity is true, I can't see that motives to kill Patrick help at all.'

'How would the mistaken identity theory work?' Ian asked Libby, his stern face relaxing a trifle.

'If someone stabbed Melanie thinking she was Patrick,' said Libby, colour seeping up her neck. 'Of course, now we know she wasn't stabbed – or rather – she was, but …' She trailed off.

'Exactly.' Ian stood up. 'I shall have a chat with DCI Murray and review the case. If I need to, I know where I can find you.' He sighed. 'Here we go again.'

'That's what Ben said,' said Libby. 'And can you find out what it was Nina Etherington wanted to talk to the police about? Or if she did? She said she would, but Murray and Wallingford hadn't heard from her last time we spoke.'

'I'll see. Oh, and Libby,' said Ian as they were leaving, 'if I come down to the Manor, will you take me over the relevant sites?'

'Won't you want one of the detectives to do that?'

'No. I want you to do it.'

'Well! He wants me!' said Libby smugly as she and Fran left the station.

'Don't you go flirting with him again,' warned Fran.

'As if I would,' said Libby, guiltily pushing down the instinctive attraction she felt for their Byronic policeman friend.

'We certainly seem to have done it again,' said Fran. 'Are we having lunch in the pub?'

'Will they let us leave the cars in the station car park?' asked Libby.

'We'll risk it,' said Fran. 'Come on.'

Their favourite Canterbury pub was tucked down a back street and their favourite barman was still behind the bar.

'Ladies!' he said, bustling towards them. 'Haven't seen you for ages. How's the lovely Harry?'

They exchanged gossip for a few moments before ordering sandwiches and soft drinks.

'So Ian took us seriously,' said Libby.

'He always does in the end,' said Fran, 'but I expect he and Murray will have to run it all by the Superintendent. I don't suppose Murray's going to be too pleased about having shortcomings in his investigation shown up, retirement or no.'

Their sandwiches arrived, overstuffed and delicious, and for a while conversation lapsed.

'Do you remember, this was where we first met,' said Libby, through a mouthful of tuna and cress.

'And you hated me because I was with Ben,' said Fran, wiping her mouth with a paper napkin. 'How could I forget?'

'There really was nothing between you, was there?' said Libby after a moment, looking down at her plate.

'Libby!' Fran was astonished. 'After all this time? You know there wasn't. There never had been. He was a client.'

Libby looked up and grinned. 'That makes it sound even worse.'

Fran spluttered over her orange juice.

Half an hour later they strolled back to the police station to find a message stuck under the wiper on Libby's windscreen.

'From Ian,' she said. 'Listen: "When you deign to come and pick up your cars –" sarky "– let the desk sergeant know. I'd like to come out to the Manor this afternoon." Suppose I didn't have time? Cheek.'

Fran laughed. 'Then I expect he'd go on his own.'

Libby bridled. 'No, he needs me to show him where everything happened.'

'It's a courtesy,' said Fran with a grin. 'After all, Ben could do the same thing, and Ben's on the spot, isn't he?'

'Oh, all right. Come on, let's go and tell the desk sergeant.'

'You go,' said Fran. 'I'm off. Let me know what happens.'

But when Libby entered the foyer of the police station Ian was already there.

'Sorry,' said Libby, 'weren't we meant to leave our cars there?'

'The car park spaces are supposed to be for people with legitimate business here,' said Ian, ushering her back down the steps. 'Now, you get going and I'll meet you there.'

'Very sure of yourself, aren't you,' muttered Libby.

'Yes,' said Ian, not turning as he walked away. Libby blushed and cursed.

Inevitably, Ian's sleek dark car was already parked in front of the Manor by the time Libby's Romeo the Renault arrived. Ian himself was gazing at the poster on the front of the Oast House Theatre.

'Shakespeare?' He turned as she came up behind

her. 'That's ambitious.'

'The Dream,' said Libby. 'Jolly fun for all the family.'

'Are you in it?'

'Me?' Libby laughed. 'And who do you think I could possibly be? An ancient witch-like Titania? Geriatric Hermia?'

He smiled. 'Maybe not. 'I can see you as a female Bottom, though.'

Libby snorted. 'That would be a whole new take on the story, wouldn't it? A lesbian Titania.'

Ian laughed. 'I meant it as a compliment. You have a talent for comedy.'

'Thanks, I think.' Libby grinned back at him. 'Come on, then. This is where I met the guests and ticked them off on my clipboard.'

'Did you by any chance put the times they arrived down?' Ian held open the Manor door for her to precede him.

'No – what a bugger. That would really have helped, wouldn't it? But I had no reason to.'

'It would, but it doesn't matter. Can you show me the rooms the guests occupied?'

'Can I pop into the office? I need to get a copy of the list, I can't remember off-hand. And I need to tell Ben you're here.'

'I'll come with you.' Ian followed her down the passage to the estate office, where Ben was poring over the accounts. He looked up, surprised.

'Hello, Ian. Come to arrest me?' He looked at Libby. 'I suppose there's no point in asking why you're here.'

Libby explained and collected the original list of

guests from her desk drawer. 'I'll pop in and let Hetty know what we're doing on the way past.'

'She's in the main kitchen,' said Ben. 'She says the one in her flat isn't big enough.'

'Well, when you're used to one the size of a church I don't suppose it is,' said Libby. 'Come on, Ian.'

Ian grinned at Ben and followed her out.

After saying hello to Hetty, Libby led Ian through the whole of the Manor, not only the public rooms and guest bedrooms, but the other areas which would have been accessible although out-of-bounds. He inspected it all thoroughly.

'And where exactly did Hetty see this Lily Cooper?'

Libby showed him the area outside Hetty's flat. 'Early morning, I think,' she said. 'Hetty's an early riser. And there was no reason for Mrs Cooper to be anywhere outside her room. Or Patrick's,' she added thoughtfully.

'Yes, that's where she'd been,' said Ian, swivelling round to see behind him.

'What are you doing?'

'Checking the topography.'

'The –? Oh, to see if this was her best way back to her room? No, it wasn't. They were both on the floor above. She didn't need to be here at all.'

'Who else was on this floor?'

'Young Nina Etherington.'

'Why do you always say "young" Nina?' Ian turned to face her.

Libby shrugged. 'Because she is. None of the other women are young – even Lily Cooper and Dee

Starkey are at least in their forties. She doesn't exactly fit with the group.'

Ian frowned. 'She didn't?'

'No. And did you find out what she wanted to tell the police?'

'No. But I haven't managed to go through all the statements yet. Right – now the huts.'

Libby led the way back to the office and collected the key to hut number five.

'I never came here during your first big case,' said Ian, as they tramped across the Manor grounds.

'I wouldn't call it that,' said Libby. 'It was all too close to home. Horrible.'

'They all are. You've just got inured to it.'

'No.' Libby shook her head. 'It's just easier to think of things as an intellectual puzzle.'

'That makes you sound cold,' said Ian, 'and you aren't.' He looked around. 'Where was the bridge? That Peter fell from?'

Libby waved. 'Over there. In fact, it's still there, what's left of it. And just back there, where that big flower bed was –' She stopped.

'Yes. The original site of the huts.' Ian looked sideways at her.

'You read up on it?'

'After the case where I first met you all, yes.' He pointed ahead. 'Are those the new huts?'

Libby let him into hut five and stood back. Nothing had been changed, except the contents of the bin and the bed linen which had been taken away for analysis. Melanie's bag had gone, but her make-up and toiletries still stood on the dressing table.

117

'Why did you take the sheets?' she asked.

'DNA,' said Ian, going into the bathroom pod.

'Ah,' said Libby, none the wiser.

He came out of the bathroom, produced evidence bags and gloves from his pocket and collected all the make-up and toiletries.

'More DNA?' asked Libby, interested.

He gave her a quick smile. 'You never know. Now, let's have a look at where she was found.'

Libby locked the door behind them. 'I'm surprised Mr Murray let me keep a key to the hut if it was still under investigation.'

'So am I,' said Ian.

Libby frowned at him, but said nothing. 'Well, you can see for yourself where she was found.' She indicated blue and white tape fluttering from posts stuck in the ground. 'Not far.'

Ian ducked under the tape and crouched down. After a moment, he stood up and looked back at the huts.

'Is there another way in here apart from the Manor? I can see the gravelled track for cars, but it seems to carry on.'

'It does, but only locals know about it,' said Libby. 'Ben and I thought of that the other day. It's not gravelled all the way, it's just a track and comes out at the top of my road.'

'So a vehicle could get here without being seen from the house?'

Libby repeated her own objections to this theory.

'But it could have come up here at night?'

'I suppose so,' said Libby doubtfully, 'Nick Forrest thought he heard a car at night.'

'What time?'

'I don't know,' said Libby, 'but you'll ask him, won't you?'

'Certainly will.' Ian ducked back under the tape. 'Come on, let's see if there are any tyre tracks further on. Or has anyone else been along here since the weekend?'

'Not to my knowledge. Ben sometimes brings the four by four along here to come home, but we've been walking over the last few days.'

They passed the huts and carried on along the rutted track towards the woods.

'Too dry to show anything,' said Ian, squatting down again. Libby admired his taut thighs beneath the gents' suiting and gave herself a mental slap on the wrist. Taut thighs indeed.

'Might as well turn back.' He stood up and turned to face her. 'I'll maybe get the team out here to have a proper look. I take it they didn't at the weekend?'

'I don't know,' said Libby, turning back towards the Manor. 'I wasn't watching what they did out here.'

'No, of course not.' He grinned at her. 'Must have been very frustrating for you.'

She grinned back. 'It was, rather. The only thing we could do was talk to some of the guests. Ben chickened out.'

'So, just the old team, then?'

'Yup – Castle and Sarjeant on the job.'

'Wolfe,' corrected Ian.

'Castle and Sarjeant sounds better though, don't you think? I suggested it to Fran.'

Ian slid her a wary look. 'But I think she prefers Wolfe.'

'Yes, of course she does.' Libby heaved a sigh. 'She's very proud of it.'

'And she'll keep it that way. Much as you seem to be keeping to Sarjeant.'

'Oh, don't you start,' groaned Libby. 'My marital preferences seem to be up for discussion by the world and his wife. No pun intended.'

'Not by me,' said Ian. 'What you do is your business. Except when it's mine.'

'Is that another warning?' asked Libby.

'Not entirely. What I'm saying is whatever you find out, or stumble across, it comes to me first. Understand?'

'That means we can help?' breathed Libby.

'God help me, yes. I may regret it, but yes. And now, can you remember as much as you can of your conversations with the guests?'

Libby beamed. 'With pleasure!'

Chapter Fourteen

LIBBY REPEATED AS MUCH as she could of the conversations she and Fran had had with Jennifer, Nina, Dee and Daniel. Nothing she had said to Lily Cooper or Patrick Joseph seemed relevant. By this time they were back at the Manor and Ian was frowning.

'There's something wrong with all this,' he said.

Restraining herself from a sarcastic "Well, dur!" Libby merely said 'Mmm?'

'There seems to be no animus towards Melanie but quite a bit towards Patrick.'

'But as I said, not enough to kill him for. If Daniel or Dee wanted Patrick to help them towards mainstream publication, it wouldn't do their cause much good to bump him off, would it?'

'No,' said Ian, 'so the only credible suspects are Patrick himself because Melanie had found out about his affair with Cooper, and Cooper herself.'

'And Patrick seemed genuinely devastated by Melanie's death. And before you say anything,' said Libby, as Ian opened his mouth to protest, 'I know that all murderers do that, but Jennifer confirmed it, saying she'd known them both for years and even babysat for Patrick and his younger sister. Also,' she added, 'it wasn't really an affair, by all accounts, more a fling. I don't even think it was continued after the writers' holiday where they all met. This was just to be another one- or two-night stand, which is what he specialised in.'

'Sounds like a great bloke,' said Ian.

'But actually quite charming. And he wasn't trying to seduce me.' Libby giggled. 'Lily Cooper was reet put out.'

'Was she?' Ian looked interested.

'Well, Patrick wasn't really taking much notice of her – in public anyway. Even Harry and Peter noticed in the pub on Friday night.'

'But she had been to his room,' said Ian. 'She admitted it –'

'Boasted, more like,' interrupted Libby.

'And so did he,' continued Ian. 'I'll have to read the statements properly.'

'Timings,' said Libby.

'Quite.' Ian twitched his eyebrows at her. 'Well, anything else you can think of before I go back and get stuck in?'

'Where did the takeaway come from?'

The eyebrows now rose in surprise. 'Very good point, Libby. I shall look into that, too. As long as they've kept the evidence,' he said with a sigh.

'Oh, come on, Ian! No one's likely to have thrown it away, surely?'

'I'm beginning to wonder,' said Ian, turning to his car. 'Say goodbye to Ben and Hetty for me.'

'Don't you want tea or coffee before you go?'

'No thanks. I just want to get going now. Enough time's been wasted.'

'Ah – the Golden Hours,' said Libby.

Ian laughed, leant forward and kissed her cheek. 'You know what, Libby? You're priceless.' He turned, got into the car and drove off down the drive.

'Are you seducing your pet policeman?' asked Ben, strolling out to join her.

Libby grinned. 'He thinks I'm priceless.'

'Well, so do I, but probably for different reasons.' Ben slid an arm round her waist. 'Come on. Mum's made lemon drizzle cake.'

When Libby got back to the cottage, she called Fran.

'Ian doesn't appear thrilled with the way the investigation's been handled so far. He thinks a lot of things have been missed.'

'Which is stupid, really,' said Fran. 'They had the classic country-house murder set-up – all the suspects in one place.'

'But did they? If, as it now looks like, it was nothing to do with Patrick, the murderer must have been an outsider.'

'Who knew all about the weekend? That's a bit improbable,' said Fran.

'Perhaps her murderer came with her?' Libby said excitedly. 'That's it! The murderer drove her here, she went and ticked herself off and picked up the keys, after all, they were labelled.'

'And how did they find the huts?'

'Not difficult. The track leads behind the theatre and is quite obvious. Then, in the middle of the night, he kills her, dumps the body and drives off down Allhallow's Lane. Nick Forrest heard the car.'

'You're forgetting something. Neither Forrest nor Fisher saw a car.'

Libby looked dashed. 'Oh. Well, perhaps they arrived – Melanie and the murderer – after Fisher and Forrest came back to the Manor before dinner?'

'Then they would have seen a car when they went back to their huts that night.'

'Perhaps they just didn't notice it?'

'Clutching at straws, Lib,' laughed Fran. 'Now, I've got to go. We are having a visitation.'

'Oh, lawks,' said Libby. 'Who from?'

Fran sighed. 'Chrissie and the baby genius.'

'No Brucie-baby?'

Fran's younger daughter had given birth to a baby girl some months previously. Her husband Bruce, even more besotted than his wife, was nevertheless being pushed out of the equation a trifle.

'Yes, I expect he'll be there, doing all the things Chrissie doesn't want to do.'

'Like changing nappies?'

'Exactly. He's changed a good deal for the better. Sorry, no pun intended. Pity I can't say the same for Chrissie.' Fran sighed again. 'Still, I'd better go and get ready for them.'

After the call, Libby went into the kitchen thanking her lucky stars that so far, none of her three children had found the urge to procreate. Her older son Dominic lived in London, as did her daughter Belinda, both in a succession of delightful though non-serious relationships. Adam, who lived – nominally – in the flat above the Pink Geranium, had been in a relationship with Fran's step-daughter Sophie for over two years, continuing even though she had been away at university. He spent equally as much time in Sophie's flat above her father's gallery-come-shop in Nethergate.

Libby began, unenthusiastically, to poke about in

the fridge for something to cook for dinner and her thoughts drifted back to the case.

The whole problem was the focus on Patrick. Why *had* Melanie decided to come to the weekend? And if the murder wasn't to do with her connection to her husband, how did the murderer know about the weekend and where she'd be?

In the middle of peeling potatoes, it occurred to her that they hadn't really done an exhaustive web search on Melanie Joseph. There were the death threats and the bomb under her car – they'd been told about those – but why exactly had she been targeted? Just because she was pro-nuclear fuel?

Libby put the potatoes on to boil, checked the lamb chops in their dish in the oven, wiped her hands and went to wake up the laptop. When Guy had looked up Melanie Joseph he had concentrated on the death threats and the bomb, but Libby found her name coming up on thousands of sites, most prominently on the Green Country website.

'That's the place to start,' she muttered and clicked on the link.

The Green Country website was huge and professional, and smacked of government. Melanie Joseph's biography was the obvious place to start looking.

Melanie Joseph, she read, was born Melanie Jacks in Devon and read politics at Cambridge, where she'd first met her current husband, novelist Patrick Joseph. 'Current?' murmured Libby. She'd been recruited as a researcher by a member of the cabinet of the day and had married a businessman with links to the party, an Edgar Solomon. 'Ah – a former husband!' said Libby. Their two children, Rachel and Zachary, had stayed with their mother after the break-up of the marriage. She had married Patrick Joseph some three years later, and had subsequently become interested in green politics. She had helped found Green Country, and here it listed all the committees and sub-committees on which she had served, at one point being named Special Advisor to the government. There was no mention of the death threats.

Libby decided to look up the link to the online encyclopaedia and found Melanie's page there. The basic information was the same, but after that came the death threats. It also appeared that Melanie had had run-ins with all political parties at one time or another, and had a knack of making the most inflammatory statements in public. Her stand over ancient monuments was militant, and she had been known to barricade certain places if she thought they were at risk. Several archaeologists had nailed their colours to her mast, but there were some who considered she went too far. Some places that were open to the public were well protected and policed, and her opponents argued that it was part of the nation's heritage that the public should be allowed to see and learn from them. Libby agreed.

'So there's plenty there for the police to look into,' thought Libby, as she went back to the kitchen, 'and they'll already be doing it. In fact, I'm surprised the Met isn't already involved.'

She wanted to share the information with Fran, but decided that she could hardly drag her away from her visiting family, and had to wait until Ben came home to talk about it.

'I'm sure they've already got the Major Crimes Squad, or whatever they're called, on to it,' said Ben. 'I didn't realise that she was such an important figure politically.'

'And if she was,' mused Libby, 'why wasn't she more security conscious?'

'It explains the false identity,' said Ben. 'I bet she had several to use, all legit.'

'Yes.' Libby's eyes turned to the laptop. 'But, you know, I'm not sure she was still quite as powerful as she had been. Most of her high-profile causes – and the bomb and death threats – were several years ago. And from the Green Country website it seems that she's now more of a figurehead than an active participant.'

'There's another angle.' Ben helped himself to more potatoes. 'Her first husband.'

'I thought of that,' said Libby. 'But why would he want to have her killed?'

'I was thinking of the religious angle.'

'Religious?'

'I would say he was Jewish, wouldn't you? And their children – two rather Jewish names.'

'Oh,' said Libby, 'you can't go by that these days. Everyone calls their children Rachel and Zachary.'

'But Solomon is a very Jewish surname. What was her maiden name?'

Libby screwed up her forehead. 'Jecks? No – Jacks. Is that Jewish?'

'Don't know.' Ben put his knife and fork together and pushed his plate away. 'Anyway,

Melanie married again, and this time to an Irish Catholic. That must have caused friction.'

'How do you know he's an Irish Catholic?'

'Guessing – again because of the name.'

'But Joseph can be a Jewish surname, too.'

Be grinned. 'Go on then, get the laptop. You know you're dying to.'

But Ben's guess was right. Patrick Brendan Joseph was born of Irish Catholic parents and appeared to have spent all his early life in the same place, where, Libby remembered, Jennifer also lived.

'Blimey,' said Libby. 'Jewish wife and children in a Catholic marriage, outspoken political activist and cuckolded wife. Lots there for the police to get their teeth into. I wonder why we haven't seen a more senior force?'

'I should imagine Ian's getting right on to it now,' said Ben. 'As I said, I expect there's a major crimes investigation going on already.'

'But why haven't we seen it?'

'Because they've decided it had nothing to do with anyone here?'

'But she was killed here, and by someone who was either already here or who knew about the weekend.' Libby scowled. 'I want to know.'

'Yes, darling.' Ben patted her hand. 'And I'm sure Ian will tell you as much as he's able.'

'If he ever bothers to come back to us,' said Libby gloomily. 'I bet that co-operation bit of his was a mere sop.'

But, to Libby's surprise, later that evening Ian rang.

Chapter Fifteen

'I'M AFRAID NOW I'VE been relegated to the man on the ground,' said Ian.

Libby sighed. 'Ben and I were wondering why the big guns hadn't been brought in.'

'You researched her, then,' said Ian, sounding amused.

'Of course! Although she doesn't seem to be as powerful as she used to be.'

'Somewhat of a cipher these days, I gather, but it's what she represents. So we've got an investigation from Scotland Yard – or interference, possibly.'

'And why hadn't Murray done all those things you thought he should have done?'

'Because he contacted Scotland Yard,' said Ian. 'I should have realised.'

'So what will you be doing?'

'I don't know, quite, but I've retrieved the take-away cartons. They came from a pizza place in Canterbury.'

'Blimey, they must have been cold by the time she ate it!' said Libby. 'They certainly didn't deliver.'

'That's what I thought. I wondered if they were dumped there to put us off the scent.'

'Really?' Libby thought about it. 'Shall I tell you what Ben and I were talking about?'

'Could I stop you?'

Libby recounted the theories she and Ben had

been discussing.

'It's all being looked into,' said Ian. 'Solomon has been living in the US for years, and Rachel and Zachary joined him as soon as they left school. They're both in university over there.'

'So they didn't much like their mother? Or their step-father?'

'No idea, but believe me Scotland Yard are on to it.' He sighed. 'I am, however allowed to investigate the – er – *small* things. Don Murray has happily handed over the case. I have to liaise on everything.'

'Oh, Ian, what a pig. So by small things – that's the pizza cartons?'

'Yes. Things they haven't noticed. The false credit card is being looked into at the highest level, of course.'

'But they should notice *everything*. Isn't that what they do?'

'We'll see. Meanwhile, best if you don't poke around too much. I think you'll probably be contacted by someone tomorrow, although they seem quite happy currently that we've covered the ground – physically, at least.'

'They're looking into the backgrounds of all the guests?' asked Libby. 'Well, of course they are.'

'Oh, yes. And there are enough subversive elements there to keep them happy.'

'Really? What?'

'Oh, Libby.' Ian laughed. 'You know I can't tell you that.'

'So they're sure it isn't anything to do with our weekend?'

'I don't suppose they're sure of anything,' said

Ian, 'but they'll carry on investigating until they are. They've already had people going over Patrick's house in the country and the London flat with a tooth comb.'

'Oh, they've got a London flat?'

'Melanie needed it, apparently, because she was – used to be – involved at the headquarters of Green Country most of the time.'

'And advising the government.'

'Until she quarrelled with all the main parties.'

'Yes, I saw that,' said Libby. 'Even the Green party?'

'She appeared to have her own idea of what "Green" meant. Anyway, I must go. I just thought you'd like to know.'

'Hoy! Wait a minute! What about Nina Etherington?'

'What about her?'

'Did she ever talk to the police again?'

'I don't think so. But she'll be spoken to now, so perhaps she'll reveal all. Now, I'm going, Libby!'

Libby relayed the conversation to Ben.

'Isn't it a bugger?' she finished. 'Now we can't look into anything. It's worse than when that awful Big Bertha –'

'Who?'

'You remember – that tarty blonde super-intendent who was involved with the business at Creekmarsh.'

'Oh, yes.' Ben grinned. 'She really didn't like you, did she?'

'And I didn't like her. But this time we really can't get involved. We could be locked up for treason, or something.'

'Talk to Fran about it in the morning,' said Ben. 'Now, nightcap? Nice cup of cocoa?'

Libby threw a cushion at him.

But in the morning, before Libby could even get dressed, there was a knock at the door. Ben had just driven up Allhallow's Lane to go and have a look at a tenant farmer's new sheep, so Libby shuffled to the door and peered out through a crack.

'Mrs Sarjeant?' A large man in a dark blue suit held up an impressive ID. Beside him, a second man, just as impassive and nearly as big, in a charcoal grey suit, held his up, too.

Libby sighed and stepped back. 'Scotland Yard.'

'Sorry to disturb you, madam,' said blue suit. 'May we come in?'

'I'd rather not have strange men in my house when I'm on my own,' said Libby. 'We can talk on the doorstep.'

Blue suit and grey suit exchanged surprised glances.

'Would you care to call our superior officer, madam?'

'No, because I don't know what number you might give me,' said Libby, reaching behind her to pick up the phone. 'You just hold on, and I'll ring DCI Connell.'

Luckily, Ian's phone call of yesterday evening had been the last call received so she was able to call back without looking up the number.

'Libby?' He sounded irritated, as he would when his personal phone rang.

'I've got two men here,' she said, 'and their

names are –' she beckoned for the two IDs to be held where she could see them '– Terence Jones and Danny Lee. They appear to have genuine IDs. I don't want to let them in unless I know they're bona fide.'

Blue suit and grey suit were now looking distinctly uncomfortable.

'Where's Ben?' asked Ian.

'Gone to work.'

'I'd send them up to the Manor, then.'

'No, he's gone to see a tenant farmer. They'd frighten Hetty.'

'I've never known anything frighten Hetty,' commented Ian. 'Let me have a word with one of them.'

Libby handed the phone to blue suit, whose conversation, once he'd introduced himself, consisted mainly of grunts, until he handed it back.

'Let them in, Lib. I'm coming over myself as they need an officer on the ground to show them around, so I'll come to you first.'

Libby switched off the phone and regarded the two men warily.

'All right,' she said, 'DCI Connell says you can come in as he's coming here himself.' She stepped back and allowed them to precede her into the sitting room.

Blue suit, whom she now knew to be Terence Jones, looked round for somewhere to sit. Libby pulled out the two chairs at the table under the window and waved a hand. Jones and Lee took their seats, still looking uncomfortable, while Libby sat on the sofa. Sidney looked up and glared.

Jones cleared his throat. 'I'm sorry if we startled you, Mrs Sarjeant,' he said. 'And of course very sensible not to let people over the threshold if you aren't sure of their identity.'

'Quite,' said Libby. 'I take it you're here about the death of Melanie Joseph? Well, I never met her, as I'm sure you've seen in the case notes or whatever you call them by now, I only spoke to her on the phone, although of course that need not have been her, especially as she gave the name Ann Marsh, neither had I met any of the other guests except my own personal friends Amanda George and Fran Wolfe.'

Jones cleared his throat again.

'And you haven't thought of anything more you can tell us since you were interviewed over the weekend?' asked Lee.

'I was also interviewed yesterday by DCI Connell, who picked up several things that had not been investigated over the weekend,' said Libby sharply. 'I don't think there's anything else I can tell you that you can't find out for yourselves.'

'You don't own this – er,' Jones whipped out a notebook and consulted it, 'Manor?'

'No, my partner Ben Wilde owns it. His mother still lives there. And neither of them had met or knew anything about any of the guests, either.'

'But you organised this weekend break?' said Lee.

'No.'

'That's not our information,' said Jones, beginning to look annoyed.

'Then your information is wrong. Lily Cooper,

whose address I'm sure you already have, organised it. We were merely the venue.'

That Jones and Lee were now both annoyed and dying to shout at her, Libby had no doubt, and hugged herself with glee.

'Now we've cleared that up,' she said, 'perhaps you'd like to go back to your car and wait for DCI Connell. As you can see, I haven't had a chance to get dressed yet.'

There was very little the two men could do unless they arrested her and, with very bad grace, they left. Libby watched them get into an anonymous dark saloon, where they were both immediately on their cell phones. Libby grinned, shut the door and went upstairs.

She'd had a shower and was halfway into her clothes when she heard the door knocker. She threw on a shirt and went downstairs.

Ian was grinning on the doorstep and the dark saloon was gone.

'I won't stay,' he said, 'but you certainly upset them. They aren't used to being answered back or refused entry, and they hadn't been briefed properly either. Luckily, Scotland Yard or not, I outrank both of them.'

'Don't sick Hetty onto them, then, or they'll never recover,' laughed Libby. 'I didn't realise Scotland Yard could be so easily intimidated. Oh, and by the way, their department used to be Special Branch, didn't it?'

'Yes, it is, and it'll be SB to us for ever,' said Ian. 'Their new title is far longer.'

'Yes, I noticed it on their ID,' said Libby. 'It's

all counter-terrorism and stuff, isn't it?'

'Among other things,' said Ian. 'Covert ops, all sorts of exciting stuff.'

'And murdered ex-politicos.' Libby shook her head. 'Off you go then. Ben will be back at the Manor soon if you need back-up.'

'All I need is to brief these goons properly,' said Ian, 'and teach them not to barge all over the territory with their great flat feet.'

'Can't see them doing covert ops,' grinned Libby.

Ian drove off and Libby rang Fran.

'So,' she concluded, 'it really is out of our hands now, although Ian doesn't seem to place much faith in Scotland Yard – or whoever they are.'

'No.' There was a pause. 'We could, of course, warn everyone.'

'Do what?'

'The guests. You've got all their phone numbers. We could call them and warn them they're going to be investigated by Scotland Yard.'

'They'll all know that by now,' said Libby. 'I expect Jones and Lee's brothers-in-arms have paid them all visits.'

'They haven't paid me one,' said Fran, 'and I was a guest.'

'Ah. But they'll have been looking into backgrounds without people knowing.'

'So we should warn them.'

'Oh, you are clever, Fran! And then we can get them chatting?'

'Precisely.'

'But why?' asked Libby. 'Do you think it isn't

politically motivated?'

'I've absolutely no idea,' said Fran, 'but she was murdered at the Manor. There must be a link to someone or something there, and I want to find it.'

'So does Ian and so do Scotland Yard. Are you suggesting we'd do a better job?'

'No, but we can always get people to talk to us. Especially as we're in the same boat as they are.'

'Solidarity sort of thing?'

'Exactly,' said Fran. 'Were you planning anything special today?'

'I hope that wasn't a pun,' said Libby. 'No, I wasn't. Are you coming here, or shall I come to you?'

'I'll come to you. Nearer the seat of operations,' said Fran. 'I'm on my way.'

Chapter Sixteen

'I FORGOT TO ASK,' said Libby as Fran sat at the table and opened her laptop, 'how were Chrissie and Brucie last night?'

'Ghastly, thanks,' said Fran.

'Ah. And baby Montana?'

Fran screwed up her face. 'I suppose I'll get used to it eventually.'

'I didn't mean her name – after all, it's not as bad as some of them you hear these days. I meant how was she?'

'She cried a lot.' Fran sighed. 'I couldn't help comparing her to Jane and Terry's Imogen.'

'That's very disloyal,' said Libby in mock disapproval. 'And Jane and Terry will have terrible trouble later, while Montana will turn into a positive paragon.'

Fran smiled. 'Yes, I know. Go on, put the kettle on and we'll make a start on these calls.'

'Lots of them will be at work,' called Libby from the kitchen. 'Try the women first.'

'On the basis that they're least likely to be at work? That's a bit sexist, isn't it?'

Libby poked her head round the kitchen door. 'No, I meant those two who shared a room. They were both of a certain age, weren't they?'

'Audrey Glenister and Bernice Weldon.' Fran ran her finger down the list Libby had printed out. 'No email address for either of them, or mobile numbers.'

'Told you they were of a certain age,' said Libby.

'What's got into you this morning?' Fran turned round to look at her friend. 'That's a bit sweeping.'

'Must be because I was upset by Scotland Yard.' Libby looked shamefaced. 'Sorry. I bet they're complete silver surfers.'

'I'll ring them, though, just in case you say something you shouldn't,' said Fran, taking out her own mobile. Libby opened her mouth to protest and shut it again with a snap.

Fran's side of the conversation was not particularly illuminating. She informed Audrey Glenister of what was happening, explained the situation and suggested she talk to her friend Bernice and come back to Fran if they wanted to talk it over. After which, she spent nearly five minutes listening to an obviously excited woman and making wind-up motions.

'Did she say anything interesting?' asked Libby, who was now sitting beside Fran at the table.

'No, although she said a lot. She did wonder if her husband's ex-job with the civil service would come up if she was investigated by Scotland Yard, but as he was in the housing department of local government I don't suppose it will.'

'She sounded excited.'

'She was. I should think this is the most exciting thing that's ever happened to her. And her friend sounds the same.'

'Who next, then?' Libby pulled the list towards her. 'Lily Cooper? She's more involved than some of the others.'

'You can do her,' said Fran. 'I deserve a rest.'

Lily Cooper sounded as though she was somewhere with a lot of people.

'Sorry, Mrs Cooper, am I disturbing you? It's Libby Sarjeant here.'

'Wait a moment.' Libby heard movement and suddenly the background noise was cut out. 'I'm at work. What did you want?'

Encouraging, thought Libby. 'Actually, Mrs Cooper, I just wanted to warn you –'

'Warn me? Are you threatening me?'

'No, no,' said Libby hastily. 'It's Scotland Yard.'

'Scotland Yard?'

Libby took a deep breath. 'You obviously know that Melanie Joseph had political links.'

'Did she?'

Bloody hell, thought Libby. 'Yes, I thought you'd know. She was a government advisor and sat on committees.'

'Oh, that.'

'Yes, well,' Libby went on, 'because of that it was thought best to bring in the specialists, so I had a visit from two Scotland Yard detectives – their department used to be Special Branch and has a new name now, but that's effectively who they are – this morning and they are investigating everyone's backgrounds. We thought we ought to warn you.'

'We? Who's we? And why me? Why did you want to warn me?'

'Fran Wolfe and I,' sighed Libby, 'and we're warning everybody, not just you. We simply thought people needed to know.'

There was a short silence.

'Well, I don't see that it's got anything to do with me,' said Lily eventually. 'I didn't even know the woman.'

'No, I don't think anyone did,' said Libby, 'not the weekend guests, anyway.'

'Except Jennifer,' said Lily, an unmistakeably sour note in her voice.

'Quite,' said Libby, 'although she knew Patrick better than Melanie.'

'I bet,' muttered Lily.

'Anyway,' Libby hurried on, 'if there's anything you want to talk about, do phone one of us.'

'Why should I want to talk to you?' said Lily rudely, and the phone went dead.

'That went well,' said Libby, and picked up her mug before repeating the conversation.

None of the other guests were answering their phones, so Libby and Fran left messages on them all, not mentioning Scotland Yard – 'just in case' said Libby.

'Well, that was a bit of a waste of time,' said Fran. 'Unless we get anything out of it when they ring back.'

'At least we know how bitchy Lily Cooper is.'

'I thought we knew that already,' said Fran.

'We guessed. Why do men go for women like that?'

'Because she was all that was left?'

'Oh, yes. We know he had a bit of a thing with Dee Starkey and he tried it on with Nina, so I suppose, yes. She was all that was left and she was desperate. She has that look, doesn't she?'

'The well preserved, over-toned look.' Fran

turned down her mouth. 'I hope to God I don't ever look like that.'

'I wonder how old she is?' mused Libby. 'Forty-five?'

'She probably wants people to think she's thirty-five,' said Fran.

Libby persuaded Fran to stay for lunch, and, to while away the rest of the morning, they took a jaunt in Fran's car to the Cattlegreen Nurseries on the outskirts of the village. Joe and "the boy", Owen, were pleased to see them and left them to wander among the rows of plants.

'Any news on that murder?' asked Joe, as he took Fran's money for a tray of bedding pelargoniums.

'No.' Libby shook her head. 'Nothing to do with us, it seems. We'll just have a plague of bluebottles for a bit.'

Joe frowned and Owen frowned harder. Libby sighed.

'I meant a lot of police around the place. Already had two this morning.'

'Must be hard for old Hetty,' said Joe, handing over change. 'Specially now old Greg's gone.'

'Oh, she's fine,' said Libby. 'Much as we all miss him terribly, Hetty has a lot less responsibility now. And Ben looks after her. The police won't bother her.'

Joe nodded. 'You take care, now,' he said. Libby grinned and patted Owen's arm. He blushed.

'The whole village knows, then,' said Fran driving back towards Allhallow's Lane.

'Well, of course they do. You ought to be used to

that by now. Don't forget the community memory's been useful to us in the past.'

'Yes.' Fran frowned as she swung the car into Allhallow's Lane. 'But we also know how different people's memories are. They get smoothed over and sanitised.'

'Hmm.' Libby shot a quick glance at her friend. 'Well, it's a bit soon for memories to start playing up in this case.'

The answerphone light was winking and informed Libby that there were three messages. The first was from Dee Starkey, the second from Daniel Hill and the third from Jennifer. Libby went into the kitchen to prepare a salad while Fran called Jennifer.

'It was lovely to hear from you so soon, but I couldn't help feeling there must be something serious going on?' Jennifer's rising lilt made it a question.

'Libby had a visit from two Scotland Yard detectives this morning,' Fran told her.

'Good heavens! Why? Oh – don't tell me – Melanie and her blasted Green Country, I suppose.'

'We've been told,' Fran went on, 'that even though her post with the organisation is merely titular these days, because of her past as a government advisor –'

'I know, I know, and the bomb and the death threats.' Jennifer sighed. 'So I suppose the case has been handed over to them and we're all going to be investigated.'

'Um, yes, I'm afraid so. At least that's what we've been told.'

'I didn't think they'd give that much away.'

'No,' said Fran, 'we were told by the detective formerly in charge of the case.'

'Wallington? Was that his name?'

'No, that was DS Wallingford, and at that time DCI Murray was in charge. It was taken over briefly by DCI Connell, and then Scotland Yard appeared. DCI Connell told us, because he'd already re-interviewed us and gone over the ground. The crime scene, that is.'

'I see.' Jennifer was quiet for a moment. 'Well, it won't be the first time.'

'Er – what won't?'

'I've been investigated.' There was a light chuckle. 'When the bomb went off, although the car was outside the flat in London, we were all questioned very thoroughly.'

'We?'

'Friends in the village. She'd been a trifle – ah – active here, too.'

'Oh?' Fran made frantic faces at Libby.

'I don't know how much you know about Green Country or Melanie's particular causes, but we have an ancient monument on the edge of the village.'

'Aah,' said Fran.

'I see you do know. In that case you'll guess that she engendered quite a lot of bad feeling here.'

'I can guess.'

'Well, there you are. I shall await questioning a second time with equanimity.'

Fran laughed. 'You can tell you're a writer.'

'Oh?'

'Your phrasing. Not exactly normal conversational stuff.'

Jennifer laughed. 'No, perhaps not. Sorry. It was kind of you to warn me.'

'Where is your village? If you don't mind me asking?'

'Dorset, on the borders of Somerset and Wiltshire. Near enough to Stonehenge for tourists to do both, and Avebury, in one visit.'

'And she objected?'

'She certainly did.'

'Well, I'm sure the police, or whoever it is, will revisit that,' said Fran. 'Have you seen Patrick since you've been home?'

'Yes, I was round there yesterday. The children are on their way home.'

'They had children? I didn't know.'

'Melanie's children, Rachel and Zachary.'

'Of course, Edgar Solomon's children.'

'You *have* been doing your research.' Jennifer sounded amused.

Fran sighed. 'I'm afraid for Libby and me it's second nature now.'

'Ah, yes. Home-grown investigations, isn't it?'

'Inadvertent, actually,' said Fran, nettled.

'Sorry, of course. I couldn't resist looking you up, either, when I got home.'

'On the internet?' Fran was surprised. 'Are we there?'

'In reports of various cases, yes. I did see a reference to you as a special advisor.' Again there was a questioning note in Jennifer's voice.

'I've done property investigation in the past.' Fran's tone put an end to any further questions.

'Really,' Jennifer said dryly. 'Pity you can't

come and have a look at our monument.'

Resisting the urge to ask why, Fran began to wind up the conversation.

'Thank you for ringing back, Jennifer, and let us know if you need to talk about anything.'

'I meant it, you know. Look it up and see if you're interested. Give my regards to Libby. Goodbye Fran.'

Libby was almost hopping up and down from foot to foot.

'What? What? What did she say?'

Fran relayed the conversation and followed Libby back into the kitchen, where they began on the salad and cold meat which were set out on the table.

'So, what do you think? Should we go down and have a look?' Libby leant forward excitedly.

'Why, though?'

'Because Jennifer asked us to. Because she's looked us up, and she obviously knows what you do.'

'What makes you say that?'

'Why else would she ask you to have a look at an ancient monument? I bet in one of those reports of the other cases it mentions your talents.'

Fran pulled a face. 'Ian never made anything of it in the press.'

'No, but it's amazing how people actually seemed to know what you did, isn't it? Think of Jane and Campbell McLean. They knew.'

Fran sighed and pushed away her plate. 'OK. We'll have a look at the area. See if we can pin it down.'

Libby rose gleefully to her feet and began clearing away. 'Go and get the laptop, then, and I'll put the kettle on.'

Fran raised an eyebrow. 'Yes, mistress.'

Libby laughed and clattered plates in the sink. 'You know you want to. Come on, Fran! Don't you feel a proper investigation coming on?'

Chapter Seventeen

'HOPELESS.' FRAN SQUINTED AT the screen. 'The whole area is littered with henges and barrows.'

'Are we assuming we should be somewhere in – or on – Cranborne Chase?' Libby peered over her shoulder.

'It seems like it. Not many actual monuments, like standing stones, it's just ditches and burial mounds.'

'Well,' said Libby swinging the laptop round to face her, 'we'll just have to call Jennifer and ask her. It looks like an interesting place anyway. I'd love to find out more of the history. It was a private hunting forest until 1828.'

'I know, Lib. I've been reading all the sites, too.' Fran sat back.

Libby's phone rang.

'Hello? Oh, Dee.' Libby waggled her eyebrows at Fran.

'What did you want?' Dee Starkey sounded nervous.

'Just to tell you the update on Melanie Joseph's murder,' said Libby.

'What? Have they found him?' Too quickly.

'Him? Who?'

'The – er – the murderer,' faltered Dee.

'No, they haven't found anybody,' said Libby, 'but we thought we ought to warn you that Scotland Yard are now looking into it.'

'What?' squeaked Dee.

Libby once again explained about Melanie's political background.

'Oh, don't I know it,' said Dee, viciously.

'You do?'

'I happen to be very interested in prehistoric archaeology,' said Dee. 'She was very much against us.'

'Oh, I know she was all for preserving ancient sites,' said Libby.

'Hardly,' spat Dee. 'She would have had everything wrapped in bubble wrap so that no one could get near it.'

'Ah,' said Libby. 'Anywhere in particular?'

'Her own bloody village in particular!'

'Oh? Where was that? They have a monument?'

'Haven't you ever heard of Bonny Henge?' Dee was incredulous. Libby was typing the words into the search engine with one hand.

'I'm afraid not,' said Libby, watching as all the sites came up and Fran clicked on the first one.

'Look it up,' said Dee, unaware that Libby was doing just that. 'I've been arrested at demos there. No wonder Scotland Yard want to investigate me.'

'Do you live near there, then?' asked Libby.

'No, I live in London. Which of course puts me in an even worse position, doesn't it? I could have bombed her bloody car.'

'So you know about that? You didn't mention it when you were here.'

'Why should I? You were all more interested in that bastard Patrick.'

'But you said you knew nothing about her.'

'I wasn't likely to put my head in a noose, was

I?'

'True. Well, thanks for coming back to me, Dee. We'll keep you updated.'

'Bonny Henge, just outside Rising Parva. Derived, possibly, from Bone Henge.' Fran turned the laptop back towards Libby. 'That was easy.'

'Look, it's a valley on the edge of Cranborne Chase. Four Risings, Parva, Magna, St Peter and Abbas. All very Dorset.' Libby clicked on a couple more sites. 'Oh, this is great!'

Fran pushed her heavy dark hair back from her face. 'So when do we go?'

'You're excited about it now, aren't you?' Libby grinned at her friend.

'It's intriguing, I'll give you that.' She pulled the laptop back towards her. 'Especially as I noticed this, look.' She clicked through another couple of links and pushed it back to Libby.

'"The Bonny Henge Ghost",' she read, '"is said to appear on moonless nights, when it walks down from the henge and through the gates of Rising Manor, whereupon a shot is heard. It is said to be the spirit of a former Lady of the Manor who shot herself after finding her lover's murdered body at the henge." Blimey! A real ghost for you to investigate!'

'Yes.' Fran's answering grin was mischievous. 'And a cover if anyone wants to know what we're doing.'

Libby's eyebrows rose. 'But it'll be obvious what we're doing. To Jennifer and Patrick it will, anyway.'

'But the police, or Scotland Yard, whoever they

are, will want to know why we're there. This is perfect cover.'

'Brilliant. OK, who's going to phone Jennifer? And we'll have to check with the men that we're all right to skive off for a few days.'

Fran laughed. 'Really? We have to ask our menfolk for permission?'

'No.' Libby was uncomfortable. 'Just check there's nothing we should be doing.'

'Fine.' Fran picked up her phone again and re-dialled Jennifer's number.

'That was quick.' There was irony in Jennifer's cut-glass voice.

'Rising Parva,' said Fran. 'The Bonny Henge ghost.'

'Ah, I see. Well, of course you'd be interested in that. Are you coming down to investigate?'

'We thought we would. Is there a pub in the village where we could stay?'

'Afraid not, not any more. There's a pub, but it doesn't let rooms. There's the Rising Arms in Rising St Peter, which is about two miles away, or there's a B&B just outside the village. I'm not sure that would suit you, though.'

'Oh? Why?'

'A Mrs Broadhurst has two letting rooms in her bungalow.' Jennifer sounded amused. 'I can't say I've ever heard any good reports.'

'Right,' said Fran. 'Well, we'll have a look on the internet and I'll give you a ring to let you know when we're coming.'

Libby had been speaking to Ben, who seemed very relaxed about the proposed jaunt. 'His last remark was "I've been expecting something like this". He didn't even tell me not to get into trouble.'

'OK, so you can look up accommodation in the Risings while I phone Guy,' said Fran. 'Start with the Rising Arms and ignore a Mrs Broadhurst's B&B.'

The choice of accommodation was narrowed down to the Rising Arms and two other B&Bs, neither of which belonged to Mrs Broadhurst. Having decided to strike while the iron was hot, that narrowed the choice still further to Potter's Farm B&B, three or four miles from Rising Parva, but close enough for exploration, who could take them for a maximum of two nights from tomorrow.

'But I'm sorry, dear, it's Saturday after that, and I've got walkers.'

'That's all right, Mrs – er – Potter?' said Libby.

'Mrs Rush, dear. Potter's just the name of the farm. Now – you don't mind sharing a room? I can do you two singles if you prefer.'

'Are they both en-suite?'

'Oh, yes, dear. You can't sell anything without en-suite these days,' said Mrs Rush.

'Just what I told Ben when we were doing up the Manor,' said Libby when she'd switched off the phone. 'Sounds all right, though. She'll do an evening meal if we like and we can take our own wine.'

'So, said Fran, standing up. 'Tomorrow morning then? We'd better take my car.'

'Had we?'

'I doubt if your Romeo would stand up to the journey,' said Fran.

'Oh, look,' said Libby. 'We haven't listened to the other two messages.'

'Dee called again, so it's only Daniel. What did he say?'

Libby pressed the button and Daniel Hill's grumpy tones issued forth.

'This is Daniel Hill returning your call. I cannot imagine what you wish to talk to me about.' And the click of the phone being switched off.

'Oh, well, we needn't bother with him then,' said Libby. 'Let's leave him till we come back home.'

But before Fran left, the phone rang again.

'Hello, is that Libby? It's Nina here. You left a message on my phone.'

'Oh, hello, Nina, yes. We're just warning everybody about Scotland Yard.'

Nina let out a startled yelp.

'Don't worry, it's just that Melanie Joseph was a political sort of person, so Special Branch are investigating everyone's backgrounds.' Libby soothed.

'Even mine?'

'Well, yes. All of us. To see if we knew her or had any connection with her.'

'I didn't.' Nina was sharp. 'I've already said. How would I know her?'

'All right, calm down,' said Libby in surprise. 'They have to find out for themselves. Oh, and by the way, did you ever get to talk to the police about – er – about whatever it was?'

'Talk to them?'

'Yes. On the Saturday evening you asked me if any of the police were still there.'

'Oh.' There was a short silence. 'Well, no.'

'If it was information, don't you think you ought to? Or you can always tell me, if you like.' Libby glanced quickly at Fran, who was leaning forward, looking interested.

'Oh – it was nothing.' Nina sounded embarrassed. 'Just –'

'Just what? Come on Nina, it sounds as though it could be important.'

'It was the row.' It came out in a rush.

'What row?'

'In Patrick's room. I heard them. Him and Lily Cooper. At least, I think it was her. It could have been Dee Starkey, I suppose.'

'When was this?' asked Libby.

'Oh, early Saturday morning, I think. I'm not really sure …' the voice trailed off.

'I still think you should tell the police,' said Libby. 'I'll give you DCI Connell's number if you like.'

'No, I'm not having anything more to do with the police, unless they come after me,' said Nina, and the phone went dead.

'I expect,' said Fran, after Libby switched off the phone, 'she was just worried at the thought of Scotland Yard. After all, it is a bit frightening to think of being investigated by them. You automatically feel guilty.'

'I suppose so,' said Libby, 'but she was so – I don't know – almost panicky.'

The following morning, Fran called to pick up Libby at half-past nine. Libby was still staggering around with wet hair and her eyes glued shut.

'Honestly,' said Fran, exasperated. 'You agreed nine thirty on the phone last night.'

'I know. I went back to sleep after the alarm went.'

'Didn't Ben wake you?'

'Yes.' Libby's eyes opened a bit wider and a tell-tale tide of red crept up her neck.

'Oh, I see,' said Fran. 'Well, you go and get dressed and I'll make you some toast.'

'I've had some,' mumbled Libby. 'Ben made it.'

'Well, go and get ready for goodness' sake,' said Fran, standing, arms akimbo, at the bottom of the stairs. 'Or we'll never get there this side of tomorrow.'

Eventually, Libby, her bag and her laptop were loaded into the car and Fran set off towards the M25.

Halfway down the A303 the rain started. Fran began to look anxious.

'Do you want me to take over?' asked Libby.

'No, it's all right. You keep navigating.'

Libby sighed. 'Oh, for a satnav.'

'It'll only send you down a one-way dead end,' said Fran. 'Look, there's a sign for Salisbury – next roundabout.'

After Salisbury they were pointed towards Blandford Forum and at last, a signpost to The Risings. After another half a mile, they came to a finger post pointing to all four Risings and two other villages.

'That way,' said Libby, pointing down a tree-lined lane.

The rain had lessened, and, peering out of the open window, Libby finally spotted the signpost for Potter's Farm. 'Lovely views,' she said.

'If you can see them through the rain,' said Fran through gritted teeth.

The farmhouse was the sort of place expatriates dream of when they think of England. However, Mrs Rush directed them to the back of the property where a large barn had been converted.

'This is you, dears,' she said, opening a stable door into a wide hall. 'One room there, the other this side. You've both got little terraces, but I'll bring your dinner here to the hall, seeing as how it's so wet. Got everything you need?'

'Thank you,' said Libby, 'it's lovely. Do we need a key to get in? We're probably going out again in a little while.'

'Are we?' muttered Fran.

'Yes, dear – here.' Mrs Rush produced two key rings. 'One for the front door here, and one for your rooms. There's a little internal phone here in the hall if you need me.'

'This is nice,' said Libby, surveying her room after Mrs Rush had left them alone. She crossed the hall to look at Fran's room, and found her sitting on the bed. 'What's up?'

'Driving,' said Fran. 'I just hate it these days.'

'I said I could take over,' said Libby. 'You're all right at home. You do loads of the driving then.'

'On my home turf,' said Fran. 'I can't even drive up to London these days.'

'I'll do it, then,' said Libby. 'It'll make a change from driving Romeo or that four-wheeled drive beast of Ben's.'

'I'll phone up Guy and get him to put you on the insurance, then,' said Fran, 'but first I'm going to take something for this headache.'

Libby patted her sympathetically on the shoulder. 'I'll get the laptop. You can do it online.'

Half an hour later, clothes unpacked, insurance sorted and rain stopped, Libby checked the directions to Rising Parva and started the car.

'Gosh, isn't it light?' she said, as they bumped out of the farm yard on to the lane. Fran winced.

'Did you let Jennifer know we were coming?' she asked, as Libby swung into the lane leading to Rising Parva.

'Had to leave a message,' said Libby. 'Beautiful countryside, isn't it?'

Cranborne Chase, even in the rain, was certainly beautiful. Rolling chalk uplands and pockets of thick woodland concealed very small villages. Even under grey skies it was spectacular.

'It's more country-ish than our bit of Kent.' Libby waved a hand at the view and Fran winced again. Libby looked sideways at her. 'Do you know, I'd never realised what a nervous passenger you were.'

'I've got worse over the years I've known you,' said Fran.

'Implying that it's my fault?'

'No, just that I'm used to driving safely and sensibly in my own car or being driven by my equally safe and sensible husband.'

'Hmm.' Libby peered through the windscreen. 'Well, I appear to have got us here safely and sensibly. Where shall we park?'

Rising Parva was a long narrow village, with a traditional duck pond, pub and church in the middle. A couple of small alleyways led off the village street and, on a slightly higher level, they could see a few large houses. Opposite the inn and almost beside the church sat a Victorian-built village hall, in front of which were marked parking bays. Libby parked in one of them and checked her phone.

'Text from Jennifer "ring when you get here".' She keyed in the number.

'She's coming to meet us,' she said when she switched off the phone. 'Do you want to look at the church?'

Fran raised an eyebrow. 'Why would I want to do that?'

'Pray that you'll be kept safe from my driving?'

Fran aimed a punch at her shoulder. 'Shut up, or I'll drive away and leave you here.'

'I've got the keys,' said Libby, grinning and going towards a glass-covered notice board filled with leaflets and posters advertising local events and services.

'And I've got the spares,' said Fran, joining her.

Jennifer arrived on foot ten minutes later.

'I think I'll join the life drawing class,' said Libby, turning to greet her, 'and Fran's going to join the craft club.'

'What about the Rising Stars?' laughed Jennifer, shaking hands. 'Just up your street, I'd have thought.'

'Rising Stars? Who are they?'

'Our am-dram group, of course!'

Libby and Fran laughed. 'Rising Stars – brilliant!' said Libby.

'So, you want to have a look at our barrow?' Jennifer turned to lead the way back on to the village street.

'I think so,' said Fran. 'I did discover several White Lady stories on the internet about this part of the world, so it's not exactly irrefutable, is it?'

'No, but we have got proof of the lady's suicide. Up here.'

They went up a track by the side of the church and climbed a small hill, coming out on a plateau.

'There,' said Jennifer.

A long lump sat in front of them, surrounded by a shallow ditch.

'Typical Iron Age barrow,' said Libby wisely.

'Interested in archaeology?' asked Jennifer, sounding slightly surprised.

'Only the television variety,' admitted Libby. 'What do you think, Fran?'

Fran was frowning. 'I can't feel anything,' she said. 'Perhaps it's too long ago.' She turned to Jennifer. 'The woman's lover was found up here, the legend says?'

'Apparently that's a fact, too. What aren't facts are her appearances up here. But then, Dorset's supposed to be a very haunted county, and as you found out, there are all sorts of ghost stories in the area.'

'And this is what Melanie was trying to protect?' asked Libby.

'No, she was trying to protect our standing stone.'

'You've got one of those, too?' Libby was surprised.

'Fairly newly discovered,' said Jennifer. 'It's further away, and,' she looked at the sky, 'it looks as though it's going to start raining again, so perhaps if you want to see it we'd better not try today.'

'We're staying for a couple of days,' said Fran. 'Perhaps we could see it tomorrow?'

'Good idea. Have you seen enough here?'

'For the moment.' Fran was frowning again. 'I'd like to come back here, too.'

'Fine. We'll have an expedition tomorrow, then,' said Jennifer. 'Shall we go back and see if they'll give us tea in the pub?'

'Yes, and you can tell us why you suggested we should come down and investigate,' said Libby.

Chapter Eighteen

THE PUB DID INDEED give them tea. The rain had started falling again as they made their way down the hill and was now driving against the windows.

'Nice weather for a short break,' said Libby, gazing dismally out at the shiny pavement.

Fran was looking at Jennifer, who caught her eye and smiled.

'I know, I'm being mysterious,' she said. 'I'm also feeling a bit embarrassed.'

'Why?' asked Fran.

'Because I've effectively brought you down here on a mere suspicion of my own, and now it doesn't seem very sensible.'

'Tell us what the suspicion is, then.' Libby turned from the window.

Jennifer looked down into her cup. 'You had to know Melanie, really,' she said finally. 'She was so driven.'

'Driven? By her politics?'

'By her causes.' Jennifer looked up. 'Before Patrick brought her back here to live, after they'd been married for about a year, this village had been going along in its little rut the same way for generations. Even our shop was still here.' She shrugged. 'That's gone of course, but we're lucky, we still have the pub – and the church, of course, although it shares the vicar with the other Risings.'

'So what changed when Patrick brought her here?' asked Fran.

'Nothing for a while, because she was so caught up in her politics and her children. She and Edgar had awful rows about them, and I'm afraid I rather sided with him, because she didn't really want them. She sent them away to boarding school as soon as they were old enough, poor little things.'

'No wonder they chose to go to America to live with him,' said Fran.

'Quite. So then Melanie started trying to take over the village. After the bomb scare, Patrick insisted they spend most of their time here. But it ended up with her staying here, and Patrick having to keep going up to London on his own.'

'Oh, dear,' said Libby, pulling a face.'

'Exactly. Everybody guessed he was seeing other women, and if Melanie knew, she never said anything. Just carried on trying to take over the WI, the parish council and anything else she could get her hands on. She was forever trying to start clubs, or hold events, and the more sycophantic among the villagers – newcomers, mostly – backed her up.'

'What did Patrick say to all this?' asked Fran.

'He didn't. He just smiled and encouraged her.'

'So that he could carry on with his own reprehensible little schemes,' said Libby.

'That's what I thought.' Jennifer nodded. 'And then, a year or so ago a metal detectorist walking along the ridge found our stone.'

'The standing stone?' said Libby.

'Yes. There's not much of it above ground, but the chap reported it, and the county archaeologists sent someone out to have a look. Unfortunately, Dorset doesn't actually have an archaeological team of its own, so it sent someone from a university. He wanted to bring a group of his students and to dig it up. Melanie, predictably, was furious.'

'Ah.' Fran and Libby looked at one another.

'You know something about this?' Jennifer looked from one to the other.

'We know someone who's been on a demo here,' said Libby. 'But is that Bonny Henge? I thought the barrow was the henge?

'It's part of the henge. A henge isn't stones or posts, it's the earthwork. Our barrow is inside the interior ditch, which you saw. We were standing on the outer bank, although it doesn't look like it from there. When we go and look at the stone you'll be able to see that there's a bank, a ditch and our barrow, which is actually a mini-henge.'

'Mini-henge?' repeated Libby.

'Because it's smaller than twenty metres across. And it appears only to have one entrance. But now the stone has been found –'

'Oh, yes, sorry. We interrupted. What happened when the students wanted to dig up the stone?' said Fran.

'They didn't actually want to remove it,' said Jennifer, 'they simply wanted to excavate down to its lowest point to date it, and then investigate whether it was a single stone or part of a ring. Being, as it appears to be, inside the ditch, it was possible that there were more.'

'And were there?' asked Libby.

'No one's been able to get the funding for the project yet. And Melanie made it as difficult as she could, going to every county and government department she could think of to delay the process. Even Patrick was getting fed up with her.'

'But I don't understand why she wouldn't want it excavated.' Libby looked at Fran. 'We were told she wanted to keep everything in bubble wrap.'

Jennifer nodded. 'She was up in arms when the site was first investigated some years ago, which was when we discovered it wasn't actually a barrow but a henge. Although there are burials in there.'

'Is that why it's called Bonny Henge? Because of the bones?' asked Fran.

'I don't know.' Jennifer looked surprised. 'It's always been called Bonny Barrow locally, even on OS maps, so it just became Bonny Henge. It made a bit of a stir in the national press because henges are comparatively rare finds these days, and we're of course in a very good area, what with Stonehenge, Avebury and Knowlton Circles all within spitting distance. So the finding of the stone was the icing on the cake as far as we were concerned. And everybody else, from the county to the university.' Jennifer sighed. 'But she went on and on about the desecration of ancient sites, got it put on the agenda of her precious Green Country –' Jennifer stopped. 'Well, there you are. That's my suspicion.'

'You think a mad archaeologist bumped her off?' Libby looked sceptical.

'Sounds silly, doesn't it.' Jennifer gave a short laugh. 'But believe me, if you'd seen some of those demonstrators ...'

'Before we actually heard that one of the guests last weekend had actually been here,' said Fran, 'we had made a connection with her stand on ancient monuments.'

'It was a guest?' Jennifer's eyebrows shot up.

Libby nodded. 'Dee Starkey. Did you have anything to do with her?'

'Last year at the writers' holiday, I did. Strange young woman – not so young, I suppose – writes erotic fiction. Pornographic, I'd call it, actually.' A faint flush could be seen on Jennifer's well-bred cheeks.

'Well, she claims to have an interest in ancient monuments.' Libby sniffed. 'Personally, I can guess what sort.'

'Oh?' Jennifer looked interested.

Fran laughed. 'Libby got involved in a murder in a Morris dancing side a couple of years ago, and they do seem to get themselves mixed up with very strange pagan rituals.'

'Like those idiots at Stonehenge at midsummer?' said Jennifer.

'Only much darker and more secret,' said Libby. 'And sometimes there are covens – or Satanists. Very Aleister Crowley. We've been there, too, haven't we, Fran?'

'You've certainly lived,' said Jennifer admiringly. 'And do you always get your man?'

'The police do,' said Libby, with a grin. 'With or without our help.'

'And you're the special investigator.' Jennifer turned to Fran. 'With your rather special skills.'

'See?' said Libby. 'I told you she'd know all about you.'

'I must admit, I thought it would be interesting to see what you got up on the mound. Not exactly because of our Lady in white, but to see if there was any connection to Melanie's murder.'

'Unless Melanie was murdered there, I wouldn't get anything about that,' said Fran. 'I'd still like to see the stone, though.'

'But you think there's real chance that someone who wanted the new dig to go ahead could have been behind her murder?' asked Libby.

'I can't see any other reason.' Jennifer shook her head. 'It seems so odd that she should have been at the writers' weekend. Why would she go? She'd never been to one before – and she wrote herself.'

'Did she?' Fran's eyebrows rose. 'What did she write?'

Jennifer looked vague. 'Non-fiction. I'm afraid I've never been interested enough to find out. I was more Patrick's friend than hers.'

'And how is Patrick?' asked Libby, while Fran returned to frowning mode.

'Shaky. Doesn't want anyone around – except me,' Jennifer added, a shade smugly, Libby thought.

'Well, do give him our best wishes,' she said. 'I suppose we ought to be getting back to our farm, Fran.'

'Oh, where did you say you were staying?' asked Jennifer.

'Potter's Farm. It's a couple of miles away, and it's lovely.' Libby stood up and Fran looked startled.

'Are we going?' she said.

'Yes, come on.' Libby started towards the door, Jennifer hurrying in her wake. 'I'm afraid we can't give you a lift, Jennifer,' she continued. 'As you can see, there's only room for two in these cars.'

Jennifer peered interestedly inside. 'Are they comfortable?' she asked. 'I've often wondered about them. I think I might feel a bit vulnerable in one.'

'They are a bit light,' said Libby, watching Fran trail across the road out of the corner of her eye. 'So.' She held out her hand to Jennifer. 'Thanks for meeting us. What time shall we say tomorrow?'

'Ten thirty? You can park here and I'll walk you up to the stone, then we can circle round and come back to the henge. I must stop calling it a barrow.'

'We left rather suddenly,' said Fran, as Libby turned the car to set off towards Potter's Farm.

'Because you'd gone into a brown study, and there is no knowing what you'll say when you're like that. It could have been something we wouldn't want Jennifer to hear.'

'Mmm.' Fran looked out of the window. 'It's just that there's something wrong.'

'Wrong?' prompted Libby, after a minute. 'How do you mean?'

'With the stuff about the stone and the henge.'

'You mean, Jennifer was making it up?'

'Oh, no, I'm sure she wasn't. But there's something wrong about Melanie.'

'Well, yes. She's dead.'

Fran huffed an irritated sigh. 'You know what I mean. The motive. The reason she's dead. No one's spotted it yet.'

'Have you?' Libby incautiously looked at Fran, who shouted, 'Look where you're going!' and grabbed the wheel.

'All right, all right.' Libby removed Fran's hand and crept slowly round a bend. 'So, come on. Do

167

you know what the motive was?'

'I think,' said Fran, 'I might.'

Chapter Nineteen

'WELL? WHAT IS IT?' Libby pulled in to a farm gateway and turned to face her friend.

'Something to do with her writing.' Fran was still frowning.

'Her writing?'

'As soon as Jennifer said she wrote, something clicked into place.' Fran shook her head. 'But I don't know exactly what.'

Libby sighed and pulled out of the gateway. 'And you said there's something wrong about the henge?'

Fran wriggled her shoulders. 'Could just be residual stuff from burials, but I did feel something up there, even though I said I didn't to Jennifer.'

'But not connected to Melanie?'

'I don't know. I don't think so.' Fran was frowning again.

Libby slid her a sideways look. 'Look, we'd better go and find somewhere that sells wine before we go back to the farm. It'll help you to think.'

Fran grinned. 'Or not. Where are we going?'

'I think we ought to head into Blandford Forum. I don't see any of these villages sporting a shop that sells wine, do you?'

Having found a supermarket in the middle of Blandford Forum and bought what Libby considered a reasonable amount of wine to see them through the next few days, they found their way back through the rain to Potter's Farm, where they found

Mrs Rush lighting the wood-burning stove in the hall between their rooms.

'Makes it more cheerful,' she said with a smile. 'What time do you want your dinner?'

They settled on seven thirty. Once they had put the wine away and hung up wet jackets, Libby pulled the table in front of the fire and they sat down with the laptop.

'What are we looking for?' asked Libby, checking the wifi connection.

'Melanie Joseph books,' said Fran, and Libby typed that into the search engine. Immediately over two thousand sites came up.

'She certainly wrote,' said Fran, 'but Jennifer was right, it's all non-fiction, or academic stuff.'

'Look here, though,' said Libby, and clicked on a link. 'A book about ancient monuments, and,' she scrolled down, 'desecration of same.'

'It's odd, isn't it,' said Fran. 'If she was so enamoured of these places you'd think she'd be fighting on Dee's side, so to speak, not trying to prevent anyone from going near them.'

'Perhaps there's something she's trying to conceal?' suggested Libby.

'In every site in Britain?'

'Oh, yes. Unless it's all camouflage to protect this site only?'

'Hardly,' said Fran. 'No, it's a puzzle. I can see the point in not wishing to disturb the dead, and of course there've been lots of protests when sites have been dug, like the one in Norfolk – Sea Henge, wasn't it?'

'Yes, I remember that, but the protest was

against its removal, wasn't it? The scientists wanted to dig it up in order to preserve it, and the protestors said it would destroy its magic.'

'Perhaps Melanie felt excavations would destroy the magic?' Fran pushed back her hair. 'I suppose we should read the book.'

'No we shouldn't.' Libby peered at the screen. 'It's hardback and costs twenty-five pounds.'

'Perhaps Patrick knows about it,' said Fran.

'Oh, sure, we can just pop along and ask him.' Libby sat back.

'Maybe not.' Fran stared at the wood-burner. 'But I bet Dee would know.'

'I thought we'd exhausted Dee as a witness?'

'Of course not,' said Fran. 'She's got a lot more to tell us.'

'You sound very certain.'

'I am.' Fran grinned. 'More certain than I am about finding anything at the standing stone or Bonny Henge.'

'Where does she live?' Libby turned once again to the computer.

'She said London. You told me.'

'Right.' Libby frowned. 'So do we go and see her?'

'We'll call her and see,' said Fran and closed the laptop. 'One thing at a time.'

Mrs Rush's dinner was excellent, as was the Chilean Syrah they drank with it. Admitting to feeling tired, Libby agreed to have an early night.

'So we can be fresh for climbing up that henge,' said Fran.

'It wasn't exactly steep.'

171

'No, but then we're doing a circular walk to the stone and back, and goodness knows what we'll do after that.'

'Find out where the rest of the guests live,' said Libby. 'Some of the others might live in the area.'

'It's a thought,' said Fran. 'Night.'

Fortunately, the rain had gone and left the sky a clear blue, with only the smallest wisps of cloud appearing and disappearing when they emerged after a substantial farmhouse breakfast the next morning.

Fran was once more behind the wheel, happier and more confident now the rain had cleared and she vaguely knew the route. Jennifer was already waiting for them in front of the village hall.

'Better day for it,' she said. 'I brought the dog, I hope you don't mind?'

Libby bent down to say hello to a grinning hound of mixed parentage with a huge, feathery tail.

'He's gorgeous,' said Fran. 'What's his name?'

'Herald,' said Jennifer. 'No idea why. He was a rescue and already named.'

'Because his tail's like a banner,' said Libby.

'Of course.' Jennifer laughed. 'I've had him three years and never thought of that.'

The went up the lane beside the church, Herald preceding them, and paused at the top, while the dog investigated a variety of interesting smells. Fran wandered over to the edge of the ditch and peered at the mound.

'How does she do this?' Jennifer quietly asked Libby, as they watched.

'She doesn't consciously "do" anything. Things appear in her head as though they're facts. As though she's actually seen them. She's tried doing it on purpose, of course, because the police occasionally ask her, but it doesn't often work. I mean,' said Libby, suddenly remembering, 'she came up with something yesterday evening about which she was quite certain and I have no idea what it might mean.'

'About Melanie?' Jennifer was watching Fran.

'No, not exactly,' said Libby. 'About someone else. No idea what it means, but I'll go along with it.'

'May I ask who? Is it someone I might know?' Jennifer turned to her, looking worried.

'No, no, don't look so bothered.' Libby grinned. 'Not you or Patrick.'

'Oh.' Jennifer's face relaxed into a relieved smile. 'Sorry. I'm very concerned about him. I know he gets a bad press about all his little affairs, but he's a kind-hearted soul really, and people are inclined to take advantage of him.'

And he of them, thought Libby, thinking of Nina, Dee and Lily.

'Did he often get asked for advice on manuscripts?' she asked aloud.

'Oh, frequently. But he didn't have the time or energy to do anything about it. The books took up all of his time.' Jennifer's expression clouded.

'Did Melanie help him?' Libby was curious.

Jennifer looked at her sharply. 'Help? In what way?'

'Act as his secretary, that sort of thing?'

'Oh, yes. Considering she had her own work to do, although it was nowhere near as much as it had been a few years ago, she was very good. She often stayed here when he went to London to do the business side of the work and followed up research projects for him.'

'Research? But I thought he wrote thrillers?' said Libby.

'Libby, really!' Fran came up to join them and looked shocked. Jennifer laughed.

'A lot of people think that writing fiction is just ploughing away until the words make sense,' she said, 'but in every work of fiction there are things which must be got right. Otherwise you pull the reader out of the story.'

'Rosie says much the same,' said Fran.

'Rosie? Oh, your Amanda George. Nice woman. Wish I could take her course.'

'She's very good,' said Fran, 'but surely you don't need a course. You've been writing for years.'

'And been paid for it,' Libby added.

'It's very nice of you, but writing a novel's a whole different technique,' said Jennifer. 'Now, shall we make a move? It's getting hotter and we don't want to be out here scorching ourselves for too long.'

Jennifer and Herald led them along a chalk ridge towards a thick line of trees. Just as they were about to drop down to them, Jennifer stopped.

'Here,' she said, and stepped over what Fran and Libby now realised was the shallow ditch which had followed them from Bonny Henge. She crouched down and pulled away some vegetation, and there,

174

set into the ground, was the top part of a dark, pointed stone.

'Oh,' said Libby, disappointed.

'It's been buried,' said Fran. 'Deliberately?'

'They don't think so,' said Jennifer, standing up and brushing her hands together. 'It's more likely natural, the same way that the ditch is now so shallow and would have been much deeper four thousand years ago.'

'Four thousand? Blimey!' Libby looked at the stone with new respect.

'If you stand here and look back, you can see the full shape of the henge.' Jennifer beckoned them across the ditch, and sure enough, Libby could see the oval shape of the mound with the ditch encircling it.

'It's obvious once you know,' said Fran. 'And there definitely are other stones here.'

'There are?' said Jennifer and Libby together.

'Yes, why?' Fran looked at them in surprise.

'We haven't found any yet,' said Jennifer. 'I told you, we haven't raised enough for a proper dig.'

'Well,' said Fran, 'they're here. Not all of them, but a good few. And,' she frowned, 'some holes.'

'Post holes?' asked Libby.

'How do I know? Just holes. I don't know anything about archaeology.'

'We need to get someone out here,' said Jennifer, 'as soon as we can.'

'I don't think any serious archaeologist would listen to me,' said Fran.

'What about the burials?' asked Libby.

'I don't know. All I know definitely is – there are

stones here.' She shivered.

'And?' prompted Libby. Fran scowled at her and shook her head slightly. Libby sighed and stepped back across the ditch to where Herald was lolling against what could be seen of the stone, his tongue hanging out.

'Shall we walk back?' asked Jennifer. 'We can carry on round the other side, which actually dips into the trees. It'll be cooler.'

'So what was that about?' hissed Libby, as she and Fran fell into step behind Jennifer and her dog.

'Something happened here, but I have no idea what or when. Something to do with death.' Fran shivered again. 'I said there was something wrong.'

'But you also said it could be residual from the burials that must be here.'

'It just doesn't feel like that,' said Fran.

'Well, it could also be the white lady's bloke. He was found up here somewhere.'

'Hmm.' Fran looked sceptical. 'Doesn't feel like that either.'

Libby sighed. 'Oh, well. No doubt more research is indicated.'

When they emerged from the trees back where they started, the sun was even hotter.

'A cool drink in the pub?' suggested Jennifer. 'Herald could do with a drink, too.'

In the empty bar with a half of lager for Libby and mineral water for Jennifer and Fran, and Herald enjoying a tin bowl of water in the doorway, Fran asked a question.

'Jennifer, you said yesterday you didn't know

176

much about Melanie's writing. But we found she'd written quite a few books, and one is actually about ancient monuments and their destruction. Surely you must have known about that? She'd have written about Bonny Henge, surely.'

'Well, yes.' Jennifer looked uncomfortable. 'But I've never read it. Patrick said ...' she trailed off.

'That it wasn't very good?' suggested Fran. Libby looked surprised.

'In so many words.' Jennifer nodded, looking even more uncomfortable. 'It sounds awful, now, but because I didn't like or approve of her, I was always ready to believe the worst about her. Even when Patrick was – well, wasn't exactly pleasant about her. Yet she really did help him a lot.'

'Was he jealous?' asked Libby. Fran and Jennifer looked at her in surprise.

'Well, she was a writer, and an academic, and she'd had a high-profile career. He could have been.'

'I suppose so,' said Jennifer slowly. 'It never occurred to me.'

'Is there any chance at all that Patrick would talk about her?' asked Fran.

Jennifer shook her head. 'He seems hell-bent on wiping the memory,' she said. 'Yesterday he was talking about burning her files.'

'He can't do that!' said Fran, outraged. 'The police would be furious.'

'I told him that.' Jennifer laughed ruefully. 'He was like a child denied a treat. God knows what he's up to now.'

'Is he at home?' asked Libby.

'He certainly is. And very unhappy about it. You see, his step-children have arrived.'

Chapter Twenty

'THEY DON'T GET ON?'

'No. They didn't get on with Melanie, either, but they've come back because they felt they should, I suppose. Edgar saw to that.'

'What was he like?' asked Libby.

'I only met him a couple of times. He and Melanie split up long before she met Patrick.'

'Ostensibly,' said Fran.

Jennifer looked startled. 'You think they might have started seeing one another while she was still married to Edgar?'

'It's not inconceivable, is it?' said Fran. 'Neither of them sound like particularly stable personalities.'

'Patrick's normally very stable,' defended Jennifer.

'But constitutionally unfaithful,' said Libby.

Jennifer subsided. 'I suppose so.'

'Anyway, Rachel and Zachary are coming to stay, are they?' said Fran.

'They're here already – at least they're in the country. And as far as I can make out, their father is with them.'

'Oh, boy!' said Libby. 'Happy families.'

'By the way,' said Fran suddenly. 'I never asked – where was the original writers' holiday?'

Jennifer and Libby exchanged surprised looks.

'Not far from here, actually,' said Jennifer. 'It was organised by a local writing association. Quite a big hotel on the coast in Devon.'

'So most of the delegates were from round here?'

'Not necessarily. The holiday was advertised in writing magazines and websites. Anyone could go. But they managed to get Patrick to run a group, being a local author, and a couple of others who live vaguely in the area.'

'It might be worth finding out who does live in the area,' said Fran. 'Who would know?'

'Lily Cooper,' said Libby. 'Although I suppose I took details when people paid – no I didn't, did I? Because they only had to give the numbers on the card. I only took phone numbers.'

'What's it got to do with Melanie, though?' asked Jennifer.

'Oh, just wondering,' said Fran vaguely. 'You don't happen to have the name of the association?'

'Well, of course, I'm a member. It's called *Writers in the South*. There's a website.' Jennifer looked at Libby and raised her eyebrows. Libby shrugged.

'Back to Bonny Henge,' said Fran. 'Who deals with the archaeology of the Chase?'

'Mainly the AONB.'

'The who?' said Fran.

'The what?' said Libby.

'Area of Outstanding Natural Beauty. There's an actual organisation, run from Cranborne itself, I believe. They've been involved in trying to get something done about the henge and the stone.'

'Can you tell me anything about the specific reasons Melanie was against – what? Was she against archaeology, or people wanting to explore the sites?' asked Fran.

'Apparently, there are many people who don't want to dig up sites because of the damage they will do. Even some archaeologists,' said Jennifer.

'But that's the whole purpose of archaeology, surely?' said Libby. 'To find out what was going on? Unless you dig it up you don't know.'

Jennifer shook her head. 'I don't understand it, but I think that was the stand she took, and she didn't want members of the public tramping all over sites, either.'

'Then half of Britain would be out of bounds,' said Fran.

'I said I didn't understand it,' said Jennifer with a short laugh. 'Or her.'

'Oh, well,' said Libby with a sigh. 'I suppose if there's nothing else we can do, we might as well get back, shall we Fran?'

Fran was looking vague again. 'I'd like to see the stone again.'

'OK.' Libby turned to Jennifer. 'Do they do lunches here?'

'Only bar food, I think,' said Jennifer. 'I suppose you could always –'

But Libby interrupted. 'No, no, we're not going to impose on you, if that's what you were going to suggest. We'll have a sandwich or something here, take a quick walk up to the stone again and go back to our B&B. We'll need to look things up on the computer.'

'You should have a tablet,' smiled Jennifer. 'Or at least a smart phone.'

'A tablet?'

'You know, a mini computer with smartphone

technology. Then you could look things up on the move. Even I've got one.'

'Oh, yes. Fran's husband's got one. I didn't think I'd ever need one.'

'We should have borrowed it.' Fran had come out of her reverie. 'I'll go and get a menu.'

Jennifer stood up and prepared to leave. 'Don't forget to ring me if you need anything else,' she said. 'I was certain there was something to find out about the henge and the stone, but I'm not sure Fran's seen anything. Or felt it, whatever it is she does.'

Fran came back with a menu and they accompanied Jennifer to the door to say goodbye to Herald.

'I hope you can find something out about poor Melanie's death. I'm sure there's some connection with the village,' said Jennifer.

'But why?' asked Fran.

'Because she'd angered so many people. And when the demonstrators came they seemed to have a personal interest in her.'

'What were they actually protesting about?' asked Libby. 'I've got very confused.'

'They maintained it had a pagan-religious significance and they should be allowed to worship there.'

'As I said before,' said Libby, 'or hold nasty Black Masses.'

'And the archaeologists were just as bad. The amateurs, anyway.' Jennifer sighed and patted Herald, who stood and grinned at them. 'Well, I'll be off then. As I said, let me know if there's anything else you want to know.'

'What were you thinking about?' asked Libby, when Jennifer had gone and they'd ordered home-cured ham sandwiches.

'Several things. If any of the weekend guests were members of *Writers in the South* they might have known about Patrick and Melanie living in the area, even though they all said they didn't know Patrick apart from meeting him at events like the holiday.'

'And?'

'Someone else as well as Dee Starkey could have been among those who were up in arms about her.'

'I don't see that the one necessarily follows the other,' said Libby, 'but I suppose it's worth finding out if any of the others come from this area. Although even then, we come up against the fact that her car wasn't there –'

'But someone here could have given her a lift. We thought about that, didn't we?'

Libby sighed heavily. 'OK. So we look into *Writers in the South*. What else?'

'Jennifer was right. There is something odd up at the stone. But I'm not sure it has to do with Melanie.'

'Is that why we're going back up there?' said Libby dubiously.

'Yes. Without Jennifer. She's been muddying the waters.'

'What? Deliberately?'

'No.' Fran looked up as the barmaid signalled that the sandwiches were ready. 'Just she desperately wants to find something up there. I

183

don't know what, but she's got an agenda.'

'She wants to prove Melanie wrong and get the archaeologists in?'

'She does, but it isn't that.' Fran got up and went to fetch the sandwiches. 'We might never find out.'

'Of course,' said Libby a little later, through a mouthful of ham, 'she's very protective of Patrick. Do you think there's more to it than that? Do you think she thinks he's the murderer?'

'Maybe.' Fran sighed. 'I wish we could talk to Patrick.'

'I expect the poor bloke's had enough people bothering him by now. I bet Scotland Yard have already been on to him.' Libby put down her sandwich. 'Funny, though, Jennifer didn't say anything about them speaking to her.'

'Perhaps they haven't,' said Fran. 'Perhaps they've looked into everyone's background and decided that most of them don't have a political motive.'

'Hmmm.' Libby thoughtfully finished her sandwich. 'Well, one thing at a time, I suppose. Back up to the monument?'

Without Jennifer and Herald, Fran took her time walking alongside the boundary ditch, looking across at the village and to the other side of the henge and the trees. At one point, she climbed to the top of the mound and walked right across it. Libby stood still and watched. Eventually she came back to the ditch.

'You can see the entrance to the henge,' she said.

'Can you? Where?'

'Where the stone post is. There's a gap. And I'm

pretty sure there are huts inside.'

'Inside?' Libby was bewildered. 'You mean, under that mound?'

'No. I mean, there used to be huts. That's the holes I could see.'

'See! I said post holes!' said Libby.

'I wouldn't know,' said Fran, walking forward towards the post. 'I think they really ought to excavate this site.'

'So do I,' said Libby, 'especially as there seem to be so many other sites in the area. It would help complete the picture. But you're not getting anything else from here? No White Lady avenging her lover?'

'No ... but it's confused.' Fran stopped in front of the stone post. 'There's something here. Something's happened here.'

Libby stood looking at her hopefully. Fran went down on her haunches and pulled away more vegetation.

'No,' she said, shaking her head. 'It doesn't make sense.'

'What doesn't?' said Libby, exasperated. 'What are you talking about?'

'I keep thinking someone died here. And no – not a prehistoric burial. And it doesn't seem like a historic death, so probably not the White Lady's lover.' She scrabbled at the back of the post, where it was stuck firmly in the ground. 'But there's no recent sign of activity.' She stood up and closed her eyes. 'No, no clearer.'

'So it was a waste of time?' said Libby, with some asperity.

'No, Libby.' Fran frowned at her. 'I'm convinced there is more here than one henge post, and something happened here, whether it was to do with Melanie or not. And I'm going to find the right person to tell.'

They drove back to Potter's Farm through rolling, partially wooded countryside, highlighted in places by fields of meadow flowers planted by farmers to increase insect and bird life.

'Isn't it beautiful?' sighed Libby. 'The quintessential English countryside.'

Fran glanced sharply sideways. 'Not thinking of relocating, I hope?'

'Couldn't afford it,' said Libby. 'Anyway, I could hardly drag Ben from his ancestral home. And what would I do without you? And Pete and Harry?'

'You'd get bored.'

'I expect I would. Look – don't miss the turning.'

Back at Potter's Farm, Libby took the laptop out onto the terrace, under the shade of the overhanging balcony.

'What are we looking for?' she asked.

'*Writers in the South*,' said Fran. 'See if there's a contact number.'

The *Writers in the South* website was fairly basic, and didn't contain a list of members, but did, however, contain details of both the weekend at The Manor, the next writers' holiday (not organised by them) and a contact number for the secretary.

'So, do we try?' asked Libby. Fran nodded and picked up her phone.

Her eyebrows rose as the call was answered

almost immediately.

'I'm afraid you don't know me,' she explained, 'but I was a guest at the weekend in Kent – oh, yes, I know, shocking. You didn't go yourself? No. But you knew Patrick and Melanie Joseph were going? No? Oh, just Patrick. Yes, of course, Lily Cooper organised it.' She paused, listening. 'Well, I'm near Rising Parva at the moment with Mrs Sarjeant who was the host of the weekend, and we wondered how many other guests lived in this area, or in your catchment area, anyway.'

She looked at Libby and made a face.

'Oh, no we wouldn't dream of intruding. We just wondered … Yes, of course.' She gestured to Libby for a pen and paper and began to scribble. 'Thank you so much.' She switched off the phone and sat back in her chair. 'Well, that was interesting.'

'Didn't she ask why you were asking all those questions?' said Libby.

'No, not once.' Fran giggled. 'I don't know what I would have said. But just look at this.' She pushed the paper towards Libby. 'Either members, or people she knows who live in this area.'

Libby looked at the list and gasped.

'All of them!' she said.

Chapter Twenty-one

'NOT NECESSARILY PEOPLE WHO live in Cranborne Chase,' said Fran, 'But in the area, from Bournemouth and Weymouth right across to Southampton, and members who live outside the area. Like Dee Starkey.'

'But why would she join an association of writers so far from her home patch?'

'Mrs Scratchall –'

'Who?'

'The secretary. She said people had to join if they wanted to go to the writers' holiday. I suppose that makes sense.'

'And Paul Fisher – he lives in north London. Audrey and Bernice – they're Bournemouth.' Libby pored over the scribbled list. 'What's this – D Hill – Daniel? – Pole?'

'Poole. Not the ideal milieu for a literary writer.' Fran grinned.

'And Lily. Well, well. Salisbury. Both of them almost on the doorstep.'

'And the fact that everyone seemed to think their affair hadn't carried on after the holiday indicates that she probably didn't know where he lived. He'd be keen to keep it *off* his doorstep, wouldn't he?' Fran unscrewed the bottle of fizzy water they'd brought out with them. 'And Nina. Where's she? Reading.'

'I can't see Nina being involved with any of this,' said Libby. 'Whatever all this is. Now, who's left. Nick Forrest. Well.' She looked up. 'Would you look at that.'

'I did,' Fran grinned. 'I wrote it.'

'Ebbesdean. Right in the middle of Cranborne Chase.'

'It doesn't mean to say any of them knew the Josephs lived here,' said Fran, 'except Jennifer. But it does make me wonder if any of them knew about Melanie's involvement with ancient monuments, in particular Bonny Henge. After all, Dee admitted she'd even been arrested here. Others could have been.'

'So are you convinced this is the real motive for her murder?' asked Libby.

'It seems more likely than anything to do with Patrick, doesn't it?' said Fran.

'Let's speak to Dee again, then.'

'She wasn't very forthcoming last time,' said Fran.

'But Scotland Yard might have been on to her by now. We could be sympathetic, especially as we now know the story behind the fight about the henge– if that's what it was.'

'Wouldn't a visit to Nick Forrest be better?' suggested Fran.

'We could do both. It's Friday, though. He didn't phone until late afternoon the other day, so he might not be home from work yet. And then, as it's Friday, he might go for a drink after work. I can leave a message and say we're in the area, though.'

'Ring them both and see what happens,' said Fran. 'Are we going to book dinner with Mrs Rush tonight, or find a pub?'

They decided to opt for a pub, as they didn't know where they might be later in the evening, and Libby left messages for both Nick Forrest and Dee Starkey. Dee called back first.

'What do you want now?' She sounded edgy and sharp.

'Have Scotland Yard been on to you yet?' asked Libby.

'What's it got to do with you?'

'We came down to Rising Parva to have a look at Bonny Henge and the post. We can see why people were angry with Melanie. The area really needs to be excavated, doesn't it?'

'No!' Dee almost shouted. 'No! It belonged to our ancestors – it's a sacred place.'

'Ah.' Libby was confused. 'But Melanie didn't want it excavated either.'

'But she didn't want anyone on the site. She wanted to fence it off and have no one allowed near it. That isn't fair.'

'Right.' Libby looked helplessly across at Fran. 'So when you demonstrated here, it wasn't to get permission to excavate?'

'No, it bloody wasn't. But there were people there who wanted that. And now,' she said, and her voice was bitter, 'I suppose they'll get their way and a dig will go ahead.'

'Only if they can get the funds,' said Libby.

'Why do they need money to do a dig?' Dee was scornful. 'But we'll stop them if they try.'

'Who's we?'

Dee's voice turned wary. 'My friends and I.'

'Are you an organised group?'

'You're worse than bloody Scotland Yard,' shouted Dee and switched off the phone.

Libby related the conversation – that which hadn't been audible – to Fran and the phone rang again.

'Hi.' Nick Forrest sounded surprised. 'Do I gather you're in my neck of the woods?'

'Quite close,' said Libby. 'We're in Rising Parva. You're not far from there, are you?'

'About ten miles, I suppose. What are you doing there?'

'Looking at Bonny Henge.'

'Oh. Isn't that where they've discovered a standing stone?'

'That's right,' said Libby cautiously. 'You know about that?'

'You couldn't not know,' said Nick, laughing. 'Not if you live round here.'

'You're not interested in archaeology, then?'

'Me? Good God, no. Although, as I said, you can't fail to be aware of it here. There's archaeology all over the place. Why did you want to see Bonny?'

'We heard about it from Jennifer Alderton.' Libby made an I-don't-know-what-I'm-doing face at Fran.

'Oh?' Nick sounded puzzled. 'And why did you want to speak to me?'

Libby opened and shut her mouth a couple of times but couldn't think of what to say. Fran put her head in her hands.

'Libby?' prompted Nick.

'Actually,' she said in a rush, 'it was about Melanie.'

'Melanie? Who – oh! Patrick's wife? Oh, right. Well, yes. Those Scotland Yard people did call me. They didn't seem that interested in me, but as I'd briefly been a member of a quasi-political party at university, I think they felt duty bound to check me out. Daft, really.'

'Oh, well, that's a relief,' said Libby.

'So, are you and your friend doing anything this evening? There's a great pub here that does food, if you fancy driving over.'

'We'd love to,' said Libby, a little too quickly. 'Wouldn't we Fran? Go and meet Nick for dinner at a pub?'

'Great,' he said. 'It's called the Barley Mow. Can you find your way here from Rising Parva?'

'Yes, I'm sure we can,' said Libby. 'We'll see you in there about eight, shall we?'

'What was the matter with you?' said Fran as Libby switched off the phone.

'I just couldn't think what to say to him. He didn't seem to know about Melanie's interest in the standing stone, or that she and Patrick lived here.'

'Good job he suggested the pub, then, wasn't it?' said Fran. 'I suggest we decide what we're going to talk to him about before we go, or we'll end up sitting in silence for the evening.'

'Let's see if there's anything interesting about Ebbesdean,' said Libby, turning to the computer.

'And we can ask him about *Writers in the South*,' said Fran. 'That should keep us going.'

The drive to Ebbesdean was idyllic, over the top of the chalk downland, looking down into shadowed valleys, until the village came into view. A church spire poking out of the top of a thick band of trees, with green and yellow fields spreading out behind painted the quintessential picture of England, as Libby again remarked.

The Barley Mow, a flint building almost next to a crossroads, stood in the centre of the village opposite a green, where there were tables, mostly occupied. Fran pulled into the car park at the side of the pub. As they got out of the car, Nick Forrest came up to meet them.

'I recognised the car,' he said, holding out a hand. 'I'm afraid I was nosy enough to have a good look at it last weekend.'

Fran shook the proffered hand. 'I don't mind. Lots of people are curious.'

'Can I get you a drink?' he asked. 'I'm at a table on the green while the light and the weather hold.'

Libby ordered lager, and Fran a mineral water, and, after escorting them to the table, Nick left them to go to the bar.

'He's not our man,' said Libby.

'Because he's young and pleasant?'

'Don't be daft. Because he doesn't have a motive.'

'He wasn't very happy with Patrick, apparently.'

'But you said that wasn't the motive,' said Libby. 'He doesn't know Melanie.'

'Didn't,' corrected Fran. 'So he says.'

Libby looked at Fran in puzzled annoyance, but just then Nick came back with a tray, three glasses and a menu.

'Strangely, they do very good fish and chips here,' he said, sitting down, 'but only on a Friday.'

'That's what I'll have then,' said Libby.

'Me too,' said Fran, 'even though I live at the seaside and could have them all the time.'

'Oh, you don't live near Libby, then?' said Nick. 'I assumed as you were a friend of hers, you did.'

'I do,' said Fran, 'just not in the same village. I live at the seaside, a few miles away.'

'My geography's not that good. I didn't realise The Manor was near the coast.' He stood up again. 'I'll pop inside and order then, shall I?'

By the time he came back again, Libby was well into her lager and had lit one of her increasingly rare cigarettes.

'Sorry,' she apologised. 'I just never get the chance these days.'

Nick grinned. 'I know. I've only just given up myself, because it was an unequal struggle.'

'High-handed bloody government,' said Libby. 'The minute they ban smoking in our own homes I leave the country.'

Nick laughed. 'It is a bit ridiculous, isn't it? After all, everyone agreed Prohibition was a bad idea. This is substantially no different. Or it would be.'

'Quite right,' said Libby. 'Eh, Fran?'

Fran laughed. 'Don't get me involved.' She looked round the little green and across to a pair of imposing gates on the opposite side of the road. 'Is that Chancery House? We found that on the internet.'

'Did you?' Nick frowned.

'We just thought we'd see where you lived,' said Libby hastily.

'Yes, that puzzled me a bit.' He picked up his beer and looked at them over the top. 'How *did* you know where I lived?'

Libby sighed. 'Time to come clean. We got in touch with *Writers in the South*.'

'Really?' His eyebrows disappeared into his hairline. 'Why?'

'To see if anyone who was there last weekend lived anywhere near the Josephs.'

He looked confused. 'And did they?'

'Yes,' said Fran. 'You do.'

Chapter Twenty-two

NICK'S MOUTH DROPPED OPEN. '*Me*?' he said. 'They live *here*?'

'In Rising Parva,' said Libby. 'Near enough.'

A range of expressions crossed Nick's face, finishing up with what looked suspiciously like anger.

'Sorry,' said Libby cautiously.

He exhaled heavily. 'I just can't bloody believe that he strung me along.'

'Eh?' Libby and Fran looked at each other.

'Sorry.' He shook his head and took a long pull of his beer. 'I should explain.'

'You don't have to,' said Fran. 'We – er –' she glanced at Libby, '– we thought you knew.'

'How would I know? I met him last year on that writers' holiday – well, you knew that – and for the mini-course that he ran he'd asked for manuscripts to be submitted to him beforehand.'

'He could have been inundated,' said Fran.

'No, it was limited to ten people and we only had to send in the first ten pages of a novel.'

'Ah. The ten people who were at the Manor last week?' said Libby. 'Now it makes sense.'

'Yes, although they weren't all writing thrillers.'

'No,' said Libby, thinking of Dee Starkey and Nina Etherington.

'Did he critique them all?' asked Fran.

'He said he had,' said Nick grudgingly, 'and to be fair, he'd done a good job on mine. But when I

196

talked to him about it he was a bit vague.'

'What about the others?' asked Libby.

'They all had critiques, but some of them weren't what they'd expected.' Nick shrugged. 'I guess they weren't in his genre.'

'But there was some bad feeling about the critiques?' suggested Fran.

'Well, not exactly.' Nick sat forward, cradling his glass. 'It was fairly obvious that he had favourites.' He looked up quickly. 'Not among the writers, among the books. He liked mine, Nina's and Dee's, surprisingly.'

Not, thought Libby.

'Anyway, he talked to us all about them when he wasn't giving his classes, you know, in the bar, and we became quite a – well – a group, you know?'

'Convivial,' said Libby.

'Exactly. And he said we must keep in touch, and as good as promised to help me with my book.'

'But you said he was vague about it?' said Fran.

Nick frowned. 'He was. He seemed only to talk about it in generalisations, not specifics.'

'As though he hadn't really read it?' asked Libby.

'Not exactly – he did know what it was about. And he did say keep in touch.'

'And did you?' asked Fran.

'Well, yes, we all did, mainly by email, and that was why we arranged last weekend. And he kept promising to meet me – get together, he said – but it was difficult with his schedule. And he let me think he lived miles away.'

'Maybe he didn't know where you lived?'

suggested Fran.

'Oh, no. He knew where we all lived. Our initial critiques came to us by post.'

'That's odd,' said Libby. 'Why not email?'

'We had to send in hard copy and a stamped addressed envelope.'

'How old-fashioned,' laughed Fran.

'How do you mean?' said Libby.

'That's what you used to do when you approached an agent or a publisher,' said Fran.

'It's still how you approach most,' said Nick. 'Very few accept initial queries by email.'

'Oh,' said Fran, abashed. 'I haven't got that far yet.'

'So he knew you lived near him.' Libby sipped her lager. 'But he must have had so many people trying to get him to read manuscripts or help them in one way or another, I expect he just wanted to keep his privacy.'

'But he kept saying he wanted to meet up,' protested Nick. 'All he had to do was say he'd meet me at the pub for half an hour.'

Privately, Libby found herself agreeing with Patrick. If this was the sort of obsessive chasing would-be authors went in for, she'd want to keep her privacy, too.

'Table thirty-five!' shouted a voice from the pub, and Nick stood up and waved. A sturdy young woman in an inadvisable short black skirt scuttled over bearing a tray on which three plates of fish and chips sat gently steaming.

'That looks lovely,' said Libby, smiling up at her. The handmaiden grunted and scuttled off.

For a few minutes they were all occupied with the application of salt and vinegar and the cracking of crisp golden batter.

'This is good,' said Libby through a mouthful of chips.

'Told you.' Nick grinned at her, calmer now.

'How much do we owe you?' asked Fran.

'No, please –' Nick began, but was interrupted by both women.

'Don't be silly, Nick. You don't know us. You're not buying us supper. Anyway, we're picking your brains,' said Libby.

'Are you?' Nick looked surprised.

'Well, yes. We wondered if any of the other weekend guests had any idea where Patrick and Melanie lived?'

Nick frowned thoughtfully. 'I don't think so. Except Jennifer, of course, and I didn't know that until she told that policeman. I didn't know where any of them lived, actually, except Paul. He lives in north London, and I've been up to stay with him a couple of times.'

'And he didn't know where anyone lived either?' said Fran.

'I don't think so. Why?'

'We're trying to find out if Melanie knew anyone who was a guest. It's just so odd that she was there and that she was murdered there. It had to be someone who knew about the weekend.'

'It needn't have been a guest, though,' said Nick, slowly. 'Any number of people knew about the weekend.'

'It wasn't advertised like the holiday,' said

Libby, 'so how?'

'*Writers in the South* knew – we initially used their message boards to get in touch before exchanging emails.'

'But not the wider general public,' said Fran. 'Only partners, husbands and wives, families.'

'I suppose so. I told a few people.'

'Friends? At work?' asked Libby.

'Well, yes.' Nick was now looking irritated.

'If they're local,' Libby persisted, 'they might have known Melanie.'

'Somebody would have told me,' said Nick.

'Hmm,' said Libby.

'What does that mean?' Nick put down his knife and fork.

'If you were talking about going to see Patrick Joseph and someone knew his wife – not unlikely as you're in the same neighbourhood – if they had a grudge against her, they wouldn't tell you, would they? But they could find out where you were going and –'

'And somehow find out that Melanie was going under cover to confront her husband?' interrupted Fran. 'I don't think so, Lib.'

'Oh.' Libby's face fell. 'I suppose not.'

'I still can't believe I didn't know they lived near here,' said Nick, shaking his head and picking up his knife and fork.

'Especially Melanie,' said Libby.

'Why Melanie?'

'Oh, we didn't get round to warning you, did we?' said Fran. 'Melanie Joseph was a former government advisor and president of Green

200

Country. Scotland Yard are interested in the case.'

'Really?' Nick looked quite bright at this information. 'Of course ! Those bombs under the car!'

'Only one bomb, actually,' said Libby, 'and death threats.'

'There you are then! It's nothing to do with us.'

'Scotland Yard don't want to believe that,' said Fran. 'They want a link between one of you and Melanie's enemies.'

'But how could any of us – why are they enemies?'

'She stood up for some controversial policies.'

'What, like wind farms? That sort of thing?'

'Well – yes,' said Libby guardedly.

'Nuclear power?'

'Yes, she had an opinion on that,' said Fran. 'And ancient monuments.'

Fran and Libby watched for Nick's reaction and were disappointed.

'Oh. Well, she didn't go short of those if she lived round here. There's practically one on every corner.' He shook his head. 'You know, I still can't believe that Patrick lived not ten miles away from me.'

'So we gather,' said Fran. 'You were never aware of any protests about local monuments?'

'I'm afraid I'm not really interested,' said Nick. 'I don't read the local papers or watch the local news. Unless it's something I can't avoid, like Bonny Henge.'

'Right.' Libby sighed. 'So you can't tell us anything?'

'No. Did you think I could?'

'You live in the same area as the victim. We hoped you might,' said Fran.

'What about *Writers in the South*?' asked Libby, after a pause for more fish and chips. 'How did you find out about them?'

'Someone at my local writers' group told me about them.' Nick was vague as he put down his knife and fork. 'They have big quarterly meetings with famous names speaking, and a lot of the smaller writers' groups like mine belong, or are affiliated, to them. Then they organise this writing holiday. It's really good and very inclusive.'

'Inclusive?' asked Libby.

'Yes. Published and – er – pre-published writers all together, and no one seems to mind.'

'Why should they?' asked Libby, wrinkling her brow.

'Published writers can be very sniffy towards unpublished,' said Fran. 'That's why Rosie's so different.'

'Rosie? Oh, Amanda George,' said Nick. 'Yes. She seemed very nice.'

'So, *Writers in the South*,' continued Libby. 'Are they a charity?'

'A charity?' Nick looked surprised. 'No, they're just a writers' group. Mainly to support the unpublished.'

'They don't have any big name sponsors, or anything like that?'

'Good lord, no. But they manage to get some good names as speakers as I said. And they had really good people running their mini-courses on the holiday. Patrick was one, of course.'

'Do they think,' said Nick later, over their second drinks, the remains of the fish and chips having been removed, 'that the people who planted the bombs –'

'Bomb,' corrected Fran.

'Bomb, then. Do the police think it was the same people who killed Patrick's wife?'

'They're obviously thinking along those lines,' said Libby.

'Didn't they catch the person who'd planted the bomb?' said Fran.

'Did they? But if that person was working for an organisation there would still be others around,' said Nick.

'And they wouldn't advertise their presence,' said Libby.

'So it could have been one of our group?' Nick looked worried. 'But they're all – they all seemed so normal.'

Libby wondered if Daniel Hill or Dee Starkey would be pleased to be called normal.

'You didn't ever hear any of them making any sort of – well, *subversive* comments?' said Fran.

'Subversive? About what?'

'Anything. The government, political correctness, the media – anything,' suggested Libby.

'No.' Nick was still looking worried. 'I think Daniel is a bit of a communist, and Dee seemed to be angry with everything, but that's about it.'

'Oh, well,' sighed Libby. 'It was worth a try. Look, if you think of anything give one of us a ring, will you, Nick?'

Nick brightened. 'Are you investigating properly, then? I'd be happy to help.'

'That's good, then,' said Fran. 'We'll call on you if we need you.'

'And did you find anything else out about the car?'

Fran and Libby looked at each other.

'Bugger,' said Libby. 'I'd forgotten the car.'

Chapter Twenty-three

'GOOD JOB HE REMINDED us about the car,' said Libby, as they drove back to Potter's Farm.

'Why?' said Fran, carefully negotiating a sharp bend in a narrow lane. 'We can't find a car.'

'No, but it's a significant part of the puzzle,' said Libby. 'She was obviously brought to the Manor in someone else's car, which makes it certain that the murderer was one of our guests.'

'We've already talked about this. It could have been someone dropping her off.'

'I know we've talked about it, and I still say – how could they when someone would have seen the car? Except that Ben says a lot of people know the back way in from the top of Allhallow's Lane.'

'But that would argue someone local. No one else would know about that,' said Fran, sighing with relief as they turned into the drive of Potter's Farm.

'Hmm,' said Libby. 'I think we need to go over all the evidence.'

'Not tonight,' said Fran, stopping the car. 'All I need now is a large drink to make up for all the mineral water I've drunk this evening.'

'But,' said Libby, when they were both supplied with glasses of wine in front of the large windows, 'we do need to decide what we're going to do next.'

Fran sighed. 'I suppose so. We could see if we could speak to Daniel and Lily. Salisbury and Poole are both within shouting distance.'

'Neither of them want to speak to us, though,'

said Libby.

'That's never stopped you before.'

Libby leant back in her chair and gazed at the ceiling. 'We could do a bit of research on them both.'

'We've looked them both up online. What else do you suggest?'

'What about Facebook? If they were on there, would it have come up when we searched for them?'

Fran nodded. 'I was thinking of visiting, though. Daniel sounds as though he might not go out to work.'

'How do you "sound" like that?' asked Libby, interested.

Fran laughed. 'I just thought he seemed retired.'

'Except for contributing to – what was it?'

'*Scriptus*. Which can't take up much of his time. Just a thought.'

'I could ring him back in the morning,' said Libby, a touch dubiously. 'After all, I didn't return his call the other day.'

'And warn him about Scotland Yard. Then we'll know if he's heard from them.'

'He might not tell us. He sounds extremely grumpy.'

'He was grumpy last weekend, so that's no different,' said Fran. 'What about Lily Cooper?'

'She put the phone down on me,' said Libby, 'and she knows about Scotland Yard, so we haven't got an excuse.'

'I wonder where she works?'

'We can hardly ask your Mrs Scratcher –'

'Scratchley.'

'Whatever. We can't ask her where Lily works. And there's no one else to ask.' Libby finished her wine. 'Perhaps I'll have a brainwave overnight.'

But it was Fran who had the brainwave.

'We can ask Mrs Scratchley, you know,' she said, wandering into Libby's room with a cup of tea.

'Huh?' Libby struggled up out of the duvet and tried to unstick her eyes.

'Ask when there's another meeting, or which groups are likely to be meeting on their own. Nick said lots of smaller groups were affiliated to the main group, didn't he?'

'Mmm.' Libby grunted and heaving her legs out of bed, staggered over to the tea tray and switched on the kettle.

'Is that a "yes" mmm? Or a "I don't know" mmm?'

'Yes.' Libby dropped a teabag into a cup. 'It's too early.'

Fran grinned and retreated. By the time Libby emerged enveloped in a cardigan, she was writing notes.

'Well?' Libby wrapped her hands round the cup and perched on the edge of a chair.

'Mrs Scratchley, who sounded rather surprised, I must say, said there won't be another *Writers in the South* meeting for another six weeks, but Daniel Hill is holding one of his literary events today just outside Poole.'

'A literary event? Bit pretentious, isn't it?'

'She gave me a link to it.' Fran pulled her laptop towards her and clicked on a link. 'There.'

Libby went to the table and bent down to have a

look. 'Live literature. Join writer Daniel Hill and others reading their work at this prestigious event. Two p.m. at the Fanbridge Centre.' She looked up. 'Where's the Fanbridge Centre?'

'Fanbridge, strangely enough. It's on the outskirts of Poole. Shall we go?'

'I think we should,' said Libby, 'even if we'll be bored witless.'

'Do you think Daniel will throw us out?'

'I'd like to see him try. So we leave Lily alone even though we're so close to Salisbury?'

'I can't see that we've got any grounds to see her or talk to her. Not legitimate ones, anyway.'

'OK.' Libby stood up straight and stretched. 'I'm going to have a shower and then Mrs Rush's breakfast. Should we call Jennifer to say goodbye?'

'After breakfast,' said Fran. 'See you in ten minutes.'

Full of Mrs Rush's bacon, eggs and fried bread, Libby and Fran paid their bill and retired to their rooms to collect their bags. Fran called Jennifer before they left.

'Oh, that's a pity,' said Jennifer, when she heard their plans. 'Patrick was saying he would have liked to see you as you were in the area.'

'Patrick?' Fran's eyebrows flew upwards and she looked at Libby. 'He wanted to see us?'

Libby nodded frantically.

'I think he wanted to say thank you to Libby.'

'Really? What for?'

'She didn't try to make capital out of the situation,' said Jennifer.

'There wasn't much she could do, was there,'

said Fran.

'And I said I thought you were both trying to solve the – er –'

'Murder,' said Fran helpfully.

'Yes. Would you have time to come over this morning before you leave?'

'I'm sure we would,' said Fran, looking at Libby again. Libby once more nodded vigorous agreement.

She was given directions to Patrick's house and switched off the phone.

'Well, what do you think of that?' she said.

'Good job we rang,' said Libby. 'I wonder why he wants to see us.'

Fran repeated Jennifer's thoughts on the matter.

'That's nice of him, if that's the case,' said Libby, 'but I also don't want any taint of association attached to the Manor.'

'Come on, then,' said Fran. 'If we want to see Patrick and get to Fanbridge to see Daniel we'd better get a move on.'

The rain had started again by the time they reached Rising Parva. Following Jennifer's directions, Fran turned right just before the village proper. A narrow lane crept up the hillside and stopped at a pair of high hedges. With unashamed tautology, a rustic plaque announced "High Hedges".

'Do we just drive in?' asked Libby, peering out of the side window.

'There's no gate, so I suppose so,' said Fran, proceeding to do just that.

A curving drive led them between dense shrubberies to a long, low flint and brick house under a thatched roof.

'Pretty,' said Fran.

'It hasn't got eyebrows,' said Libby.

Fran stopped the car and looked an enquiry.

'Steeple Farm has windows in the thatch and they look like beetling eyebrows. Or the thatch does. I've always been a bit spooked by it.' Libby got out of the car.

'What is Ben going to do with Steeple Farm?' asked Fran, shutting the car door.

'It's not his, you know that. It technically belongs to his Aunt Milly, Peter's mum, so it will be up to Pete and his brother to do something with it when his mum dies.'

'Pity Ben did all that work to it though,' said Fran, with a sideways look at Libby, who sighed.

'I know, and it would have been a good idea to live there, but number seventeen's my home – I own it and I can do what I like there. I'm perfectly happy for Ben to live there with me, but I really don't want to move.' She walked up to the front door. 'I hope we're expected.'

But the door was opened before she had time to ring the old-fashioned bell at the side.

'I'm so pleased you could come,' said Patrick, drawing her inside. 'And Mrs – Wolfe, was it?'

'Fran, please,' said Fran, feeling waves of something grey and murky flowing from the man who was smiling so sadly at her.

'And Libby,' said Libby. 'It's awfully nice of you to see us.'

'Oh, I'm in your debt,' said Patrick, leading them into a comfortable sitting room, with two big sofas

210

upholstered in a faded terracotta either side of a wide fireplace which contained the largest wood-burning stove Libby had ever seen.

'Please sit down,' he said. 'Jen's in the kitchen getting coffee. Or would you prefer tea?'

'Coffee's fine,' they said in unison.

'No, really.' Patrick sat down opposite where they sat side by side. 'I would have come to you, but I'm a bit – well, paranoid, I suppose you could say – about going out at the moment. That's why I'm so grateful to you for not saying anything to the media about – um – well, about –'

'Melanie's death?' said Libby. 'No need to thank me. Why would anyone want to talk to me about it, anyway?'

Patrick smiled. 'The media will look at every angle. Has no one come after you yet? Your local television station? One of the redtops?'

'No.' Libby shook her head. 'Have they been after you?'

'No.' Patrick frowned. 'I'm not sure why.'

'Scotland Yard,' said Fran succinctly.

'Oh.' Patrick seemed to shrink into himself. 'Of course. Jennifer told me.'

'They haven't spoken to you?' Libby was surprised.

'Not yet.' He sighed. 'Doubtless they will. I can't think it's out of respect for the feelings of a recently widowed man.'

'Has no one spoken to you since you came home?' asked Fran.

'From the police? Only a DCI Connell, but I gathered he was from the local force. I suppose I shall be investigated by the Special Operations people again. I can't think why they haven't already been here.' His voice was now sounding querulous. Jennifer appeared carrying a tray.

'If they haven't been already, they aren't seriously considering you as a suspect,' she said soothingly. 'Hello, Fran, Libby.'

She looked younger, thought Libby. Her hair, previously neatly folded back in a pleat, was loose and her linen shirt and trousers far more becoming.

'That's true,' said Patrick, brightening, 'but I still think it was magnanimous of you not to go to the media.'

'I wouldn't know where to go,' said Libby, disingenuously and mendaciously. 'Anyway, if I had, I expect Scotland Yard would have stopped me.'

'Not if you'd got in on the first day,' said Patrick. 'I gather it took a while to get passed up the line.'

'Oh?' said Fran. 'I thought you'd only heard through Jennifer about Scotland Yard.'

'Inspector Connell told me it had been passed on when he rang on Monday.'

'He never –' began Libby indignantly, and subsided at a look from Fran. Jennifer shot her a sharp glance, but Patrick didn't seem to notice.

'It's not as if I'm not used to it,' he said tiredly. 'We've had it all before. Guards on the place here and the flat in London. Endless questions and sifting through our acquaintances. They never found out who did it.'

'And of course,' said Libby, accepting a cup

from Jennifer, 'there was all the business at Bonny Henge.'

'Don't remind me,' he said. 'If only she'd stayed out of the spotlight. Odd though, that the media haven't been on to me.'

'Yes,' said Libby, 'especially as it was reported on the internet almost immediately. Certainly on the Sunday.'

'I expect Scotalnd Yard put a muzzle on the media,' said Fran. 'But no one can muzzle the internet.'

'So do you think the Bonny Henge business was why she was killed?' asked Libby. Fran frowned at her again.

'That's all right,' said Patrick. 'I'd rather talk about it, if you don't mind. Jennifer says you've been looking into it a bit.' He gave an unconvincing laugh. 'Two Miss Marples, eh?'

'Fran is a special investigator, Patrick,' said Jennifer, again sounding a little like Nanny in the nursery. 'She helps the police sometimes. I wanted to get them both down here to see if they could find anything. I couldn't think of any other reason Melanie would –' she looked round at Libby and Fran and made a face, 'well, that Melanie would die.'

'No, I see that.' Patrick nodded and gazed down at his cup. 'It was kind.'

Jennifer made a sound between a snort and a sigh of exasperation. 'It wasn't kind, Patrick. I wanted to make sure they didn't try and set you up like they did last time.'

Chapter Twenty-four

'SET YOU UP?' SAID Libby and Fran in chorus.

'They didn't really.' Patrick shifted uncomfortably in his seat and threw Jennifer an irritated look. If she's hoping to take Melanie's place, thought Libby, she's got a long way to go.

'It was thought,' said Jennifer, sitting up very straight and assuming Nanny-knows-best tones again, 'that a group of what I can only call anarchists tried to implicate Patrick in the death threats and the bomb under the car. Melanie had a very high profile then.'

'That's why she all but retired from public life and moved down here permanently,' said Patrick. 'I kept the flat on as I have to go up to town frequently, but she was happy to stay here. Until,' his voice grew bitter, 'that blasted standing stone.'

'Can you tell me exactly what her feelings were about it?' asked Fran. 'I don't mean to be intrusive, but she didn't want it either excavated or left as it is now.'

'She didn't want it *defiled*,' said Patrick. 'Those were her exact words. "I don't want it defiled." She felt it had – oh, I don't know – a religious significance, or a cultural one, and it should be preserved. She felt digging would disturb the spirit of the place, but hordes of people swarming all over the site would also disturb and possibly destroy it.' He shrugged. 'I could see what she meant, in a way.'

'So can I,' said Libby, 'but I don't suppose either the archaeological community or the druids, or whoever they are, would agree with her.'

'You're right,' said Jennifer. 'The strange thing is, as you saw yesterday, no one seems to have tried either yet. I know the funds for an excavation haven't been forthcoming, but you'd think someone would be around now and then with a theodolite or something.'

'A theodolite?' said Libby, interested. 'Do they use those in archaeology?'

'They have to survey the site before digging,' said Patrick. 'I set a book on a dig once.'

'And the druids haven't been back, either?' asked Libby.

'I don't know that they're druids,' said Jennifer, 'but no. Mind you, there were some arrests at the last protest.'

'We know.' Libby looked from Jennifer to Patrick and took a chance. 'Dee Starkey was one of them.'

Jennifer's face tightened, and Patrick's mouth fell open.

'Dee? She's been here?' he said.

'Not to the house. She wouldn't have known where it was, but,' said Libby, ignoring the warning looks Fran was sending, 'she did know Melanie lived here. I think she was possibly the only one of your fellow guests who did last weekend. It was Dee who told us about Bonny Henge.'

Now Patrick was looking hunted. 'You won't tell her where I live, will you?'

'Of course not.' Libby looked surprised. 'Why

on earth should we? We're just trying to make sense of the situation. I don't want opprobrium attached to the Manor any more than you want it attached to you. We all know what media scandals can do to people. And you don't want to affect any future books.'

'I shan't write any more.' Patrick shook his head and seemed to shrink into the corner of the sofa. 'I can't bear it.'

'Don't be silly,' said Nanny-Jennifer coaxingly, 'of course you will.'

But Patrick just shook his head again and gazed at the fireplace.

Fran's phone rang. She stood up hastily, fishing it out of her pocket and sending a quick glance Libby's way.

'Excuse me,' she said, backing towards the door. 'I ought to take this.'

'Why do you think you won't write any more?' asked Libby, to cover the silence after Fran had left the room.

'Melanie was my rock,' said Patrick. Libby couldn't resist a quick glance at Jennifer's face, which was stony. 'In fact,' he went on, 'I think I might move away from Dorset altogether. I don't need the house any more, the children don't live here, and I've got the flat.'

This time Jennifer did show some emotion. Horror? Distress? Libby couldn't make up her mind. Fran came back into the room and resumed her seat.

'Sorry about that,' she said. 'It was the police.'

'Oh?' said Libby, while Patrick and Jennifer both looked startled.

Fran smiled gently. 'Nothing to worry about,' she said. 'Do carry on. I interrupted.'

'Patrick was just saying he might sell this house and move to London permanently,' explained Libby.

'I wouldn't make any rash decisions just yet, Paddy,' said Jennifer. 'After all, this has been your home since you were a boy.'

'I think that's why I need to go, Jen.' He gave her a tired smile. 'There's no one left here for me.'

Jennifer looked as though she'd been stabbed. 'But look at all the friends you've got here!' she stammered.

'The dinner party and point-to-point set?' Patrick laughed. 'All they'd miss is a tame minor celeb to open fêtes. At least in London I've got friends in the business. Real friends.'

He's got no idea what he's doing, thought Libby, watching the two of them.

'You don't have any writer friends around here, then?' asked Fran. 'I thought you did. Nick Forrest only lives at Ebbesdean, and Daniel Hill's not far away in Poole.'

A faint colour appeared along Patrick's cheekbones. 'Yes, I know. I had to send back their critiques before last year's holiday. But –'

'They weren't friends, Fran.' Jennifer had regained Nanny status. 'I told you, if you remember.'

'Of course.' Fran smiled at her. 'So you didn't see Lily Cooper either? Salisbury's not far.'

'No.' Patrick's face closed. 'They were not friends. Merely people I met whom I was tutoring.'

217

Don't push it, Fran, thought Libby, but Fran had obviously made whatever point she wanted to and was lifting her coffee cup.

'Actually, we're going to see Daniel this afternoon,' Libby said brightly. 'He's doing some sort of live literature event.

Both Patrick's and Jennifer's faces expressed disgust.

'Don't go!' said Patrick. 'He'll be absolute shite. He did something at the holiday, and of course, all the other so-called literary morons followed suit. It was excruciating.'

'Oh.' Libby was taken aback. 'I thought I might be a bit bored, but I didn't think it would be that bad.'

'Is it performance poetry?' asked Fran.

'It's meant to be,' said Jennifer. 'I found it intensely embarrassing.'

'Not very good, then,' said Libby.

'We didn't think so,' said Jennifer.

'Did you go to the holiday together?' asked Libby. 'Or was it a coincidence?'

'No,' said Patrick.

'Yes,' said Jennifer.

'What I mean is,' said Jennifer, her colour matching Patrick's. 'Patrick said he'd been asked to tutor this part-time course, and as I was trying to write a novel in between commissions, I thought it would be fun to go and see if I could kick-start myself. Then I met Nina, and the others were OK, especially Audrey and Bernice, so when this get-together was mentioned I decided to go. And when I heard Amanda George had been asked to talk to us, that was the icing on the cake.'

'Must have been convenient,' said Fran. 'At least you could travel in the same car.'

'I went straight from London,' said Patrick, not looking at Jennifer.

'Right.' Libby smiled vaguely. 'Well, we won't take up any more of your time, Patrick. It was kind of you to see us, and I'm so very sorry about your wife.'

Patrick stood up with the air of a guardsman going on parade.

'It was kind of you to call,' he insisted politely. 'And thank you once again for keeping a low profile.'

'We shall continue to do so,' said Fran. 'Thank you, Jennifer.'

It was Jennifer who showed them out.

'I'm sorry about that,' she said as she accompanied them through the front door. 'He's not himself yet.'

'How do you mean?' asked Libby.

'Oh, all that stuff about not writing any more and moving to London. He'll change his mind again.'

'You certainly seem to know him very well,' said Fran. 'And it's hardly surprising he doesn't really know what to do yet. It's only been a week since Melanie was found.'

'Good heavens, so it is,' said Libby. 'It's Saturday again!'

'If you need my help on anything, you know where to find me,' said Jennifer, shaking hands with them both. 'And as for Lily Cooper – I'm pretty sure she did know where they lived. I'm not saying

219

anything else,' she looked over her shoulder, 'because I don't want to worry him.'

'OK,' said Fran. 'If necessary, I'll call you again.'

'Well, that was interesting, wasn't it?' said Libby, as they drove back down the drive. 'And what did the police want? Who was it really?'

'It was the police.' Fran looked left and right before pulling on to the main road. 'It was Ian.'

'Was it? Cor! What did he want? Did you tell him where we were?'

'Wait a sec.' Fran pulled into a farm gate and turned off the engine before turning towards Libby. 'Brace yourself. Melanie wasn't killed at the Manor and she'd been dead well over twelve hours before she was found.'

Chapter Twenty-five

'SO, YES, I DID tell him where we were, and he told me not to say anything, obviously.' Fran tapped the steering wheel. 'So I don't know where that leaves us.'

'Good God.' Libby stared out of the window at the stunning view. 'So that means – what does it mean?'

'It means her body was dumped during the night, and someone went to the trouble of setting the scene in the hut. So where was the body until it was dumped? Do you think the killer put it in the hut?'

'It was obviously an attempt to implicate Patrick. Otherwise why leave the handbag with all the credit cards and driving licence so prominently displayed? Someone meant us to think Melanie had come disguised as Ann Marsh to confront Patrick about his infidelities.'

'They forgot the car, though,' said Fran. 'They should have brought her down in her own car and left it there. And it might not be to deliberately frame Patrick, but simply to divert suspicion.'

'Odd way to go about it,' said Libby. 'You know, while we were in Patrick's house, I'd begun to think perhaps it was Jennifer all along, to get rid of Melanie and claim Patrick for herself, but if the whole idea was to frame Patrick that's a non-starter. She's potty about him.'

'I wonder why she portrays herself as a borderline elderly pearls-and-twinset type in public when she's so much more attractive in real life,' said Fran.

'So she can keep close to Patrick with no one being any the wiser,' said Libby. 'She can assume her ex-babysitter persona and be no threat to his various inamorata.'

'But you'd think she would want to pose a threat to them,' said Fran.

'No, because at the moment, Patrick only sees his old friend Jen, who's been there all these years for him to lean on, and I'll bet he uses her to hide behind if one of the ladies gets a bit too persistent. Then she can pop out in her best when they're alone.'

'Makes sense.' Fran nodded, pursing her lips. 'And she did look so much nicer today – and younger.'

'And it's all wasted.' Libby sighed sympathetically. 'He's not going to hang around. He'll be off to London and the high life as soon as he decently can, leaving her behind.'

'She was shattered when he went on about his so-called friends, wasn't she?' said Fran. 'He didn't even notice.'

'Anyway, it couldn't have been Jennifer,' said Libby. 'I give her an alibi myself. I saw her arrive *and* take her case out of the car. I think I might have noticed if she'd had a body in it. I ticked her off and watched her go in and up the stairs, and I was on front-door duty for a good while after that. Come to think of it,' she sighed, 'I can give most of them an alibi for the same reason.'

'Perhaps,' said Fran slowly, 'she was hidden

nearby before Friday.'

'Eh?' Libby turned in shock. 'Bloody hell, Fran. Where did that come from? And, come to that, where would she have been hidden?'

'I was just thinking,' said Fran, 'if someone had bothered to check out the place before last Friday, they could have come up and dumped the body somewhere nearby. In the woods, maybe?'

'That wouldn't work,' said Libby firmly. 'There would be forensic evidence of – of – well, leaves and things. And if the body had been there overnight, wouldn't there be, um, deteriorations? What happens about rigor?'

'It was just an idea. I'm trying to work out how she got there. So are the police.'

'There will be forensic evidence of the killer in the hut, won't there? It would take time to set everything up, and they couldn't possibly do it without leaving traces. Not unless they had a police boiler suit. And a mask and gloves.'

'Do they have masks? I thought that was only doctors and nurses,' said Fran.

'I think so.' Libby was frowning. 'After all, it's a procedure of a sort, isn't it?'

'Well, whatever it is, the police are stepping up the investigation.'

'Do I take it Ian's back in the loop now?'

'Apparently.' Fran laughed. 'He sounded quite cock-a-hoop. I told him we'd ring him when we got home. I think Scotalnd Yard, or whoever they are, have got a bit fed up because it doesn't look remotely like a political or terrorist murder.'

'So they'll let Ian and the team back in? That's

good,' said Libby with satisfaction.

'Anyway, you can see why I wasn't to let on to Jennifer and Patrick. If she was killed before she went to Steeple Martin, they could be in the frame.' Fran shook her head. 'Although if Patrick was in London and Melanie was down here I don't see how that would work.'

'He was very quick to say that, wasn't he?' said Libby. 'Do you think it wasn't true?'

'Jennifer wasn't too sure,' said Fran. 'I wonder where he really was.'

'And more importantly,' said Libby, 'where *she* was.'

'Jennifer or Melanie?'

'Melanie. That's probably the most important thing.'

'The other important thing,' said Fran, slowing down to look at a road sign, 'is that the whole thing was premeditated. Someone booked in as Ann Marsh.'

'Ah, but it could have been Melanie herself, and someone else knew her plans. Anyway, you're right, it was definitely premeditated.'

'I wish I could get something on it,' said Fran, with a sigh, 'but there's nothing. There was a lot of negative energy coming off Patrick this morning, though.'

'Has he got something to hide?'

'I would say so. And we also ought to try and look at Lily Cooper again.'

'After what Jennifer just said, yes. I'd forgotten that in the shock of what you told me.' Libby peered out of the window. 'Where are we?'

'Going round the outskirts of Wimborne Minster,' said Fran. 'I've been there before. There's a lovely old hotel in the square.'

'So we're nearly there? Should we stop for lunch?'

'What, in Wimborne? No, I'd rather get to Fanbridge first. There's bound to be somewhere there we can get a sandwich.'

'OK,' said Libby, who had been thinking more in terms of something alcoholic to sustain her through Daniel Hill's event.

However, when they found Fanbridge, which was fairly non-descript and suburban, the only place that appeared to have food of any sort was the Fanbridge Centre itself, a modern building next to a pound shop. The Gallery Restaurant overlooked what appeared to be a multipurpose space which today was set up with an optimistic amount of chairs around a small dais.

'Perhaps we could stay up here and watch?' whispered Libby, as they collected their pre-packaged sandwiches and exorbitantly priced cans of drink.

Fran looked doubtfully at the bored waitress behind the counter. 'I don't know. It would be easier to leave from here if we got bored, but that isn't the point, is it? We want to speak to Daniel.'

'It would also be easier to read or do a crossword up here if we get to hair-tearing boredom,' said Libby.

'Have you got a book with you?'

'Yes,' said Libby triumphantly. 'Haven't you?'

'No. I suppose I could go and find a newspaper

or a magazine. There's got to be a shop somewhere.'

'There are magazines over there,' said Libby, pointing to a table by the front entrance. 'They're probably local ones, but better than nothing.'

'Right,' said Fran, standing up. 'I'll go and pinch a couple.'

Libby watched as she went back down the stairs and went to the table. It didn't look as though there was much of a selection, but suddenly Fran's head shot up, she grabbed a newspaper and a magazine and quickly came back up the stairs. Then Libby saw the reason. Daniel Hill appeared in the doorway, flanked by two other people. Fran flopped down in her chair and pushed back her hair.

'That was close.'

'Mind you,' said Libby, 'we could have talked to him now and saved ourselves the agony of the performance.'

'I suppose we could.' Fran peered over the balcony rail to where Daniel, in apparently the same knitted waistcoat he had worn last week, was setting up a table with the help of his acolytes, two women of indeterminate age, one with hair in a plait and large glasses, the other with cropped grey hair and small glasses. Just as she began to draw back, Daniel looked up.

'Bugger!' whispered Libby. 'He's seen us!'

'It was you who said we should have talked to him before the performance,' said Fran, watching as Daniel turned to speak to the two women, who both looked up at the gallery. 'So what do we say now?'

'He'll know we came here to see him,' said Libby. 'Come on, let's finish our sandwiches and then we'll go down. Pity, I'm sure we would have loved his readings.'

Fran coughed on a sandwich.

Daniel had taken no notice of them since he'd first looked up, but Libby got the impression it was a studied ignorance. When she and Fran approached from the body of the performance space, the two acolytes turned towards them, but Daniel, though he must have heard them, didn't.

'Daniel, just the man.' Libby raised her voice to performance pitch.

Slowly he turned round, his face more bulldog-like than ever.

'What do you want?' he snapped. 'I said I had nothing to say to you.'

'Why?' Libby widened her eyes at him. 'We only wanted to warn you about Special Branch.'

The two acolytes' faces registered alarm.

'Well, Scotland Yard, anyway,' amended Libby. 'Have they been in touch already?'

The shifty eyes provided their own reply and Fran smiled gently.

'We've just been talking to Patrick and Jennifer,' she said, 'so we thought we ought to talk to you as well.'

'I haven't got long,' muttered Daniel.

'No, we know your event starts at two,' said Libby. 'Shall we sit down for a moment?'

Daniel reluctantly led the way to the back row of chairs, deliberately ignoring the other two women who watched with shocked faces.

'How did you find me?' he said, as soon as they sat down.

'Through *Writers in the South*,' said Fran. 'They don't appear to mind passing on details.'

'That's an infringement of personal liberty,' said Daniel.

'Well, of the Data Protection Act, anyway,' said Libby, trying not to grin.

'We only wanted to speak to you as a friend of Patrick's,' said Fran craftily, 'as he's being looked into, too.'

Daniel looked slightly less pugnacious and grunted.

'It all seems so odd, you see,' said Libby, taking her cue. 'Patrick would seem to be the only one who had a motive for killing his wife, yet we know he didn't.'

Daniel sniffed. 'One of those women. Bound to be.'

'Women?' said Libby.

'Jennifer whats-her-name or bloody Lily Cooper.'

'What makes you say that?' asked Fran.

'Jealous, weren't they?' He sniffed again and brushed ineffectually at his front, where traces of ash still lurked.

'Of Melanie?' prompted Fran.

'Huh. Thought they bloody stood a chance. Course they didn't.'

'I can see Lily might have wanted to step into Melanie's shoes –'

'Bed, more like,' grunted Daniel.

'But Jennifer had been a friend since Patrick was a child,' continued Libby.

'She was the same. Must have been one of

them.'

'So you don't think there's anything in Scotland Yard's investigations into Melanie's political past?' said Fran.

Daniel looked uncomfortable and fixed his eyes on a point above their heads. 'Wouldn't know.'

'Did you know anything about her days with Green Country or as a government advisor?' asked Libby.

'What would I know?' There was a slightly patchy colour beginning to show on Daniel's cheeks, Libby noticed gleefully.

'So, you've never written about her?' she said. 'Not in *Scriptus*, of course, but in one of your other publications.'

'What other publications?' His eyes were wide open now and staring at Libby, who was put on the spot.

'I'm sure you remember,' said Fran, 'otherwise why would Scotland Yard have come after you?'

'They didn't "come after me" as you put it,' said Daniel, now highly indignant. 'Yes, I used to contribute to a couple of magazines that were critical of Green Country's policies. A lot of people did.'

'But self-confessed anarchists?' asked Fran gently.

Daniel's colour was now alarmingly high. 'Look, I had nothing to do with the silly whore's death. If I'd wanted to kill anyone it would have been him, the puffed-up bloody pulp-peddler. Couldn't be bothered with anyone like me, could he? Or that pipsqueak Nick Forrest. It didn't matter that he

229

could have helped us, and even come to events. And what he did –' He stopped abruptly.

'So you knew he lived locally?' put in Libby quickly.

'Course I did. We weren't supposed to – our manuscripts were all sent to the *Writers in the South* secretary to preserve anonymity.' He made a sound of disgust. 'But it wasn't exactly difficult to find out where he lived.'

'Nick Forrest said he didn't know,' said Fran.

'He might not have,' admitted Daniel grudgingly, 'but Lily and Dee did.'

'That's hardly all of you,' said Libby mildly. 'What about Paul Fisher?'

'Who? Oh, that other queer little Nicky palled up with. Dunno.'

Fran's face showed blatant distaste. Libby rushed in.

'Surely not? They both struck me as nice people.'

'You saying queers aren't nice?' He gave a bark of laughter. 'Mind you, you're right.'

'No,' said Libby, 'I wasn't. As it happens, some of my best friends are gay, and I've even been an attendant at a civil partnership. I phrased my remark badly.'

'Well, you two –' he looked from Fran to Libby with a sneer, '– obviously lezzers–'

He got no further, as two ringing slaps connected with both his cheeks. Astonished, Libby and Fran watched open-mouthed as the two acolytes dragged him off his chair, then dismantled everything they had set up on the dais. Daniel got to his knees and crouched in the aisle, watched interestedly from the gallery by the staff.

'You're not a couple,' said the slimmer acolyte, turning to Libby and Fran. 'We are, and we can see that. We'd begun to have our doubts about this self-important pig, but he was our best way into writing and writers.' She gave a short laugh. 'I think we'd better think again.'

The other woman came up and put an arm round her. 'I guess we had,' she said, 'particularly if he's mixed up in murder.'

'I'm not mixed up in anything!' Came a strangled and gasping cry from the floor. The women took no notice.

'Will you go ahead with the event?' asked Fran.

'He might.' The younger woman glanced distastefully at Daniel. 'We won't be here.'

'Are you members of *Writers in the South*?' asked Libby.

'No.' The plaited one sighed. 'He said it was –' she turned to her friend. 'What did he say?'

'Proletarian.' Silver hair snorted. 'Honestly. I think we might join now. We didn't know he was a member.'

'I only joined –' began the voice from the floor.

'To get close to Patrick. Yes, we gathered that,' said Libby. 'You pathetic little worm. I pity your cat.'

'Hodge is a very well looked after cat!' Daniel gasped, struggling to his feet.

'Hodge!' said four women in unison, and laughed.

'Look,' said silver hair, turning her back on him,

'if we can help in any way – not that we know what's going on – but we'd be happy to.' She fished in the pocket of her quilted gilet and pulled out a wallet. 'Here.' She handed over a card. 'We'll even keep an eye on him if you want.'

Libby held out her hand. 'That's great, thank you. We live in Kent, so it would be good to have an impartial ear to the ground, so to speak.'

Silver hair shook the proffered hand. 'Can you tell us what's going on? I'm Virginia, by the way – don't laugh – known as Ginny, and this is Sarah.'

Fran introduced herself and Libby and led the way out of the Centre.

'Anyone fancy a drink?' said Libby. 'Or isn't there a pub near here?'

'In Fanbridge?' Sarah squinted through her large glasses. 'You must be joking! There's a nice one in Wimborne, if that isn't too far? We live there.'

'Great!' Libby smiled happily. 'Lead on, then, and we'll tell you the whole story.'

Chapter Twenty-six

IN THE BAR OF the hotel in Wimborne, Fran and Libby between them related the story of Melanie Joseph's murder.

'Well,' said Ginny, when they'd finished, 'I knew Melanie lived near here because she was involved with the Bonny Henge protests. It was all over the news. I didn't connect her with Patrick, though.'

'That's what I find puzzling,' said Fran. 'When the police asked if anyone knew Melanie or Patrick everyone except Jennifer said no.'

'It doesn't look as though anybody actually *knew* them,' said Libby, 'but they did know where they lived, which no one has admitted to before.'

'I think Nick was telling the truth,' said Fran. 'I don't think he knew.'

'No, and I wonder what Daniel thought he knew about Nick and Paul Fisher? I mean,' said Libby, 'we know they spent some time together in between the holiday and the reunion, but I wouldn't have thought Nick was gay.'

'Daniel is just a nasty old homophobe,' said Sarah. 'He's never sounded quite so unpleasant as he did just now, but we always felt he was laughing at us, didn't we?' She looked at her partner. 'And it's worse for us, because it seems that gay men are accepted more than we are.'

'I think that's true,' said Libby. 'Our friends Peter and Harry have said the same. They're accepted completely and rarely come up against any prejudice, but I know Harry says the women do. He's a member of an LGBT group, although he says he's not altogether comfortable with people being lumped together in a grey area.'

'What's LGBT?' asked Fran.

'Lesbian, Gay, Bisexual and Transgender,' explained Libby.

'It doesn't quite cover it, he's right,' said Fran. 'And as for coming up against prejudice, what about that case last winter?'

'Cy, you mean? Well, yes, I suppose there was homophobia there,' said Libby, but –'

'Are you actually investigators, then?' asked Sarah, looking quite excited.

'We help the police sometimes,' said Libby, looking warily at Fran.

'I used to do property investigations,' said Fran, repeating her almost-true explanation. 'But this one is a bit different. No one's asked us to look into it.'

'It just happened on my premises,' said Libby. 'It makes a difference.'

'Well, as I said earlier,' said Ginny, 'if there's anything we can do, let us know. If you really would like a local ear.'

'Two,' said Sarah, grinning happily at Ginny, who patted her hand.

'This is my number,' said Libby, scribbling on a beer mat. 'If you read or hear anything that you think might be useful, would you ring? I'd say send an email, but I might not pick that up quickly enough.'

'I'm not entirely sure I followed the whole

story,' said Ginny, 'or that I'll remember all the names, but I'll remember Patrick and Melanie.'

'We'd better get going,' said Fran, standing up and holding out a hand. 'It was lovely to meet you.'

'And you,' said Ginny, while Sarah impulsively gave Libby a kiss.

'You must come up to Kent and meet Peter and Harry,' said Libby. 'They've got a great veggie restaurant. Mainly Mexican.'

'How did you know we were veggie?' asked Sarah.

'I didn't,' said Libby, in some surprise. 'There's a coincidence.'

'Although,' she said to Fran in the car, 'it shouldn't have come as a surprise. They look like eco-warriors.'

'What does an eco-warrior look like?' asked Fran, turning onto the A31 towards Ringwood. 'And don't say "like them".'

Libby grinned. 'I liked them, and they'll be good spies.'

'Not sure we need spies,' said Fran, 'in fact, I'm not sure that coming down here wasn't a bit of a waste of time.'

'How can you say that?' gasped Libby. 'Think of what we've found out!'

'OK, what?' said Fran.

'That there were more people who knew where Melanie lived, for a start. And you think there's more than just one post at that henge. And that Patrick's critiques were not quite what was expected.' Libby frowned. 'Although I don't know why that's helpful.'

'It could be,' said Fran. 'Remember Nick and Daniel, at least, were trying to get closer to Patrick. They both wanted him to give them a bit more advice – or help. And he avoided them all. I expect Lily Cooper also tried, but he wouldn't have let her get close.'

'Except at the writers' weekend,' said Libby. 'There can't be any other reason she was floating round the place in a nightie at five thirty in the morning.'

'I wonder,' said Fran. 'Did Patrick confirm she'd been with him?'

'Can't remember. Would we know if he had anyway?'

'I just wondered if he could have sent her away,' said Fran, cautiously pulling out to overtake a lorry.

'Even if he had,' said Libby, 'she couldn't have gone off and killed Melanie in a fit of pique. Melanie was already dead by then.'

'And what about Nina hearing that row?' said Fran. 'It must have been Lily she heard, not Dee.'

'What time did she say it was?' Libby turned to Fran. 'Early morning?'

'The same time Hetty saw Lily outside her room. That fits.'

'But no one else heard a row. Hetty would have done, surely?' Libby frowned at the windscreen.

'So why would Nina lie about it? Anyway, she hasn't told the police, so it doesn't matter.'

'I'm beginning to think there's more to Nina than we first thought,' said Libby. 'She doesn't add up, somehow.'

'Well, she certainly hasn't got a motive for

killing Melanie. And frankly, I really can't see any other motives.' Fran sighed. 'None of the writers had any sort of motive to kill her, certainly not in the pre-planned way it happened. It must be something to do with the henge. Or her political connections. Or something.'

'In that case, presumably Scotland Yard will turn it up,' said Libby.

'Not necessarily, if it's the henge,' said Fran. 'And how seriously will Scotland Yard take that?'

'We'll have to look into the protests more closely when we get home,' said Libby.

'Hmm.' Fran negotiated a roundabout. 'We should have done that while we there. We didn't even bother to find the local museum. How stupid was that?'

'I suppose we should have done. We could have asked Jennifer. She was the one who got us down there and showed us the henge.'

'And I'm still not sure why she did that,' said Fran.

'Because she wants the murderer found? And didn't think Scotland Yard would take the henge stuff seriously?'

'I'll call her when I get home,' said Fran. 'Apart from anything else, I want to ask her about the museum, or who to get in touch with anyway.'

'I expect the archaeologists are used to slightly strange people butting in on their sites,' said Libby, and received a punch on the arm.

The drive back to Kent took longer than the drive down had, despite the sunshine, and Libby didn't let herself into number seventeen until after eight o'clock. Ben stood up and came to kiss her.

'How did it go?'

'Tiring, informative and a bit puzzling,' said Libby. 'I'll tell you all about it as soon as I've got a large drink.'

Half an hour later, in a dressing gown and on her second whisky, Libby concluded: 'And Fran says she's not sure why we bothered to go.'

Ben frowned at the fireplace. 'It does seem to me you didn't keep your eye on the ball.'

'Oh, really?' Libby scowled.

Ben patted her hand. 'Don't be daft. No, what I meant was, Fran said she thought that something had happened near the standing stone, and even Jennifer thought that. You didn't bother to go back to that or the story of the ghost. Who was she?'

'The White Lady. Well, that's what we called her. I think on the internet site Fran found it called her the Bonny Henge Ghost, but as it hasn't been known as a henge for long it must have been called something else before then. The Rising Manor ghost, perhaps.'

'Did you even go to Rising Manor?'

'No. We forgot all about it. It didn't seem important somehow.'

'I suppose it isn't. But you were going to use it as a cover. And what about Fran's first moment? When she saw Mrs J drinking?'

'I think we forgot about that, too.' Libby sighed. 'We're slipping, aren't we?'

'No doubt you'll get back on form now you're home,' said Ben, slipping an arm round her. 'And you must be exhausted after all that travelling. How about an early night?'

Libby put down her glass.

'When you spoke to Ian yesterday,' said Libby on
the phone to Fran late on Sunday morning, 'he said
Melanie'd been dead over twelve hours.'

'He said at least twelve hours. Apparently rigor
had gone off completely and there was something
about ambient temperature.'

'And what about what killed her? All we know is
that the stabbing was post-mortem.'

'He didn't say. He was mainly calling because
Guy told him where we were and he wanted to stop
us saying anything to – well – to anybody.'

'We haven't, have we?' said Libby. 'But listen,
Ben said last night we forgot all about you having
that moment with Melanie drinking. And writing.
You said it was something to do with her writing.
And we didn't go into the ghost at all.'

Libby heard Fran sigh. 'I know, I know. I don't
know honestly what we *did* do, I said that yesterday.
But I also said I'd ring Jennifer today and ask about
the museum.'

'What about Rising Manor? We didn't look for
that either.'

'But the ghost story is nothing to do with
Melanie's story,' said Fran. 'It was only going to be
a cover. And we didn't need it.'

'Oh, all right. So it was a waste of time, then?'

'Well, no. We learnt a bit more about Patrick and
Jennifer, a lot more about Daniel and Nick, and saw
a lovely part of the country. I'm sure if we put it all
into context and tell Ian everything we learnt, we'll

find it's been useful.' Libby heard a yawn. 'Anyway, now I'm going to put a roast in the oven and spend the rest of the day on the beach with a book. I'll talk to you tomorrow.'

'Bother,' said Libby.

'What?' Ben appeared from the kitchen and handed her a mug of tea.

'Fran doesn't want to talk about it. She's going on the beach with a book.'

'Sensible woman,' said Ben. 'We could go and join her, if you like. We haven't got to go up to Mum's for lunch today.'

'Don't make it sound as though it's a chore,' said Libby, 'I love your mum's Sunday lunches.'

'So do I, but it's great when she actually deigns to accept an invitation to go out to someone else's, even if it's only to Flo and Lenny.'

'*Only* Flo? She of the matchless meat pie? Not to mention the wine.'

Ben laughed. 'You know what I meant. Now, do you want to go down to Nethergate? We could have lunch at The Swan. Or The Sloop.'

'No, I think Fran might want to be left alone today. I'm a bit much if you have to put up with me unrelieved for three days.'

'I'm glad you realise what a hero I am,' said Ben, kissing her on the nose. 'Shall I see if Harry's got room for us at lunchtime, then?'

'That'd be nice.' Libby beamed. 'Now I shall go and get dressed and you needn't follow me up there, either.'

Harry booked them in towards closing time at The Pink Geranium, and by the time Ben and Libby

240

arrived, there were only a couple of tables occupied. Reading a newspaper at the large pine table in the right hand window sat Peter, a glass of red wine in front of him.

'Here you are, dears,' he said. 'Harry's put us here. He'll join us, too. I'll go and get drinks.'

Harry came back with him carrying a bottle and three glasses. 'This'll do to be going on with,' he said. 'I shall go and create something lovely in the kitchen and then come and join you to eat it. I've kept the Pollo on, petal, just for you.'

'But it's meat!' said Libby.

'I am capable of keeping separate equipment to deal with it, duckie. And it's gone down a storm. So, do you want some?'

He departed with their order and Peter poured wine.

'So, come on, you old trout,' he said. 'Tell us what you've been getting up to in Dirty Dorset?'

Chapter Twenty-seven

LIBBY REPEATED THE SALIENT points of the visit to Cranborne Chase, twice, because Harry had to hear it too when he joined them.

'So there we are,' she said, forking up refried beans. 'All muddled up and we don't know what we got out of it.'

'Two nice new friends from Wimborne, by the sound of it,' said Peter.

'You know what,' said Harry leaning back in his chair and twirling his wine glass, 'I think you've got to look at Patrick a bit more closely.'

Libby frowned. 'Why? He does seem genuinely devastated.'

'That could be guilt,' said Ben.

'But we still have all the same problems,' said Libby. 'How did she get there? When and where was she killed? I saw Patrick arrive and he didn't have anyone with him.'

'In the boot?' suggested Peter.

'I suppose if she came with any of the writers she must have come in a boot,' said Libby.

'And the set up in the Hopper's Hut. That would have been easy for him – he'd have access to all her stuff.' Harry leant forward again and picked up the wine bottle.

'But he didn't leave the Manor at any time until he went to the pub with Lily Cooper and Nick Forrest.'

'He didn't have to do it until he dumped the body

during the night,' said Peter. 'No one went over there before you and the police did in the morning.'

'What about the take-away?' asked Ben.

'It came from a Pizza place in Canterbury,' Libby said, 'and it wasn't delivered, it was brought in. I think Ian had someone looking into it.'

'There's another problem,' said Peter. 'The booking. It was made by a woman, and the credit card was genuine. Did he have an accomplice?'

Libby stared at him. 'Of course! Jennifer! She'd do anything for him.'

'Hold on,' said Ben. 'Would she help him kill his wife so that he could continue his affair with someone other than her? More likely to help if she thought she was going to be the favoured one.'

'That's true.' Libby chewed her lip. 'It would make sense if Jennifer killed her though. She admits she didn't like her.'

'But the same applies,' said Peter. 'It doesn't sound as if Patrick has any romantic interest in her at all.'

'No.' Libby sighed. 'He was awful to her while we were there, although he didn't know he was, if you see what I mean. He doesn't want to write any more and he's going to sell the house and live permanently in his London flat. And he was scathing about the local friends – who must be hers, too.'

'Perhaps he made her think there was a chance for her?' suggested Harry. 'So she acted on it?'

'The whole scene when you were there could have been a set-up,' said Peter. 'I mean, it was a bit odd that he should ask to see you to thank you, wasn't it?'

'Yes, we thought that at the time,' said Libby slowly. 'You could be right. I wonder if it was?'

'There's another thing to consider, too,' said, Ben, helping himself to more wine. 'She was killed at least twelve hours before she was found. And she'd already been found by seven thirty. The medical examiner didn't get to the body until at least half an hour later, so we're saying the latest time of death would be eight the night before. So was she killed at the Manor, or was she already dead and the body taken there? Seems an awful lot of trouble to go to.'

'We decided it was planned,' said Libby, 'but I'm really not sure how anyone could have got her there if she was still alive.'

'By saying she would be able to confront her husband or catch him *in flagrante*?' said Harry.

'Maybe,' said Libby doubtfully, 'but if that's the case, it would have to be someone who knew her quite well, and we haven't come up with anyone who did.'

'Except Jennifer,' said Ben.

'But I like her!' said Libby.

'I expect most murderers have their fans,' said Harry.

'Oh, I'm fed up with it.' Libby picked up the bottle and discovered it was empty. 'Can I fetch another one, Hal?'

'You stay there, petal, I'll get it.' Harry got up.

'Fed up?' said Ben. 'Do you mean you'll step away from it?'

Peter snorted. 'That'll be the day. She says it

every time, but she never does.'

Harry returned with an open bottle. 'Trouble is, you'll still be involved because you *are* involved. It was your business and you met all the guests except the victim. You can't get out of it, really, can you?'

'I suppose we could even be suspects,' said Libby, turning to Ben. 'Blimey!'

'I expect Murray and Ian have excluded you,' said Peter. 'They know you too well.'

'Ah, but people always say that on TV, don't they?' said Harry, as he finished topping up glasses. '"But so-and-so would never kill anybody!" and he's just finished wiping out half the town.'

'Well, I might still be in the frame as a witness,' said Libby, 'but I can stay out of the investigation. Ian would be thrilled if I did.'

'After you've told him what you found out in Dorset,' said Ben. 'And after you've thought of some other little angle you hadn't thought of before.'

Harry and Peter laughed. Libby scowled.

It was much later, while Ben and Libby sat in the garden of number seventeen that Libby's mobile rang.

'Are you back yet?' asked Ian.

'Yes. I'm in the garden with Ben,' said Libby, mouthing "Ian" at Ben.

'I need to ask you a few more questions. Will you be around in the morning if I go to the Manor?'

'Do you want both of us?'

'I'm going to ask Fran, but I might have to go and see her. I don't want to put her out.'

'Actually, I meant did you want Ben as well, but

he'll be at the Manor anyway. I'm sure Fran will come up. Can you tell me what it's about?'

'Apart from what you were doing in Dorset harassing witnesses?'

'Oh,' said Libby.

Ten minutes later the phone rang again.

'Are you coming?' asked Libby.

'Of course. What did he say to you?' said Fran.

'Said we'd been harassing witnesses in Dorset.'

'Yes, he said the same to me, but I don't think he was serious.'

'Has he received a complaint?'

'I've no idea, but don't forget he called me while we were at Patrick's, so he knew what we were doing.'

'Daniel might have told on us,' said Libby.

'*We* didn't knock him off his chair,' said Fran.

'Oh, well, we'll find out in the morning,' said Libby. 'See you at ten.'

Ian was already closeted in the estate office with Ben when Libby arrived at nine forty-five the next morning.

'Shall I go and get coffee?' she asked.

'Mum's on the case,' said Ben.

'I'll go and give her a hand, then.'

'No, Libby, please sit down,' said Ian, 'it'll give me a chance to talk to you without Fran.'

Libby looked alarmed.

'Nothing serious,' Ian soothed, 'I just wanted to know if Fran had any of her – what is it you call them? Moments? – Since I last saw you. She's sometimes not inclined to tell me.'

'Because she still thinks you might not believe

her.' Libby pulled a chair up to the desk and sat down.

'You know I take her seriously,' said Ian. 'So, did she?'

Libby frowned. 'Well, she thought she saw Melanie drinking something. That was before we went away. I don't know how she knew it was Melanie, because she'd never seen her. Then, she thought something had happened at this place in Rising Parva.'

'The monument?' said Ian.

'Oh, you know about that?' said Libby. 'Actually, it's a henge, and a recently discovered standing stone. Melanie was making a bit of a fuss about it.'

'Yes, we know about that. And the fact that one of your guests had demonstrated there. Against Melanie.'

'Not so much against her personally, I don't think,' said Libby.'

'But she was the personification of what they were up against,' said Ian.

'Yes, perhaps. Anyway, there were two groups against her for that. The druids, or whoever they were, and the archaeologists.'

'So Fran was feeling something of that?' asked Ian.

'She didn't say so. She said something nasty had happened, I think, but she didn't explain. Then she felt there was something emanating from Patrick when we saw him on Saturday. But I said that was probably because his wife had been murdered.'

'And how did you think he seemed?'

'A bit – diminished. He certainly appears devastated. We were very surprised that he should have asked to see us. In fact –' Libby stopped and looked at Ben.

'Yes? In fact what?' Ian leant forward.

'We were wondering if it wasn't a put-up job. Asking us there.'

Ian leant back again. 'I would have wondered that too. So he did actually ask you?'

'We'd already met Jennifer, who had suggested we go down to Rising Parva.'

'Why?' Ian was frowning.

'She seemed convinced that Melanie's death was something to do with the henge, or the standing stone, or both. She knew somehow about Fran's – um – gift, and she thought she – Fran – would pick up something that would help.' Libby looked at Ben again. 'I'm afraid we've begun to get suspicious about her, though.'

Ian sighed. 'Start at the beginning. No, wait. We'll have coffee and you can tell me when Fran's here.'

On cue, the door opened and Fran ushered Hetty and a large tray into the room.

'And now,' said Ian, when coffee had been poured and distributed and Hetty had retired to her kitchen, 'you can start with Jennifer's invitation, why you went and what you found. And don't,' he said with a warning look, 'leave anything out.'

248

Chapter Twenty-eight

IT TOOK HALF AN hour for Fran and Libby to relate the events of three days in Dorset, especially as each of them spent some time correcting the other.

'So who complained about us?' Libby finished up.

'No one. Patrick told me he'd seen you when I called him to ask for another interview.'

'He said he'd wondered why nobody had been in touch,' said Fran.

'Scotland Yard were too busy chasing their tails over a political motive,' said Ian.

'And have they given up on that?' asked Libby.

'I doubt it. They'll be trawling through all the suspects they questioned or suspected when the bomb incident happened.'

'And the death threats?' said Ben.

'And the death threats.' Ian picked up the coffee pot hopefully, and put it down again.

'I'll get some more,' said Libby.

'In a minute,' said Ian. 'One of the things Scotland Yard have been doing is looking into links any of last weekend's guests might have had to the previous events.'

'Well, we knew that.' said Libby. 'Some of them received phone calls.'

'But what about the business of the protestors at the henge?' asked Fran. 'Weren't Scotland Yard interested in that?'

'You think that had something to do with the

murder?' Ian looked interested.

'I don't know. Jennifer seems to think so.'

'You thought something nasty had happened up on the henge, didn't you?' said Libby. 'Could it be that?'

Fran shook her head. 'I don't know.'

'The other thing is how Melanie got here,' said Libby, turning back to Ian.

'We have thought of that, Libby,' said Ian with a smile. 'We've now set in motion a forensic check on all the cars. Should have been done before, but not realising that she'd been dead longer than we thought didn't help. That's why I called Patrick yesterday. All the local forces will be contacting the guests.'

'So nothing we did is going to hinder or help?' said Fran.

'If you'd mentioned Melanie drinking something earlier it might have done. Tox screen came back finally.'

'And?' prompted Libby.

'Was she poisoned?' said Fran.

'No, she was suffocated as far as the scientists can tell. I'm sure you remember, Fran, the difficulties there.'

'Aunt Eleanor, yes.' Fran stared into the past. 'But why would my mentioning drinking helped?'

'Because she was given ketamine first.'

'Oh, God.' Libby shook her head. 'This gets worse.'

'So our murderer really planned this,' said Fran. 'It wasn't a spur of the moment thing where the body had to be dumped somewhere.'

'No. So it was someone who knew her quite well,' said Ian.

'But that's only Patrick and Jennifer,' said Libby. 'No one else knew her. That's what we've been trying to find out.'

'Either someone's lying or it's someone who wasn't here as a guest last weekend,' said Ben.

'Well, obviously someone's lying – the murderer is for a start, if he or she was here,' said Ian, 'but finding someone who could have planned this and knew enough about this venue who *wasn't* here will be frankly Herculean.'

'So what are you going to do?' asked Libby.

'I had hoped you might have come up with something,' said Ian, 'but as you haven't, I'm afraid it's going to be a descent on Dorset to dig up all her friends and acquaintances.'

'Patrick's dinner party circuit,' said Libby.

'What?' asked Ian and Ben together. Libby explained.

'He almost seemed to despise them,' said Fran.

'Jennifer was part of the same circle we think,' Libby said, 'so she'll be able to give you names and addresses if Patrick doesn't.'

'She'll probably know more of them than Patrick anyway,' said Fran. 'Pity we didn't ask while we were down there.'

'I don't see how you could,' said Ian. 'You aren't the police.'

'No, we know.' Libby sighed. 'I do find it so frustrating.'

'I daresay.' Ian gave her a wry smile. 'Now, did you say something about more coffee?'

251

Libby took the tray back to the kitchen where Hetty shooed her out and promised to bring fresh coffee in five minutes.

'So will you go down there yourself?' she asked on returning to the office.

'I shall have to. I'm taking DS Wallingford with me, but we can't afford to take anyone else. I'll have to rely on good relations with the local force and hope they can spare me a couple of people.'

'I was going to call Jennifer today because I wanted information about the museum,' said Fran. 'I assume I don't say anything about this?'

'If she's in touch with Patrick she'll know,' said Ian. 'I've already booked in to see him tomorrow morning. We're going down this afternoon.'

'Couldn't you have seen him sooner? He's got longer to get his story right, or hide the evidence if you don't see him until tomorrow,' said Libby.

Ian laughed. 'As I spoke to him yesterday he's already had plenty of time, and I'm pretty sure he'll have told Jennifer.'

'Unless he's avoiding her,' said Fran. 'He looked rather as though he was getting a bit fed up with being mothered when we saw him Saturday morning.'

'That's true,' Libby agreed, 'and she's not as much in his confidence as she thinks she is. Will you try and see Daniel Hill?'

'I certainly shall.' Ian grinned. 'I shall encourage him to make a complaint about you.'

Hetty appeared with a refreshed tray, interrupting Libby's indignant response.

'Who will do the forensic examination on the

cars?' asked Fran, bringing them back to the subject. 'You or the Dorset force?'

'Dorset, but we'll have to have it on our budget, probably,' said Ian. 'If one of the cars turns anything up then it will be brought back to Kent for further tests.'

'Surely something will turn up,' said Libby. 'Melanie had to get here somehow, especially as she couldn't do it under her own steam.' She thought for a moment. 'And what about that credit card? Did you find out about that?'

'Yes, and it was hers, issued by the MOD.'

'Ministry of Defence?' said Fran. 'Why them?'

'I don't know. Spooks keep themselves to themselves. She was once a person of considerable interest to certain sections of society and had a few aliases. That's where Scotland Yard are snooping around now. The MOD are keeping an eye on them.'

'Heavens above!' said Libby. 'A crime of national importance.'

'It does seem more likely, then,' said Fran, 'that the murderer is somehow connected to that part of her life.'

'Certainly, rather than being murdered because she was someone's wife,' said Ian.

'That's what we've said all along,' said Libby. 'At first glance it looked as if the only people with a motive were Patrick himself and Lily Cooper. Now it looks as though it's only Patrick and Jennifer Alderton.'

'Let's hope we can find a link somewhere, then,' said Ian.

'Preferably a car with traces of her in the boot,' said Libby.

Ian finished his second cup of coffee and stood up. 'Sorry to bother you even further, but can I have another look round the hut where Melanie stayed?'

'Help yourself,' said Ben. 'Have you still got a key?'

Ian produced it out of his pocket. 'I'll have to get SOCOs in to have another go at the ground, too, if that's all right. Now we know she must have been transported we need to find traces of the vehicle, although that'll be nigh impossible after over a week.'

'And we've had rain,' said Fran.

'And I've never believed in the sort of detective who finds a thread of cotton on a twig and immediately recognises it as coming from the victim's coat,' sniffed Libby.

'But she does believe in a batty woman who has visions,' smiled Fran. Ian smiled back at her.

'Can we come?' asked Libby, as Ian made to leave the office.

'I suppose so, but keep out of the way.'

Libby turned to Ben and gave him a quick kiss. 'You don't mind, do you?'

He patted her hand. 'Course not. Should I be expecting you to disappear back to Dorset tonight?'

'I'd love to – apart from leaving you, of course – but I don't think Ian would be very pleased!'

Fran and Libby plodded behind Ian as he made his way slowly towards the Hoppers' Huts, his eyes on the ground.

'Ben wanted to know if we were going back to

Dorset,' said Libby. 'I said Ian wouldn't like it.'

'I was thinking that myself,' said Fran. 'I'd like to go to the museum and see what I can find out about the henge.'

'Really?'

'Yes, really.'

They stopped and looked at one another.

'And do we tell Ian?' asked Libby.

'I think we have to,' said Fran. 'And I think it would be better if we stayed somewhere nearer to the museum so we can be right out of his way.'

'Or even in that nice hotel in Wimborne?' said Libby.

They both turned to look at Ian who was by now a long way ahead.

'Come on,' said Fran. 'Let's go and tell him.'

Chapter Twenty-nine

UNSURPRISINGLY, IAN DIDN'T SEEM enthusiastic about the return to Dorset.

'I suppose I can't stop you,' he said, 'but don't come near me or anyone I'm talking to. Museum – fine. If you want to investigate that henge, ask me first.'

'As we don't know exactly where he'll be, we can't get near him, can we?' muttered Libby as she and Fran went back to the Manor.

'You know what he means,' said Fran. 'Now we'd better break the news to our better halves that we're going away again.'

'And find somewhere to stay. Remember Mrs Rush said she was full up from Saturday? It's summer holiday time, so I doubt there'll be much available.'

Leaving Ian to ferret about around the Hoppers' Huts until his SOCOs arrived, there was very little available, they discovered on the internet in the estate office, but strangely, the Barley Mow in Ebbesdean had two rooms.

'Had a cancellation, dear,' said the female voice on the other end of the phone. 'Family's got measles. Poor sods. Do you know where we are?'

'Oh, yes,' said Libby. 'We had fish and chips with you last Friday.'

'Did you?' The voice sounded pleased. 'You'll know we do good food then. So, when are you coming?'

Guy, less sanguine about the repeat visit than Ben, had asked that they didn't go until the following day. Fran went back to Nethergate to soothe her spouse and Libby promised Ben an extra-special meal that evening to compensate for her further absence.

'Not that it does, of course,' he said several hours later, sitting down to a selection of home-made curries. 'If I had to make a choice, I'd have you over the curry.'

'That sounds uncomfortable,' said Libby.

The following morning, Fran parked her little car behind Libby's Romeo the Renault and transferred her luggage into Ben's four by four.

'He says it's much more comfortable for a long journey,' said Libby. 'And we can take more.'

'You can,' said Fran. 'I've only got what I was taking anyway.'

'It does mean I'll be doing all the driving,' said Libby, 'so we won't be going out much in the evenings.'

Fran laughed. 'Of course we won't! Anyway, we're staying in a pub this time. Shall we tell young Nick we're going to be there?'

'We'd better, because I think the Barley Mow may be his local and he might be peeved if we show up without warning him.'

'And he said he'd like to help, didn't he?' said Fran. 'Although I don't know how.'

'He knows the area,' said Libby. 'Come on, let's go and say goodbye to Ben and then we can be on our way.'

The journey this time was accomplished in better

time and in sunshine. Libby did take a wrong turning once they left the main road, but found her way back fairly quickly, and soon they were approaching Ebbesdean in its little hollow once again.

They were in time for a late lunch at the Barley Mow, which was much quieter than it had been the previous Friday. The landlady, a voluptous blonde, was pleased to see them.

'Can't be doing with losing bookings these days, dear,' she said. 'Manna from heaven, you two.'

'Thank you,' said Libby. 'Mrs – er?'

'Just call me Yvonne. Now the kitchen's not closed, so what will you have?'

Settled outside with sandwiches and drinks, Libby and Fran reviewed their plans.

'I think we should tell Ian where we're staying,' said Fran. 'Just so he knows we're doing as we're told.'

'OK, and leave a message for Nick Forrest. Then what?'

'Ask Yvonne about the museum. Then, if it's open, we can go there.'

Yvonne herself came out to collect their plates. There was no sign of last Friday's handmaiden.

'Musem?' she said. 'Well, there's the one in Salisbury, or there's ours, look.' And she nodded across the road.

'Chancery House?' Fran said in surprise. 'We saw something about that on the internet. I didn't realise it was a museum.'

'Oh, it's more than a museum.' Yvonne perched herself on a bench beside them and fished out a packet of cigarettes. 'Don't mind, do you? Don't get much of a chance.'

'No, I'll join you,' said Libby. 'Go on, what about Chancery House?'

'It's what they call a living museum,' said Yvonne, settling down more comfortably. 'You know, places all set up and working just like it used to be in the old days. They got what they call "rescued" buildings and they teach things like woodwork. Very popular.'

'Is it open today?' Libby looked across at the closed gates.

'Yeah, every day. But that's not the main entrance. You have to go along the lane here and round the bend.'

'Do they have any prehistoric stuff?' said Libby.

'Stone age, you mean?' Yvonne wrinkled her pencilled eyebrows.

'Well, yes. You know, like –' Libby frowned.

'Flint weapons,' supplied Fran. 'That sort of thing.'

'Oh, I wouldn't know about that, dear. I've only been in there when they do village events. They have a fête and a Christmas fair, see?'

'Do they have any local history exhibits?' asked Fran. 'About the area? Or would we have to go to Salisbury for that?'

'Oh, they got stuff in the main house all about the Chase, dear. Why don't you pop round and have a look? Bit pricey – I think it's about a tenner to get in. I got a leaflet inside. Hang on, I'll get it. Another drink?'

'What do you think?' asked Libby when Yvonne

had departed in search of her leaflet and two cups of coffee.

'It is a bit expensive, but it might be worthwhile. On the other hand the Salisbury Museum might be cheaper, or even free.'

Yvonne came back with coffees and a handful of leaflets. 'Look see, there's no actual museum in Cranborne itself,' she said. 'All the old stuff went to Salisbury.' She put one of the leaflets down. 'And this is ours. Probably got what you want, eh? What was it exactly you was looking for?'

'Have you heard of Bonny Henge?' asked Libby.

Yvonne was scornful. 'Heard of it? I should bloody say so. The stone they found – all over the local news it was. Some silly cow getting herself all het up over it.'

'Yes, we heard something about that,' said Fran, kicking Libby under the table to keep her quiet. 'Nick Forrest – do you know him?'

'Nick? Course I do. He's a regular. Was it him who brought you here?'

'Yes. He didn't know much about what went on in the area, but he knew about that.'

'Well, there's stuff about that over there, I'm pretty sure. In the main house it would be.'

'That's great, thank you, Yvonne,' said Libby. 'We'll certainly go and have a look. What time do you serve dinner?'

'Any time from six thirty. Now, got everything you want? I'll see you later then.'

They pored over the leaflets. Salisbury had what was called the Pitt-Rivers Wessex collection, which looked fascinating, and there were other collections in Shaftesbury, Blandford and Wimborne but although the Chancery House leaflet said nothing about it, Yvonne had said there would be something about Bonny Henge there. So, finishing their coffees and returning the cups to the bar, they left the pub and set off up the lane.

As Yvonne had said, the main entrance to Chancery House was just round the bend, and far more impressive than the gates opposite the pub. Large signs either side of a wide entry announced "Chancery House Living Museum" with details of opening times beneath. They walked through the entry and along a dusty track to where a booth and barrier had been set up.

'Half price,' said the affable grey-moustached man inside the booth. 'It's nearly three now and we close at five.'

'Thank you,' beamed Libby, and handed over a ten-pound note.

They made their way towards the imposing mansion. 'Georgian?' said Fran, and climbed the steps. Inside a helpful guide immediately stepped forward and handed them a map and a set of headphones.

'Actually,' said Libby, 'we were wondering if you had anything about Bonny Henge?'

'Oh, of course.' The woman, in a pleated skirt and pearl-buttoned cardigan had been sent from central casting, Libby was sure. 'This way,' she went on. 'You'll also find some material about our Rising Parva ghost there, too, although of course in those days it was thought to be a barrow.' She frowned. 'Actually, now I think about it it probably wasn't known as a barrow either in those days.'

'When did the ghost – er – die?' asked Fran.

'1778. The events did actually happen, although I'm not sure there's any provenance for the ghost story. Here we are.' With a flourish, their guide indicated a large, well-lit glass case containing various archaeological finds and many photographs. 'The ghost story's further along.'

'Thank you,' said Fran, 'this is just what we wanted.'

'Pleased to help,' beamed the guide and disappeared back the way they'd come.

Libby and Fran stood staring at the exhibition, daunted.

'I don't know where to start,' said Libby.

'At this end and work our way along,' said Fran.

In between the pieces of broken pottery and flint arrowheads were framed information pages in copperplate script. They learnt when the barrow had first been excavated, when it had been discovered to be a henge and finally, underneath a large photograph of what they recognised as the standing stone, a somewhat newer-looking page in plain Times New Roman told the story of the discovery of the stone and all its implications. There was no mention of any protests, for or against excavation, simply a statement that investigations were ongoing.

'But they aren't,' said Libby, as they stood back to survey the whole display case.

'No, but as soon as funding's available there will be.' Fran moved on to the smaller case.

'I know we've been considering this whole Bonny Henge thing as being a possible motive, but could it really? It seems so unlikely, unless Melanie stood in the way of funding somehow.' Libby peered into the second case. 'I like this Lady in White picture. Very Victorian.'

'I still think it's to do with her writing,' murmured Fran. 'Look at the highwayman!'

'Her writing? But she hadn't published anything for years. Still you were right about the drinking, so you might be right about this.'

'Thanks.' Fran made a face. 'Come on, look at this ghost story.'

In 1778, it appeared that the daughter of the owner of Rising Manor had slipped out at night to meet her highwayman lover on top of Bonny Henge, known then as Bonn Hill. Finding his body mutilated, she walked down from the hill, into the Manor, took one of her father's flintlock pistols and shot herself. The highwayman, one Peter Radcliffe, was later buried at a crossroads some way from the village, his lady, Margaret, the other side of the crossroads. Sightings of Lady Margaret had been reported from the mid-nineteenth century onwards.

'Trust the Victorians,' said Libby. 'I said it was a Victorian picture, didn't I?'

'You did. And what it's got to do with Melanie's murder I have no idea.' Fran stood back and sighed. 'In fact what anything's got to do with it I don't know.'

Libby looked at her uneasily. 'But you wanted to come down again. You said you wanted to go to a museum.'

'I know.' Fran sighed again. 'I don't know what's driving me on this one. I can't seem to see any connections with anything, and yet there's this certainty that there's something to find out.'

'Well, yes,' said Libby. 'A murderer, for one thing.'

Fran wandered back along the Bonny Henge case. 'And I thought there'd be more to find out about this. We already knew all this.'

'Come on then,' said Libby. 'We've still got well over an hour left. We can have a look at these rescued buildings. Get our fiver's worth.'

'Oh, yes, I owe you that,' said Fran. 'Yes. Let's go and look at buildings.'

Chapter Thirty

BACK AT THE BARLEY Mow, Fran and Libby retired to their rooms, ostensibly to rest and then get ready for dinner downstairs but, naturally enough, both switched on laptops.

Libby made herself a cup of tea from the hospitality tray, put her feet up on the bed and rested the laptop on a pillow.

'Do you know,' she said out loud to herself, 'I don't know why we're here, either. And I don't know what we're looking for. Or who.'

She sighed, took a sip of very hot tea and opened her email programme. To her surprise, there were three addressed to her persona at the Manor.

The first was from Paul Fisher.

Mrs Sarjeant, I apologise if I was less than polite when you called last week. I have since received visits from detectives and my car has been forensically examined, even though I informed the officers that I hadn't used it to go to the Manor. In fact, several of us met up at Victoria Station and shared a taxi when we reached Canterbury. I realise now that you were trying to be helpful. If you hear anything else about the investigation, I'd be very pleased if you let me know'

'Hmm,' thought Libby.

The next was from Bernice Weldon. Libby had to think for a moment to remember who she was.

Dear Mrs Sarjeant,
Last week Mrs Fran Wolfe rang my friend Audrey Glenister to tell us that Scotland Yard would be likely to investigate us over the death of Melanie Joseph. Both of us have subsequently been interviewed and even our cars are now being examined, though only mine was used to take us to the station. We arranged to meet up with Paul Fisher and Nick Forrest to share a taxi from Canterbury. I assume this is because it is thought that Mrs Joseph was transported in someone's car to The Manor? We can't seem to find out anything else, although we have been in touch with the other members of our little group by email, but some of them appear to have either left the group or not bothered to reply.
We wondered if you had heard anything more?
Best wishes
Bernice Weldon.

The last, most surprisingly, was from Dee Starkey.

I've got some information. Don't know who to go to. Scotland Yard detectives didn't seem to know much about the case. Is that one we saw at The Manor still in charge?

Libby hit reply.

'The Senior Investigating Officer is now DCI Connell, who is based in Kent but is currently in Dorset. I can tell him you are trying to get in touch, if you like.'

Libby slid off the bed and went to knock on Fran's door.

'Look,' she said, displaying the laptop screen.

Fran sat down on her own bed and read the emails.

'I've only replied to Dee, telling her I'll tell Ian she wants to get in touch. What do you think?'

Fran shook her head. 'No idea. What information can she have? And why didn't she tell anyone at the time?'

'Or when the Scotland Yard people went to see her?'

'She says they didn't seem to know about the case. I wonder if she tried to tell them? Or if she's only just realised she has information?' Fran looked back at the screen. 'Oh, hello! You've got another email.'

Dorset? Is he looking at Bonny Henge? Tell him I need to speak to him.'

'From Dee, look.' Libby sat beside Fran on the bed. 'Do we tell him?'

'I think so.' Fran reached for her mobile. 'Shall I send him a text? He'll be cross if his phone rings.'

'You do that and I'll reply to the other two,' said Libby.

She was just finishing off a reply to Bernice

Weldon when Fran's phone rang.

'Hello, Ian.' Fran put her thumb up at Libby. 'Yes, Libby got an email from Dee Starkey. Here, I'll hand you over.'

Libby took the phone. 'Ian? Yes Dee Starkey says she has some information for you. She guessed you were at Rising Parva and it seems urgent.'

'How did she "guess" I was in Rising Parva?' Ian's voice put the word in quotation marks.

'I'll read you her email and my reply.' Libby did so. 'Then she emailed back almost immediately: *Dorset? Is he looking at Bonny Henge? Tell him I need to speak to him.*'

Ian sighed. 'I suppose I should be grateful.'

'I expect she would have got in touch somehow,' said Libby. 'Oh, and I've had two of the other people on, both telling me their cars have been done over when they didn't even use them for the weekend.'

'I assume you mean forensically examined? Yes, I heard that. But then, none of those four people were ever seriously suspects, even though young Forrest lives in the area and is a journalist.'

'A *what*?' yelped Libby.

'A journalist.'

'He told us he never knew what was going on in the area,' said Libby, practically hyperventilating. 'He was *lying*!'

'It would appear so.' Ian sounded amused.

'I bet there's a connection, then,' said Libby. 'Why lie to us?'

'Or even to us?' said Ian.

'You don't seem bothered.'

'His car is being examined and his story looked at again, but I doubt very much if he has a motive. And if he left home early in the morning to go to Salisbury Station as he said, and met up with his friend Paul and the two ladies from Bournemouth in London, when could he have done it?'

'I still want to know why he lied,' said Libby.

'Perhaps to try and get a story out of you?' suggested Ian.

'Oh, bloody hell!' Libby exploded. Ian was openly laughing now. Fran carefully removed the laptop from her friend's lap.

'OK, OK, enough,' said Ian. 'Have you got this Starkey woman's phone number?'

'No. You'll have it, though.'

'Yes, I was just hoping to save time,' said Ian. 'Thanks for letting me know. Go carefully, now. Where are you going this evening?'

'Nowhere,' said Libby. 'We're eating here. And probably eating Nick Forrest, too, if he comes in.'

'Be gentle,' said Ian, and rang off.

Libby relayed the conversation.

'He could be some other sort of journalist,' said Fran. 'You know, for a trade magazine or something.'

'I thought all journalists kept an eye on the news,' said Libby. 'Especially local news.'

'You could ask Peter,' suggested Fran. 'He's quite a high flyer these days, isn't he? He'd know all about the business.'

'Yes, he does opinion pieces and guest editorial stuff. Political comment mostly.' Libby thought for a moment. 'I doubt if he'd know Nick's name though. I think our best bet's to corner the little blighter and make him talk.'

'You said he was nothing to do with it last Friday,' said Fran, handing back the laptop.

'I know. He's so innocent-looking. Doesn't look like a journalist.'

'Neither does Peter or Jane. Or even Campbell McLean.' Fran stood up.

'And I suppose they cover all aspects, don't they?' Libby also stood up, closing the laptop. 'Peter does the big stuff, Jane's on the local paper and Campbell's local TV news. Nick could be any one of those.'

'Or none,' said Fran, switching on her kettle. 'Have you had tea?'

'Bother,' said Libby. 'I left it getting cold in my room. See you later.'

Five minutes later she was back in Fran's room.

'Another email, look,' she said, turning the laptop to face Fran. 'And I didn't even know she had my email address.'

'Hello, Libby
I'm sorry if I was a bit abrupt on the phone. As you said, the police have come to take my car away for forensic testing. Lucky then that I have the use of the vet's van to get to and from work. It's very handy sometimes.
I hope you find out about Mrs Joseph's murder and why it happened. At least it can't be anything to do with us, can it? Will you let me know?
Best wishes

'Is it me, or does she sound anxious?' said Libby.

Fran was frowning again. 'Yes, she does, but as I said before, it's probably the stress of being investigated. We'll get in touch if there's anything we *can* tell her.'

At six thirty Libby knocked on Fran's door again.

'Going down?' she asked.

'Coming.' Fran picked up her handbag and phone. 'Did you do any more research after the emails?'

'No.' Libby led the way downstairs. 'I couldn't think what to do. I don't know what we're doing here either, now. Or who we're investigating.'

'No more do I.' Fran sighed. 'I really hoped there'd be something more in the museum.'

'But what?' Libby held open the door to the bar.

'I don't know.'

They went to the bar, where they were served by a different handmaiden who wore a similarly unfortunate skirt. Taking their drinks and a menu to a table by a window, they prepared to stake out the main entrance in case Nick Forrest appeared.

'Meanwhile,' said Libby, sipping her wine, 'try and think what it is you thought we ought to find at the museum.'

Fran leaned her elbows on the table, frowning. 'I really don't know. I expected to find something that was a revelation; something that would connect Melanie to it and explain why someone would have murdered her for that connection.'

'I wonder why they all said they didn't know her or where they lived?' mused Libby. 'What did Daniel say? He, Lily and Dee knew. Well, we knew Dee did.'

'There's got to be a connection,' said Fran, banging her glass on the table. 'There's just got to be. Why is it there all the time?'

'Er – eh?' Libby was startled.

'I mean, it's constantly in my head. And Jennifer wanted us – me – to come down to see it. Why?

'Don't ask me. I'm just being nosy, like always. Come on, what do you want to eat?'

When they had both chosen local beef and ale pie, Libby returned to the subject.

'Now, writing. It was a writing weekend. Melanie couldn't have come because she wanted to learn to write a novel, because this was a reunion, but perhaps she genuinely wanted to come to be with her husband?'

'Rubbish. In that case, why not come with him? And why use an alias? We know the name's genuinely hers, so Patrick would have known it.'

'OK, that's got that out of the way. So what did she write? Non-fiction? Do you think she wrote about the henge? Or the ghost?'

'Might have done,' said Fran. 'We can look that up tomorrow. I'm not going upstairs to get a laptop now.'

'No, and anyway,' said Libby, 'look who's just come in.'

She was beside Nick Forrest before he even had time to order his drink. She beamed impartially at both him and the barmaid and said 'I'll get this.'

Looking surprised, but not nervous, Nick allowed himself to be conducted to the table where Fran sat smiling at him.

'I didn't expect you two back here so soon,' he said. 'Cheers.'

'We didn't think we would be, either,' said Libby. 'But then, neither did we know we'd been talking to a journalist.'

Libby had hoped he would choke on his beer, or something equally theatrical, but disappointingly, he just sighed.

'I suppose it was too much to hope for,' he said, 'that you wouldn't find out.'

'Well, of course we would,' said Libby. 'We have police contacts, remember.'

'I know. I've been reading up on you both since last Friday.' He took a long swallow of his beer.

'Reading up – oh, the internet.' Fran shook her head. 'I forget that other people can look us up as well as the other way round. Although I'm surprised that there's anything about us on there.'

'You *would* be surprised,' said Nick.

'Someone else said that recently,' said Libby. 'But apparently our cases get reported in the local press and then it goes online.'

Fran laughed. 'Our cases? That makes us sound important.'

'Oh, you know what I meant,' said Libby, 'the cases we've been involved with, then.'

'So you're actually working this case, are you?' Nick looked from one to the other.

'Why don't you tell us instead, young Forrest, why you didn't tell us you were a journalist and why you lied about having no knowledge of anything that went on in the area.' Libby sat back and picked up her wine, ready for a good story.

'I wasn't sure what you were doing down here last week, and I thought if I told you who I was – or what I was, more accurately – you'd never tell me anything. So I shut up. I thought I might get something out of it, but I didn't.'

'How do you mean, you didn't?' asked Fran.

'I work for a regional newspaper, yes, but I'm actually a music journalist. I freelance for some of the London mags and do interviews and reviews at the local level. I rarely get involved in news material, but you're right, of course, I couldn't fail to be unaware that Melanie Joseph was involved with Bonny Henge. But I really didn't know they lived in Rising.'

'You said you didn't get anything out of it – us. What did you mean?' asked Libby.

'I was hoping I could get a bit of a local scoop. Even if it wasn't my field, my editor would have been quite pleased if I had. But you didn't tell me anything, really. Except that Patrick lived at Rising Parva, and they wouldn't have published that under the circumstances. We're quite a caring lot, actually.'

'No door-stepping?' said Fran.

'No. Or even phone hacking!' He grinned mischievously. 'But I realised, when I looked you up, with your police contacts you'd know what I did as soon as I was mentioned. I take it you did report on our meeting?'

'Yes,' said Libby, 'of course. And on our

meeting with Patrick, and Daniel.'

'You saw Patrick?' Nick looked surprised.

'Yes. Briefly.' Fran didn't expand further.

'And Daniel.' Nick looked down at his beer. 'Well, well, well.'

Fran and Libby waited.

'OK, what did that mean?' asked Libby eventually.

'It explains why he rang me on Saturday evening and threatened me.'

Chapter Thirty-one

'HE *WHAT*?' SAID FRAN and Libby together.

'I couldn't understand what he was on about at first.' Nick shook his head and finished his pint. 'Before I say any more, can I get you two another drink?'

By the time Nick was back with three more drinks, Fran's and Libby's meals had arrived.

'Are you eating here?' asked Libby, knife and fork poised.

'No, I've already eaten,' said Nick. 'You carry on.'

'We were going to,' said Libby. 'Go on, then, tell us about Daniel.'

'I'm not sure I should, really,' sighed Nick. 'It seems like telling tales, but I've mentioned it now, so I suppose I'll have to.

'Last year at the writers' holiday Daniel started out quite friendly. Not as grumpy as he seems now. But gradually he realised that no one was looking up to him and he was considered just as much of a beginner as the rest of us.'

'Except you aren't,' said Fran. 'And if you're a music journalist, why didn't we find any mention of you on the net?'

'Because I don't write under my own name. Reviewers often have a pseudonym to protect them – especially music reviewers. Some of the fans can be a trifle – well, let's just say vocal.

'Anyway, Daniel decided he would confide his

annoyances to me one night when we'd been drinking in the bar. I'd been with Paul, but he'd already gone up to his room, and I was very surprised when Daniel came to sit with me.' He stopped and stared down at the table.

'He made a pass at you?' suggested Fran, gently. Libby looked at her, astonished.

Nick looked up and gave her a quick smile. 'How did you know?'

'He's so aggressively homophobic.' Fran returned to her pie. 'And he mentioned something about you and Paul when we saw him. It was that which led to our disagreement with him.'

'Ah.' Nick sat contemplating his drink until someone hailed him from the bar. He waved back, but didn't move.

'What was your disagreement with him?' he said eventually. 'What happened?'

'We asked to speak to him at this place where he was doing Live Lit –'

'Oh, God,' said Nick.

'Yes,' said Libby. 'And he then accused you and Paul of being gay, us of being gay and then his two female helpers, who are, in fact, a couple, slapped his face and took us for a drink.'

'Succinctly put,' applauded Fran. 'That's it, essentially, Nick. So why did he threaten you?'

'Why do you think? He was obviously very upset about something, and very flustered. He just threatened to damage my career if I ever told anyone about what had happened between us. Oh, and tell everyone about Paul and me.'

'Oh?' Libby raised an eyebrow.

Nick sighed again. 'It's hardly a secret. On the holiday Paul and I got together, and the night Daniel came on to me his line was now that Paul had left me on my own I'd need someone else.' He shuddered. 'He was so insulting. It made me creep.'

'We thought he was wrong,' said Libby. 'Sorry.'

'That's all right, but I thought you would have spotted it, not that any of us go round advertising as so many people think we do.'

'Why me?' said Libby.

'Your friends who supplied the lovely Mexican food. You seem close to them.'

'So you thought my gaydar would be finely tuned?' Libby laughed. 'It is usually.'

'So how would Daniel damage your career?' asked Fran.

'He was going to publish my real name on all the music fan sites for one thing. And, presumably, on Twitter and Facebook. Despite his public disapproval of social networking, I know he uses them. I've had a look and seen what he puts up there.'

'Hell hath no fury,' said Libby.

'Yes, it was a bit like that,' said Nick. 'Anyway, he was just about as nasty as possible. Left a very unpleasant taste. I rang Paul and told him and we decided to ignore him, but I didn't know what it was that had upset him in the first place. I do now.'

'Do you think,' said Fran, pushing her empty plate away, 'that he is nasty enough to have done something to Melanie to hurt Patrick?'

'Yes, I think he is, but he'd have been far more likely to have hurt Patrick, and I don't think it would have been physical. More like a smear campaign.'

'He did know where Patrick lived, he admitted it,' said Libby. 'He said he, Lily Cooper and Dee knew. I assume through *Writers in the South*.'

'They seem to be very free with giving out private information,' said Nick, a little huffily.

'Good job for us,' said Libby. 'Although Ian will have all the names and addresses now, anyway.'

'Ian?' queried Nick.

'Our favourite DCI,' said Libby. 'Ian Connell.'

'Oh, yes. He called me about the car.'

'Well, now we've cleared that up,' said Fran, observing that Nick looked thoroughly deflated, 'do you want to go and join your friends?' She nodded towards the bar.

'Not really.' He gave her a sad little grin.

'Another drink, then?' Fran stood up.

'No, let me –'

'No, you bought the last one,' said Libby. 'Come on, you look fed up now. Sorry if we've brought up things you would rather have not thought about.'

'That's OK.' Nick shrugged. 'Paul and I still see one another, though not as much as we would like. Last weekend was a bit of a bonus. Except for Daniel. Bloody creep.'

'Hey!' Libby was struck by a thought. 'Last weekend. You and Paul were in Hoppers' Huts four and six, with Melanie between you. Didn't you – um –' she paused.

'Spend the night together?' Nick smiled. 'Yes, of course we did. It was when Paul was going back to his hut he found the body.' He made a face.

'Horrible.'

'Ah! I wondered why it was so early,' said Libby, as Fran came back to the table.

'What was early?' she asked. Libby explained.

'And you didn't hear anything except the car?' said Fran.

'Nothing. Why?'

Fran and Libby looked at one another. Fran gave the slightest of nods.

'If you haven't gathered already,' said Libby, 'the police think Melanie was already dead when she arrived at the Manor, and someone set up the room to look as if she'd been there. She also booked in under an alias, but the evidence in the room showed who she really was. Where the body was until it was dumped near the huts we don't know.'

'You mean we could have been next door to a dead body all night?' Nick looked horror-struck.

'What difference would it make if it was in the hut or outside?' asked Fran.

'None I suppose.' Now he looked uncomfortable. 'So they want to check the cars – I guessed why – but I didn't even take my car. What was the alias?'

'Can we tell him that?' asked Libby.

'Probably not,' said Fran. 'So tell us. Last week you knew nothing about Melanie and little about anything going on in the area.'

'Except Bonny Henge,' he said defensively.

'Except Bonny Henge. But now you can tell us what else you know about the area, in case there's anything we could use.'

'Use?'

'Tell our friendly policeman,' said Libby.

'I think you've probably got everything I know by now.' He heaved another sigh. 'Daniel is a pain in the backside – whoops!' He grinned. 'I didn't mean that. Jennifer – well, you've seen yourself what Jennifer's like.'

'Don't tell me you knew Jennifer, too?' said Libby.

'Only because of the writers' holiday. And of course, she lives in Rising Parva, too, doesn't she? It looked to me as if she was very protective of Patrick, even when I didn't know they'd known one another before. She's a journo, too.'

'Yes, we know, but wants to write fiction. Funny, isn't it, that so many of you on that course were already published elsewhere?'

'Often the case. Sometimes, people don't consider you a proper writer until you've had a novel published.'

'Our friend Rosie says that,' said Libby.

'Rosie?'

'Amanda George. You met her.'

'Ah, right. So what exactly are the police looking for?'

'Not sure we can tell you any more,' said Fran warily.

'Let me have a guess then?' He leant forward, looking like an eager puppy.

'Go on then,' said Libby, 'but we might not tell you if you're right or wrong.'

He frowned in concentration for a moment. 'Right. If Melanie was dead before she was taken to the Manor – oh, hang on. Perhaps she wasn't. Was she taken there alive and then stabbed?'

Fran and Libby didn't look at one another.

'We – they – don't think so,' said Libby.

'Right. So whoever took her knew her, or her habits. And there was a lot of her stuff in the hut, was there?'

They nodded.

'So whoever it was could get into the house in Rising Parva and knew where to find stuff. Or – no, they could get into the house and just go through all the rooms to find stuff that looked right.'

'You've forgotten that it had to be someone who knew she was intending to go to the weekend,' said Fran.

'So it had to be someone who she knew well!' said Nick in triumph. 'So it must be Jennifer!'

'Must it?' said Fran.

'Well, no one else knew her, did they?'

'Most people have said they didn't know her, or where she and Patrick lived, but so far we haven't any real proof of that,' said Libby. 'Patrick isn't admitting to knowing any of the guests better than the others.'

'Except the ones he went to bed with,' said Nick.

'Dee and Lily,' said Fran.

'He tried it on with Nina, too, but I don't think he got very far.'

'She says he didn't,' said Libby.

'So you've got to find out first who took their cars to Kent. That rules out Paul, me, Audrey and Bernice.'

'Dee lives in London, so I can't see her driving all the way down here, can you? And she doesn't strike me as the sort of person Melanie would have known.' Libby sipped her wine. 'Socially, I mean.'

'Nina drove, but she's even more unlikely,' said Fran. 'I thought at first she'd come with Jennifer, but apparently not.'

'You see?' said Nick. 'It all points to Jennifer.'

'I'm still not convinced of that,' said Libby, 'even though it looks most likely.'

'Are you sure it isn't anything to do with the time of her life that she spent in government – or advising it?' asked Nick.

'Certainly could be, but it doesn't alter the fact,' said Libby cheerfully, 'that someone still had to kill her and take her there, knowing where she lived and knowing what she planned to do. It had to be someone who knew her, and knew about the Manor. So if wasn't a guest at your weekend do, someone had to get in and out of the Manor grounds at least twice without us seeing them.'

'Twice?' Nick raised his eyebrows.

'Once to sign her in. Do you remember, I came in and asked if everybody was there on the Friday night? That was because she – or who she was pretending to be – had been ticked off on my clipboard and the keys to her hut had gone. Then to dump the body. We don't know at what time the scene in the hut was stage-managed.'

'Very complicated.' Nick frowned. 'Someone had it planned thoroughly, didn't he, or she?'

'Yes, and that's really all we know at the moment,' said Fran. 'We came down here to see if we could find out about who she knew, or how she lived, but we haven't been very successful so far.'

'Well, you found me and Daniel last week,' said

Nick. 'That was fairly successful.'

'So,' said Fran, 'to get back to what you know about the area. You know about Bonny Henge. What exactly do you know about it?'

'Used to be Bonny Barrow, and then some years ago they decided it was a henge. Then a year or so ago they found a standing stone and think there might be more up there. It's a small henge with probably only one entrance. And there are groups who want to protect it and groups who want to excavate it. Oh, and there's the White Lady of Rising Parva.' He grinned. 'Not exactly scientific fact.'

'You know a lot more than you let on,' said Libby.

'I know, and I'm sorry, but none of that helps find who killed Melanie Joseph, does it?'

'I suppose not, but it's interesting that you know all that. Because if you know it, so must the others,' said Fran.

'Only if they live in the area,' said Nick. 'But you can find out all about the White Lady wherever you are.'

'On the internet, yes,' said Libby doubtfully.

'Oh, no, I didn't mean that. I meant the book about her. Fictionalised, of course, but I think it sold quite well. By someone called Ann Marsh.'

Chapter Thirty-two

SILENCE. NICK LOOKED FROM Fran to Libby and back. 'What did I say?'

Libby cleared her throat. 'Just a bit of a shock, that's all.'

'I said it was to do with writing,' muttered Fran.

'Sorry – what?' Nick peered at Fran, who deliberately picked up her wine and took a large swallow.

'Nothing,' said Libby. 'Tell me, Nick, have you read it? How did you come to hear of it?'

'It was in all the local bookshops and anywhere that could possibly sell books. I expect they've got it over the road. I've never read it.'

'You mean in Chancery House?' said Fran. 'We didn't see it and we asked about Rising Parva. The guide even showed us the exhibit for the White Lady.'

'Well, maybe they haven't any longer, but you'd find it online.' Nick picked up his glass. 'Come on, what's this about?'

'You're a journalist,' said Fran. 'You already know more about the case than you possibly should, and we're certainly not going to give you any more.'

'You knew the name.' Nick narrowed his eyes. 'Didn't you? Ann Marsh? Who is she?'

'She's – connected to the case,' said Libby. 'But we're not going to tell you how.'

'Why?'

'Because we will have to tell the police what

you've told us and we would get into serious trouble if we said any more,' said Fran.

'I could tell them myself.' Nick sat back, looking belligerent.

'OK, that would be great,' said Libby with relief.

'Oh.' Nick frowned. 'Well, actually what would I say?'

'There's a book about the White Lady of Bonny Henge written by someone called Ann Marsh. That's what you told us.' Fran was becoming brisk.

Nick sighed. 'OK, you can do it.'

'Gee, thanks,' grumbled Libby.

'Look, I don't know the significance, do I? So why would I report it? No, it's better that you two do it.' He pushed his chair back. 'And now, if you don't mind, I will go and join my mates. Thanks for the drinks.'

'And thanks for the information,' said Fran. 'I expect we'll see you again.'

'Not if he sees us first,' said Libby, as Nick was absorbed into the group at the bar.

Fran got up. 'I'm going to look that book up online. Coming?'

'No, I'm going to go outside and have a cigarette. I'll follow you.'

'Aren't you interested? This is the most fascinating thing we've discovered so far.'

'Of course I'm interested, but it'll wait for twenty minutes, won't it?'

Fran sighed. 'All right. See you in a bit.'

Libby took her drink to one of the tables outside. It was still quite light, although she could see lamps coming on in some of the houses round the green.

She lit her cigarette and rested her elbows on the table, trying to make sense of what they'd just learnt. If Melanie Joseph had written a book about her local ghost under the name of Ann Marsh, what exactly did it mean? And did it matter? She knew Fran was convinced that it did, because she'd had the feeling Melanie's murder was to do with writing, but to Libby's non-writerly brain it didn't add up.

'Still got the dreadful habit, I see,' said a voice, and Libby nearly spilt her wine.

'Ian!' She looked up at him and saw DS Wallingford hovering behind looking uncomfortable. 'Is this an official visit?'

'No, I'm not going to arrest you. Where's Fran?'

Libby opened her mouth, shut it again and grinned. 'There!' she said as Fran appeared from the door of the pub, laptop in hand.

'Ian – what are you doing here?' she said.

'Lovely welcome from both of you, I must say. I'm off duty, and I knew you were here, so I dragged poor Barry here along as driver.'

'If you're off duty, perhaps you won't want to see this then,' said Fran.

Ian cast his eyes up. 'Great. But let me get a drink, first.'

'Nick Forrest's in there,' warned Libby.

'Is he? Would I be right in thinking he helped you to whatever information you think you've got for me?'

Libby nodded.

'Well, it doesn't matter for the moment because he and I have never met. You can introduce me later. What can I get you to drink?'

Libby had another glass of wine, but Fran, always more sensible, declined and Ian went into the pub followed by DS Wallingford.

'What is it?' said Libby, when they'd gone.

'Here.' Fran turned the laptop screen, and there was the cover of a book, with the same ghostly picture they had seen earlier that day at Chancery House, superimposed over a traditionally dark silhouette of an isolated house.

Libby scrolled down to the description of the book, which appeared to be a gothic time slip novel based around the legend of the White Lady. There was nothing about the author, and when Libby clicked on the name nothing more came up.

'Look, it only came out six months ago,' Fran said. 'It's got to have something to do with her murder.'

Ian and Barry Wallingford appeared carrying drinks and sat down on the benches either side of the table.

'So what is it?' Ian asked, after his first pull at his pint. Fran turned the laptop screen towards him.

'I don't see –' he began, frowning. 'Oh, Ann Marsh. So?'

'The book's about the local ghost who walks from the henge to Rising Manor. And it only came out six months ago.' Libby shrugged. 'I don't know what it means, either, but Fran's sure it means something.'

'It's got to be Melanie. I know Ann Marsh isn't an unusual name,' said Fran, 'but as it's about her local legend it's got to be her. Although she's only written non-fiction before, and this is very much in the romantic-gothic genre.'

'We were both surprised when we heard,' said Libby, 'because it was such a coincidence, but I don't see that it has anything to do with her murder.'

'And how did you hear?' asked Barry Wallingford, making them all jump.

'Nick Forrest,' said Fran. 'He brought us here when we came down before, and after you'd told us he was a journalist we rather hijacked him when he came in this evening. He admitted he knew slightly more about the people and set-up than he'd told us before and then said that anyone could find out about the White Lady because of the book written about her. The name rather took us by surprise.'

Ian's face darkened. 'You didn't tell him why?'

'No, of course not. Do you want to talk to him yourself?'

'I suppose I ought to.' Ian frowned at the laptop screen. 'Did he tell you anything else?' He turned to Wallingford. 'This is all off the record, Barry, but they've been very helpful in the past. Not that I expected anything this evening.'

'I recognised Mrs Sarjeant's name when I first went to the Manor.' He grinned at Libby. 'Then I realised why you'd backed off the case.'

'Didn't do me much good, did it? Go on then, did this Forrest tell you anything else?'

Libby and Fran told him about Daniel's threat and the background to it.

'That didn't make sense, either,' said Libby. 'Why would Daniel threaten Nick just because we'd been to see him?'

'He thought Nick would reveal all,' said Fran. 'I can see how he worked it out. He knew we were working our way through the members of the writing weekend, and if we told anyone about how he'd behaved towards us, someone else might agree and wade in with their own story. And Nick did.'

'The other thing was,' said Libby, 'and I don't suppose he'll thank me for telling you this, he and Paul Fisher spent the night together in Nick's hut. It was when Paul was going back to his own that he found the body.'

'That was why it was so early,' said Barry Wallingford.

'Just what I said.' Libby beamed at him. 'So, do you want to talk to Nick?'

Ian and Barry looked at each other. Barry nodded.

'I suppose so,' said Ian. 'One of you point him out to me.' He stood up.

'I'll go and fetch him,' said Fran. 'It would be kinder.'

'All right, but you two are not – repeat *not* – sitting in on the interview.'

'OK, boss,' grinned Libby, and collecting the laptop and her glass, stood up.

'No,' said Ian, 'you stay here. We'll go to one of those tables over there.' He indicated the green, just as Fran arrived with a bewildered-looking Nick.

'DCI Connell, Mr Forrest,' said Ian holding out his hand. 'And this is DS Wallingford, whom I believe you've already met.'

'What's this about? The book? I don't know anything about it.' Nick shook Ian's hand as if it might turn into a snake.

'Just come over here, Mr Forrest,' said Ian, 'and we'll explain. Nothing to worry about. Can I borrow the laptop, Fran?'

The three men walked across the green, while Libby and Fran watched.

'What do you suppose Ian will ask him?" said Libby.

'Why he didn't say he and Paul were together that night, I expect, and what he knows about the book.'

'But that was such a throw-away remark, when he mentioned the name,' said Libby. 'He doesn't know anything about it.'

'He might know more than he thinks,' said Fran slowly.

'Eh?' Libby turned to stare at her friend. 'Not another "moment"?'

'No.' Fran shook her head. 'I just wondered – oh, it's too far-fetched to be possible.'

'Go on, what? You can't leave it like that.'

'No, it's daft.' Fran looked across at the three men on the green. 'I'll wait until they come back and ask Nick then.'

'That's not fair,' said Libby.

Fran shrugged. 'You'll hear then, won't you? If I tell you now, you'll tell me how bonkers it is and then I won't ask.'

Libby harrumphed and lit another cigarette.

Ten minutes later, by which time darkness had fallen, Nick walked back towards them between Ian and Barry Wallingford.

'Nick,' said Fran, as he approached. He looked at

her without hostility, which quite surprised Libby.

'I was wondering,' continued Fran, while Ian and Barry Wallingford stood aside looking as baffled as Libby, 'if, when you went on that writers' holiday, you knew what your fellow delegates' books were about?'

'Books?' Nick looked baffled now, too.

'Sorry, the manuscripts you'd submitted to Patrick before the course.'

'Well, they weren't books, only ten pages or so with a synopsis.'

'Were any of them finished?'

'I don't know. Mine wasn't, and Paul's wasn't. Not sure about the others.'

'Didn't you discuss them during Patrick's course?'

'Yes, we had to read out a part of what we'd submitted and discuss it, each of us in turn. We didn't all do it on the same day.'

Fran leant forward. 'And do you remember what any of them were about?'

Nick looked startled. 'No – well not properly. I remember Daniel's – it was about someone going to have a sex change in Singapore.' Nick wrinkled his nose. 'Ironic, in a way.'

'Fran, I hate to interrupt,' said Ian, 'but can you tell us what you're getting at?'

'I was just wondering,' said Fran, going a bit pink, 'if any of the books submitted to Patrick were a time slip novel about the White Lady of Bonny Henge.'

Chapter Thirty-three

EVERYONE LOOKED AT FRAN. Then everyone looked at Nick, who was gaping.

'What made you think of that?' said Ian. 'What books submitted?'

Libby explained, as Nick seemed incapable of speech.

'But I don't think there were any,' he said when Libby had finished.

'Any romances?' asked Fran.

'No obvious ones that I remember,' he said slowly. 'We were all supposed to have submitted something in Patrick's genre, but he did say several would fit other genres better.'

'And you would only have heard short pieces from each read out?' said Libby.

Ian and Barry Wallingford were listening with puzzled interest.

'Exactly,' said Nick, 'so I don't know. Can I go now?'

'Yes, sorry,' said Fran, looking in the light from the pub windows even pinker. Nick disappeared and the two policemen sat down.

'Right – what was that about?' asked Ian.

'I told Libby I thought it was daft,' said Fran, 'but I just wondered when I realised what the book was about if Melanie had pinched the idea from one of the writers who submitted to Patrick.'

'But why would any of the writers have written about the ghost of Rising Parva?' asked Libby.

'It still wouldn't be worth killing for,' said Ian. 'If somebody had a real grievance it would be better to fight it out in court, surely.'

'No would-be writer could afford that,' said Fran.

'Anyway,' said Libby, 'the manuscripts were submitted to Patrick, not Melanie.'

'She could have seen them,' said Fran. 'Jennifer said she helped Patrick.'

'I don't see how it helps to find her killer,' said Ian.

'No,' said Fran. 'Sorry. I said it was daft.'

'What about Dee Starkey?' asked Libby. 'Did you get hold of her?'

'No, I had to leave a message. If you feel like it you could email her again and tell her I've tried to speak to her. If it's as urgent as she told you it was she'll ring either you or me.'

'Nina emailed, too,' said Libby. 'She seemed a bit anxious.'

'I don't think they've found any forensics in her car,' said Ian, 'although I haven't had a full report on it.'

'You know,' said Fran slowly, 'she could easily be the person who wrote about The White Lady. She's a romance fan, isn't she?'

'So's Jennifer,' said Libby, 'and she's far more likely to have written about a ghost in her home village. Anyway, we don't know that Melanie stole the idea from anybody.'

The subject was dropped and the evening slid easily into a mildly enjoyable social occasion, but as Ian and Wallingford stood to leave, Fran said, 'Is there any way we could ask for copies of those manuscripts?'

Ian frowned. 'I can't see why, and they'd have been destroyed by now, wouldn't they?'

'Not by the writers,' said Fran with a small smile.

'Would Joseph have kept copies?' asked Wallingford.

'No, but he might have kept copies of his critiques,' said Libby. 'Is it worth asking?'

Ian sighed. 'We're seeing him tomorrow again. We've had people going through his house. I'll mention it.'

'Is he a suspect then?' said Libby.

'Of course he is.' Ian looked surprised. 'The most obvious one.'

'But we don't think he did it, do we?' said Libby, as she and Fran climbed the stairs to go back to their rooms.

'I don't know. The police can't have thought so, or they would have been questioning him much more thoroughly than they have done. There must have been some reason not to suspect him in the beginning.'

'I suppose so.' Libby halted outside her door. 'So what made you think about Melanie pinching that idea?'

'I kept thinking about her writing. It was the only thing that made any sense.' She shrugged. 'But even that didn't make sense, either.'

'I have to agree with Ian,' said Libby. 'I can't see that killing someone who had pinched your idea would make sense. You'd want a fight in the open, so you could claim it for your own and perhaps make some money from it.'

'I know.' Fran sighed. 'The only people with any kind of real motive are Patrick, Jennifer because she was jealous of Melanie, and Lily Cooper for the same reason. And Lily didn't know her well enough to meet up with her and give her ketamine before the weekend. Well, didn't know her at all, in fact.'

'Let's sleep on it,' said Libby. 'Then tomorrow we'll track down a copy of the White Lady, or whatever it's called.'

The next morning they were served breakfast in a small private parlour behind the bar.

'I looked that book up last night,' said Libby, pouring tea. 'It's actually called *Rising Lady*.'

'So did I,' said Fran, 'and it does actually look quite good. It's got lots of five-star reviews.'

'We'll go and find a bookshop, shall we? I don't want to spend another entrance fee at Chancery House.'

It appeared that neither of them wanted to talk about Melanie Joseph's murder that morning and instead they went to Salisbury in search of bookshops.

It wasn't hard to find one, nor was it hard to find many Patrick Josephs on the shelves. It was harder to track down Ann Marsh, but Libby eventually found *Rising Lady* in General Fiction.

'No photograph,' said Fran, as they pored over it.

'And a very sparse biog,' said Libby. 'Are we going to buy it?'

'It would be cheaper online,' said Fran.

'Oh, come on, Fran! If everybody did that we wouldn't have any real bookshops,' said Libby. 'Besides, I can't wait all that time to read it. I'll buy it. Blimey!'

'What?'

'Look – a cover quote from Patrick Joseph!'

'That seals it, then,' said Fran, taking the book from Libby and marching towards the till.

They found a cafe with tables outside in the sunshine and sat down to read the first few pages of *Rising Lady* together.

'I can't believe Jennifer didn't know about this,' said Libby, after a waitress had delivered their coffee. 'They must have publicised it in Rising Parva. In all the Risings.'

'You'd think so,' agreed Fran. 'After all, somebody must have noticed it somewhere, or it might have caught someone's eye online.'

'If they were trying to keep her identity quiet they wouldn't want to publicise it locally,' said Libby.

'But they've got it in Chancery House, Nick thought.'

'We don't know they have,' said Libby, 'and, as I said last night, you'd have thought the lady there would have told us if it was, especially as they had this drawing displayed.'

'Perhaps they actively kept it away from the area,' said Fran.

'Which argues that there is something dodgy about it.'

'It's all supposition,' said Fran, leaning back and pushing the book away from her. 'I don't know why

I'm bothered about it.'

'Neither do I, but it's intriguing,' said Libby, picking up the book and reading a few more lines. 'In fact, so's the book. I'm looking forward to it.'

'Lily Cooper lives here,' said Fran, staring down the street as though expecting to see the woman appear.

'So she does.' Libby put the book down. 'Were you intending to call on her?'

'Just saying. It's actually much closer to the Risings than I thought.'

'Has she jumped to the top of the list?'

Fran sighed. 'I don't know. I can see her killing Melanie by accident if she and Patrick had been discovered, but not with this sort of deliberation. Someone really wanted Melanie out of the way permanently.'

'So why would that be?' Libby looked resigned. 'She must have been a threat to someone.'

'Sorry, Libby.' Fran gave her friend a smile. 'I know I'm being a pain.'

'I don't know if we're trying to find things out or not, frankly,' said Libby. 'I think we might just as well go home again.'

'All right.'

Libby looked surprised. 'Really?'

'Just let's go to Rising Parva once more and show Jennifer this book.'

'Ian might not like us going if he's there,' said Libby doubtfully.

'We'll call him. But let's call Jennifer first in case she's not home.'

'We're going now?'

'Why not? And we can always have lunch in the pub there again.'

Jennifer was in, and though surprised to hear from Fran, said yes, she would meet them at the pub in half an hour.

'Poor Patrick's had the police in the house for two days,' she said. 'I've been taking him meals. And they've been all over my car, too.'

'Not pleasant, is it?' said Fran. 'Thanks, Jennifer, we'll see you in half an hour.'

'Do you realise,' said Libby, as they finished their coffee, 'we've met Jennifer three times in her home village, yet we've never been to her house.'

'I don't think that's particularly remarkable,' said Fran. 'I know lots of people quite well who've never been to my house.' She picked up her phone again. 'Better tell Ian where we'll be.'

But Ian's phone went straight to voicemail, and Libby and Fran decided not to call his official phone as it could quite easily, as he had told them before, impede an investigation.

Rising Parva looked much as it had every other time they'd been there. If the police had a presence there, it was out of sight, presumably at Patrick's house.

Jennifer had not arrived, so they sat on a bench outside the pub and waited for her.

'I wonder what she'll say,' said Libby, who held the book face down on her lap.

'That's what we're here for,' said Fran. 'To find out. Look, here she comes.'

Jennifer, summery in pale blue linen, with her hair loose, approached from the direction of the henge with Herald, who waved his plumed tail and beamed at them.

'Hi!' she said. 'Nice to see you again.' There was a faint question in her voice.

'We just wanted to ask you something,' said Fran. 'Do you want to go inside? We're going to have lunch here, but we can stay here if you like.'

'No, here's fine.' Jennifer allowed Herald to have a drink at the dog bowl and sat down on the bench beside Libby.

'We asked you about Melanie's writing,' said Fran, 'and you said you didn't take much notice. But we thought you must have known about this.'

Libby held out *Rising Lady* and watched Jennifer's face turn white. Her hand fluttered up to her chest and her eyes went frantically from Fran to Libby and back.

'You obviously did know,' said Libby, putting the book back in her lap. 'And it's equally obviously important.'

Jennifer sat in silence for so long that Herald padded over, whined and put his head on her knee. Fran leant across Libby and put her hand on Jennifer's arm.

'Would you like a drink? Water? Brandy?'

Jennifer shook her head and seemed to break the spell. 'No – I – I think I'd like tea.'

'I'll go and ask,' said Libby. 'Milk?'

When Libby had gone inside the silence fell again, only now Jennifer was rhythmically stroking Herald's head.

'They'll bring tea out,' said Libby. 'I didn't know what to order you Fran.' She sat down and looked expectant.

'I don't know where to start.' Jennifer continued looking down at Herald.

'Can you confirm that Ann Marsh is – or was – Melanie Joseph?' asked Fran.

'Yes.' Jennifer almost whispered.

'And you knew it?'

'Yes.'

'So what about this book?' asked Libby, getting impatient. Just then Jennifer's tea was brought out and set on a wrought-iron table.

'The book?' prompted Fran.

'I – er – I helped her with it.'

'Honestly!' said Libby, exasperated. 'Why haven't you told anybody this before?'

'It didn't seem relevant.' Jennifer cleared her throat and reached out for her mug.

'But it means you must have known her much better than you allowed people to think,' said Fran. 'You could hold the clue as to why she was murdered.'

'No,' whispered Jennifer, shaking her head.

'Tell us why this has upset you so much,' said Libby, 'and why, come to think of it, you thought no one would find out?'

'Why should they?' said Jennifer, looking up.

'Somebody would have come across this book, just as we did,' said Fran. 'And from there it would have been a short step to asking the police to get hold of the publishers and find out who the author was. An author who's just been murdered, so this is quite relevant.'

'But no one would have known I helped,' said

Jennifer, her eyes returning to the book.

'No, neither would we, but you gave yourself away.' Libby sighed deeply. 'There must be some reason this has frightened you.'

Jennifer drank some of her tea.

'Look, Jennifer,' said Fran, 'I'm really sorry for you, but you must see that your closeness to Melanie means you'll be able to help the police. DCI Connell's here in Rising Parva now, so –'

'He's with Patrick. I can't talk to him,' Jennifer interrupted.

'Oh, come *on*, Jennifer!' said Libby. 'What is it? Why is the fact that you helped Jennifer write it so worrying?'

'Because,' Jennifer drew herself upright in her seat and put the mug on the table, 'because I didn't help her. She helped me. This is my book. She stole it.'

Chapter Thirty-four

THOUGHTS AND SUSPICIONS TUMBLED over one another in Libby's mind, thoughts that were mirrored in Fran's face. Jennifer stood up.

'Where are you going?' said Libby.

'Home,' said Jennifer.

Fran picked up Herald's lead. 'Not yet,' she said.

'You know perfectly well we'll only send the police to see you,' said Libby. 'So be reasonable and tell us all about it. We'll see if we can help.'

'You can't help,' said Jennifer, but she sat down again.

'Alcohol might,' said Libby. 'I'm going to get you a glass of wine. I'm driving, so I'll have a shandy. You, Fran?'

When Libby had gone, Fran handed Herald's lead back to Jennifer, who took it but didn't move.

'How much does Patrick know about this?' asked Fran.

'Most of it,' said Jennifer.

'And he's said nothing to the police?' Fran was frowning. 'Why on earth not?'

'To protect me, probably,' said Jennifer, although she didn't look convinced.

Libby came back with the drinks and sat down on another bench that she pulled up to face the one on which Jennifer and Fran were sitting. 'That's better,' she said. 'Now, begin at the beginning, Jennifer.'

After a moment's thought, Jennifer picked up her

wineglass, took a sip and began her story.

'You know I wanted to write a novel? That was why I went on the writers' holiday last year. I already had the idea, in fact, I'd written most of it. Patrick suggested I should go, but we decided we wouldn't say we were already friends because it would cause accusations of favouritism.' She took another sip of wine. 'He said it was a great source of ideas, as well everything else.' Her eyes flickered suddenly.

'He'd been before, then?' said Fran.

'Yes, he was a regular. There and some other conferences.'

'So you went along? And submitted the first ten pages to him first?' said Libby.

'Yes.'

'And Melanie saw the manuscript?' said Fran.

'Yes.'

'And offered to help? Come on Jennifer, give us a hand here,' said Libby.

Jennifer took a deep breath. 'Melanie knew it was mine, and asked if she could see any more of it. Well, of course, I gave it to her, and when I got back from the writers' holiday she was very encouraging and helped by pointing out a couple of the historical details I'd missed, and then helped me finish it. Then she said she would help me find an agent and a publisher.' She fell silent again.

'So,' said Libby, 'she submitted the book as her own. What – to Patrick's publishers? As herself?'

'Yes. When I found out – as of course I did when I found a copy in their house – I almost fainted from shock. Literally. She made it sound so speciously reasonable. I would never have had a hope, didn't I know how difficult it was these days for a new author, at least my work had seen the light of day. Eventually, I threatened to sue. Luckily, I still had the book on my own computer, and backed up on CD and memory stick.' She gave a small twisted smile. 'You don't work in publishing without learning that.'

'What did she do?' asked Fran. 'Had she had an advance?'

'Yes, she had. Not a large one, but apparently Patrick's publishers don't normally publish that sort of book, so they were taking a risk. But it was doing quite well. After I confronted Patrick with it, he said he hadn't known what was going on and would have stopped her if he'd known, but I'm pretty sure he did know – just didn't want to.'

'So what happened next?' asked Libby.

'Patrick told her to give me the advance. And they both signed a letter to the publishers, with me countersigning, asking that my name should be included on the cover in any future editions. And that I should receive the royalties.'

'Well, that's great!' said Libby. 'So why were you so upset when we showed you the book?'

'Because that letter was never sent.' Jennifer looked up. 'And I never received the money from the advance. And I knew how it would look. As if I'd killed her because she'd stolen my book.'

'But your best chance was to keep her alive to challenge her – to do as you said, and sue,' said Fran.

'No, I couldn't do that,' said Jennifer, her eyes

dropping to her lap again.

'Why not?' Libby was getting exasperated again.
'It was your right.'

'But Patrick –' began Jennifer.

'Ah. You're protecting Patrick.' Libby shook her
head. 'He doesn't deserve it, if you ask me.'

'No, you don't understand,' said Jennifer. 'It
would have meant the end of Patrick.'

'How do you mean, the end?' asked Libby. 'Did
he depend on her that much? You said she helped
him, but to that extent?'

'She helped him a lot.' Jennifer's lips snapped
shut, as if she were forcibly holding back words that
threatened to burst out and destroy everything.

They sat in silence for a moment, then Fran said:
'You said you didn't like her much. And that you
didn't take much notice of her own writing. If that
was the case, why did you let her help you with the
book?'

'I – well, I suppose because I thought she would
be better equipped than I was, and I would never ask
Patrick.'

'And he never commented himself on your
manuscript?' said Libby.

'No, but we'd already decided that.' Jennifer
finished her glass of wine. 'And I ought to get back
now.'

'Back where?' asked Libby.

'What?' Jennifer looked startled. 'Oh – er –
home.'

'Not Patrick's?' said Fran.

'The police are there, aren't they?' said Jennifer.

'I should think so,' said Libby. 'DCI Connell

told us they would be.'

'DCI –' Jennifer looked frightened now. 'Will you tell him?'

'Of course,' said Fran. 'You know we will.'

'Of course.' Now Jennifer sounded almost relieved. 'And then he'll talk to Patrick, won't he?'

'I expect so, even if we can't see that this had anything to do with Melanie's murder,' said Libby.

Jennifer stood up and hesitated. 'Thank you for talking to me first,' she said.

'We couldn't very well have told the police anything about the book until you told us, could we?' said Libby. 'Anyway, the police already know about the book.'

Jennifer's eyes widened.

'But not, of course, that you wrote it,' said Fran. 'We didn't know that until you told us.'

'We simply thought there might be something in the fact that Melanie wrote it under a pen-name – if she did, which we also didn't know conclusively – that could have given us a clue to her murderer.'

Jennifer swallowed hard and lost the colour she'd regained over the past ten minutes.

'Go on, you go off home,' continued Libby. 'We'll be in touch, or the police will, if there's a need to.'

Jennifer nodded and, without another word, picked up Herald's lead again and turned abruptly.

'There's more to this,' muttered Fran, as they watched Jennifer walk away.

'But what?' said Libby. 'I don't understand it. Why has she kept out of it for so long? Look.' She opened the book at the publishing history page. 'It was only published a few months ago. Melanie must have rushed it through with the publishers.'

'In case Jennifer found out too soon?' suggested Fran.

'I don't know, but I don't see how the Josephs could have hoped to keep it quiet. The publishers must have agreed not to publicise Melanie's real identity, but it would have come out eventually. And to be honest, who would believe Jennifer? Remember all those other plagiarism claims by unknown writers against famous ones? They're always thrown out of court.'

'Primarily because the unknown writers haven't got enough money to pursue it,' agreed Fran. 'Do you think we need to tell Ian now?'

'Yes, so he can ask Patrick about it. Although I still don't see what bearing it has on the murder,' said Libby.

'There's something that Jennifer wasn't telling us. And she's still scared. So perhaps whatever that is, it *does* have a bearing on the murder.' She fished her phone out of her pocket. 'And we don't know that Ian's actually at Patrick's, do we?'

The phone once more went to voice mail, so, taking a deep breath, Fran called Ian's official phone. She was answered within seconds.

'Yes?'

'There's something you need to know. Jennifer Alderton wrote that book, *Rising Lady*. Melanie stole it.'

There was a short silence.

'Where are you?'

'At the pub in Rising Parva,' said Fran. 'I left

308

you a voice mail saying we were coming to see Jennifer Alderton.'

'Is she with you?'

'No, she said she was going home.'

'Damn. I'll send someone to pick her up.'

'Are you with Patrick?' asked Fran.

'Yes. I'll talk to him now.'

The phone was switched off and Fran pulled a face at Libby.

'He's going to talk to Patrick and pick Jennifer up. I thought he might ask us to go up there.'

'Of course he wouldn't,' said Libby. 'We've already interfered too much. We might as well have lunch and go home, as we planned.'

They ordered shepherd's pie and waited for it on the bench outside.

'You read about that sort of thing happening, don't you? Or writers thinking it will happen.'

'You do?' Libby asked.

'Writers submit manuscripts, get rejected and think that someone at the agency or the publishers have pinched the idea.'

'This wasn't the publisher or agent, though, it was another writer,' said Libby. 'That must happen.'

'I still don't understand how she got the publishers to take her on, though. It's so hard to get published at all and she was unagented and didn't want to trade on her own name.'

'We know why she didn't want to trade on her own name,' said Libby. 'Because it wasn't her work.'

'The publishers wouldn't have known that.' Fran shook her head. 'Still don't get it.'

Their shepherd's pie arrived just as Fran's phone trilled again.

'Might need your input again,' came Ian's tired voice. 'Something's come up.'

Fran put down her fork. 'What? What do you want us to do?'

'I think you could come up here. The Joseph's house. You know where it is, don't you?'

'Yes.' Fran was frowning. 'But why do you need us? And can we finish our lunch first?'

'All right.' Ian sighed. 'I'll tell you when you get here.'

They finished their lunch as quickly as possible and set off towards Patrick's house.

'This is giving me indigestion,' complained Libby. 'Why do you think he wants us?'

'I have no idea,' said Fran. 'It seems highly unlikely.'

DS Wallingford – Libby still couldn't think of him as Barry – let them in to Patrick's house and ushered them into the sitting room, where Ian sat on an upright chair by a small table and Patrick and Jennifer sat miserably opposite each other either side of the fireplace. Ian nodded, grunted and stood up, jerking his head towards a door at the back of the room. Libby and Fran followed him through it.

'What's up?' said Libby. 'What have they said? Why did you want us?'

They found themselves in a long kitchen that had been extended into a conservatory. Ian turned to face them.

'I don't know what it is about you two,' he said heavily, 'but whenever you're involved things just get more and more complicated.'

Libby felt herself blushing and noticed that Fran had gone pink, too.

'But *we* don't make things complicated,' she protested.

'No, you just uncover the complications,' said Ian. 'And I suppose I'm grateful. If you hadn't found out about that bloody book, we wouldn't know what we do now.'

'But what? All we found out was that Melanie had pinched the book Jennifer had written because she saw what Jennifer submitted to Patrick for the writers' holiday.'

'She saw it all right,' said Ian. 'Because it was to Melanie that the books were submitted.'

'What?' said Libby and Fran together.

'Patrick hadn't written his books for years. Melanie wrote them all.'

Chapter Thirty-five

FOR A LONG MOMENT there was a stunned silence.

'*Melanie* wrote them?' Fran said eventually in a strangled voice.

'Apparently she'd been helping for years before she took a back seat from public life, because he'd hit some sort of writer's block.' Ian shrugged. 'Can't say I'd know what that is. So when she had more time on her hands it seems that she more or less took over.'

Libby shook her head. 'I don't understand it. Why wouldn't she want her own name on the books?'

'Because it was Patrick who had the name. She would have had to build up a following,' said Fran.

'But she could have done it on the back of her public persona,' said Libby. 'Like those celebrities who write books. They don't sell because they're good books, they sell because of the name.'

'Well, she did it this time with the Ann Marsh pseudonym and Jennifer's book.' Fran frowned. 'This makes it even more mad. I wonder why?'

'It lets Joseph out as a suspect,' said Ian. 'He wouldn't have wanted Melanie out of the way.'

'No wonder he said he wouldn't write any more,' said Libby.

'Did Jennifer know all this?' asked Fran.

'Not until after Melanie died, so she says,' said Ian. 'Then Patrick told her.'

'She would have talked to him about her own

book,' said Fran. 'Is that how she found out?'

'She didn't say so, but it makes sense.' Ian rubbed a hand over his face and sighed. 'The reason I wanted to talk to you two is because I want to find out about the other writers. Did they have any idea about this? Could this be a motive for Melanie's murder?'

'Because they felt cheated by Patrick you mean? Because he was supposedly critiquing their work and running workshops when he wasn't even writing the books?' Libby frowned. 'But why us? Shouldn't DS Wallingford or someone do it?'

'You've already had contact with them, and I think they're more likely to respond to you than to a heavy-handed copper,' said Ian. 'I thought you'd be pleased.'

'Of course we are,' said Fran, with a severe look at Libby. 'I suppose we should start with Dee as she's been trying to get in touch with you. Have you heard from her yet?'

'No.' Ian levered himself upright from the worktop where he'd been leaning. 'I don't know why, as she told you it was urgent. Try her again, and then move on to someone else.'

'Why did you bring us up here to tell us?' asked Libby as they went back to the sitting room.

'It was that or come down to you at the pub, and I didn't want to do it in public. Also, I thought you might want to talk to Jennifer and Joseph before you talk to anyone else.'

'Right.' Fran nodded. 'Will you go now?'

'Out of the room, yes. I want to see what the SOCOs have got. They've more or less finished.'

Ian collected DS Wallingford and left Libby and Fran in the sitting room with Jennifer and Patrick.

'Why didn't you tell the police any of this before?' Libby asked, sitting on the sofa and glaring at Patrick.

He cleared his throat. 'I – er – didn't think it was relevant.'

Libby snorted. 'Your wife and ghost-writer is killed and you didn't think it was relevant? I can see now why you stopped writing books yourself.'

Patrick was now bright red. 'I resent that remark.'

'Resent away, chummy. It'll all come out now in any case.' Libby looked at Jennifer. 'At least your stolen book will now come up, and should be put right.'

Jennifer opened her mouth, looked at Patrick and closed it again.

Fran sat down beside Libby. 'I really don't understand you two. Why did you think it would be possible to keep this from the police? And why would you?'

'I told you,' said Jennifer, her voice beginning to crack. 'I thought it would give me a motive.'

'But it clears *you*,' said Fran to Patrick. 'You must see that.'

'Er – yes.' Patrick's colour had subsided. He now looked simply frightened.

'Come on, then, what else is there?' asked Libby. 'Obviously there's something. What else are we going to find out? That you actually did kill your wife?'

'Of course not,' said Patrick. 'And I don't see

what it's got to do with you anyway.'

'Nothing, I suppose,' said Libby with a shrug. 'But as you can see, we often work with the police and we have been asked to this time.'

'So is there anything else you want to tell us?' asked Fran. 'Anything you know about the other writers who were there last weekend?'

'No, nothing.' Patrick was still looking apprehensive.

'You know nothing about them except the contact you had through *Writers in the South* and last year's holiday?' said Libby.

'Nothing. And the email group we set up to organise last weekend,' said Jennifer. 'You know all this already.'

'I daresay we do,' muttered Libby.

'In that case we'll get off,' said Fran standing up. 'I hope if you think of anything else you'll tell either one of us or the police.'

'Of course.' Jennifer nodded. Patrick said nothing, but watched them leave the room with worried eyes.

'Bloody hell!' Libby burst out as they stepped out of the front door into the sunshine. 'What are they hiding, those two? And why?'

'I can only think that they really did murder Melanie.' Fran was frowning as they walked down the lane back towards the village hall, where they had once again left the car. 'Or one of them did and is protecting the other.'

'Can't you feel that?' Libby watched her friend closely. 'I mean, you always said it was about her writing, and it looks as though it is. Or could be.'

'We still don't know it is,' said Fran. 'That's why Ian wants us to talk to the other writers. I expect the investigations into her old public life are still going on.'

'Yes, and for all we know it could be something entirely different. You know,' said Libby, enthusiastically embracing a whole new scenario, 'a long-lost illegitimate child or misappropriated will, or –'

'Abduction by aliens,' interrupted Fran, grinning. 'Meanwhile, if we can find a wifi connection, shall we try and raise Dee Starkey by email?'

No wifi was to be had in the village, however, and as neither Fran nor Libby had a smartphone and Dee's telephone number was locked away in Libby's email account, they had no way of reaching her until they reached home.

'Same goes for all of them, actually,' said Libby. 'How annoying. I would have liked to see Lily Cooper while we were here.'

'I doubt if she would have liked to see us,' said Fran. 'Come on. We'll go home and do it from there. We don't have to interview people face to face.'

'No, but at least they can't escape so easily if they're in front of us,' said Libby. 'They can put the phone down on us, though.'

Libby dawdled through the narrow lanes of Cranborne Chase to allow them a last look at the stunning beauty of the rolling chalk grassland and ancient woodlands. In a dip between hills, the spire of the church at Ebbesdean appeared and vanished at a turn in the lane.

'Glorious,' sighed Libby. 'I wish …'

'No, you don't,' said Fran. 'You'd never see anyone if you lived here.'

'I don't see Dom and Bel very much as it is,' said Libby. 'They could come here just as easily as to Steeple Martin.'

'They grew up in Kent, Lib,' said Fran. 'When they come to you they can also see all their old friends. And what about Adam? He lives there now.' She slid a look sideways at her friend. 'And what about us?'

Libby smiled. 'I know. Just day-dreaming. Perhaps we could buy a caravan and come and park it here?'

Fran laughed. 'Oh, yes! I can just see you and Ben in a caravan.'

They hit far more traffic on the way home, and Libby was aware of tense shoulders and a stiff neck by the time they'd made their way round Canterbury and were on the home straight. Fran had left her car outside number seventeen, and decided to come in for a cup of tea before driving on to Nethergate.

'You can have tea,' said Libby, 'I'm having a large glass of wine.' She flung her arms round Ben. 'I've missed you.'

'Shall we have a quick look at Dee's email while I have my tea?' suggested Fran.

'Still on the trail, eh?' said Ben. 'Go on, then. I'll make the tea. We're booked in at Harry's later Lib.'

'Again? Lovely.' Libby beamed and unearthed her laptop from her luggage.

'Nothing more from her,' said Fran, after they'd read and re-read the previous day's emails.

317

'Where's her phone number?'

Libby tracked down the numbers of everyone who'd been at the Manor when Melanie had been murdered, and this time wrote them down. 'That way we won't lose them,' she said. 'Which one of us is going to ring her?'

But Dee's phone went straight to voicemail.

'Odd,' said Libby. 'And we haven't got her landline number, have we?'

'Ian will have,' said Fran. 'We could ask him for it?'

'Suppose so,' said Libby doubtfully. 'She's in London, isn't she? I really don't want to have to go chasing after her in person now we've got home.'

'We could try through *Spank Monthly*,' suggested Fran. Ben raised his eyebrows as he handed her a mug. Fran grinned at him.

Libby brought up the home page of the magazine. 'There's only a contact form here,' she said, 'but we could try it. We won't get a very swift answer, though.'

'I don't know what information she could have had anyway,' said Fran as Libby closed the laptop. 'We agreed she was an unlikely person for Melanie to know, and she'd have not been able to get all the personal stuff to set up the room, not coming from London.'

'No, I suppose we can discount anyone who came from London,' agreed Libby. 'Mind you, that's only Nick, Paul Fisher and, well, Patrick himself, I think. He said he came straight from the London flat, didn't he?'

'Yes, so there might have been stuff there he

could have taken.' Fran was thoughtful.

'But not her body,' said Libby.

'Jennifer could have brought that up,' said Fran.

'So they were in cahoots? That's why they looked so frightened today?'

'Could be, but I'm sure Ian and his team would have found some sort of evidence if that was the case.' Fran stretched. 'We could talk round corners for ever on this one. Let's call it a day and start the ring round tomorrow.'

'I'll email you the phone numbers – no, you take the list I wrote. I'll write them out again. And we'll do what we did before, divide them up.' Libby stood up. 'Will we have to speak to Nick again? I think he's had enough of us.'

'I think we will,' said Fran, opening the front door. 'This is new information, after all. We didn't talk to him about this.'

Ben and Libby walked slowly towards The Pink Geranium an hour later. It was still light, but the lights were on inside the eight-til-late, the pub and the restaurant. Adam opened the door for his mother.

'Hello, darling,' she said giving him a kiss on the cheek. 'Are you on duty tonight?'

Adam indicated his long white waiter's apron. 'No, Ma, I wear this for fun. You're at the back tonight, no room in the window.'

The Pink Geranium was indeed crowded. 'Feast or famine,' said Harry, popping his head out of the kitchen to say hello. 'Remember last December when we had the snow and we were empty?'

'You know you said someone from Dorset must

319

have taken Melanie's body and her clothes up here?' said Ben, after Adam had brought them a bottle of red and taken their order.

'Yes,' said Libby, who'd regaled him with the events of the last two days while she'd showered and changed.

'And the room was booked, by credit card, in the name of Ann Marsh?'

'Yes.'

'And you think the booking was genuine?'

'Yes,' said Libby, exasperated. 'What are you getting at?'

'Couldn't it be,' said Ben slowly, making patterns on the table with his fork, 'that somebody else on the course – holiday, or whatever – told Melanie about what Patrick was up to, and offered to take her with them? Then she would have left under her own steam.'

Libby looked at him with a dawning awareness. 'And therefore –' she said.

'And therefore,' continued Ben, 'no one needed to rifle through the house, she could have taken herself and her belongings anywhere in the country and been killed and transported from there.'

'Even London,' breathed Libby.

'Especially London,' said Ben.

Chapter Thirty-six

SO TAKEN WAS LIBBY with the new theory that she wanted to call Fran and Ian immediately.

'It'll keep until tomorrow,' said Ben, laying his hand over hers, 'and if I've thought of it, you can be sure Ian has.'

'Oh.' Libby was deflated. 'I suppose he has. He'll be looking through all the phone records, won't he?'

'Bound to be. Or some other poor bugger will be. We never see the boring side of police work, do we?'

'No, poor souls. The paperwork they have to get through is enormous.' Libby picked up her glass. 'Oh, well, I'll tell Fran tomorrow before she starts phoning anybody.'

'You could send her a text,' said Ben. 'Then she'll know in advance not to start making the phone calls before she's spoken to you. And, by the way, what exactly are you supposed to be talking to these people about?'

'If they knew about Melanie writing the books. Mind you, I don't think any of them did, or they would have denounced Patrick, especially as several of them were quite open about not liking him much.'

'Didn't you say someone made a comment about him avoiding talking about the books?'

'Oh, yes. And I actually said: "As though he hadn't read them?" And I was right! Melanie had.

And written the critiques. And, I suppose, she sent them all back to the writers. Which means she knew where they all lived and Patrick might not have. Nick seemed resentful about that.'

'Why?'

'He couldn't believe Patrick hadn't bothered to get in touch as he'd promised. As Nick said, they only lived ten minutes apart. It wouldn't have hurt Patrick to make the effort to see him for a brief chat. But if Melanie had never told Patrick where any of the writers lived, he wouldn't have known that Nick was round the corner.' Libby shook her head. 'It explains quite a lot, really.'

'What I can't understand is why Melanie let it go on. She was doing all the work and Patrick was getting all the glory,' said Ben.

'I don't know either.' Libby lifted her head to smile at her son as he placed a plate of tacos in the middle of the table. 'Thanks, Ad.'

'Go on, then, send that text before we start on the meal and then we can concentrate on the food without interruptions,' said Ben.

Libby sent the text and received an impatient text in return. She smiled and put the phone back in her new bag, which had finally replaced the basket she had been carrying around for years.

'Once we get you a new winter coat the change of image will be complete,' Ben had commented when she first brought it home.

After their meal, Harry and Adam joined them for a drink before clearing up ready for the following day.

'No Donna tonight?' said Libby, as she poured

wine.

'Not feeling well, apparently,' said Harry with a sniff. 'Playing hookey with the new husband, more likely.'

'Not so new, now,' said Libby, 'and they can't have that much time together, with him working eighty-hour weeks at the hospital.'

'I reckon she's pregnant,' said Adam.

Harry's face darkened. 'She'd better not be.'

'Oh, Harry, you can't say that,' laughed Libby. 'I remember you worrying about it when she'd only just announced her engagement.'

'She's my right hand,' said Harry, aggrieved. 'I don't know what I'd do without her.' He patted Adam's hand. 'No offence, mate.'

'None taken,' said Adam, amused.

'Well, whatever the reason, I hope she's better and back soon,' said Libby.

'So where were you off to again?' Harry leant back in his chair. 'Leaving the old man all by his lonesome again so soon.'

Libby explained where she and Fran had been, and about the discovery that Melanie had been writing Patrick's books.

'Should you tell them that?' asked Ben. 'It might not be made public.'

'Of course it will,' said Libby. 'Do you think that's the sort of secret that could be kept? Someone at the publishers will let it out, you can bet.'

'Or the police,' said Adam.

'Not on Ian's watch,' said Ben.

'I wonder,' mused Libby, 'if the publishers actually knew?'

'No reason why they should,' said Ben. 'I would have thought Patrick would keep it quiet or he might lose his contract.'

'Do writers have contracts?' asked Harry.

'I think so,' said Ben. 'Not quite sure how they work, but it would be like sailing into the mist without one.'

'Hang on, though,' said Harry, frowning. 'If the publishers didn't know, wouldn't Patrick have been breaking his contract somehow by not writing the books himself?'

'That's true,' said Libby. 'I shall look into it tomorrow. Somehow.'

The next morning Fran was on the phone before eight o'clock, wanting to know what new theories had sprung up. Libby repeated both Ben's London theory and Harry's broken contract one.

'So how would we find out about that?' asked Fran, when she'd finished. 'I don't think Patrick will tell us.'

'Jennifer might,' said Libby. 'After all, she's going to have to try and get *Rising Lady* back.'

'And that's going to be a nightmare,' said Fran. 'I wish the letter Patrick and Melanie wrote had been sent. It would have made it much easier. I doubt if the publishers will hand over the rights to Jennifer just like that.'

'Well, where shall we start today and who with?' asked Libby.

'Have you checked your email to see if Dee's been in touch?' said Fran. Libby hadn't, and did so.

'There's an email from *Spank Monthly*, though,' she said. 'Hold on – I'll read it.

Dear Libby –

'How familiar!'

– we haven't heard from Dee Starkey for over a month, although she has an outstanding commission from us which has now missed the deadline. If you should hear from her, please ask her to contact me.

There. So that's a dead end.'

'Right.' Fran was silent for a moment. Then, 'How about we do this together after all? We'll only end up constantly on the phone to each other. Shall I come up to you?'

'No,' said Libby. 'You always come here. I'll come down to you. Then we can have an ice cream from Lizzie and I can sit on the beach. And perhaps go and see Jane and Imogen.'

'OK,' laughed Fran. 'I'll tell Guy I won't be available for the shop – again!'

'Oh, dear, is that what you should be doing?'

'Only lunchtime relief, and I don't suppose he'll mind. See you when you get here. I'll have the kettle on.'

The drive to Nethergate from Steeple Martin was a pleasant one, and as Libby passed the end of Canongate Drive and dropped down towards the town and the sea, she reminded herself how lucky she was to live in an area like this, despite her brief flirtation with Dorset. From the top of the town, she looked out on to the curve of Nethergate Bay, with its lighthouse at the tip of the left headland and locally named Dragon Island in the middle.

'Picture-postcard perfect,' said Libby to herself, as she let in the clutch and began the steep descent.

At the bottom of the high street was the square, with the old Swan Inn opposite. Off to the right was Victoria Place and Cliff Terrace, where Jane and Terry Baker's Peel House stood, and to the left, Harbour Street, where, overlooking the sea on the opposite side of the road, stood Fran's Coastguard Cottage.

Libby found a parking space right down at the bottom of Harbour Street near the Blue Anchor cafe, and waved at Mavis, who was setting out her tables outside on the hard.

Fran had the kettle on and had set up her laptop on the table in her little backyard, where Balzac the cat lay curled up in his favourite plant pot. He lifted his head and chirruped at Libby.

'Not easy reading the screen,' commented Libby, pulling herself and the table further into the shade.

'We won't need that so much, will we? I thought we were going to be phoning people,' said Fran, putting a cafetière and two mugs on the table. 'You don't want biscuits, do you?'

'No,' said Libby wistfully.

'So, where do we start?' Fran sat down with the list of numbers in front of her. 'Nick and Paul will both be at work again, but Lily might answer even if she is at work. And Nina.'

'Then there's Audrey and Bernice. And Daniel, but he won't talk to us.'

'He might,' said Fran. 'I'll try him first.'

Fran didn't give him a chance. As soon as he answered his phone with a gruff 'Hill', she began.

'Daniel, this is important. Did you know that Melanie Joseph was, in fact, the real author of Patrick Joseph's books?'

After a short silence a burst of language that would, in the words of Alan Jay Lerner, make a sailor blush, emerged.

'I take it you didn't,' said Fran.

'He was making fools of us all,' declaimed Daniel. 'I shall sue.'

'But what for?' asked Fran. 'I imagine he's going to get into enough trouble when this gets out. The only thing you could complain about is that he led the workshops under false pretences. The real writer of those books actually did critique your work.'

'No wonder it was a worthless critique,' snapped Daniel, 'and no wonder he wouldn't discuss the book with me. Pointless exercise altogether.' And the line went dead.

'That was odd,' Fran said to Libby. 'Apart from the rather theatrical swearing and declamations, he didn't actually say he knew or didn't know.'

'Suspected, perhaps?' said Libby, adding milk to her coffee.

'Maybe. Your turn now.'

'Audrey, then, the one whose husband used to work for the council.' Libby pulled the list towards her, and punched in the number on her phone.

'Hello, dear, nice to hear from you again. Is there any news?' Audrey asked comfortably, obviously settling in for a nice chat.

'Well, there is, actually,' said Libby, 'although not quite the sort of news you might expect.'

'Oh?'

'Well, I'm sure this is all going to come out eventually, so you might as well know now,' Libby continued. 'Can I ask you if you and Bernice were pleased with your critiques from Patrick?'

'Pleased?' Audrey sounded surprised. 'Well – yes, I suppose so. I mean, they weren't quite what we'd been expecting, and he hardly referred to them at all when he was doing his workshops last year.'

'No, that's understandable,' said Libby, taking a deep breath. 'You see, Audrey, Patrick didn't write the critiques. He didn't even write his own books.'

Audrey made a sound like gas escaping. 'Didn't – didn't – write?'

'No. Oh, he wrote the earlier ones, but for the last few years Melanie wrote them all. And did the critiques.'

'Melanie?' Audrey burst out. '*Melanie*? That misguided tree-hugger? Said she was Green but supported nuclear power. And coal. I ask you. I don't want her critiquing my work!'

'Oh, so you knew who she was after all?' said Libby, raising her eyes at Fran.

'Of course we did. You couldn't live anywhere near Rising Parva and not know who she was.'

Libby gasped. 'You knew she lived there all along?'

'Well, no. Not actually lived there. But we knew she lived in the area. Oh, my word, you just wait until I tell Bernice. Or were you going to tell her, dear?'

'I was, yes, straight after I'd phoned you.' Libby indicated to Fran that she was to dial Bernice's number now. 'But anyway, you had no idea that was going on?'

'No, I Did Not. And I shall want my money back from that holiday. False pretences, that's what it was.'

'It wasn't their fault,' protested Libby mildly, hearing Fran begin her explanation to Bernice on the other phone. '*Writers in the South* didn't know either. If anyone should be paying compensation it's Patrick himself.'

'I shall certainly be taking this up with –' Audrey paused '– with someone, anyway. Thank you for telling me, dear. Oh – is it anything to do with her murder?'

'We don't know yet,' said Libby. 'But I'll keep you posted.'

Fran finished her own call and they compared notes.

'So, both outraged,' Libby summed up, 'but Bernice worried about something else, you thought.'

'Yes. She wasn't quite as voluble as Audrey, and almost seemed as though she half expected it, but on the other hand it *wasn't* what she expected.'

'Curiouser and curiouser,' said Libby. 'Shall we try Dee again?'

'Might as well,' said Fran, and Libby dialled the number. To her intense surprise, it was answered, not by Dee, but by a man.

'Is Dee there, please?' she asked hesitantly.

'I'm afraid not,' said the man pleasantly. 'Who's calling, please?'

'Um, this is Libby Sarjeant. Could you ask if she could call me back?'

'Thank you, Ms Sarjeant,' said the voice. 'Goodbye.'

'Well!' said Libby. 'That was a bit rude.'

But within seconds her mobile rang and she snatched it up.

'Dee?' she said.

But it wasn't Dee. It was Ian.

Chapter Thirty-seven

LIBBY'S INSIDES PERFORMED THAT manoeuvre normally referred to as the heart turning over, or possibly one's stomach sinking.

'Ian?' she croaked. 'What's happened?'

'You just tried to call Dee Starkey.'

'Yes.'

Ian sighed. 'I needn't have done this, you know. But I decided I'd better. Dee Starkey's dead.'

Libby turned her head to meet Fran's worried gaze. 'Dead?' she repeated. 'How?'

'It appears to be murder,' said Ian. 'I can't tell you any more.'

'What happened? When?'

Ian sighed again. 'I told you. I can't tell you any more. I'll call you later. Are you and Fran talking to the other writers?'

'In the middle of it,' said Libby.

'In that case don't say anything – anything, do you understand? – about this.'

Libby switched off the phone and reached a shaking hand for her coffee.

'Dee's dead?' said Fran.

Libby nodded. 'Why don't you look surprised?'

'We should have guessed when we couldn't get hold of her.'

'You don't assume someone's dead just because you can't get hold of them!'

'But if they've got in touch with you, it's a police matter and they say it's urgent, wouldn't you get suspicious?'

'We didn't,' said Libby, 'but I suppose, looked at like that, we should have been. So should Ian.'

'He – or somebody in the investigation – obviously was,' said Fran. 'Or they wouldn't have found her.'

'So why was she killed? Because of the information she said she had for us?' Libby shivered. 'God, I can't stop shaking.'

'Have a cigarette,' said Fran magnanimously. 'I'll even find you something for an ashtray.'

When she got back with a small terracotta dish, Libby had lit a cigarette and was staring into space.

'Do you know what,' she said slowly, 'it's becoming clear that everyone on that bloody weekend knew more about Patrick and Melanie Joseph than they said at first.'

'And there's something very odd about the weekend itself,' said Fran.

'Eh? What do you mean?'

'They told us and the police they'd got together for that weekend because they'd bonded so closely on the writers' holiday that they wanted a reunion. But they're not like that at all, are they? They didn't seem particularly close last weekend, and some of them are positively antagonistic to the others. So why were they there?'

Libby looked horrified. 'You're not suggesting some kind of perverted Orient Express murder, are you?'

'I don't know what I'm suggesting,' said Fran, 'just that they all knew more than they were saying and few of them liked each other, so there must have been another reason for the weekend.'

'Do you think Dee was going to tell us what that reason was?'

'It's possible.'

'Shall we get on with calling people then?' said Libby. 'Ian says we mustn't talk about Dee, but how about we now ask what the real reason was for the weekend?'

'I think Daniel and Bernice at least thought that was what we were going to ask them,' said Fran. 'Revealing that Patrick hadn't written his own books was almost – I don't know – an anti-climax. Even with all Daniel's blustering.'

'Audrey seemed genuinely bemused, though,' said Libby.

'It's as if they knew something about Patrick but this wasn't it,' mused Fran.

'Yes – and look how Jennifer and Patrick were yesterday. How scared they were. There's something they're hiding and they're worried someone's going to find out.'

'And somehow the others know about it.' Fran shook her head. 'But it's silly. If the others know something detrimental why don't they come out and say so?'

'No idea. Let's call Lily Cooper and see if she'll let down her guard.'

'I don't suppose she will, but we might as well try. I'll do it, shall I?' Fran pulled the list of numbers towards her and picked up her phone.

'Hello?' Lily's tone was brisk.

'Ms Cooper,' Fran began, 'this is just to let you know there have been developments in the case of

Melanie Joseph.'

The tone turned wary. 'Oh? That's not the Sarjeant woman, is it?'

Fran winced. 'No, Ms Cooper. New information has come to light.' Better Lily Cooper took her to be a police officer than admit who she was, Fran decided, wishing she'd concealed her number. 'It appears that Patrick Joseph didn't write his own novels.'

'So he's been –' Lily Cooper burst out and then stopped. 'Not written –? What exactly do you mean?'

Fran wanted to ask what she'd meant, but decided it could get complicated. 'Apparently all his more recent books were written by his wife. Who also did all the critiques for the writers' holiday.'

Lily Cooper's language was almost as ripe as Daniel Hill's had been.

'I'm sorry, Ms Cooper,' interrupted Fran, 'but there's one other thing. Can you tell me the real reason for the reunion weekend?'

Silence.

'Only it has become apparent,' continued Fran, in her best formal language, 'that you all knew more about Melanie and Patrick Joseph than you were prepared to admit, and neither did you appear to get on very well with each other.'

More silence. Fran could almost hear Lily thinking. 'Ms Cooper?' she prompted.

'Er – I'll think about it.' The voice was now positively shaky. 'Can I come back to you?'

'We'll be in touch,' said Fran, and switched off the phone.

'Well done, Inspector Wolfe,' said Libby. 'She's obviously rattled.'

'Very.' Fran sighed. 'I just don't get it.'

'I'll tell you who we should call,' said Libby. 'Young Nina. She's surely the most likely to tell us. Remember how uncomfortable she was at the Manor?'

'We could ask Rosie to talk to her,' said Fran, in a moment of inspiration.

'So we could! Fran, that's brilliant!' Libby finished her coffee. 'Shall we call Rosie now?'

'We can see if she's willing to do it,' said Fran. 'I suppose I'd better not say anything about Dee, had I?'

'No, but tell her everything else,' said Libby.

While Fran related the story of the Melanie Joseph investigation to an obviously incredulous Rosie, Libby poured herself another cup of coffee and wandered round the tiny back yard. Balzac jumped off his plant pot and wound himself between her legs.

Fran switched off the phone.

'Rosie says she's got one of those conference phones in her office, which means we could hear everything Nina said and we could chip in, too. She says wouldn't this evening be best if Nina works?'

'It's a mobile number,' said Libby, looking at the list, 'so she might answer it anyway. Can't we go over and try now?'

'I think Rosie's busy. We can't just barge in. Besides, don't you think we ought to run it past Ian?'

'We've got to wait for him to call us,' said

Libby. 'OK, then, we'll carry on cold calling. Who's left?'

'Only the two men, Nick and Paul. I don't suppose we'll get them either.'

'We've got Nick's mobile number now,' said Libby. 'We could try.'

'Your turn then,' said Fran. Libby punched in the number.

'Nick Forrest.'

'Hello, Nick, it's Libby.'

'Libby! Are you still here?'

Libby tried a small laugh. It didn't sound convincing. 'No, no, we're back in Kent. Nick, there's a bit more information about Patrick and Melanie. And you put us on to it, really.'

'I did? What are you talking about?'

'You know that book, Rising Lady? And it turned out it was written by Melanie Joseph?'

'So it was, was it? I don't think you'd confirmed that.'

'Yes, it was. Only it wasn't.'

'Eh?'

'It was published by her under the name of Ann Marsh, which was an alias she used while she was on official government business, and she still had the credit card in that name, which was how she managed to book in to the Manor.' Libby paused for breath.

'Yes?' said Nick. 'And?'

'Only it wasn't her book. It had been written by Jennifer Alderton.'

'Jennifer? But how?'

'Melanie saw Jennifer's submission for the

writers' holiday workshop and offered to help her with it.'

'Ah,' said Nick, sounding guarded.

'And it turns out that not only did Melanie write all those critiques, but she had also been writing Patrick's books for several years.'

'She *what*?'

'Sorry, but it does sort of change things in the investigation. So the police –'

'The police know this, do they?'

'Of course.' Libby was surprised.

'In that case – look, Libby, were you asked to tell me this?'

'Yes, and to ask you what the real reason for the reunion was. It's become apparent –'

'Yes, yes, I know all that. Look I'm going to call Paul. Do you want me to call you back, or shall I call your Inspector? I've got his card.'

Libby valiantly suggested he call Ian direct.

'All right, but I might call you afterwards,' he said. 'I'm sure you're bursting with curiosity.'

'You could say that,' said Libby dryly, and switched off the phone. She looked at Fran. 'Did you get all that?'

'Most of it. Perhaps Rosie won't need to talk to Nina after all.'

Deciding there was nothing more they could do until they heard back from either Nick or Ian, they took the coffee things indoors and wandered across the road to the beach. The usual young families were there, protected by windbreaks, burying fathers in the sand and building sandcastles. A few tots in droopy swimsuits and floppy hats squealed at the wavelets and shook small buckets.

'Ice cream,' said Libby, so they walked back across the road to Lizzie's tiny shop front and bought ice cream that tasted like it used to.

When they'd finished their ice creams they wandered down to the Blue Anchor where Bert, captain of the *Sparkler*, and George, captain of the *Dolphin*, sat in their usual seats with large white mugs in front of them.

'Not going out today?' asked Libby, nodding at the two boats bobbing gently at the end of the little jetty.

'Not enough trade,' grunted Bert.

'Little'uns don't want to go. Trouble on boats they are,' said George indicating the families on the beach. 'What you two up to then? No good, I'll be bound.'

Libby smiled. 'You wouldn't believe us if we told you,' she said. 'Are we ready for lunch, yet, Fran?'

'We've only just had ice cream. Don't think I could manage anything right now.'

'Right.' Libby sat down gloomily at one of the little tables and stared out to sea.

George looked from one to the other and heaved himself to his feet. 'Go on, Bert,' he said. 'Go and ask Mavis for the lunch. Come on, you two pesky females.'

'What?' said Libby and Fran together.

'You need a bit of a blow. Lost a pound and found sixpence, the pair of you. Us'll just have a little trip round the island, shall us?'

Libby beamed. 'Oh, George, how lovely! I'd

love that.'

'So would I.' Fran stood up. 'Thank you George. How did you know we were fed up?'

'Wouldn't make no actresses, you two. 'Sides, I bet it's some old murder you've got yourselves into. Make anybody narky, that do.'

Bert returned with a basket of baguettes, the lunch he and George usually served to passengers on their trips, and they moved down the jetty to the *Dolphin*. Five minutes later, they were chugging towards Dragon Island, Bert and George huddled over the wheel together, Libby and Fran sitting in the stern, the breeze and spray in their faces.

'That's better,' said Libby. 'George was right. We needed a blow.'

'I just hope we don't get a call from Ian or Nick while we're out here,' said Fran. 'It'd spoil it.'

'We won't,' said Libby, confidently. 'Neither of them would get back to us that quickly.'

So George piloted them round the lighthouse headland, where they stopped to eat their baguettes, then back across the bay and round the back of Dragon Island. And, as George turned to approach the jetty, Libby's phone rang.

Chapter Thirty-eight

'I'VE JUST HAD A call from Nick Forrest,' said Ian. 'I gather you told him to call me.'

'Yes, but I didn't know exactly what about.' Libby watched as George climbed ashore to tie the *Dolphin* up, and hoped he wasn't going to make her get off in the middle of the phone call.

'You're going to have to explain that. Carry on – I've got five minutes.'

'Right.' Libby looked at Fran and made a face. 'Well, we were doing what you asked us to, and we sort of added on a question. We asked them what the real reason was for the weekend, as they didn't seem to be all that friendly with each other. And it's turned out that they all knew far more about Melanie and Patrick than they let on. They all seemed very surprised about Melanie having written the books, but as though they were expecting something else.'

'Hmm,' said Ian. 'And what about Ben's idea you were talking about earlier?'

'Ben's – oh, yes. He said why couldn't Melanie have gone to someone else's place, been killed there and transported down. If you see what I mean.'

'I see what you mean. It is actually something we'd thought of.'

'Oh, right. So,' said Libby hesitantly, 'what did Nick say?'

'I can't tell you that,' said Ian, 'but he probably will, despite being warned not to talk about it.'·

'And did it help?'

'I think so. And now I'm going to have to go and solve a murder. I'll probably speak to you later.'

Bert was waiting to help them off the *Dolphin*, and Libby and Fran thanked him and George profusely.

'Just what we needed,' said Fran.

'We owe you a pint,' said Libby. 'In fact, would you like one now?' She waved a hand towards The Sloop, the pub at the end of the jetty.

'Might have to go out again later,' said George. 'Better not. We'll keep you to it, though.'

'So, what did he say?' asked Fran, as they walked back towards Coastguard Cottage.

'Not a lot, really. Nick called him, but he wouldn't say what about.'

'Is it worth calling Nick back?'

'Well, he did say he would tell me, and Ian thought he would, too. Must say, I'm intrigued now.'

'And what about Dee?'

Libby shook her head. 'Nothing.'

'Well, we've no one left to ring, so what do we do now?'

'Not much we can do until we go to Rosie's this evening to talk to Nina. Did she say what time?'

'No. I'll give her another ring.'

'And I'll ring Nick again.' Libby perched on the little sea wall and took out her mobile.

'You said you'd ring me,' she said when Nick answered.

'Yes. Hang on a minute.' There was the sound of voices and a door slamming. 'That's better. I know I said I'd tell you, but your Inspector said I shouldn't talk about it.'

'And he's just phoned me and told me you'd tell me.'

'If you're sure …' Nick sounded doubtful.

'I'm sure.'

'Right.' Libby heard a deep sigh. 'It was when you said that Jennifer had written that book.'

'What was?'

'What made me stop and think. You see, she was the only one we didn't know about.'

'Nick, you're not making sense. Who didn't know about her?'

'All of us.'

'*All* of you? You mean the group at the Manor?'

'Yes. Except Jennifer, and, of course, Patrick.'

'This is about the real reason behind the weekend, is it?'

'You said you knew there must be another reason.'

'We did. And now you're going to tell me. Start at the beginning.'

'The beginning,' said Nick. 'Difficult to know where that was.'

'The writers' holiday last year?'

'Actually before that. Several of us had met at writers' days and the odd conference. And we all knew Patrick.'

'Knew – what, before the holiday?'

'All of us at one time or another had submitted work to him before an event. It was one of his particular selling points. But last year we did it deliberately.'

'Explain.'

'Over the last few years several of us had recognised our own work in Patrick's published books. The whole plot, and even, sometimes, whole chunks of text.'

'Good God!' said Libby. 'So why hadn't you challenged him?'

'Daniel did. A couple of years ago. Patrick more or less said he hadn't done it deliberately, and these idea were always floating round in the ether. And then Bernice tried. Hers was a bit trickier, because her story had been more women's fiction, and it had been turned into crime, but there were chunks of text in there. She got the same answer. We all chose his workshop at the holiday and submitted synopses that would appeal to Patrick and sat back to see what happened. But it seemed to have backfired.'

'Why was that?' asked Libby.

'There wasn't a book. He said it was due to be published this September. Actually, that's right – it's already up for pre-order online.'

'Meanwhile, of course, Melanie had been pinching Jennifer's. She hardly had any work to do, as it was already written.'

'And she'd been doing that for the last few years with all of us.' Nick swore under his breath, but Libby heard.

'So what was the point of this weekend? Mass retribution?'

'Something like that, but we hadn't got the book we expected to be out. But we all took our original work, and we all had copies of the books that had been based on them. I say all, it wasn't all of us, and there were a couple of other people outside our group who were affected.'

'How many? There can't have been that many over the few years Melanie's been writing them.'

'That's the thing – he suddenly became more prolific, doing two books a year. No wonder.'

'And why didn't you include Jennifer?'

'Because no one had ever met her before. She was a newcomer. We couldn't understand why she was there. We know now, of course.'

'And this is what you told DCI Connell?' said Libby.

'Yes – after I'd talked to Paul. He was one of the ones affected.'

'Who were the others?'

'Daniel, Bernice, Dee and Nina.'

'*Nina*?'

'She was the most upset of the lot,' said Nick.

'I didn't think she'd actually written a novel,' said Libby.

'No – you see, that's the point. Most of us were only submitting ten pages, or a chapter, or five thousand words, but also a detailed synopsis. So Patrick could – and did – argue that it could hardly be plagiarism if he'd written the whole book after that. It was stealing the ideas that was so unpleasant. But there's no legislation for that.'

'What about Lily? Surely she wouldn't have slept with him if she knew about all this?'

'Oh, she knew, but she didn't care. She's been following him around the circuit for years, so she'd heard all the gossip. She was useful, because he had no suspicion of anything else being on the agenda if she was organising things. He knew she was just after sex, and that suited him fine. Mind you, he tried it on with everyone else, too.'

'Managed it with Dee. Oh –' Libby broke off.

'Yes. That was a bit … Didn't understand it myself. Paul said Dee was trying to get him to admit it by using sex.'

Libby thought about it for a bit. 'So why didn't any of you tell the police about this after Melanie's body was found?'

'We didn't even know it was Melanie, did we? Then when we found out we decided it would only complicate matters, as it couldn't be anything to do with us. It must have been someone from another part of her – or their – life. Or Patrick himself.'

'Yes.'

'But now …' he stopped.

'Yes, now it looks as though it might have something to do with one of you,' said Libby.

'I still don't see how, if none of us knew Melanie was writing Patrick's books.'

Libby sighed. 'And I don't see that there's a motive for murder in there, frankly. I mean, I can see how peeved you'd be if someone had stolen your work, and I can see how you might want to get your own back somehow, or at least get an acknowledgement, but murder?'

'I know. And I'm sorry if we've made life more complicated for the police, but I really don't think any of us seriously thought we could be involved. And then you two started –'

'Sniffing around, I know,' said Libby. 'Well, I think our job here is done. Thanks for telling us,

Nick. I hardly think we need to talk to Nina now.'

'No, I wouldn't. She was very upset about it all. She wouldn't want reminding.'

Libby switched off the phone and turned to see Fran staring at her.

'Did you get any of that?' she asked.

'Not much,' said Fran, 'except that it was a bit – what? Startling.'

Libby slid off the wall and they began to walk back to Coastguard Cottage as she explained.

'You're right,' said Fran when Libby finally came to a halt. 'It doesn't actually explain the murder, nor is it a real motive. And what about Dee?"

'I think she must have found out about Melanie writing the books. That's what she must have wanted to tell Ian.'

'But that wouldn't be enough to kill her for,' said Fran.

'It might if you were Melanie's killer.'

'Do you think they've all been in touch with each other while we've been traipsing round talking to them all?' said Fran, unlocking her front door.

'Who was it said that people seemed to have left the group? I bet that's because they thought they ought to keep a low profile. And I bet Daniel won't have spoken to anybody.' Libby followed Fran inside and dumped her bag on the floor. 'Cor, what a day.'

Fran's landline began to ring.

'Rosie, hi,' said Fran. Libby watched as Fran's expression turned to a puzzled frown.

'OK, I'll get back to you,' she said and put down

the phone.

'Apparently, Rosie called Nina to warn her we were going to call later, and the woman who answered said she'd gone away to visit friends for a few days. And offered the opinion that it might be the woman who stayed with her a couple of weeks ago.'

'Melanie?' gasped Libby.

'That is quite a huge leap,' said Fran, 'and "a couple of weeks ago" could mean anything, not right at the time of the conference.'

'But it is a coincidence. Where does she live? Swindon?'

'Reading.'

'Oh, bother. Not London, then.'

'Dee's in London.'

'But she's dead,' said Libby. 'Anyway, come to think of it, what's London got to do with anything?'

'I'm not sure. Think we went off the rails a bit there.'

'It was Ben's idea last night, and me saying even London. We were thinking if she'd gone to stay in the flat Patrick could have brought her down. Or Dee could.'

'But she could have gone anywhere,' said Fran.

'Or nowhere. The original idea of the murderer picking her up at home might be right.'

'Or even of Lily or Jennifer bumping her off out of jealousy.'

'Oh, dear,' said Libby. 'Perhaps we need tea.'

While Fran was making tea, Libby's phone rang again.

'Libby, have you spoken to everybody now?'

'Except Paul Fisher and Nina, yes. But Nick spoke to Paul. What's up, Ian?'

'We need to establish the whole group's whereabouts for the day before yesterday.'

'Well, that lets Jennifer, Patrick and Nick out. We know where they were,' said Libby. 'Don't know about any of the others. Is that when Dee was killed?'

'That's when the phone was switched off, and that's the last time you heard from her, so we assume so.'

'And did she live alone? For some reason we assumed she was married.'

'She was.'

'Oh! So when did her husband last see her? Was he away?'

'We didn't find her at home, Lib. In fact, we didn't find her at all. Jennifer Alderton did. On Bonny Henge.'

Chapter Thirty-nine

'BONNY HENGE?' GASPED LIBBY. Fran came out of
the kitchen and stared at her.

'Yes. So it doesn't let anyone out.' Ian gave an
exasperated sigh.

'We're hoping to speak to young Nina later, if
we can find her mobile number, because she's away
visiting friends, apparently. Do you want us to say
something to her? Oh, God.'

'What?'

'Suppose Nina's been – well, we couldn't get
hold of Dee. Now we can't get hold of Nina –'
Libby tried to control the rising panic in her voice.

'Don't jump to conclusions, Lib,' said Ian gently.
'Don't worry about trying to get hold of Nina. We'll
do that if we need to. But you can't be sure of
anyone's actual whereabouts on Tuesday evening?'

'Only Nick's, and you know that yourself. But
Bonny Henge? Right under your nose? And we
were there on Wednesday.' Libby shuddered. 'Oh,
this is awful.'

'Don't worry about it, Lib. Tell Fran, of course,
and when we've sorted it all out I'll let you know.'

Libby switched off the phone.

'Dee was found on Bonny Henge,' said Fran.

'How did you know?' Libby's eyes opened wide
in surprise.

'It was fairly obvious from your side of the
conversation. So what does Ian want us to do now?'

'Nothing. He just said to tell you.' Libby took a

deep breath. 'Jennifer found her.'

'Sit down,' said Fran. 'I'll make the tea.'

'I'm going out into the garden to have a fag,' said Libby. 'If you don't mind, that is.'

'Of course not. Go on.' Fran stood aside to let Libby past.

'I think,' she said a few minutes later, coming out with two mugs, 'we've had enough shocks today. Now we don't have to speak to Nina, I think we should settle for going back to the bosom of our families and forget the whole thing.'

'Forget it? I don't see how. And Melanie was actually found at the Manor, so how can I ever forget it?' Libby shook her head. 'No, I'll have to live with this one. But we're not going to do any more writers' weekends. The odd painting one, maybe. But no more writers.'

'Writers aren't all like this lot, Lib.' Fran pushed a mug across the table. 'Rosie says she's never met a bunch like this, and most conferences are completely different. And she's never heard of this sort of plagiarism anywhere else.'

'Still, you can't plagiarise a painting, can you?' said Libby.

'No, but art forgers can copy them,' said Fran with a grin. 'Guy's done a couple of copies in the past. Not for criminal reasons, but for TV and film.'

'Really?' Libby was interested and diverted. 'I never knew that. How did that work?'

'TV adaptations or biopics of real people, where their portraits were used.'

Libby nodded. 'Perhaps we could do a weekend on copying.' She sighed. 'Oh, it's no good. I can't think about anything else except Dee now, poor cow.' She drank some tea and pushed it aside. 'I'm going home, Fran. You were right about family bosoms.'

'Are you all right to drive?' asked Fran. 'You don't look it.'

Libby stood up and smiled shakily. 'I don't know why it's affected me so much. Look at you, you're all right. Well, shocked, of course, but you haven't gone all wobbly. But I can drive. And I promise I'll let myself be looked after.'

All the same she took the drive from Nethergate to Steeple Martin very carefully. When she got to the village, instead of going on to Allhallow's Lane, she turned left into the Manor Drive intending to put part of her plan into action by letting Hetty look after her until Ben could take over.

To her annoyance, however, there were cars parked in front of the house. Frowning, Libby climbed out of the Renault and went into the house. She hesitated in the hall, trying to decide whether to go to the estate office in search of Ben, or the kitchen to see Hetty. Hearing Ben's voice coming from the kitchen, she turned left.

'Oh!' She came to a sudden halt in the doorway. 'Nina! Whatever are you doing here? Rosie was trying to get hold of you.'

Nina, still fragile-looking in pink cotton, got nervously to her feet. 'I know. I'm sorry to turn up like this, but when I phoned home and my flat mate told me that Amanda George had called me and hadn't left a number, this was the only place I could think of where I might find out how to get in touch with her.'

'Oh, that's all right, then.' Libby smiled in relief and came forward to give the girl a hug. 'We were worried about you.' She turned to Ben and threw her arms round him, too. 'Hello, you. I've had a bad day. Hello, Het. Sorry to burst in.'

Ben pushed her into a chair at the table as Nina resumed hers.

'Got the kettle on, gal.' Hetty gave her a pat on the shoulder.

'Worried about me?' said Nina.

'Bad day?' asked Ben.

'To answer you both,' Libby smiled at them, 'yes, a bad day. And you know we couldn't get hold of Dee, Ben? Well, when we couldn't get hold of Nina either, we feared the worst. Well, I did.'

'Why?' said Ben and Nina together.

'Because when Dee was found, she was dead.'

Hetty turned round from the Aga, Ben's mouth fell open and Nina shrank back in her chair. 'Dead?' she whispered.

'I'm sorry, Nina, yes.'

Nina swallowed. 'Why was Amanda George trying to get hold of me?'

Libby frowned at the change of subject. 'Actually on behalf of the police.' She slid the two queries together. It didn't seem to matter which came first, now. 'They wanted to know how much you knew about the plagiarism story and where you were on Tuesday night.'

Nina looked disappointed. 'Oh. I thought she might have wanted to talk to me about my writing.'

Libby and Ben exchanged puzzled looks.

'So did you know about the plagiarism?' said Libby. 'We only just found out about it.'

'We all did,' said Nina. 'It was awful. So unfair.'

'Well, Dee obviously found out about something else, because if you all knew it couldn't have been a motive for murder. You were going to tackle Patrick together, weren't you?'

'Oh, yes. It's a pity we didn't.' Nina frowned.

This really doesn't add up, Libby thought, and decided to take a chance.

'Although, of course, as Melanie wrote the books anyway, it probably wouldn't have achieved much,' she said.

'Yes, once we knew Melanie had been writing the books it changed everything.'

There was a short, charged silence.

'Who knew that?' asked Libby, in as normal a tone as possible.

Nina shrugged. 'I don't know.'

'But you said "we" knew. Who's we?'

Nina went pink, but didn't say anything.

'So how did you find out?' asked Libby, waggling fingers at Ben out of sight of Nina.

'Melanie told me.' Nina looked surprised.

'You said you didn't know Melanie. You also said you didn't know Patrick. Yet we now know that a synopsis and ten pages of one of your books had been used by him – or Melanie – at least two years ago.'

'I didn't know Melanie then.' Nina was still looking surprised. 'Why would you think that?'

'You knew her well enough for her to tell you she'd been writing the books.'

Nina was beginning to look wary. Ben had silently slid from the room. Libby glanced quickly up at Hetty, who gave her the slightest of nods and placed one hand carefully on the handle of a large frying pan that stood on the Aga.

'So,' said Libby brightly. 'You hoped Amanda George would talk to you about your book.'

Nina's face transformed. 'Yes! You remember how much she liked my writing and said she was sorry I lived so far away? I thought perhaps she wanted to see some more, and perhaps mentor me. After all, if my story was good enough for Melanie to use in one of Patrick's books – *Dark Service*, it was – then I must be good enough.'

'You have to remember, though, that it was really only the idea Melanie used, not the whole thing.'

'She used nearly all of my first chapter.'

'She did that with the others, too, didn't she?'

'But I was the only one who decided that Patrick needed a lesson. No one else was going to do anything except this silly idea of confronting him at the weekend here. So I called Melanie –'

'How did you get her number?' interrupted Libby.

'I found it in Jennifer's mobile address book.'

'And how did you know to look there, and when did you do that?'

'Last year on the holiday.' She shrugged. 'Jennifer wasn't that clever and I overheard her and Patrick talking. So I looked.'

'You certainly put on a good performance here the other week,' said Libbby, straining her ears for the sound of a car, or preferably, cars.

'Yes, it was good, wasn't it?'

'So, you called Melanie.' Libby wanted to keep her talking.

'Yes, to tell her about Lily and Dee after the holiday. I thought that was a good excuse. But she just laughed. She said she always knew about his little peccadilloes, as she called them. So then, a month ago, I called her again and said they were planning to meet up here again. It was her idea to come here.'

Libby noticed Hetty's hand closing round the handle of the frying pan and hoped she wouldn't have to use it.

'How was she going to arrive without Patrick knowing? That was the point, I take it?'

'That was her suggestion. She thought it was clever. She came to me. I was to drive her down. And then when she came, she told me all about it. The books. Everything.' Nina's eyes strayed to the window and Libby's heart, already banging about and making her quite uncomfortable, sped up so much she was breathless.

'So that's it.' Nina stood up. 'Well, I'll go now, if that was all Mrs George wanted there's no point in me staying is there?'

Hetty was looking incredulous and still clutching the frying pan. Libby hastily took Nina's arm.

'Come on,' she said, praying that Ben, at least, was outside the door. 'I'll see you out. That was your car outside was it?'

'Oh, yes,' Nina said happily. 'It's been all over the place in the last few days.'

'I'll bet,' said Libby. 'Rising Parva on Tuesday, wasn't it?'

Nina turned to look at Libby, her face suddenly a mask of horror, as Ben led DC Sharif into the kitchen.

Several hours later, the usual suspects, as Harry insisted on calling them, gathered in the back yard of The Pink Geranium.

'So how come you had that Sharif bloke there?' asked Harry.

'He was already there,' said Ben. 'Ian had sent him over.'

'His was the other car in the drive,' said Libby, 'but I didn't recognise it.'

'And why had Ian sent him over?' asked Peter.

'He checked up on Nina – he'd already done it before he spoke to me – and found that she'd called Dee on Tuesday. Mobile records. I don't know why he didn't just check all of them.'

'I expect he did,' said Ben.

'I'm still confused,' said Guy. 'What was Nina's story from the beginning?'

'She was the most upset about Patrick's – as she thought – use of her idea. They all were, and last year's holiday was an attempt to get him to admit it, and to present him with another idea, which they would carefully document and use against him if it did appear in print. She knew nothing about Melanie writing the books, and neither did she know about Jennifer's book being stolen.' Libby paused for a mouthful of wine. 'But she managed to get the Josephs' home number and call Melanie to tell her about Patrick sleeping with Dee and Lily.'

'Yes, I've got that,' said Guy, 'but what happened this year? And why did she kill Dee?'

'Melanie apparently thought it would be a good joke to appear at the weekend and not only confound Patrick but his ladies, too. And Nina, who is quite obviously a bit mad, wanted some kind of revenge. So when Melanie arrived at her flat and told her the truth about the books, she flipped,' said Ben.

'Well, she didn't actually, she planned it, carefully, she thought,' corrected Libby. 'She thought if she killed Melanie, Patrick wouldn't be able to produce any more books, so he'd be doubly paid back, losing his wife and his reputation in one go. So she administered the ketamine –'

'How did she get hold of that?' asked Fran.

'Don't you remember?' said Libby. 'She told us she worked for a vet.'

'Eh?' said Harry.

'Ketamine is used in veterinary medicine,' said Ben. 'Especially equine medicine. I suppose if I'd known about her job …'

'You would have known she was a killer?' said Fran. 'I doubt it. Let's face it, she was the most unlikely looking murderer.'

'Anyway, Lib, carry on. Nina gave Melanie the ketamine. And?' Peter topped up glasses all round.

'Got her and her bag into the boot of her car, which is actually a large van, on account of transporting animal cages. She actually talked about the van, saying she often used it. Of course, the car was tested for forensics, not the van. Anyway, she calmly drove her down here, and in the middle of the night set up the scene as we found it next morning. Even the knife was a surgical knife, and veterinary nurses have access to surgical suits and gloves, and she had those with her. Despite being completely barmy, she planned it very cleverly.'

'What about the check-in?' asked Fran.

'She didn't say, but I expect she kept an eye on who was arriving and nipped out to pinch the key and tick the name when no one was looking.'

'What about the stab wound?' asked Peter.

'We don't know that either, but as it was done post-mortem it could have been done here or before they left Reading.'

'And Dee? Why was she killed, and why at Rising Parva?' asked Fran.

'Dee had called Nina to find out if the police had seen her yet, and somehow, we don't quite know how, Nina must have let something slip about Melanie writing the books. And Dee was furious. Told Nina she was going down there now to confront Patrick.'

'And presumably emailed you at the same time,' said Fran. 'And she knew from your reply Ian was in Dorset. I suppose she thought she would tell all to the police as well as confronting Patrick.'

'That's what it looks like,' said Libby. 'Anyway, Nina shot down to Rising Parva, nearer to her than it is to Dee's London home, and called Dee to say they could confront Patrick together and to meet at Bonny Henge, as Dee knew where that was.'

'But why kill her?' asked Guy.

'I've told you, Nina let something slip, we think.

Anyway, Nina thought Dee would say something about her knowing that Melanie had been writing the books, and as far as Nina knew at that time nobody else knew. So it was safer to kill Dee.' Libby shook her head. 'Not sure she was thinking very clearly by then.'

'So why on earth did she admit to you that she knew about Melanie?' asked Peter.

'Ah, there I was a bit sneaky,' said Libby, 'I dropped it in the conversation as though I knew she knew. And when she didn't act surprised, but confirmed what I said, it all fell into place.'

'You were already suspicious of her, then?'

'A bit, yes. Her story about the row between Patrick and Lily didn't ring true somehow.'

'So why did she make up that story?' Harry asked.

'She must have hoped to point the finger at Patrick, or Lily, I suppose. After all, she went to all the trouble to bring the body here and set up the hut, when she could have dumped it deep in a wood somewhere, so she must have thought the police would suspect someone here, presumably Patrick, and the row story was to give them a nudge.'

'Did she tell you all this today?' said Fran.

'After DC Sharif appeared, all she wanted to do was talk. And she wanted me to stay, so I did. So did Ben and Hetty. Until Sharif's back-up arrived.'

'Poor Hetty,' said Fran.

Ben and Libby laughed. 'Poor Hetty!' said Libby. 'She was standing there with an iron frying pan ready to bop Nina on the head.'

'So all's well that ends well,' said Harry. 'Shall

we have another bottle?'

'It hasn't ended well for some of them,' said Libby. 'Patrick has completely lost all his credibility, and I'm not sure that his publishers won't have some sort of case against him. I suppose the other writers will be careful who they send material to in the future and may have lost faith in the whole business. It doesn't look as if Jennifer is likely to step into Melanie's shoes, either. I expect Patrick will quietly disappear.'

'Lily Cooper might take him on,' said Fran. 'She was never as committed to writing as the others.'

'What about you, Fran?' asked Ben. 'Will you carry on?'

'Of course.' Fran smiled round at them all. 'Rosie's been so helpful, and I understand the business much better now. I might even write this whole case as a story.'

'Blimey!' said Harry. 'Watch it, kids. We might all end up in a book.'

'In that case,' said Peter, 'we definitely need another bottle.'